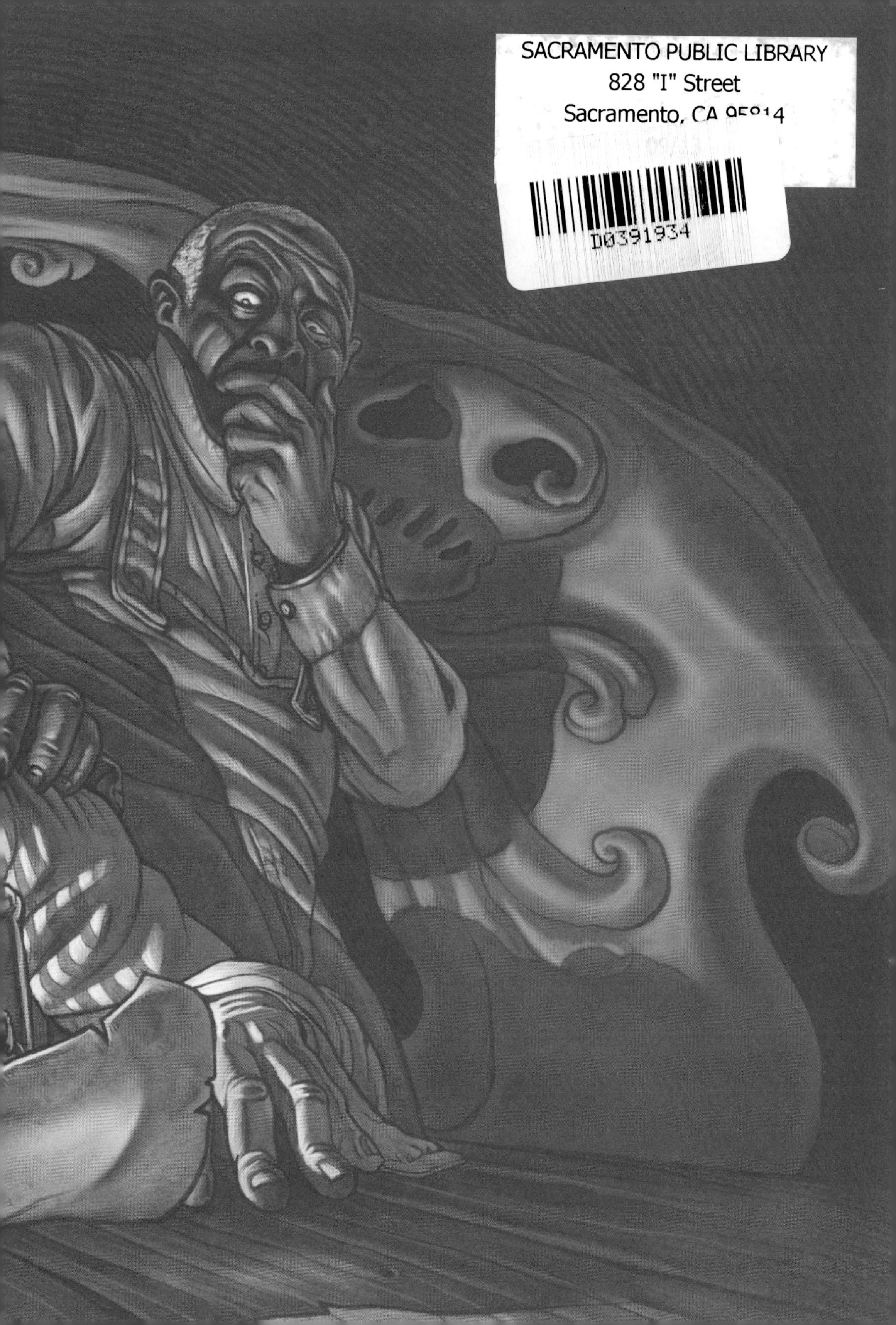

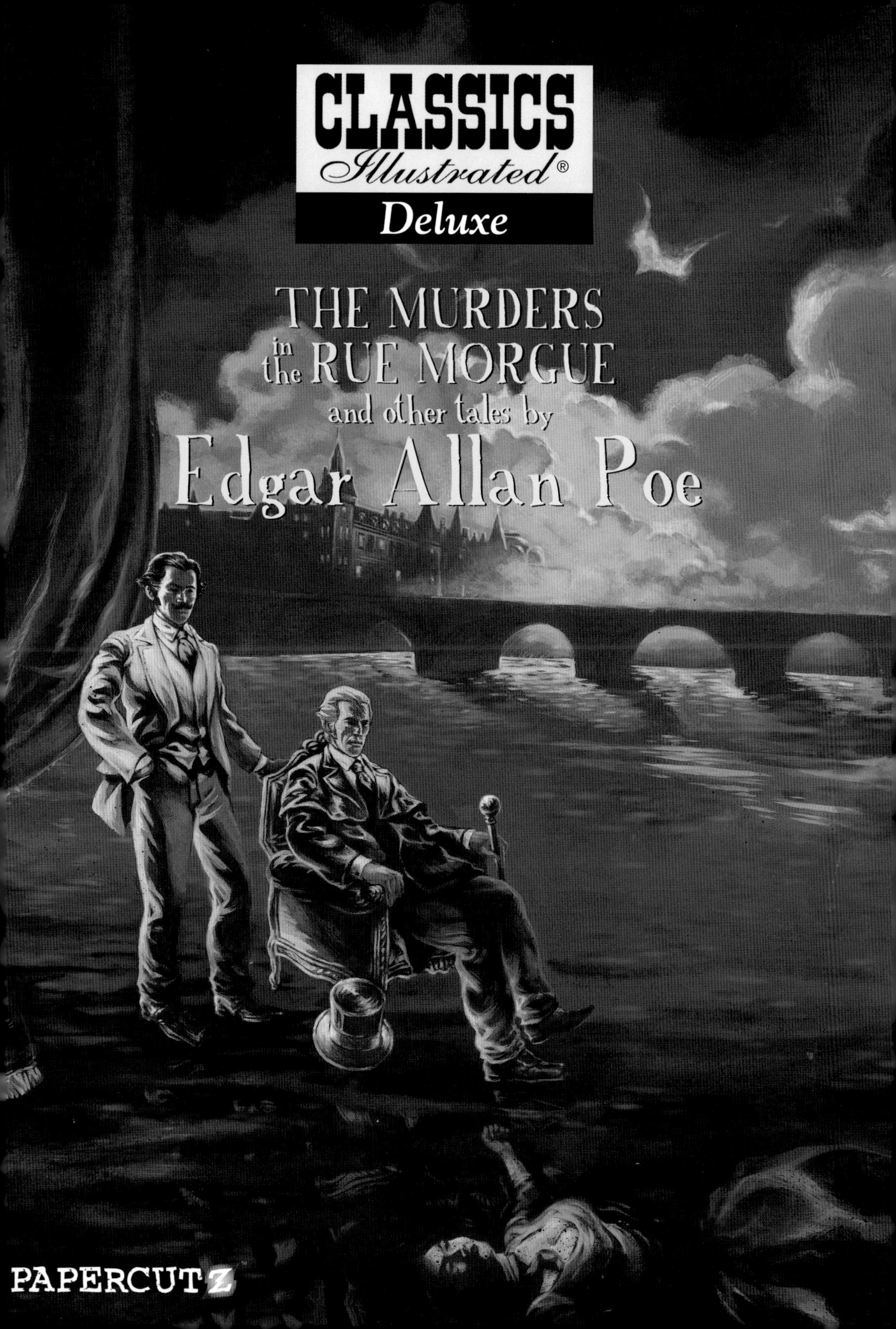
CLASSICS
Illustrated®
Deluxe
THE MURDERS
in the RUE MORGUE
and other tales by
Edgar Allan Poe
PAPERCUTZ

# CLASSICS ILLUSTRATED DELUXE
## GRAPHIC NOVELS FROM PAPERCUTZ

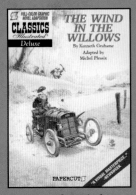

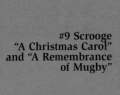

# CLASSICS
## *Illustrated* ®
## *Deluxe*

#10

# "The Murders in the Rue Morgue" and Other Tales
## by Edgar Allan Poe

Adapted by
### JEAN DAVID MORVAN and CORBEYRAN
Script

### FABRICE DRUET and PAUL MARCEL
Art

## PAPERCUTZ ™
New York

*To Richard Corben.*
*To Marc, for his inimitable interpretation of the little beetle on a long-ago Christmas night.*
*To Caroline, my treasure of love.*
*To my two gold-bugs, Valentin and Baptiste.*
*P.M.*

*Thanks to Charles Baudelaire for his brilliant translation.*
*J. D. M.*

*To Lazare, my son born this year*
*To Isabelle,*
*To my wife and my family, for their support,*
*To Sylvain and Marie, for their friendship.*
*F. B.*

*Thanks to Maëlle, my star, my planet.*
*And thanks, lastly, to Jean David Morvan, for his talent and trust.*
*F. D.*

"The Murders in the Rue Morgue" And Other Tales
by Edgar Allan Poe
"The Murders in the Rue Morgue" and "The Mystery of Marie Rogêt"
Jean David Morvan – Writer
Fabrice Druet – Artist
"The Gold-Bug"
Corbeyran – Writer
Paul Marcel – Artist
Joe Johnson – Translation
Big Bird Zatryb – Lettering and Production
John Haufe and William B. Jones Jr. – Classics Illustrated Historians
Beth Scorzato – Production Coordinator
Michael Petranek – Editor
Jim Salicrup
Editor-in-Chief

ISBN: 978-1-59707-431-5 paperback edition
ISBN: 978-1-59707-432-2 hardcover edition

Papercutz books make be purchased for business or promotional use. For
information on bulk purchases please contact Macmillan Corporate and
Premium Sales Department at (800) 221-7945 x5442.

Printed in China
August 2013 by New Era Printing LTD.
Unit C, 8/F, Worldwide Centre
123 Tung Chau St., Kowloon, Hong Kong

Distributed by Macmillan
First Papercutz Printing

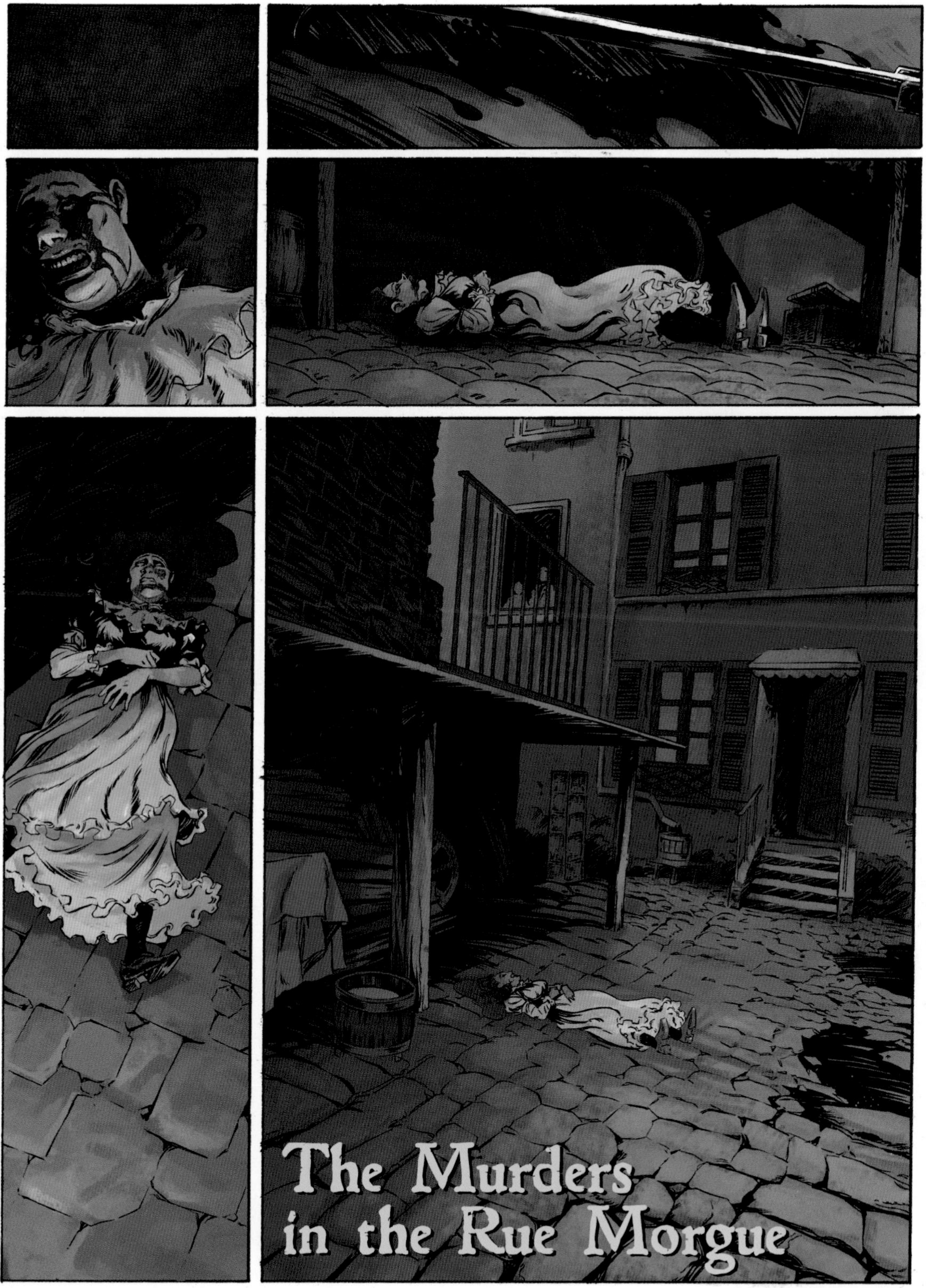
The Murders in the Rue Morgue

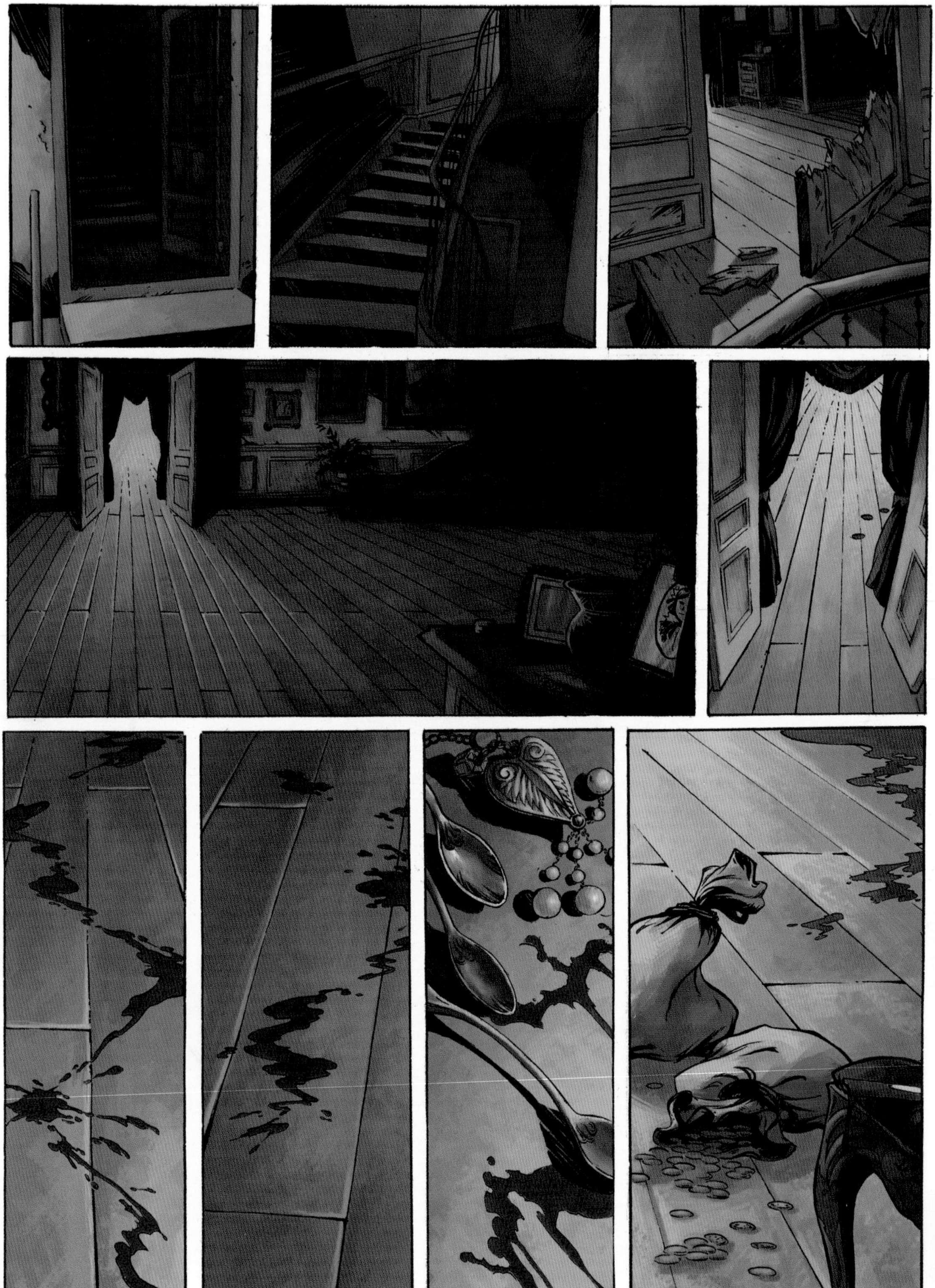

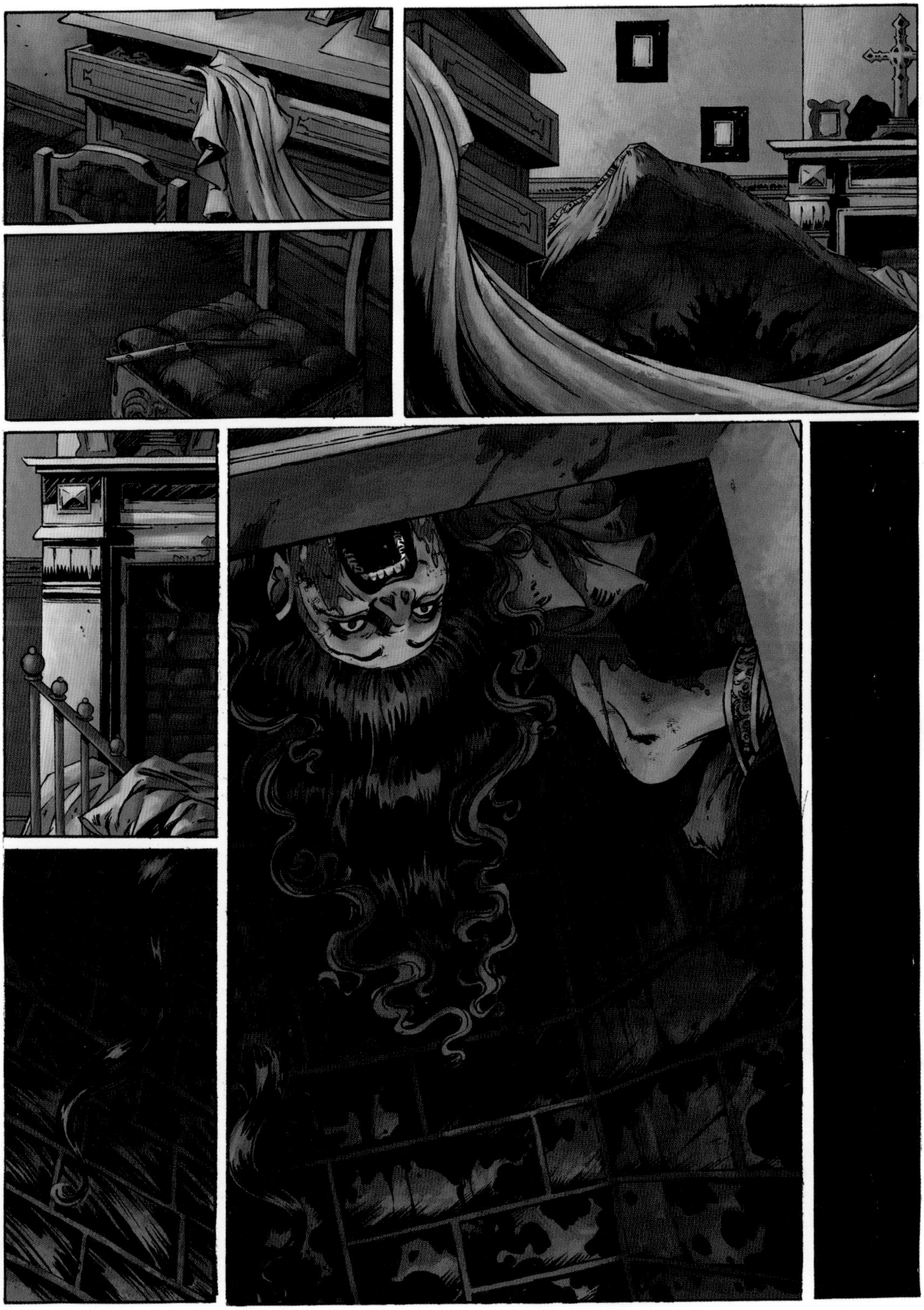

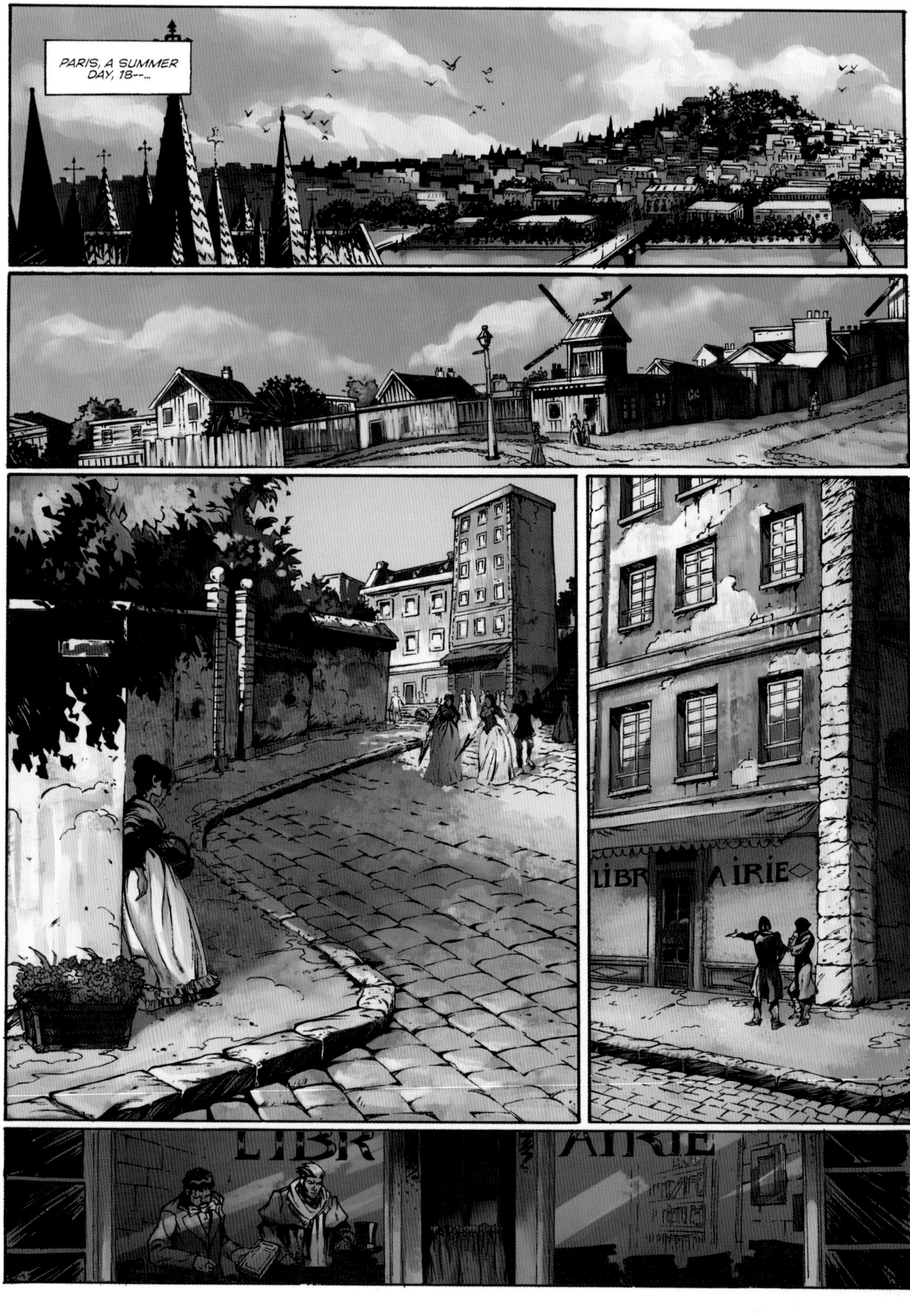
PARIS, A SUMMER DAY, 18--...
LIBR AIRIE
LIBR AIRIE

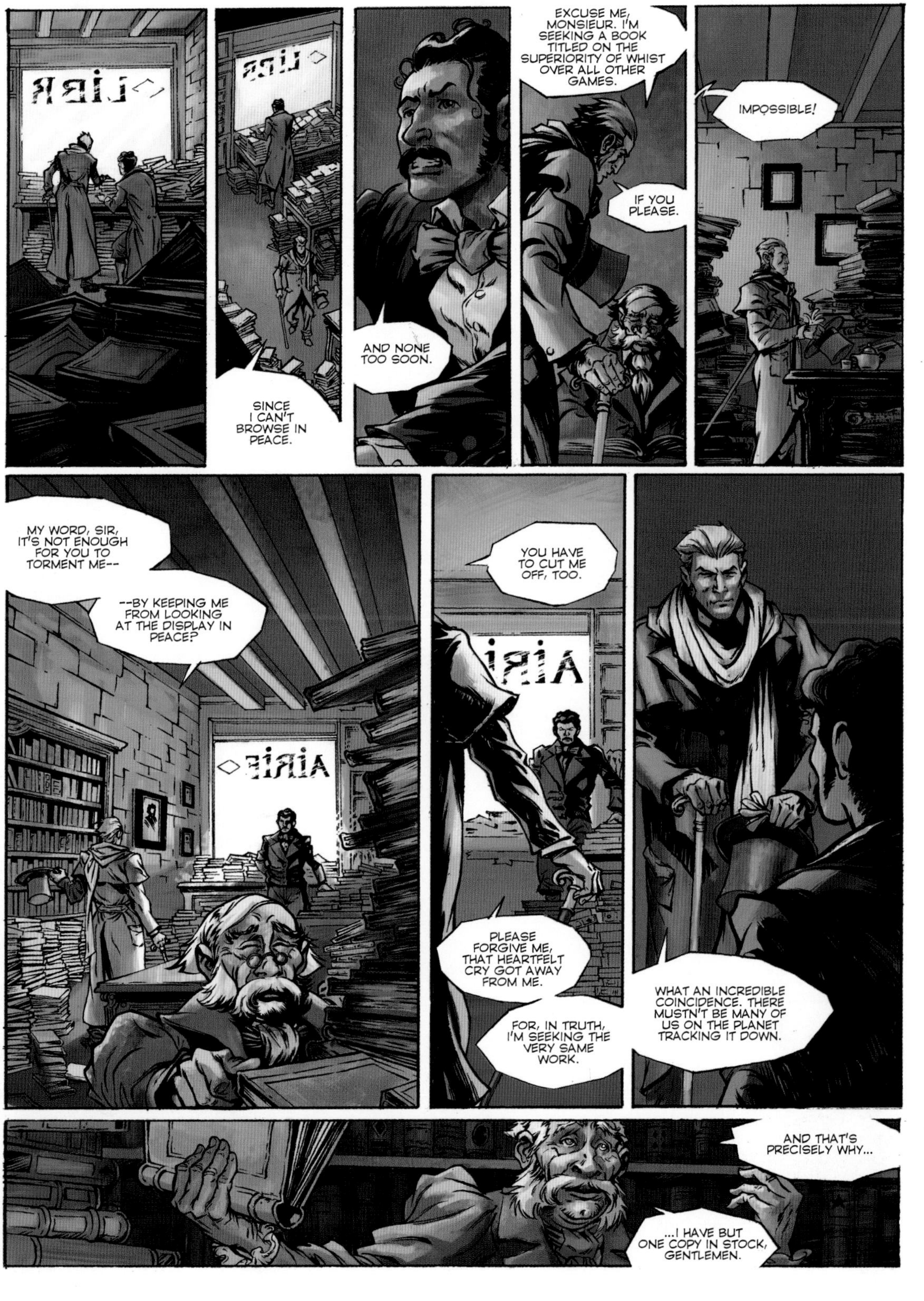
SINCE I CAN'T BROWSE IN PEACE.
AND NONE TOO SOON.
EXCUSE ME, MONSIEUR. I'M SEEKING A BOOK TITLED ON THE SUPERIORITY OF WHIST OVER ALL OTHER GAMES.
IF YOU PLEASE.
IMPOSSIBLE!
MY WORD, SIR, IT'S NOT ENOUGH FOR YOU TO TORMENT ME--
--BY KEEPING ME FROM LOOKING AT THE DISPLAY IN PEACE?
YOU HAVE TO CUT ME OFF, TOO.
PLEASE FORGIVE ME, THAT HEARTFELT CRY GOT AWAY FROM ME.
FOR, IN TRUTH, I'M SEEKING THE VERY SAME WORK.
WHAT AN INCREDIBLE COINCIDENCE. THERE MUSTN'T BE MANY OF US ON THE PLANET TRACKING IT DOWN.
AND THAT'S PRECISELY WHY...
...I HAVE BUT ONE COPY IN STOCK, GENTLEMEN.

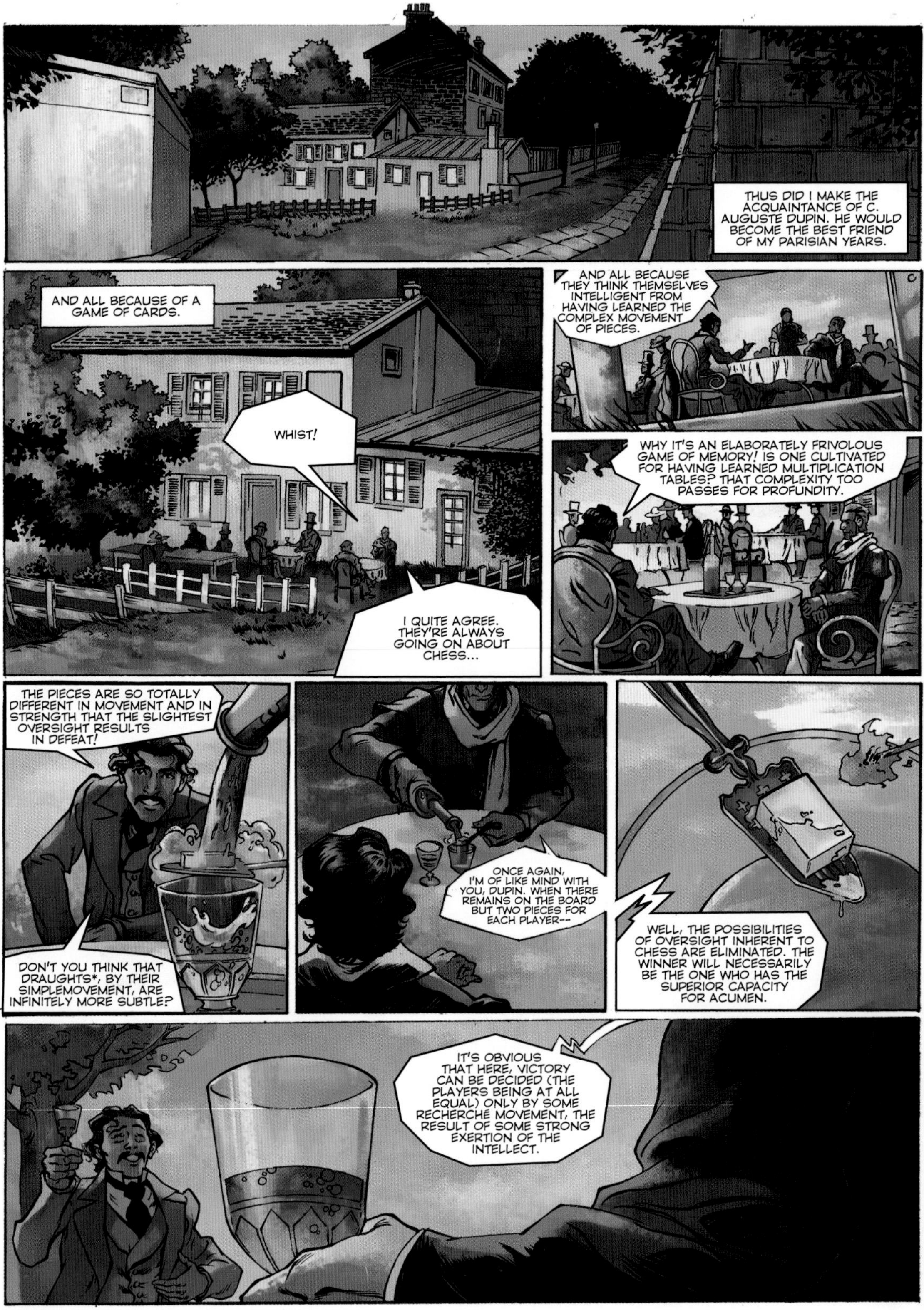
THUS DID I MAKE THE ACQUAINTANCE OF C. AUGUSTE DUPIN. HE WOULD BECOME THE BEST FRIEND OF MY PARISIAN YEARS.
AND ALL BECAUSE OF A GAME OF CARDS.
WHIST!
I QUITE AGREE. THEY'RE ALWAYS GOING ON ABOUT CHESS...
AND ALL BECAUSE THEY THINK THEMSELVES INTELLIGENT FROM HAVING LEARNED THE COMPLEX MOVEMENT OF PIECES.
WHY IT'S AN ELABORATELY FRIVOLOUS GAME OF MEMORY! IS ONE CULTIVATED FOR HAVING LEARNED MULTIPLICATION TABLES? THAT COMPLEXITY TOO PASSES FOR PROFUNDITY.
THE PIECES ARE SO TOTALLY DIFFERENT IN MOVEMENT AND IN STRENGTH THAT THE SLIGHTEST OVERSIGHT RESULTS IN DEFEAT!
DON'T YOU THINK THAT DRAUGHTS*, BY THEIR SIMPLEMOVEMENT, ARE INFINITELY MORE SUBTLE?
ONCE AGAIN, I'M OF LIKE MIND WITH YOU, DUPIN. WHEN THERE REMAINS ON THE BOARD BUT TWO PIECES FOR EACH PLAYER--
WELL, THE POSSIBILITIES OF OVERSIGHT INHERENT TO CHESS ARE ELIMINATED. THE WINNER WILL NECESSARILY BE THE ONE WHO HAS THE SUPERIOR CAPACITY FOR ACUMEN.
IT'S OBVIOUS THAT HERE, VICTORY CAN BE DECIDED (THE PLAYERS BEING AT ALL EQUAL) ONLY BY SOME RECHERCHÉ MOVEMENT, THE RESULT OF SOME STRONG EXERTION OF THE INTELLECT.

*A BOARD GAME KNOWN AS "CHECKERS" IN AMERICA

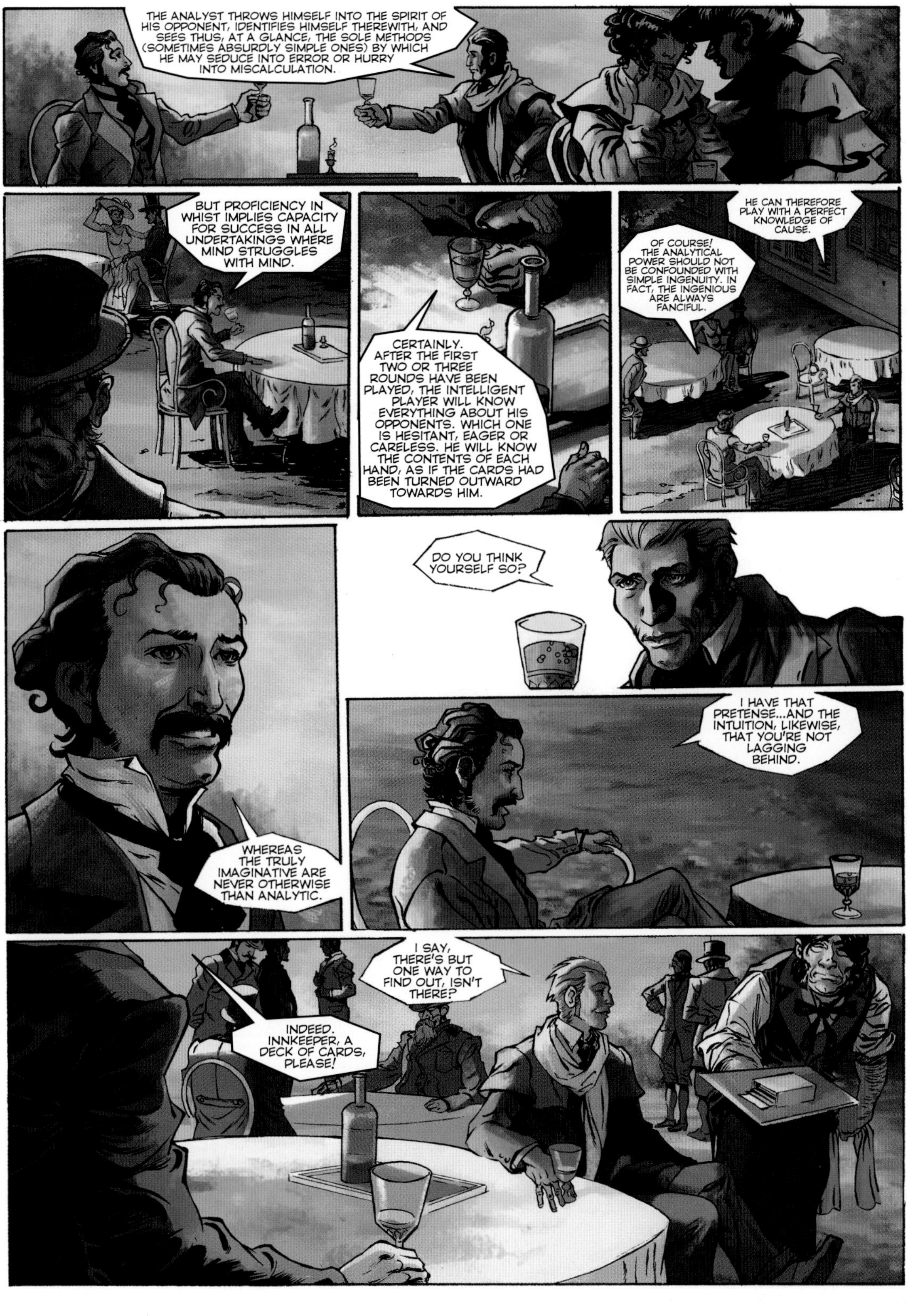
THE ANALYST THROWS HIMSELF INTO THE SPIRIT OF HIS OPPONENT, IDENTIFIES HIMSELF THEREWITH, AND SEES THUS, AT A GLANCE, THE SOLE METHODS (SOMETIMES ABSURDLY SIMPLE ONES) BY WHICH HE MAY SEDUCE INTO ERROR OR HURRY INTO MISCALCULATION.
BUT PROFICIENCY IN WHIST IMPLIES CAPACITY FOR SUCCESS IN ALL UNDERTAKINGS WHERE MIND STRUGGLES WITH MIND.
CERTAINLY. AFTER THE FIRST TWO OR THREE ROUNDS HAVE BEEN PLAYED, THE INTELLIGENT PLAYER WILL KNOW EVERYTHING ABOUT HIS OPPONENTS. WHICH ONE IS HESITANT, EAGER OR CARELESS. HE WILL KNOW THE CONTENTS OF EACH HAND, AS IF THE CARDS HAD BEEN TURNED OUTWARD TOWARDS HIM.
HE CAN THEREFORE PLAY WITH A PERFECT KNOWLEDGE OF CAUSE.
OF COURSE! THE ANALYTICAL POWER SHOULD NOT BE CONFOUNDED WITH SIMPLE INGENUITY. IN FACT, THE INGENIOUS ARE ALWAYS FANCIFUL.
WHEREAS THE TRULY IMAGINATIVE ARE NEVER OTHERWISE THAN ANALYTIC.
DO YOU THINK YOURSELF SO?
I HAVE THAT PRETENSE...AND THE INTUITION, LIKEWISE, THAT YOU'RE NOT LAGGING BEHIND.
I SAY, THERE'S BUT ONE WAY TO FIND OUT, ISN'T THERE?
INDEED. INNKEEPER, A DECK OF CARDS, PLEASE!

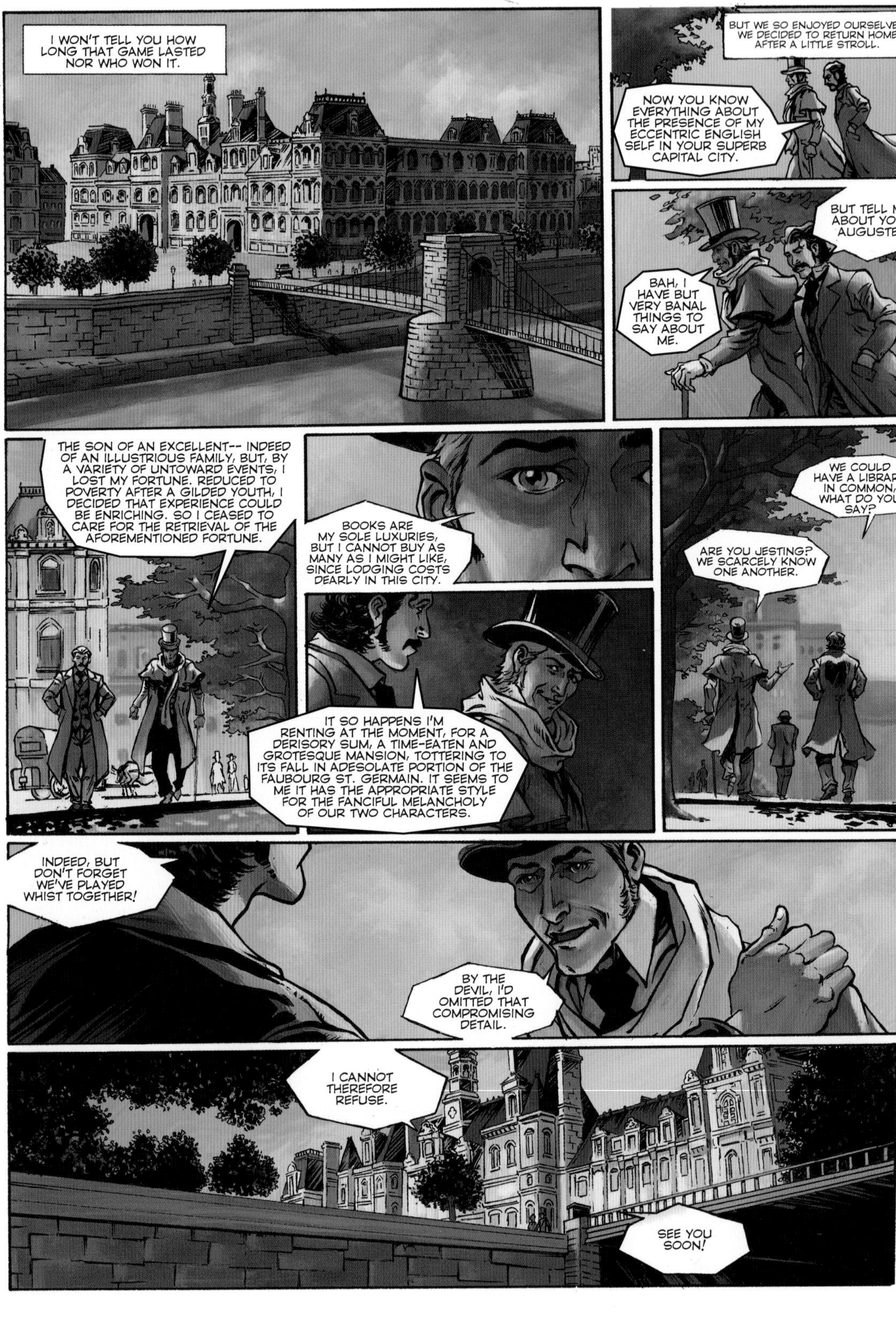
I WON'T TELL YOU HOW LONG THAT GAME LASTED NOR WHO WON IT.
BUT WE SO ENJOYED OURSELVES WE DECIDED TO RETURN HOME AFTER A LITTLE STROLL.
NOW YOU KNOW EVERYTHING ABOUT THE PRESENCE OF MY ECCENTRIC ENGLISH SELF IN YOUR SUPERB CAPITAL CITY.
BUT TELL ME ABOUT YOU, AUGUSTE.
BAH, I HAVE BUT VERY BANAL THINGS TO SAY ABOUT ME.
THE SON OF AN EXCELLENT-- INDEED OF AN ILLUSTRIOUS FAMILY, BUT, BY A VARIETY OF UNTOWARD EVENTS, I LOST MY FORTUNE. REDUCED TO POVERTY AFTER A GILDED YOUTH, I DECIDED THAT EXPERIENCE COULD BE ENRICHING. SO I CEASED TO CARE FOR THE RETRIEVAL OF THE AFOREMENTIONED FORTUNE.
BOOKS ARE MY SOLE LUXURIES, BUT I CANNOT BUY AS MANY AS I MIGHT LIKE, SINCE LODGING COSTS DEARLY IN THIS CITY.
IT SO HAPPENS I'M RENTING AT THE MOMENT, FOR A DERISORY SUM, A TIME-EATEN AND GROTESQUE MANSION, TOTTERING TO ITS FALL IN ADESOLATE PORTION OF THE FAUBOURG ST. GERMAIN. IT SEEMS TO ME IT HAS THE APPROPRIATE STYLE FOR THE FANCIFUL MELANCHOLY OF OUR TWO CHARACTERS.
WE COULD HAVE A LIBRARY IN COMMON, WHAT DO YOU SAY?
ARE YOU JESTING? WE SCARCELY KNOW ONE ANOTHER.
INDEED, BUT DON'T FORGET WE'VE PLAYED WHIST TOGETHER!
BY THE DEVIL, I'D OMITTED THAT COMPROMISING DETAIL.
I CANNOT THEREFORE REFUSE.
SEE YOU SOON!

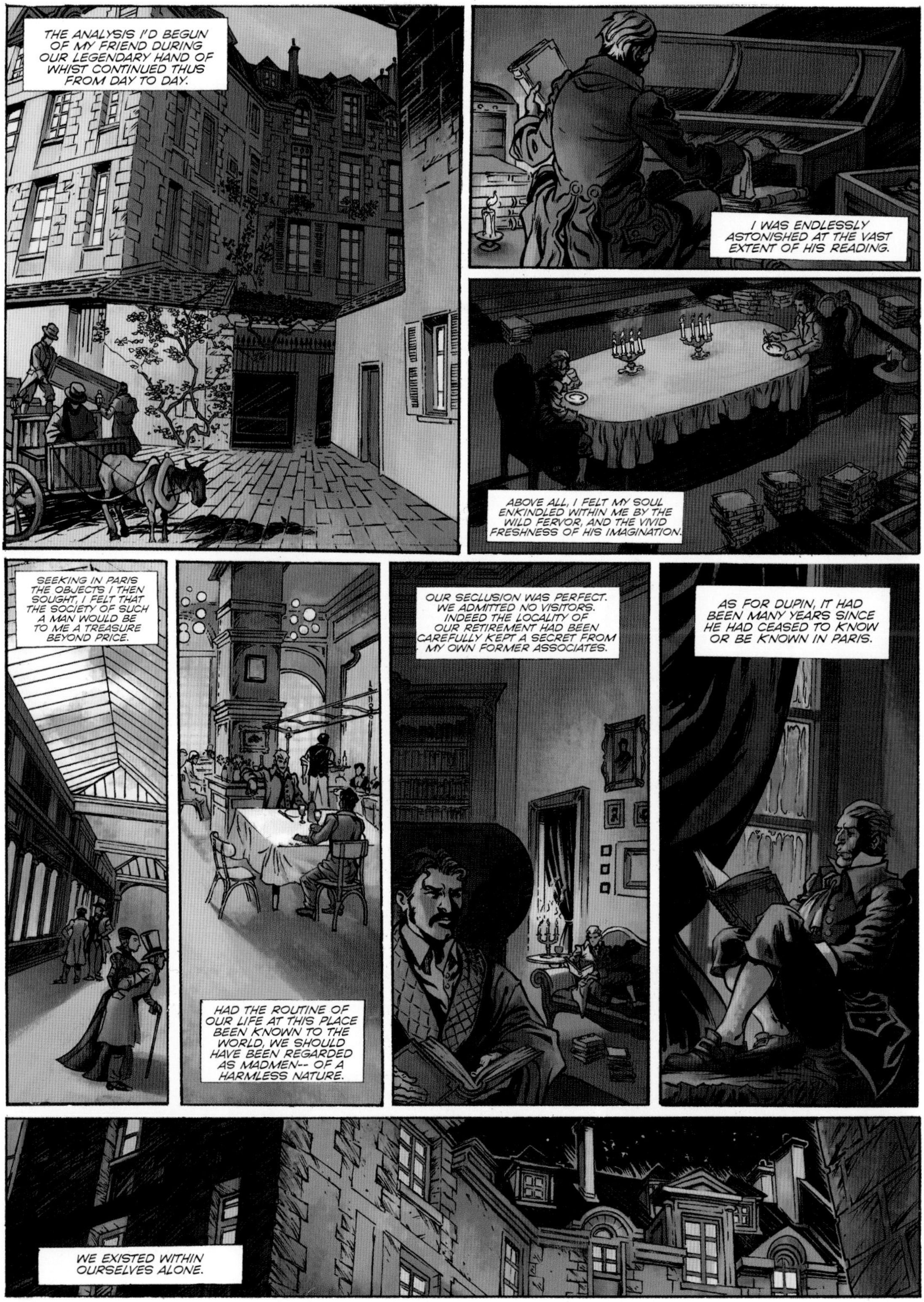
THE ANALYSIS I'D BEGUN OF MY FRIEND DURING OUR LEGENDARY HAND OF WHIST CONTINUED THUS FROM DAY TO DAY.
I WAS ENDLESSLY ASTONISHED AT THE VAST EXTENT OF HIS READING.
ABOVE ALL, I FELT MY SOUL ENKINDLED WITHIN ME BY THE WILD FERVOR, AND THE VIVID FRESHNESS OF HIS IMAGINATION.
SEEKING IN PARIS THE OBJECTS I THEN SOUGHT, I FELT THAT THE SOCIETY OF SUCH A MAN WOULD BE TO ME A TREASURE BEYOND PRICE.
HAD THE ROUTINE OF OUR LIFE AT THIS PLACE BEEN KNOWN TO THE WORLD, WE SHOULD HAVE BEEN REGARDED AS MADMEN-- OF A HARMLESS NATURE.
OUR SECLUSION WAS PERFECT. WE ADMITTED NO VISITORS. INDEED THE LOCALITY OF OUR RETIREMENT HAD BEEN CAREFULLY KEPT A SECRET FROM MY OWN FORMER ASSOCIATES.
AS FOR DUPIN, IT HAD BEEN MANY YEARS SINCE HE HAD CEASED TO KNOW OR BE KNOWN IN PARIS.
WE EXISTED WITHIN OURSELVES ALONE.

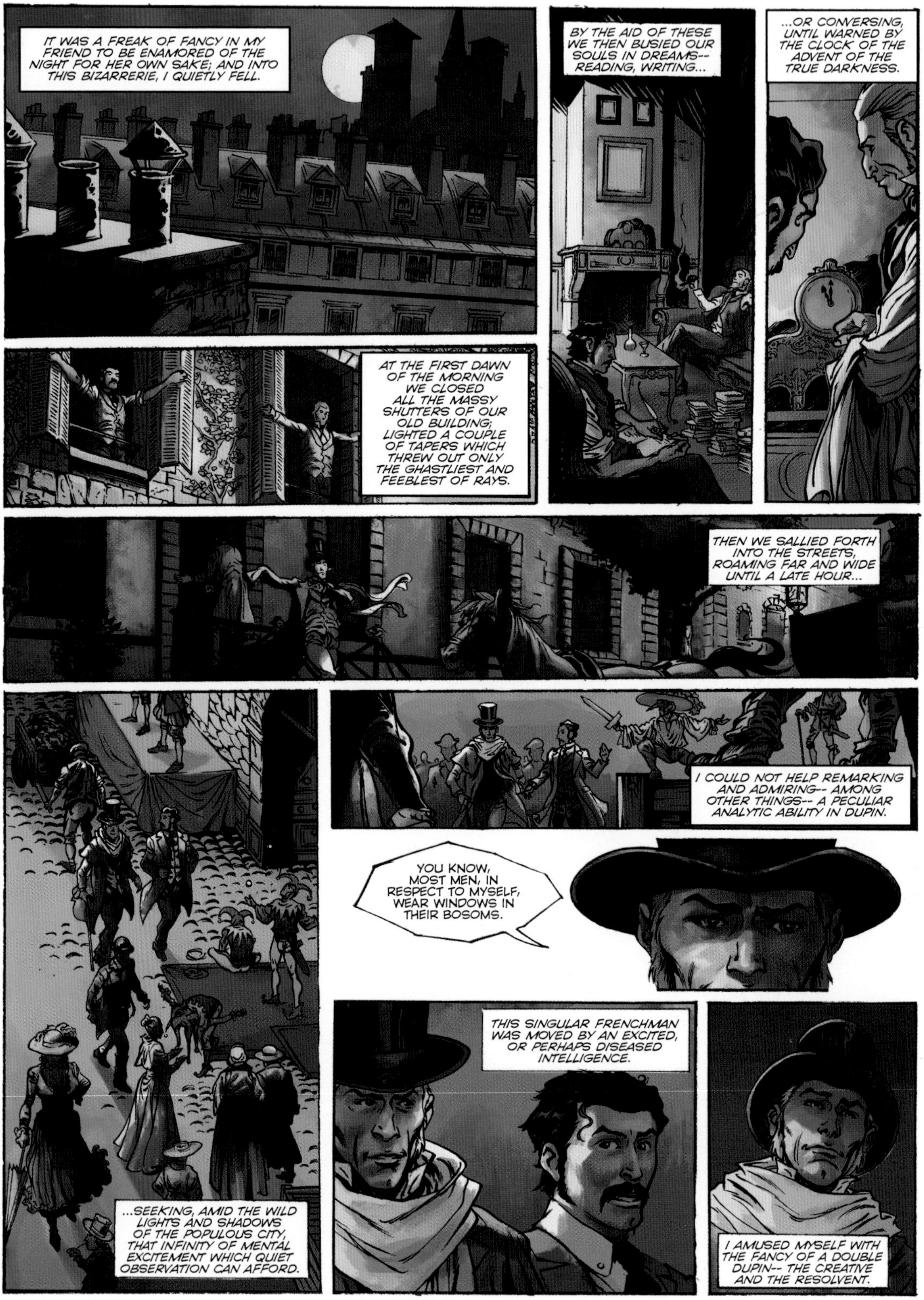
IT WAS A FREAK OF FANCY IN MY FRIEND TO BE ENAMORED OF THE NIGHT FOR HER OWN SAKE; AND INTO THIS BIZARRERIE, I QUIETLY FELL.
AT THE FIRST DAWN OF THE MORNING WE CLOSED ALL THE MASSY SHUTTERS OF OUR OLD BUILDING; LIGHTED A COUPLE OF TAPERS WHICH THREW OUT ONLY THE GHASTLIEST AND FEEBLEST OF RAYS.
BY THE AID OF THESE WE THEN BUSIED OUR SOULS IN DREAMS-- READING, WRITING...
...OR CONVERSING, UNTIL WARNED BY THE CLOCK OF THE ADVENT OF THE TRUE DARKNESS.
THEN WE SALLIED FORTH INTO THE STREETS, ROAMING FAR AND WIDE UNTIL A LATE HOUR...
...SEEKING, AMID THE WILD LIGHTS AND SHADOWS OF THE POPULOUS CITY, THAT INFINITY OF MENTAL EXCITEMENT WHICH QUIET OBSERVATION CAN AFFORD.
I COULD NOT HELP REMARKING AND ADMIRING-- AMONG OTHER THINGS-- A PECULIAR ANALYTIC ABILITY IN DUPIN.
YOU KNOW, MOST MEN, IN RESPECT TO MYSELF, WEAR WINDOWS IN THEIR BOSOMS.
THIS SINGULAR FRENCHMAN WAS MOVED BY AN EXCITED, OR PERHAPS DISEASED INTELLIGENCE.
I AMUSED MYSELF WITH THE FANCY OF A DOUBLE DUPIN-- THE CREATIVE AND THE RESOLVENT.

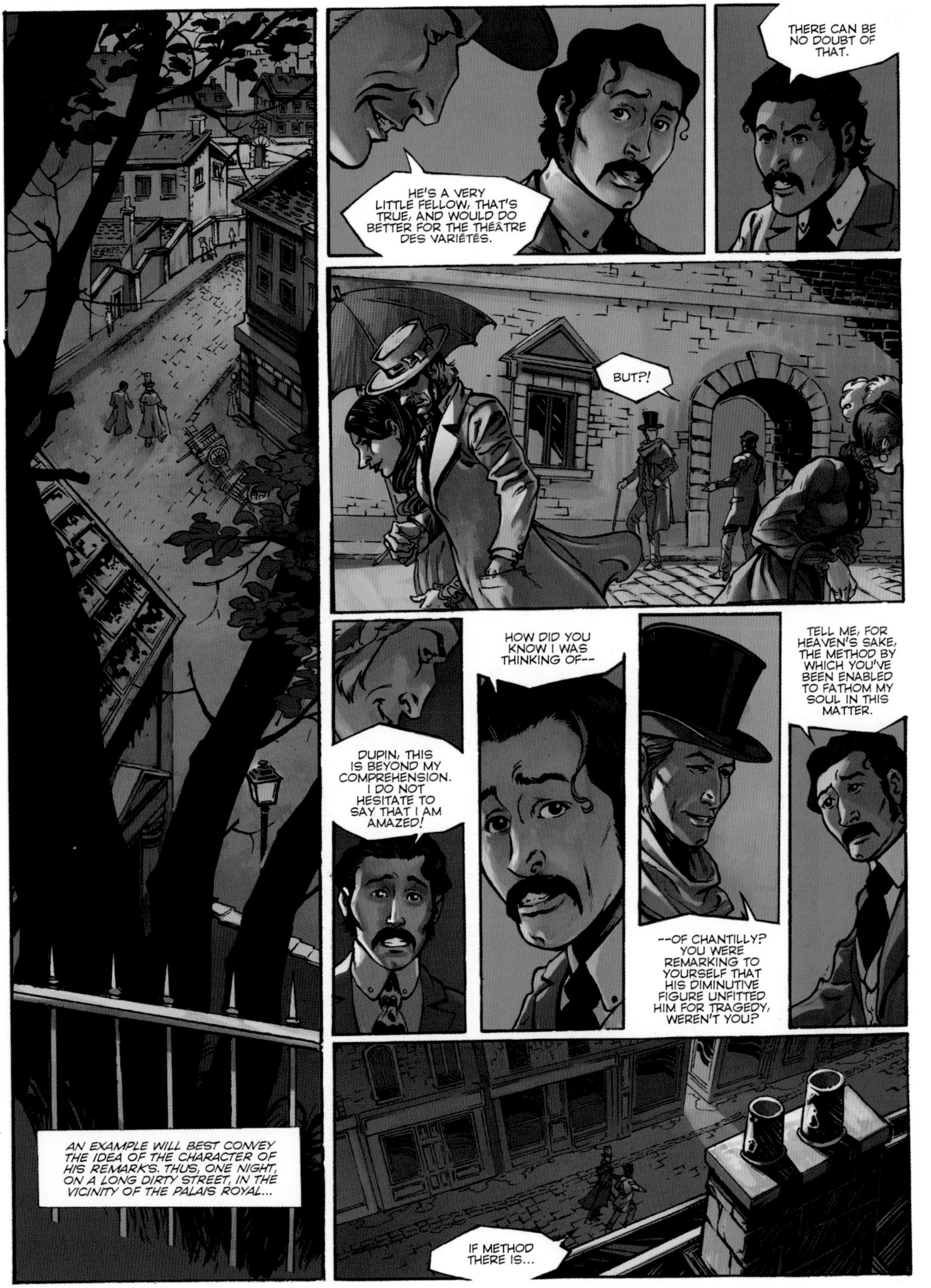
AN EXAMPLE WILL BEST CONVEY THE IDEA OF THE CHARACTER OF HIS REMARKS. THUS, ONE NIGHT, ON A LONG DIRTY STREET, IN THE VICINITY OF THE PALAIS ROYAL...
HE'S A VERY LITTLE FELLOW, THAT'S TRUE, AND WOULD DO BETTER FOR THE THÉÂTRE DES VARIÉTÉS.
THERE CAN BE NO DOUBT OF THAT.
BUT?!
DUPIN, THIS IS BEYOND MY COMPREHENSION. I DO NOT HESITATE TO SAY THAT I AM AMAZED!
HOW DID YOU KNOW I WAS THINKING OF--
--OF CHANTILLY? YOU WERE REMARKING TO YOURSELF THAT HIS DIMINUTIVE FIGURE UNFITTED HIM FOR TRAGEDY, WEREN'T YOU?
TELL ME, FOR HEAVEN'S SAKE, THE METHOD BY WHICH YOU'VE BEEN ENABLED TO FATHOM MY SOUL IN THIS MATTER.
IF METHOD THERE IS...

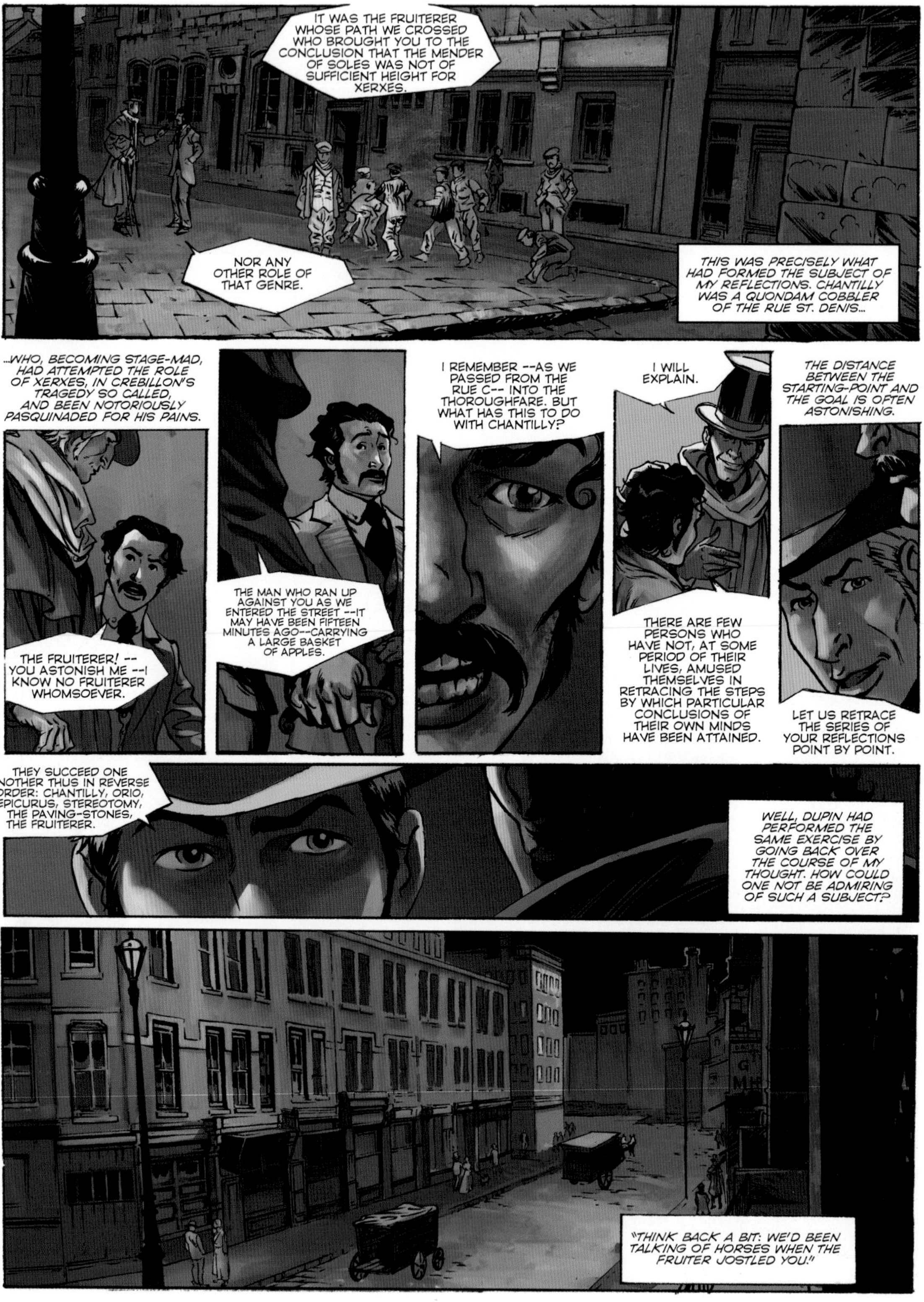
IT WAS THE FRUITERER WHOSE PATH WE CROSSED WHO BROUGHT YOU TO THE CONCLUSION THAT THE MENDER OF SOLES WAS NOT OF SUFFICIENT HEIGHT FOR XERXES.
NOR ANY OTHER ROLE OF THAT GENRE.
THIS WAS PRECISELY WHAT HAD FORMED THE SUBJECT OF MY REFLECTIONS. CHANTILLY WAS A QUONDAM COBBLER OF THE RUE ST. DENIS...
...WHO, BECOMING STAGE-MAD, HAD ATTEMPTED THE ROLE OF XERXES, IN CREBILLON'S TRAGEDY SO CALLED, AND BEEN NOTORIOUSLY PASQUINADED FOR HIS PAINS.
THE FRUITERER! --YOU ASTONISH ME --I KNOW NO FRUITERER WHOMSOEVER.
THE MAN WHO RAN UP AGAINST YOU AS WE ENTERED THE STREET --IT MAY HAVE BEEN FIFTEEN MINUTES AGO--CARRYING A LARGE BASKET OF APPLES.
I REMEMBER --AS WE PASSED FROM THE RUE C-- INTO THE THOROUGHFARE. BUT WHAT HAS THIS TO DO WITH CHANTILLY?
I WILL EXPLAIN.
THERE ARE FEW PERSONS WHO HAVE NOT, AT SOME PERIOD OF THEIR LIVES, AMUSED THEMSELVES IN RETRACING THE STEPS BY WHICH PARTICULAR CONCLUSIONS OF THEIR OWN MINDS HAVE BEEN ATTAINED.
THE DISTANCE BETWEEN THE STARTING-POINT AND THE GOAL IS OFTEN ASTONISHING.
LET US RETRACE THE SERIES OF YOUR REFLECTIONS POINT BY POINT.
THEY SUCCEED ONE ANOTHER THUS IN REVERSE ORDER: CHANTILLY, ORIO, EPICURUS, STEREOTOMY, THE PAVING-STONES, THE FRUITERER.
WELL, DUPIN HAD PERFORMED THE SAME EXERCISE BY GOING BACK OVER THE COURSE OF MY THOUGHT. HOW COULD ONE NOT BE ADMIRING OF SUCH A SUBJECT?
"THINK BACK A BIT: WE'D BEEN TALKING OF HORSES WHEN THE FRUITER JOSTLED YOU."

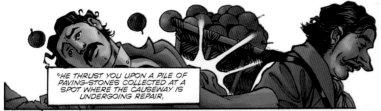

"HE THRUST YOU UPON A PILE OF PAVING-STONES COLLECTED AT A SPOT WHERE THE CAUSEWAY IS UNDERGOING REPAIR,

"YOU STEPPED UPON ONE OF THE LOOSE FRAGMENTS, SLIPPED, AND SLIGHTLY STRAINED YOUR ANKLE.

"YOU CONTINUED ON WITHOUT UTTERING A WORD, BUT I SAW YOU GLANCING, WITH IRRITATION, AT THE HOLES AND RUTS IN THE PAVEMENT.

"SO THAT I SAW YOU WERE STILL THINKING OF THE STONES, UNTIL WE REACHED THE LITTLE ALLEY CALLED LAMARTINE, WHICH HAS BEEN PAVED, BY WAY OF EXPERIMENT, WITH THE OVERLAPPING AND RIVETED BLOCKS."

"HERE YOUR COUNTENANCE BRIGHTENED UP, AND I GUESSED YOU MURMURED THE WORD 'STEREOTOMY,' A TERM VERY AFFECTEDLY APPLIED TO THIS SPECIES OF PAVEMENT.

" I KNEW THAT YOU COULD NOT SAY TO YOURSELF 'STEREOTOMY' WITHOUT BEING BROUGHT TO THINK OF ATOMIES, AND THUS OF THE THEORIES OF EPICURUS...

"...FOR WE'D DISCUSSED THIS SUBJECT THAT THE VAGUE GUESSES OF THAT NOBLE GREEK HAD MET WITH CONFIRMATION IN THE LATE NEBULAR COSMOGONY.

"I FELT THAT YOU COULD NOT AVOID CASTING YOUR EYES UPWARD TO THE GREAT NEBULA IN ORION.

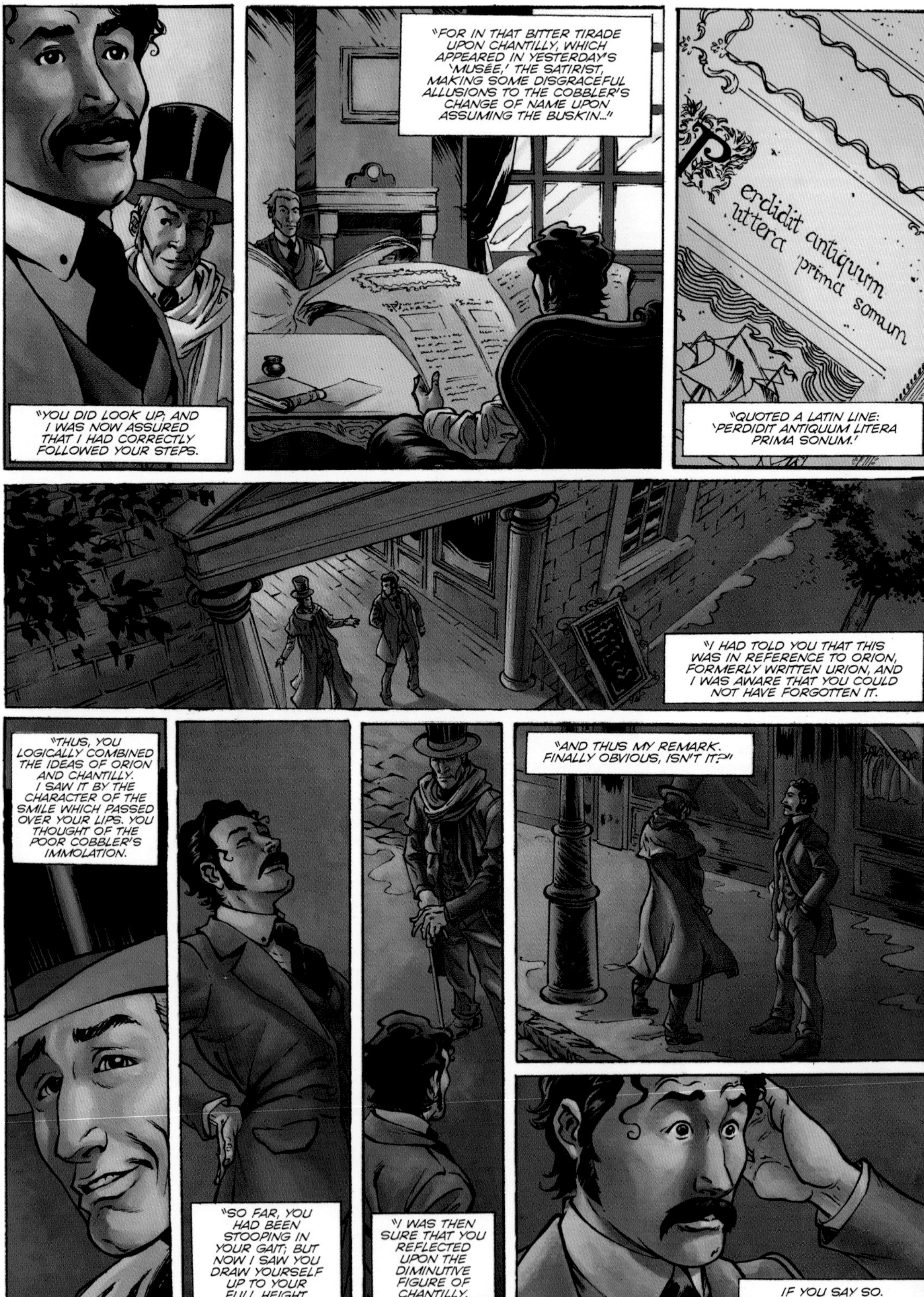
"YOU DID LOOK UP; AND I WAS NOW ASSURED THAT I HAD CORRECTLY FOLLOWED YOUR STEPS.
"FOR IN THAT BITTER TIRADE UPON CHANTILLY, WHICH APPEARED IN YESTERDAY'S 'MUSÉE,' THE SATIRIST, MAKING SOME DISGRACEFUL ALLUSIONS TO THE COBBLER'S CHANGE OF NAME UPON ASSUMING THE BUSKIN..."
Perdidit antiquum littera prima sonum
"QUOTED A LATIN LINE: 'PERDIDIT ANTIQUUM LITERA PRIMA SONUM.'
"I HAD TOLD YOU THAT THIS WAS IN REFERENCE TO ORION, FORMERLY WRITTEN URION, AND I WAS AWARE THAT YOU COULD NOT HAVE FORGOTTEN IT.
"THUS, YOU LOGICALLY COMBINED THE IDEAS OF ORION AND CHANTILLY. I SAW IT BY THE CHARACTER OF THE SMILE WHICH PASSED OVER YOUR LIPS. YOU THOUGHT OF THE POOR COBBLER'S IMMOLATION.
"SO FAR, YOU HAD BEEN STOOPING IN YOUR GAIT; BUT NOW I SAW YOU DRAW YOURSELF UP TO YOUR FULL HEIGHT.
"I WAS THEN SURE THAT YOU REFLECTED UPON THE DIMINUTIVE FIGURE OF CHANTILLY.
"AND THUS MY REMARK. FINALLY OBVIOUS, ISN'T IT?"
IF YOU SAY SO.

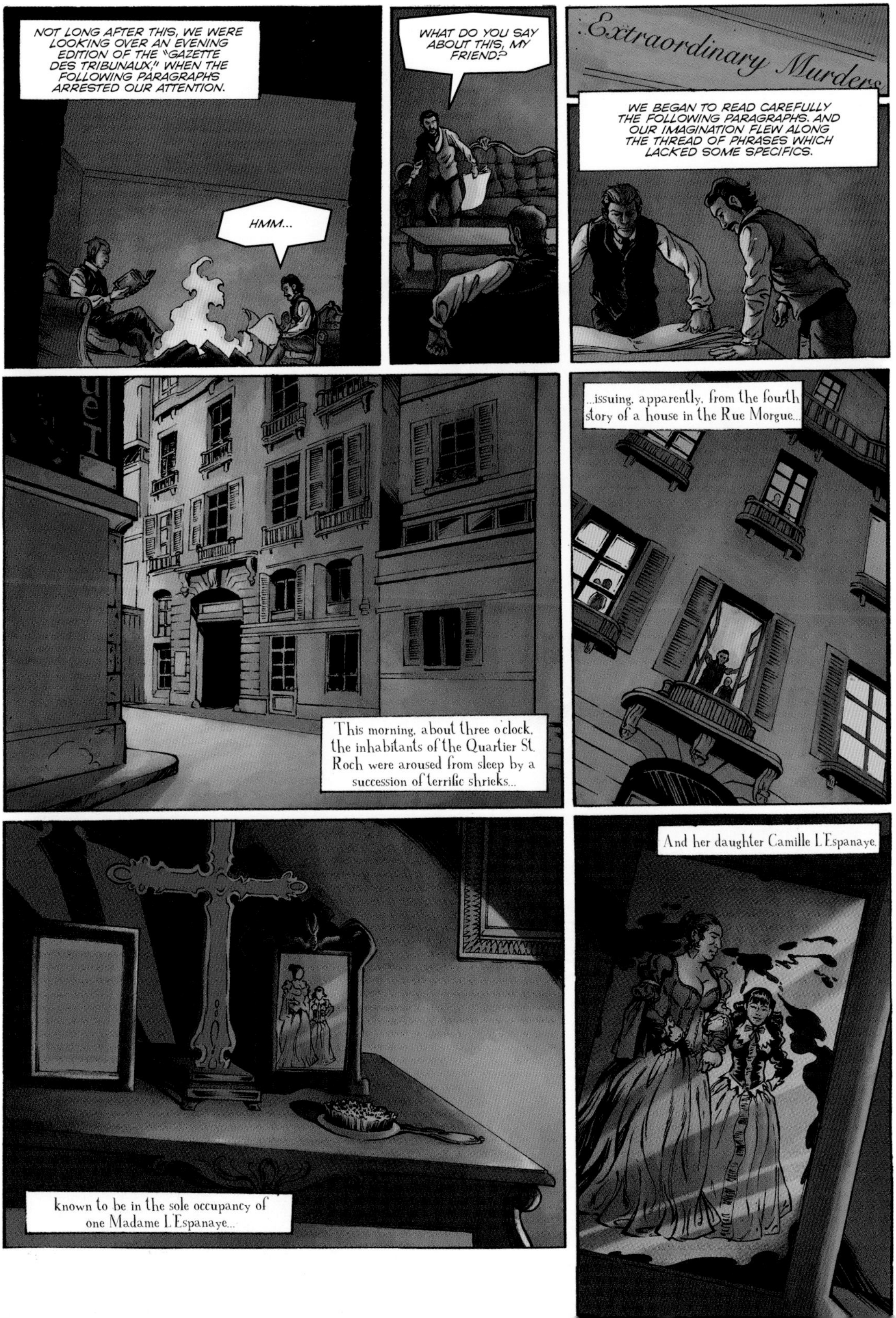

NOT LONG AFTER THIS, WE WERE LOOKING OVER AN EVENING EDITION OF THE "GAZETTE DES TRIBUNAUX," WHEN THE FOLLOWING PARAGRAPHS ARRESTED OUR ATTENTION.
HMM...
WHAT DO YOU SAY ABOUT THIS, MY FRIEND?
Extraordinary Murders
WE BEGAN TO READ CAREFULLY THE FOLLOWING PARAGRAPHS. AND OUR IMAGINATION FLEW ALONG THE THREAD OF PHRASES WHICH LACKED SOME SPECIFICS.
This morning, about three o'clock, the inhabitants of the Quartier St. Roch were aroused from sleep by a succession of terrific shrieks...
...issuing, apparently, from the fourth story of a house in the Rue Morgue...
known to be in the sole occupancy of one Madame L'Espanaye...
And her daughter Camille L'Espanaye.

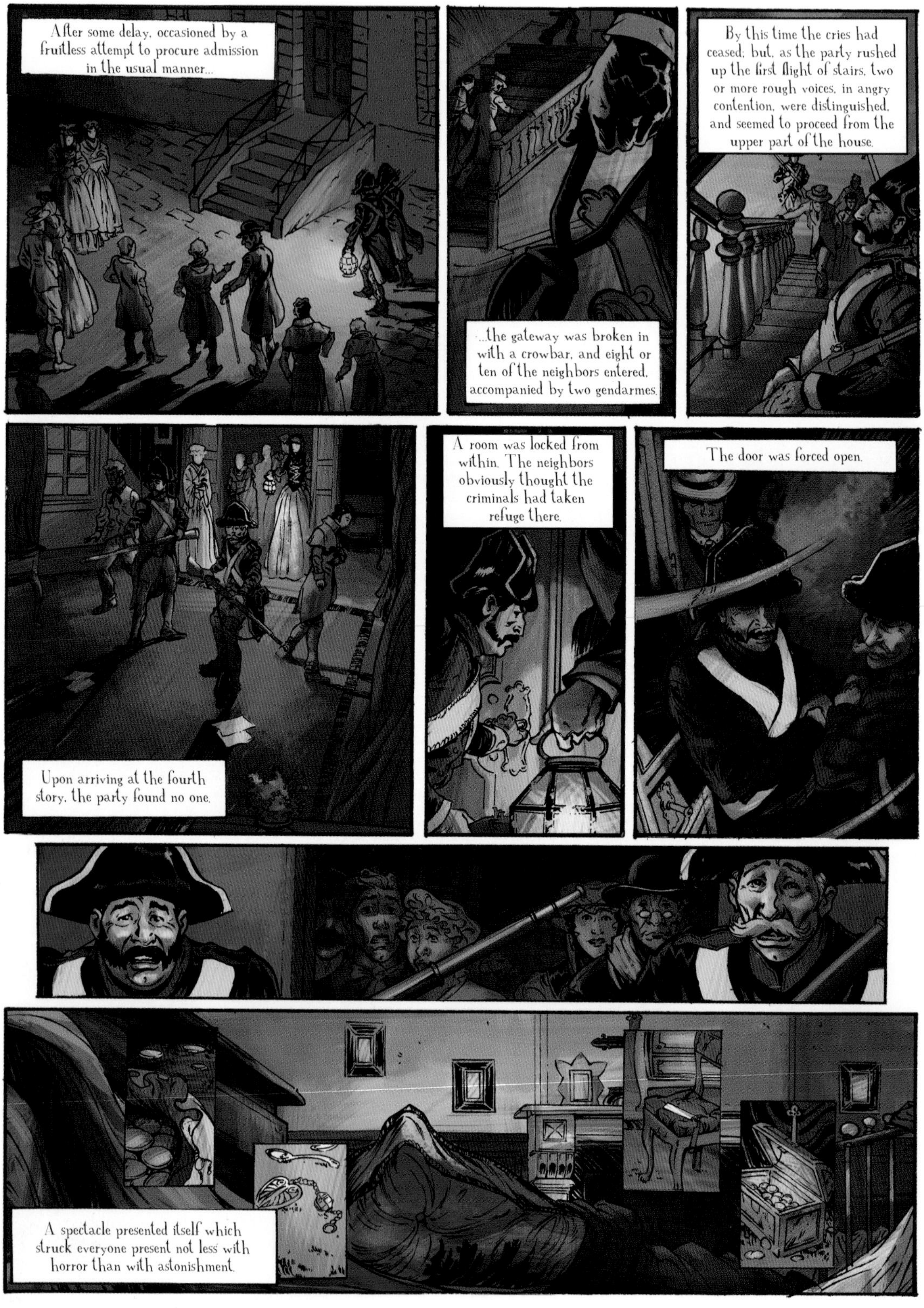
After some delay, occasioned by a fruitless attempt to procure admission in the usual manner...
...the gateway was broken in with a crowbar, and eight or ten of the neighbors entered, accompanied by two gendarmes.
By this time the cries had ceased; but, as the party rushed up the first flight of stairs, two or more rough voices, in angry contention, were distinguished, and seemed to proceed from the upper part of the house.
Upon arriving at the fourth story, the party found no one.
A room was locked from within. The neighbors obviously thought the criminals had taken refuge there.
The door was forced open.
A spectacle presented itself which struck everyone present not less with horror than with astonishment.

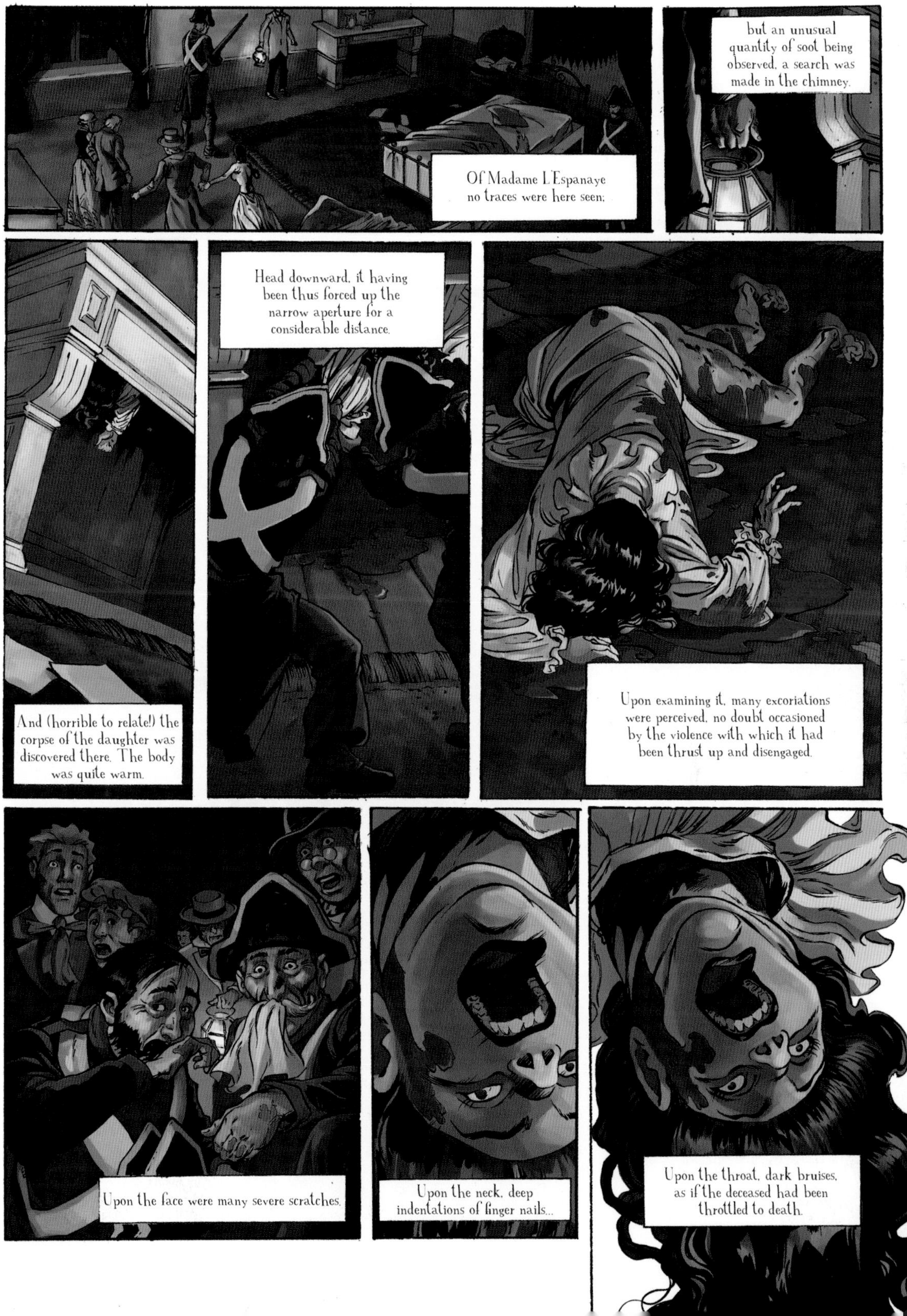
Of Madame L'Espanaye no traces were here seen;
but an unusual quantity of soot being observed, a search was made in the chimney.
And (horrible to relate!) the corpse of the daughter was discovered there. The body was quite warm.
Head downward, it having been thus forced up the narrow aperture for a considerable distance.
Upon examining it, many excoriations were perceived, no doubt occasioned by the violence with which it had been thrust up and disengaged.
Upon the face were many severe scratches.
Upon the neck, deep indentations of finger nails...
Upon the throat, dark bruises, as if the deceased had been throttled to death.

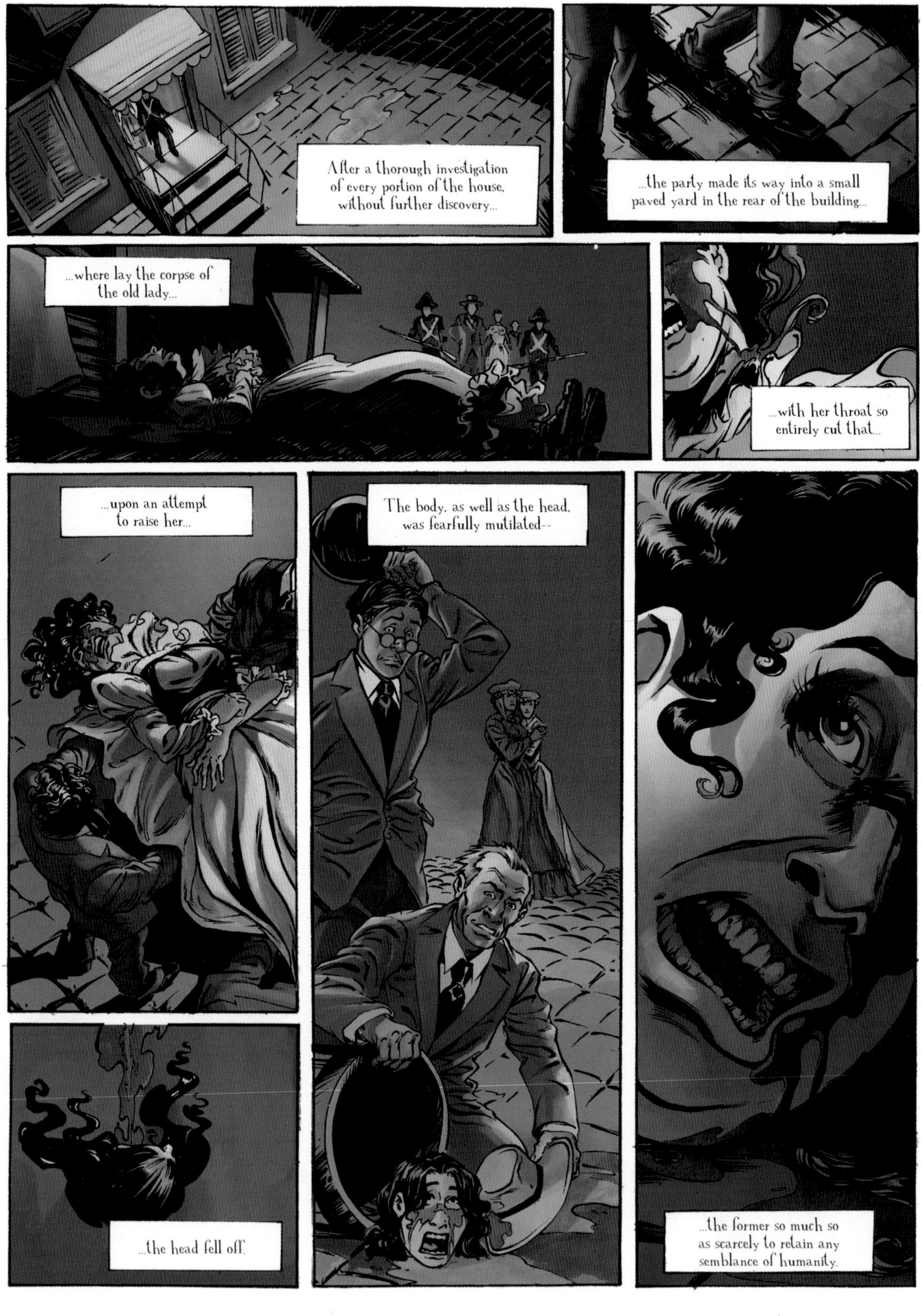
After a thorough investigation of every portion of the house, without further discovery...
...the party made its way into a small paved yard in the rear of the building...
...where lay the corpse of the old lady...
...with her throat so entirely cut that...
...upon an attempt to raise her...
...the head fell off.
The body, as well as the head, was fearfully mutilated--
...the former so much so as scarcely to retain any semblance of humanity.

To this horrible mystery there is not as yet, we believe, the slightest clue.

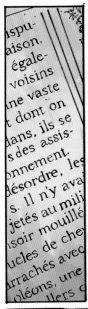

INTERESTING...

SINISTER...

WE SPENT THE REST OF THE NIGHT AND THE FOLLOWING DAY LOSING OURSELVES IN CONJECTURES ON THE AFFAIR.

ALL THE WHILE KNOWING WE STILL LACKED TOO MANY CONCRETE ELEMENTS TO BE ON THE MARK.

WE WERE AMONG THE FIRST TO BUY THE NEXT DAY'S PAPER!

BUT NOT THE LAST, FOR THE DOUBLE MURDERS IN THE RUE MORGUE SEEMED TO EXCITE THE PUBLIC.

WE WOULD HAVE BEEN HARD PRESSED TO FIND THIS MACABRE VOYEURISM INAPPROPRIATE.

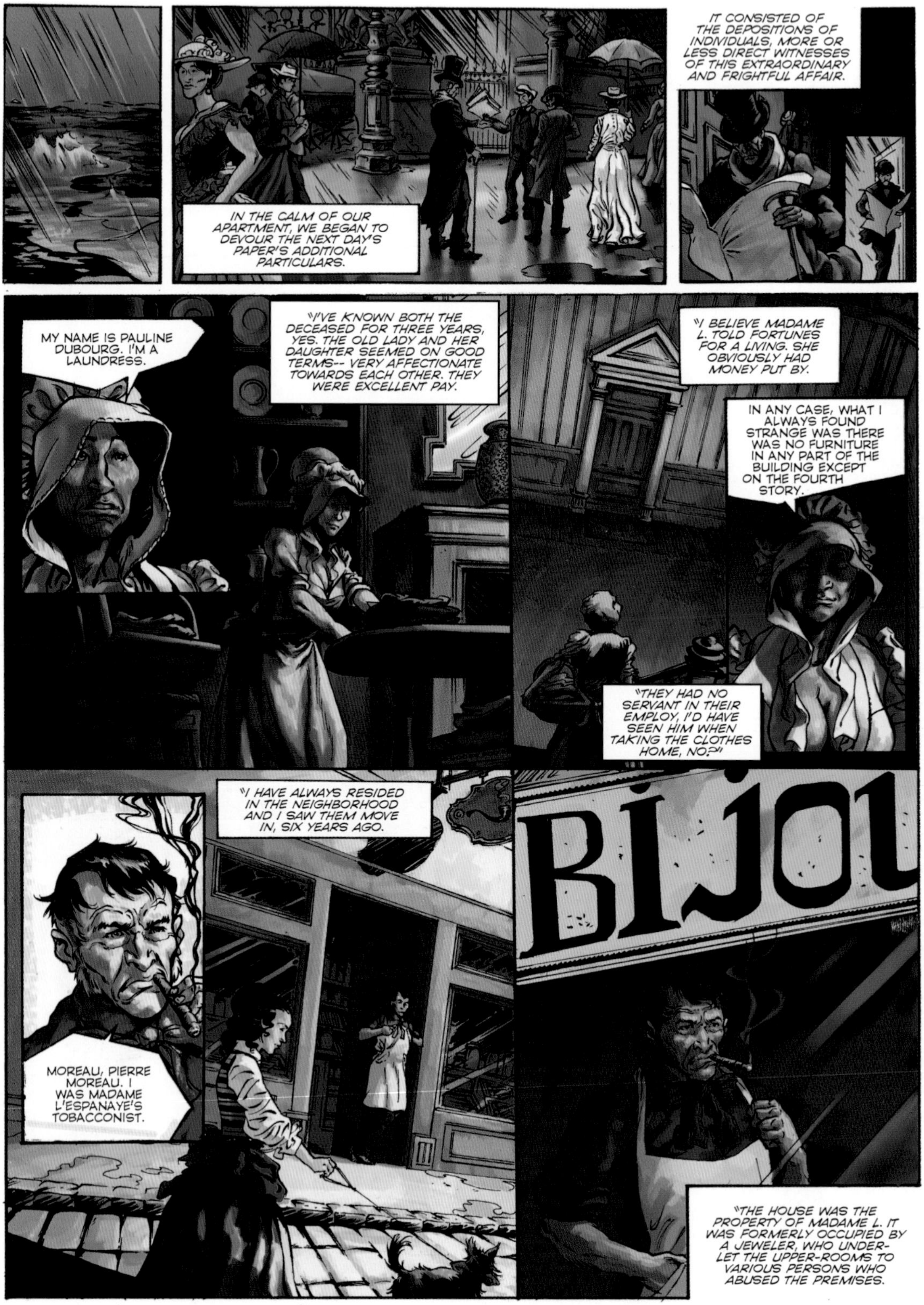
IN THE CALM OF OUR APARTMENT, WE BEGAN TO DEVOUR THE NEXT DAY'S PAPER'S ADDITIONAL PARTICULARS.
IT CONSISTED OF THE DEPOSITIONS OF INDIVIDUALS, MORE OR LESS DIRECT WITNESSES OF THIS EXTRAORDINARY AND FRIGHTFUL AFFAIR.
MY NAME IS PAULINE DUBOURG. I'M A LAUNDRESS.
"I'VE KNOWN BOTH THE DECEASED FOR THREE YEARS, YES. THE OLD LADY AND HER DAUGHTER SEEMED ON GOOD TERMS-- VERY AFFECTIONATE TOWARDS EACH OTHER. THEY WERE EXCELLENT PAY.
"I BELIEVE MADAME L. TOLD FORTUNES FOR A LIVING. SHE OBVIOUSLY HAD MONEY PUT BY.
IN ANY CASE, WHAT I ALWAYS FOUND STRANGE WAS THERE WAS NO FURNITURE IN ANY PART OF THE BUILDING EXCEPT ON THE FOURTH STORY.
"THEY HAD NO SERVANT IN THEIR EMPLOY, I'D HAVE SEEN HIM WHEN TAKING THE CLOTHES HOME, NO?"
MOREAU, PIERRE MOREAU. I WAS MADAME L'ESPANAYE'S TOBACCONIST.
"I HAVE ALWAYS RESIDED IN THE NEIGHBORHOOD AND I SAW THEM MOVE IN, SIX YEARS AGO.
BIJOU
"THE HOUSE WAS THE PROPERTY OF MADAME L. IT WAS FORMERLY OCCUPIED BY A JEWELER, WHO UNDER-LET THE UPPER-ROOMS TO VARIOUS PERSONS WHO ABUSED THE PREMISES.

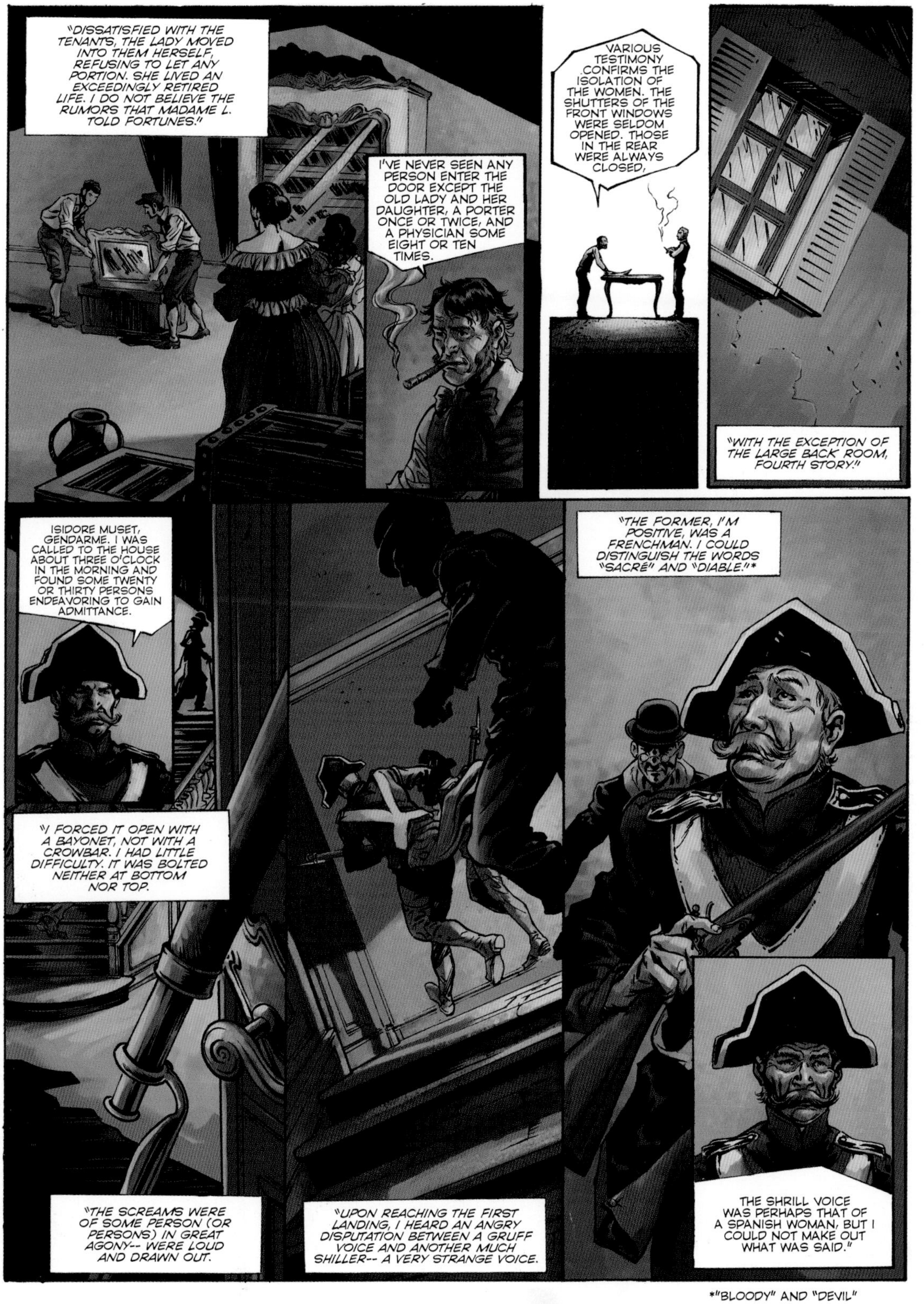
"DISSATISFIED WITH THE TENANTS, THE LADY MOVED INTO THEM HERSELF, REFUSING TO LET ANY PORTION. SHE LIVED AN EXCEEDINGLY RETIRED LIFE. I DO NOT BELIEVE THE RUMORS THAT MADAME L. TOLD FORTUNES."
I'VE NEVER SEEN ANY PERSON ENTER THE DOOR EXCEPT THE OLD LADY AND HER DAUGHTER, A PORTER ONCE OR TWICE, AND A PHYSICIAN SOME EIGHT OR TEN TIMES.
VARIOUS TESTIMONY CONFIRMS THE ISOLATION OF THE WOMEN. THE SHUTTERS OF THE FRONT WINDOWS WERE SELDOM OPENED. THOSE IN THE REAR WERE ALWAYS CLOSED,
"WITH THE EXCEPTION OF THE LARGE BACK ROOM, FOURTH STORY."
ISIDORE MUSET, GENDARME. I WAS CALLED TO THE HOUSE ABOUT THREE O'CLOCK IN THE MORNING AND FOUND SOME TWENTY OR THIRTY PERSONS ENDEAVORING TO GAIN ADMITTANCE.
"I FORCED IT OPEN WITH A BAYONET, NOT WITH A CROWBAR. I HAD LITTLE DIFFICULTY. IT WAS BOLTED NEITHER AT BOTTOM NOR TOP.
"THE SCREAMS WERE OF SOME PERSON (OR PERSONS) IN GREAT AGONY-- WERE LOUD AND DRAWN OUT.
"UPON REACHING THE FIRST LANDING, I HEARD AN ANGRY DISPUTATION BETWEEN A GRUFF VOICE AND ANOTHER MUCH SHILLER-- A VERY STRANGE VOICE.
"THE FORMER, I'M POSITIVE, WAS A FRENCHMAN. I COULD DISTINGUISH THE WORDS "SACRÉ" AND "DIABLE."*
THE SHRILL VOICE WAS PERHAPS THAT OF A SPANISH WOMAN, BUT I COULD NOT MAKE OUT WHAT WAS SAID."

*"BLOODY" AND "DEVIL"

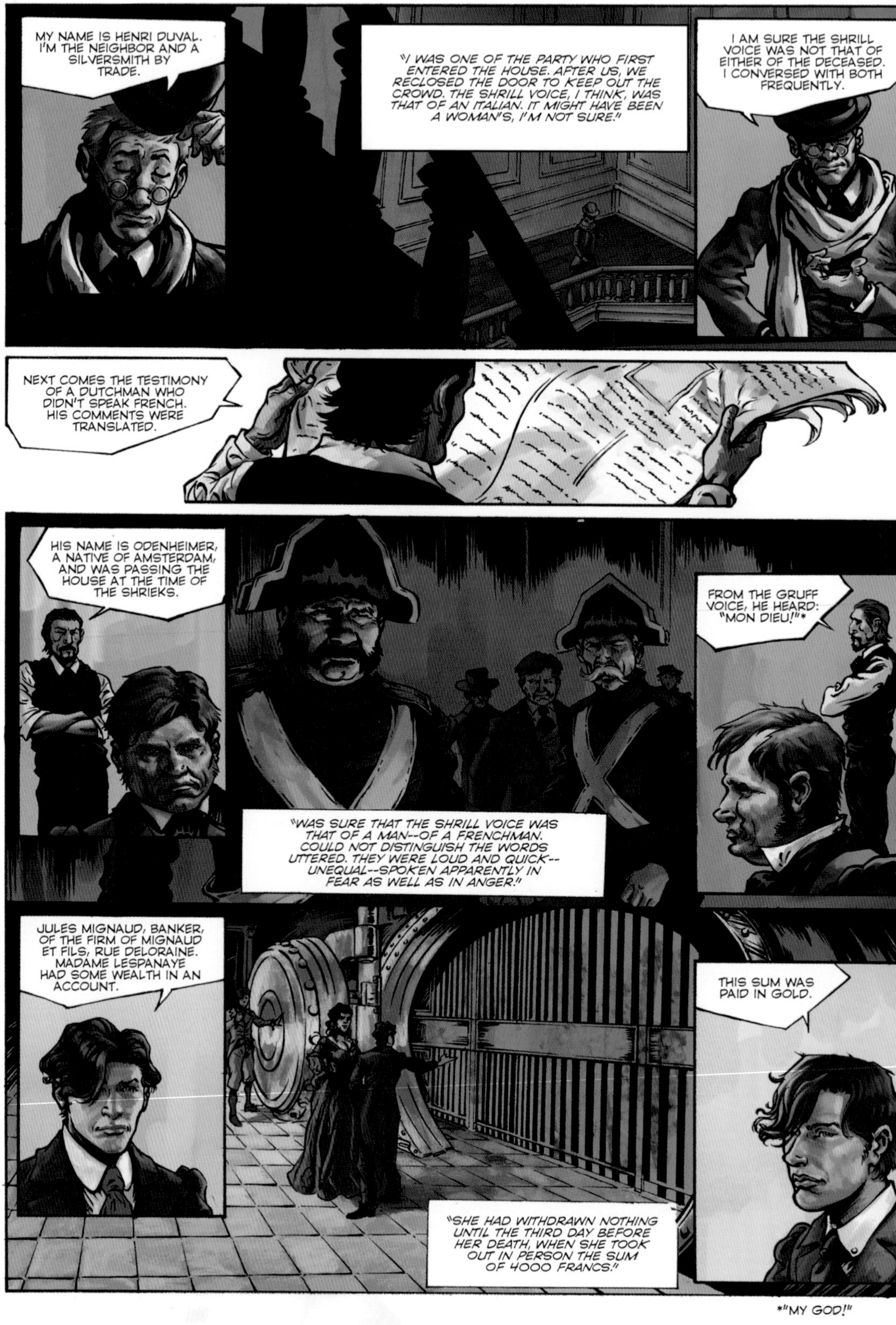
MY NAME IS HENRI DUVAL. I'M THE NEIGHBOR AND A SILVERSMITH BY TRADE.
"I WAS ONE OF THE PARTY WHO FIRST ENTERED THE HOUSE. AFTER US, WE RECLOSED THE DOOR TO KEEP OUT THE CROWD. THE SHRILL VOICE, I THINK, WAS THAT OF AN ITALIAN. IT MIGHT HAVE BEEN A WOMAN'S, I'M NOT SURE."
I AM SURE THE SHRILL VOICE WAS NOT THAT OF EITHER OF THE DECEASED. I CONVERSED WITH BOTH FREQUENTLY.
NEXT COMES THE TESTIMONY OF A DUTCHMAN WHO DIDN'T SPEAK FRENCH. HIS COMMENTS WERE TRANSLATED.
HIS NAME IS ODENHEIMER, A NATIVE OF AMSTERDAM, AND WAS PASSING THE HOUSE AT THE TIME OF THE SHRIEKS.
"WAS SURE THAT THE SHRILL VOICE WAS THAT OF A MAN--OF A FRENCHMAN. COULD NOT DISTINGUISH THE WORDS UTTERED. THEY WERE LOUD AND QUICK--UNEQUAL--SPOKEN APPARENTLY IN FEAR AS WELL AS IN ANGER."
FROM THE GRUFF VOICE, HE HEARD: "MON DIEU!"*
JULES MIGNAUD, BANKER, OF THE FIRM OF MIGNAUD ET FILS, RUE DELORAINE. MADAME LESPANAYE HAD SOME WEALTH IN AN ACCOUNT.
"SHE HAD WITHDRAWN NOTHING UNTIL THE THIRD DAY BEFORE HER DEATH, WHEN SHE TOOK OUT IN PERSON THE SUM OF 4000 FRANCS."
THIS SUM WAS PAID IN GOLD.

*"MY GOD!"

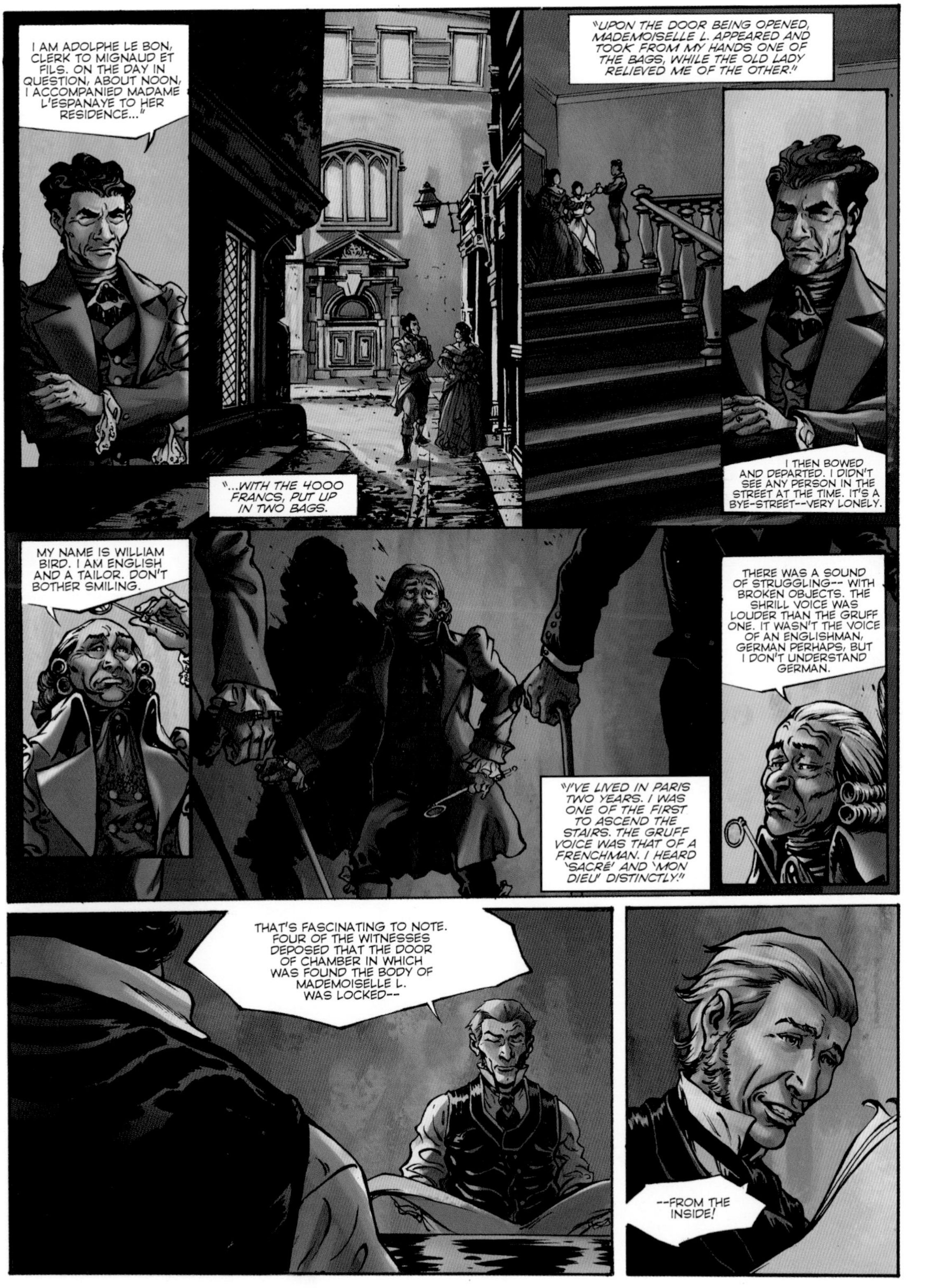
I AM ADOLPHE LE BON, CLERK TO MIGNAUD ET FILS. ON THE DAY IN QUESTION, ABOUT NOON, I ACCOMPANIED MADAME L'ESPANAYE TO HER RESIDENCE..."
"...WITH THE 4000 FRANCS, PUT UP IN TWO BAGS.
"UPON THE DOOR BEING OPENED, MADEMOISELLE L. APPEARED AND TOOK FROM MY HANDS ONE OF THE BAGS, WHILE THE OLD LADY RELIEVED ME OF THE OTHER."
I THEN BOWED AND DEPARTED. I DIDN'T SEE ANY PERSON IN THE STREET AT THE TIME. IT'S A BYE-STREET--VERY LONELY.
MY NAME IS WILLIAM BIRD. I AM ENGLISH AND A TAILOR. DON'T BOTHER SMILING.
"I'VE LIVED IN PARIS TWO YEARS. I WAS ONE OF THE FIRST TO ASCEND THE STAIRS. THE GRUFF VOICE WAS THAT OF A FRENCHMAN. I HEARD 'SACRÉ' AND 'MON DIEU' DISTINCTLY."
THERE WAS A SOUND OF STRUGGLING-- WITH BROKEN OBJECTS. THE SHRILL VOICE WAS LOUDER THAN THE GRUFF ONE. IT WASN'T THE VOICE OF AN ENGLISHMAN, GERMAN PERHAPS, BUT I DON'T UNDERSTAND GERMAN.
THAT'S FASCINATING TO NOTE. FOUR OF THE WITNESSES DEPOSED THAT THE DOOR OF CHAMBER IN WHICH WAS FOUND THE BODY OF MADEMOISELLE L. WAS LOCKED--
--FROM THE INSIDE!

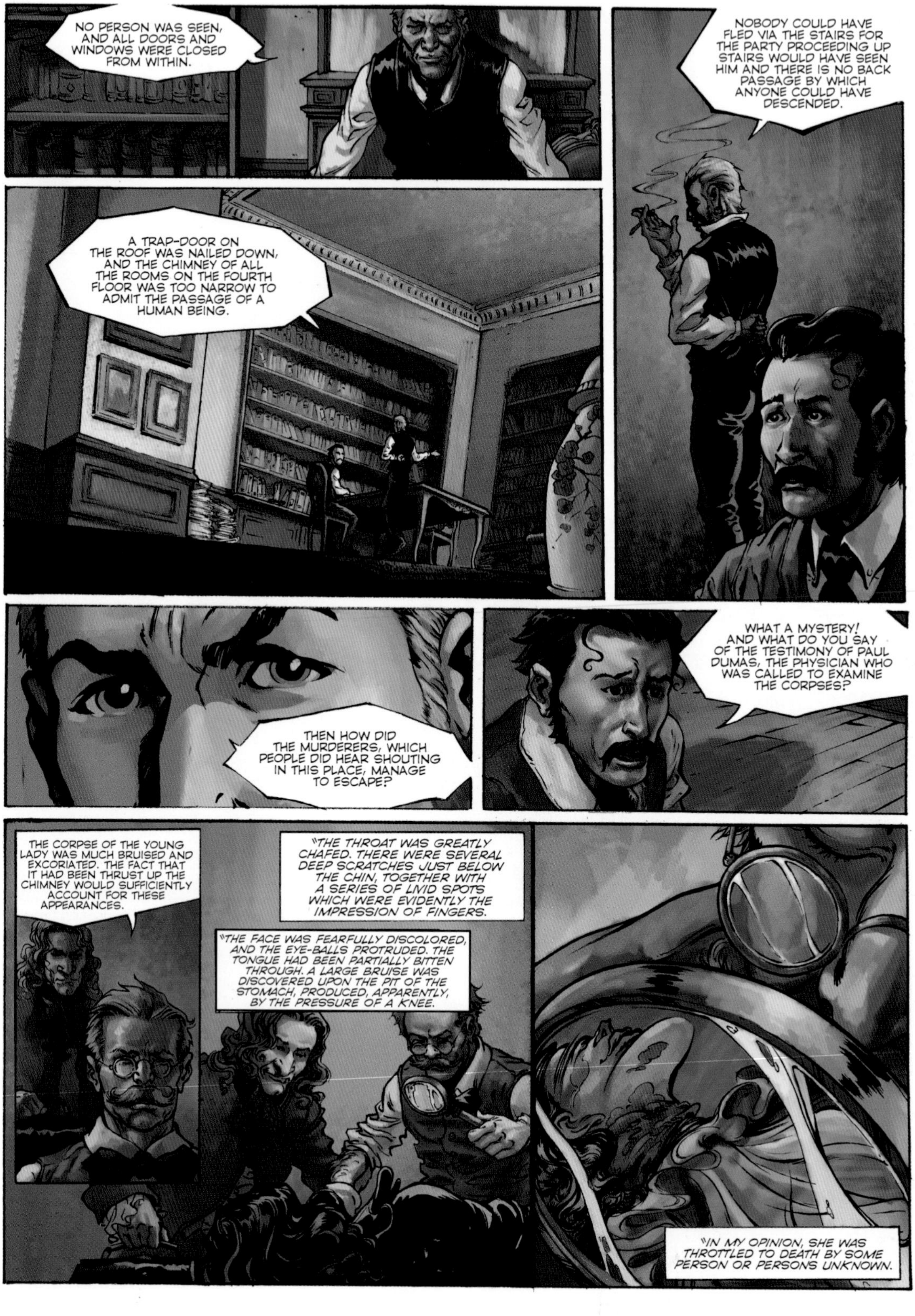
NO PERSON WAS SEEN, AND ALL DOORS AND WINDOWS WERE CLOSED FROM WITHIN.
NOBODY COULD HAVE FLED VIA THE STAIRS FOR THE PARTY PROCEEDING UP STAIRS WOULD HAVE SEEN HIM AND THERE IS NO BACK PASSAGE BY WHICH ANYONE COULD HAVE DESCENDED.
A TRAP-DOOR ON THE ROOF WAS NAILED DOWN, AND THE CHIMNEY OF ALL THE ROOMS ON THE FOURTH FLOOR WAS TOO NARROW TO ADMIT THE PASSAGE OF A HUMAN BEING.
THEN HOW DID THE MURDERERS, WHICH PEOPLE DID HEAR SHOUTING IN THIS PLACE, MANAGE TO ESCAPE?
WHAT A MYSTERY! AND WHAT DO YOU SAY OF THE TESTIMONY OF PAUL DUMAS, THE PHYSICIAN WHO WAS CALLED TO EXAMINE THE CORPSES?
THE CORPSE OF THE YOUNG LADY WAS MUCH BRUISED AND EXCORIATED. THE FACT THAT IT HAD BEEN THRUST UP THE CHIMNEY WOULD SUFFICIENTLY ACCOUNT FOR THESE APPEARANCES.
"THE THROAT WAS GREATLY CHAFED. THERE WERE SEVERAL DEEP SCRATCHES JUST BELOW THE CHIN, TOGETHER WITH A SERIES OF LIVID SPOTS WHICH WERE EVIDENTLY THE IMPRESSION OF FINGERS.
"THE FACE WAS FEARFULLY DISCOLORED, AND THE EYE-BALLS PROTRUDED. THE TONGUE HAD BEEN PARTIALLY BITTEN THROUGH. A LARGE BRUISE WAS DISCOVERED UPON THE PIT OF THE STOMACH, PRODUCED, APPARENTLY, BY THE PRESSURE OF A KNEE.
"IN MY OPINION, SHE WAS THROTTLED TO DEATH BY SOME PERSON OR PERSONS UNKNOWN.

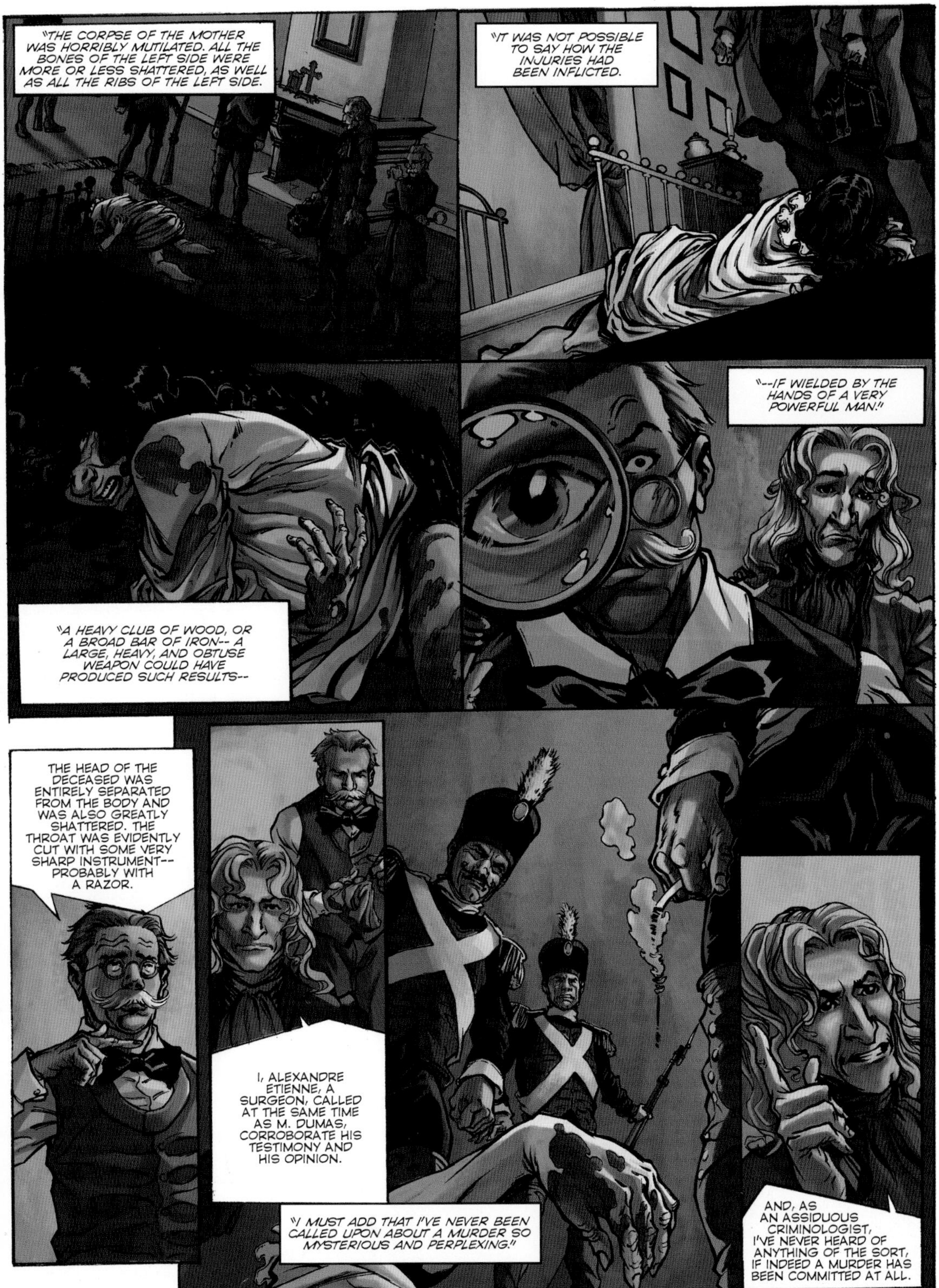
"THE CORPSE OF THE MOTHER WAS HORRIBLY MUTILATED. ALL THE BONES OF THE LEFT SIDE WERE MORE OR LESS SHATTERED, AS WELL AS ALL THE RIBS OF THE LEFT SIDE.
"IT WAS NOT POSSIBLE TO SAY HOW THE INJURIES HAD BEEN INFLICTED.
"A HEAVY CLUB OF WOOD, OR A BROAD BAR OF IRON-- A LARGE, HEAVY, AND OBTUSE WEAPON COULD HAVE PRODUCED SUCH RESULTS--
"--IF WIELDED BY THE HANDS OF A VERY POWERFUL MAN."
THE HEAD OF THE DECEASED WAS ENTIRELY SEPARATED FROM THE BODY AND WAS ALSO GREATLY SHATTERED. THE THROAT WAS EVIDENTLY CUT WITH SOME VERY SHARP INSTRUMENT-- PROBABLY WITH A RAZOR.
I, ALEXANDRE ETIENNE, A SURGEON, CALLED AT THE SAME TIME AS M. DUMAS, CORROBORATE HIS TESTIMONY AND HIS OPINION.
"I MUST ADD THAT I'VE NEVER BEEN CALLED UPON ABOUT A MURDER SO MYSTERIOUS AND PERPLEXING."
AND, AS AN ASSIDUOUS CRIMINOLOGIST, I'VE NEVER HEARD OF ANYTHING OF THE SORT, IF INDEED A MURDER HAS BEEN COMMITTED AT ALL.

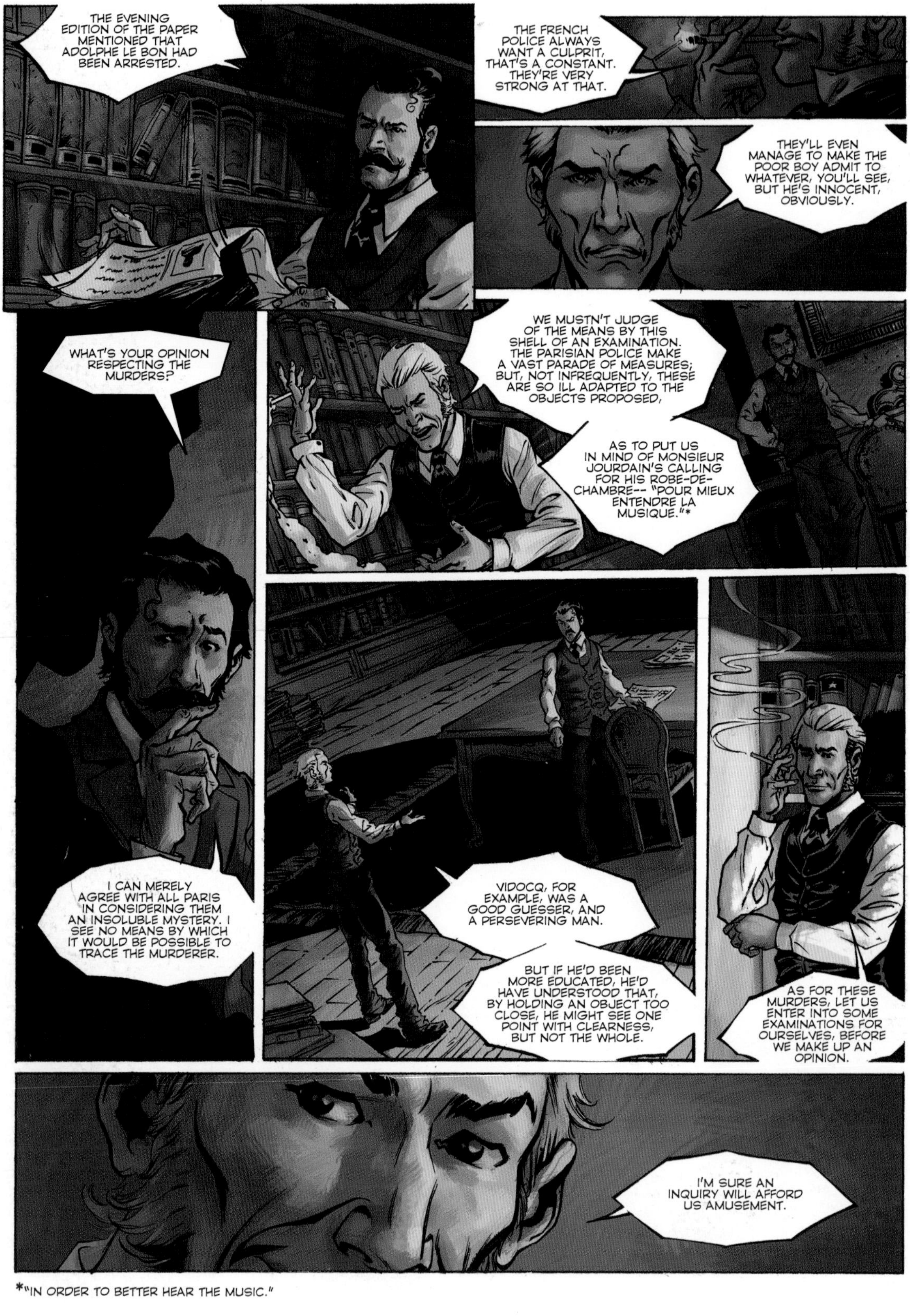
THE EVENING EDITION OF THE PAPER MENTIONED THAT ADOLPHE LE BON HAD BEEN ARRESTED.
THE FRENCH POLICE ALWAYS WANT A CULPRIT, THAT'S A CONSTANT. THEY'RE VERY STRONG AT THAT.
THEY'LL EVEN MANAGE TO MAKE THE POOR BOY ADMIT TO WHATEVER, YOU'LL SEE, BUT HE'S INNOCENT, OBVIOUSLY.
WHAT'S YOUR OPINION RESPECTING THE MURDERS?
WE MUSTN'T JUDGE OF THE MEANS BY THIS SHELL OF AN EXAMINATION. THE PARISIAN POLICE MAKE A VAST PARADE OF MEASURES; BUT, NOT INFREQUENTLY, THESE ARE SO ILL ADAPTED TO THE OBJECTS PROPOSED,
AS TO PUT US IN MIND OF MONSIEUR JOURDAIN'S CALLING FOR HIS ROBE-DE-CHAMBRE-- "POUR MIEUX ENTENDRE LA MUSIQUE."*
I CAN MERELY AGREE WITH ALL PARIS IN CONSIDERING THEM AN INSOLUBLE MYSTERY. I SEE NO MEANS BY WHICH IT WOULD BE POSSIBLE TO TRACE THE MURDERER.
VIDOCQ, FOR EXAMPLE, WAS A GOOD GUESSER, AND A PERSEVERING MAN.
BUT IF HE'D BEEN MORE EDUCATED, HE'D HAVE UNDERSTOOD THAT, BY HOLDING AN OBJECT TOO CLOSE, HE MIGHT SEE ONE POINT WITH CLEARNESS, BUT NOT THE WHOLE.
AS FOR THESE MURDERS, LET US ENTER INTO SOME EXAMINATIONS FOR OURSELVES, BEFORE WE MAKE UP AN OPINION.
I'M SURE AN INQUIRY WILL AFFORD US AMUSEMENT.

*"IN ORDER TO BETTER HEAR THE MUSIC."

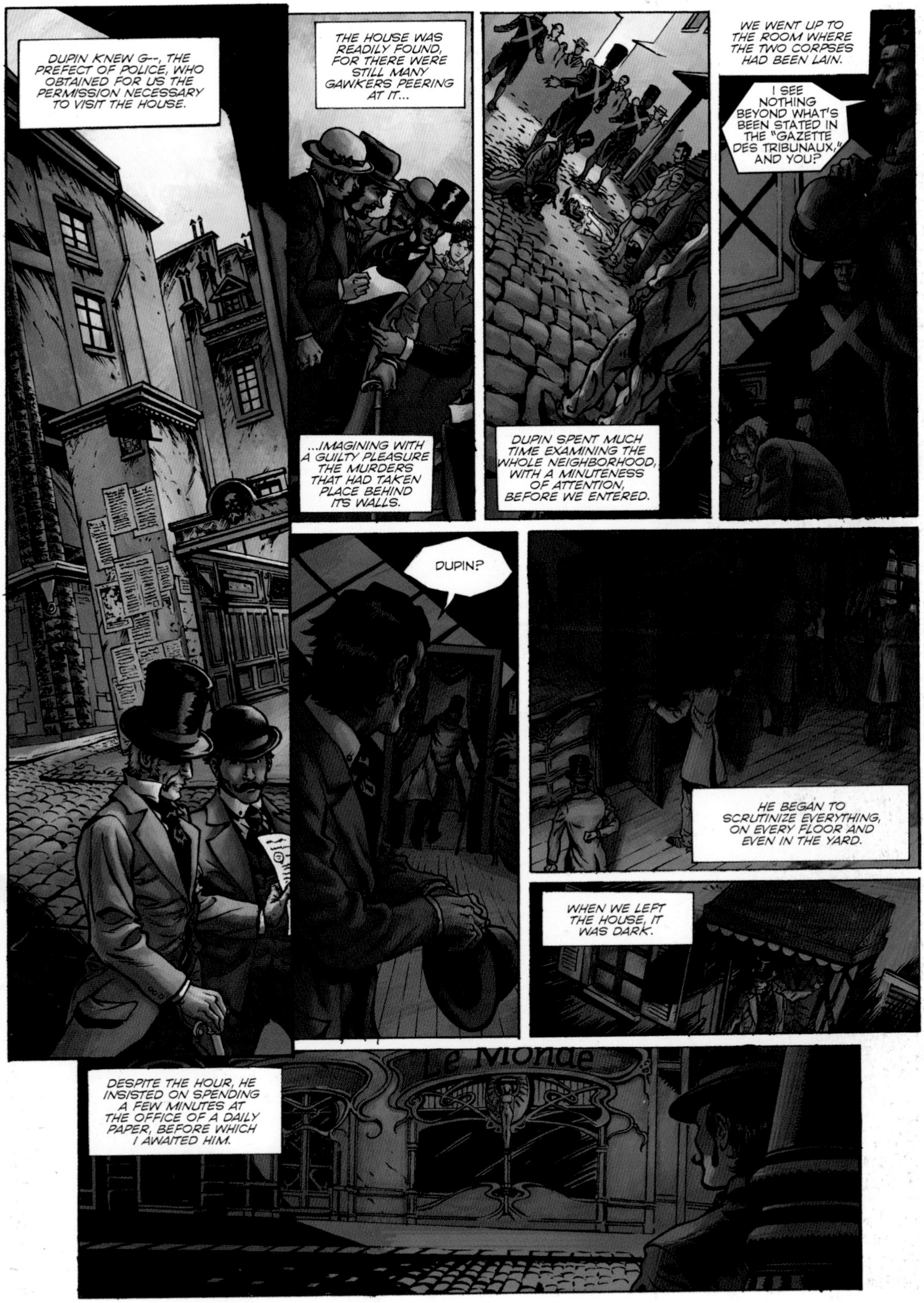

DUPIN KNEW G--, THE PREFECT OF POLICE, WHO OBTAINED FOR US THE PERMISSION NECESSARY TO VISIT THE HOUSE.
THE HOUSE WAS READILY FOUND, FOR THERE WERE STILL MANY GAWKERS PEERING AT IT...
...IMAGINING WITH A GUILTY PLEASURE THE MURDERS THAT HAD TAKEN PLACE BEHIND ITS WALLS.
DUPIN SPENT MUCH TIME EXAMINING THE WHOLE NEIGHBORHOOD, WITH A MINUTENESS OF ATTENTION, BEFORE WE ENTERED.
WE WENT UP TO THE ROOM WHERE THE TWO CORPSES HAD BEEN LAIN.
I SEE NOTHING BEYOND WHAT'S BEEN STATED IN THE "GAZETTE DES TRIBUNAUX," AND YOU?
DUPIN?
HE BEGAN TO SCRUTINIZE EVERYTHING, ON EVERY FLOOR AND EVEN IN THE YARD.
WHEN WE LEFT THE HOUSE, IT WAS DARK.
Le Monde
DESPITE THE HOUR, HE INSISTED ON SPENDING A FEW MINUTES AT THE OFFICE OF A DAILY PAPER, BEFORE WHICH I AWAITED HIM.

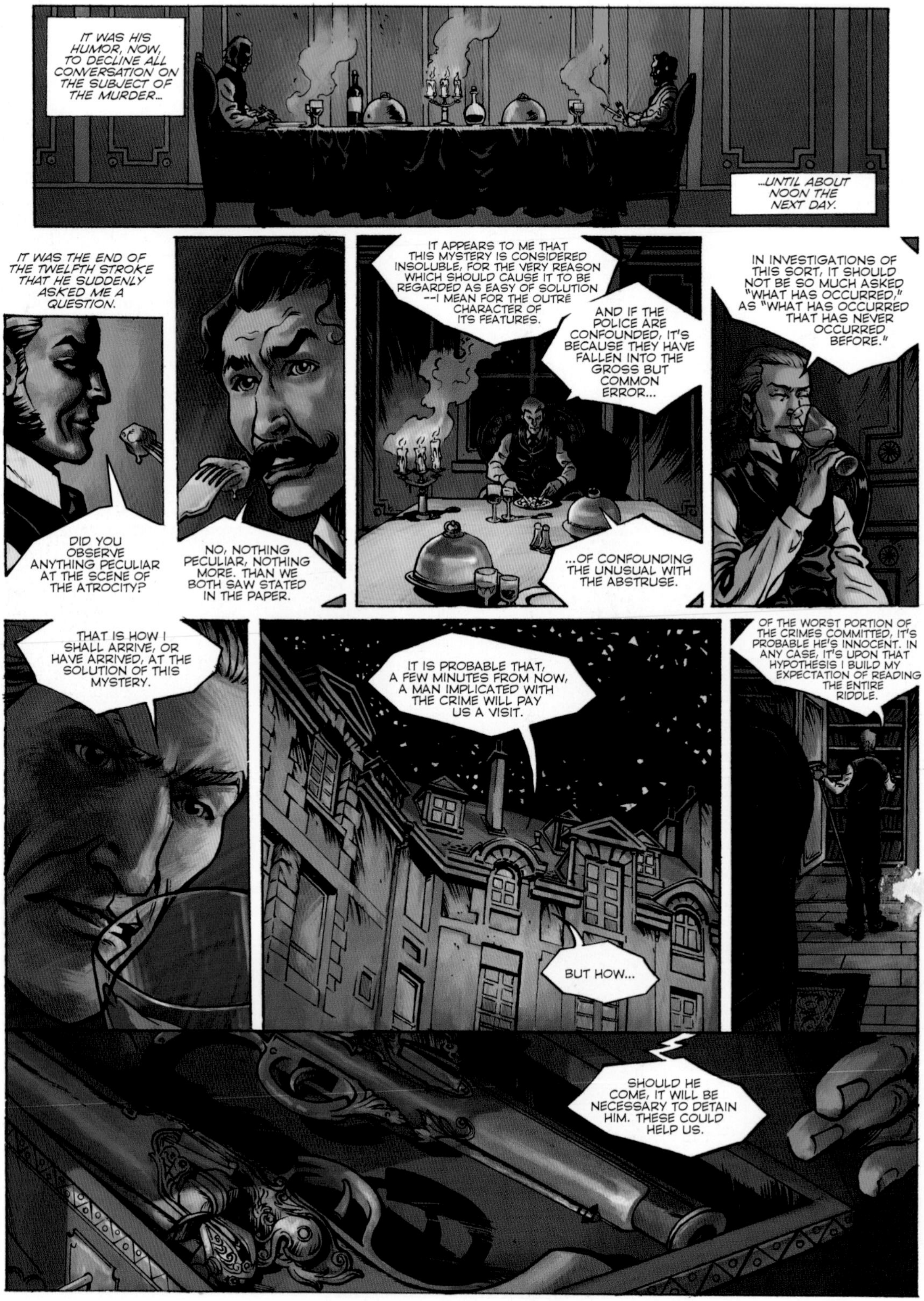
IT WAS HIS HUMOR, NOW, TO DECLINE ALL CONVERSATION ON THE SUBJECT OF THE MURDER...
...UNTIL ABOUT NOON THE NEXT DAY.
IT WAS THE END OF THE TWELFTH STROKE THAT HE SUDDENLY ASKED ME A QUESTION.
DID YOU OBSERVE ANYTHING PECULIAR AT THE SCENE OF THE ATROCITY?
NO, NOTHING PECULIAR, NOTHING MORE. THAN WE BOTH SAW STATED IN THE PAPER.
IT APPEARS TO ME THAT THIS MYSTERY IS CONSIDERED INSOLUBLE, FOR THE VERY REASON WHICH SHOULD CAUSE IT TO BE REGARDED AS EASY OF SOLUTION --I MEAN FOR THE OUTRÉ CHARACTER OF ITS FEATURES.
AND IF THE POLICE ARE CONFOUNDED, IT'S BECAUSE THEY HAVE FALLEN INTO THE GROSS BUT COMMON ERROR...
...OF CONFOUNDING THE UNUSUAL WITH THE ABSTRUSE.
IN INVESTIGATIONS OF THIS SORT, IT SHOULD NOT BE SO MUCH ASKED "WHAT HAS OCCURRED," AS "WHAT HAS OCCURRED THAT HAS NEVER OCCURRED BEFORE."
THAT IS HOW I SHALL ARRIVE, OR HAVE ARRIVED, AT THE SOLUTION OF THIS MYSTERY.
IT IS PROBABLE THAT, A FEW MINUTES FROM NOW, A MAN IMPLICATED WITH THE CRIME WILL PAY US A VISIT.
BUT HOW...
OF THE WORST PORTION OF THE CRIMES COMMITTED, IT'S PROBABLE HE'S INNOCENT. IN ANY CASE, IT'S UPON THAT HYPOTHESIS I BUILD MY EXPECTATION OF READING THE ENTIRE RIDDLE.
SHOULD HE COME, IT WILL BE NECESSARY TO DETAIN HIM. THESE COULD HELP US.

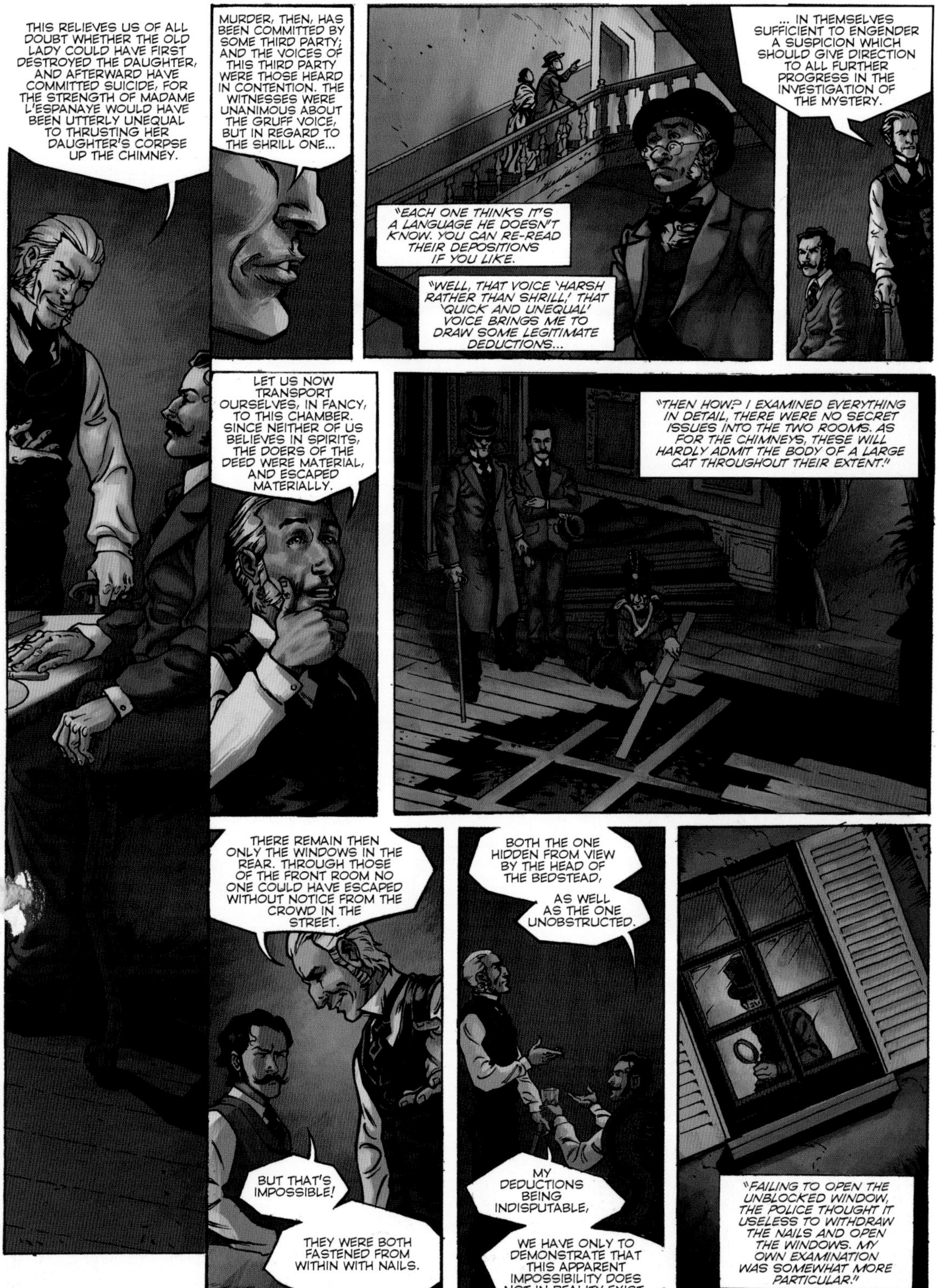
THIS RELIEVES US OF ALL DOUBT WHETHER THE OLD LADY COULD HAVE FIRST DESTROYED THE DAUGHTER, AND AFTERWARD HAVE COMMITTED SUICIDE, FOR THE STRENGTH OF MADAME L'ESPANAYE WOULD HAVE BEEN UTTERLY UNEQUAL TO THRUSTING HER DAUGHTER'S CORPSE UP THE CHIMNEY.
MURDER, THEN, HAS BEEN COMMITTED BY SOME THIRD PARTY; AND THE VOICES OF THIS THIRD PARTY WERE THOSE HEARD IN CONTENTION. THE WITNESSES WERE UNANIMOUS ABOUT THE GRUFF VOICE, BUT IN REGARD TO THE SHRILL ONE...
"EACH ONE THINKS IT'S A LANGUAGE HE DOESN'T KNOW. YOU CAN RE-READ THEIR DEPOSITIONS IF YOU LIKE.
"WELL, THAT VOICE 'HARSH RATHER THAN SHRILL,' THAT 'QUICK AND UNEQUAL' VOICE BRINGS ME TO DRAW SOME LEGITIMATE DEDUCTIONS...
... IN THEMSELVES SUFFICIENT TO ENGENDER A SUSPICION WHICH SHOULD GIVE DIRECTION TO ALL FURTHER PROGRESS IN THE INVESTIGATION OF THE MYSTERY.
LET US NOW TRANSPORT OURSELVES, IN FANCY, TO THIS CHAMBER. SINCE NEITHER OF US BELIEVES IN SPIRITS, THE DOERS OF THE DEED WERE MATERIAL, AND ESCAPED MATERIALLY.
"THEN HOW? I EXAMINED EVERYTHING IN DETAIL, THERE WERE NO SECRET ISSUES INTO THE TWO ROOMS. AS FOR THE CHIMNEYS, THESE WILL HARDLY ADMIT THE BODY OF A LARGE CAT THROUGHOUT THEIR EXTENT."
THERE REMAIN THEN ONLY THE WINDOWS IN THE REAR. THROUGH THOSE OF THE FRONT ROOM NO ONE COULD HAVE ESCAPED WITHOUT NOTICE FROM THE CROWD IN THE STREET.
BUT THAT'S IMPOSSIBLE!
THEY WERE BOTH FASTENED FROM WITHIN WITH NAILS.
BOTH THE ONE HIDDEN FROM VIEW BY THE HEAD OF THE BEDSTEAD,
AS WELL AS THE ONE UNOBSTRUCTED.
MY DEDUCTIONS BEING INDISPUTABLE,
WE HAVE ONLY TO DEMONSTRATE THAT THIS APPARENT IMPOSSIBILITY DOES NOT IN REALITY EXIST.
"FAILING TO OPEN THE UNBLOCKED WINDOW, THE POLICE THOUGHT IT USELESS TO WITHDRAW THE NAILS AND OPEN THE WINDOWS. MY OWN EXAMINATION WAS SOMEWHAT MORE PARTICULAR."

SINCE THEY DID ESCAPE THAT WAY AND SINCE THE WINDOWS WERE NONETHELESS CLOSED, IT'S BECAUSE THE LATTER HAD FASTENED THEMSELVES. I WAS CERTAIN THERE WAS A CONCEALED SPRING.

"THERE WAS NONE ON THE FIRST WINDOW, BUT UPON THE ONE IN FRONT OF WHICH THE BEDSTEAD WAS LEANED...

"THE NAIL SEEMED INTACT, BUT IN FACT, THE HEAD OF IT WAS BROKEN. WHEN I OPENED THE WINDOW, THE HEAD WENT UP WITH IT.

"ONCE I CLOSED THE WINDOW, THE SEMBLANCE OF THE WHOLE NAIL WAS AGAIN PERFECT."

LET US SPEAK NOW OF ACCESS. ABOUT FIVE FEET AND A HALF FROM THE CASEMENT IN QUESTION THERE RUNS A LIGHTNING-ROD.

THE SHUTTERS ARE A SINGLE PIECE, NOT A FOLDING DOOR AND MEASURE FULLY THREE FEET AND A HALF BROAD.

IF SWUNG FULLY BACK TO THE WALL, THEY REACH TO WITHIN TWO FEET OF THE LIGHTNING-ROD.

BY EXERTION OF A VERY UNUSUAL DEGREE OF ACTIVITY AND COURAGE, ONE COULD HAVE THEM PASSED FROM THE ROD TO THE SHUTTER. AND SUPPOSING THE WINDOW OPEN...

PUSH AGAINST THE WALL TO CLOSE THE SHUTTER AND THUS EFFECT AN ENTRANCE INTO THE ROOM.

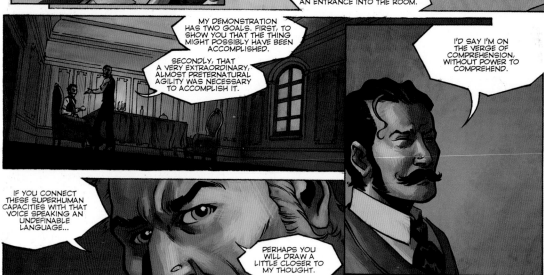

MY DEMONSTRATION HAS TWO GOALS. FIRST, TO SHOW YOU THAT THE THING MIGHT POSSIBLY HAVE BEEN ACCOMPLISHED.

SECONDLY, THAT A VERY EXTRAORDINARY, ALMOST PRETERNATURAL AGILITY WAS NECESSARY TO ACCOMPLISH IT.

I'D SAY I'M ON THE VERGE OF COMPREHENSION, WITHOUT POWER TO COMPREHEND.

IF YOU CONNECT THESE SUPERHUMAN CAPACITIES WITH THAT VOICE SPEAKING AN UNDEFINABLE LANGUAGE...

PERHAPS YOU WILL DRAW A LITTLE CLOSER TO MY THOUGHT.

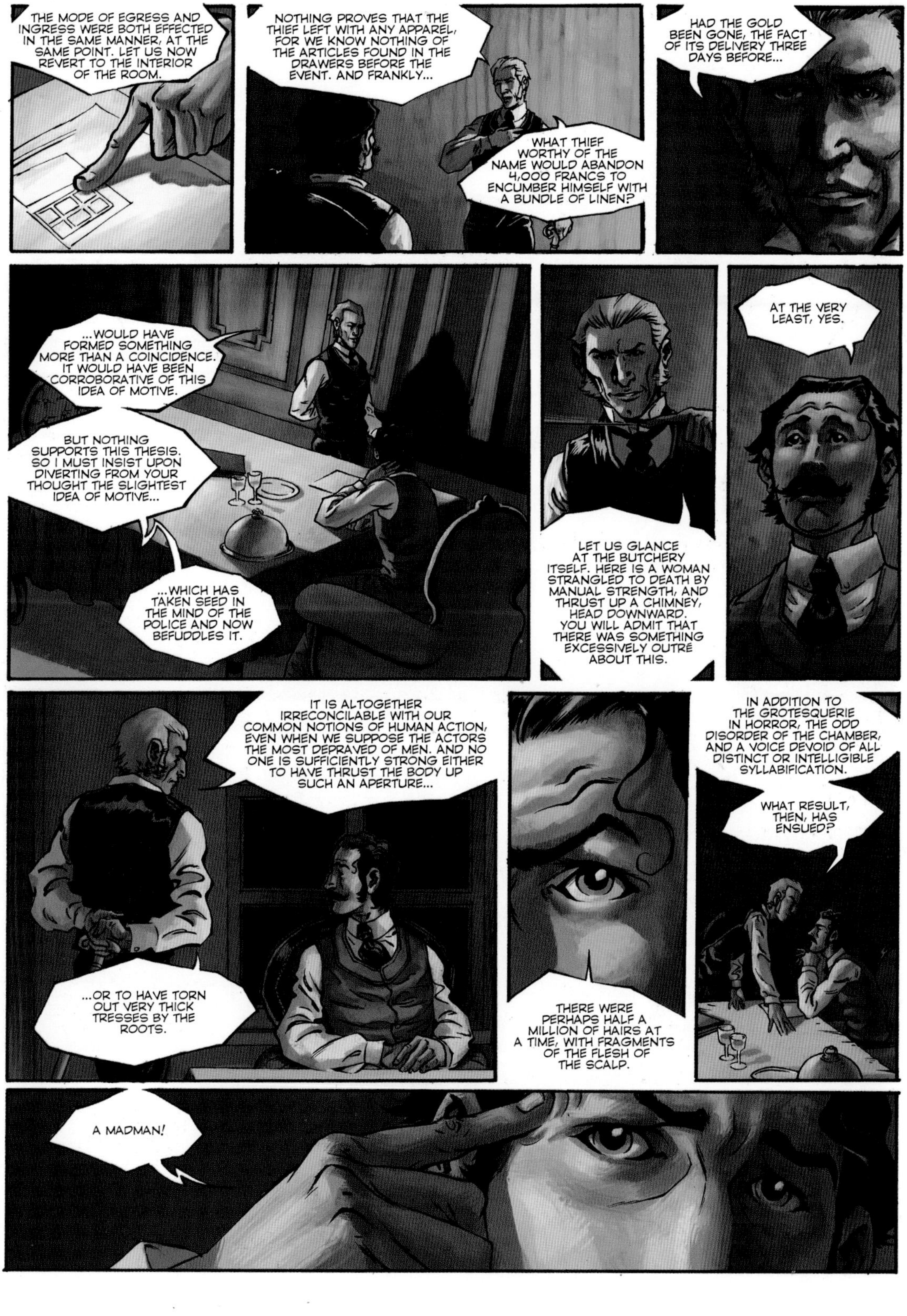
THE MODE OF EGRESS AND INGRESS WERE BOTH EFFECTED IN THE SAME MANNER, AT THE SAME POINT. LET US NOW REVERT TO THE INTERIOR OF THE ROOM.
NOTHING PROVES THAT THE THIEF LEFT WITH ANY APPAREL, FOR WE KNOW NOTHING OF THE ARTICLES FOUND IN THE DRAWERS BEFORE THE EVENT. AND FRANKLY...
WHAT THIEF WORTHY OF THE NAME WOULD ABANDON 4,000 FRANCS TO ENCUMBER HIMSELF WITH A BUNDLE OF LINEN?
HAD THE GOLD BEEN GONE, THE FACT OF ITS DELIVERY THREE DAYS BEFORE...
...WOULD HAVE FORMED SOMETHING MORE THAN A COINCIDENCE. IT WOULD HAVE BEEN CORROBORATIVE OF THIS IDEA OF MOTIVE.
BUT NOTHING SUPPORTS THIS THESIS. SO I MUST INSIST UPON DIVERTING FROM YOUR THOUGHT THE SLIGHTEST IDEA OF MOTIVE...
...WHICH HAS TAKEN SEED IN THE MIND OF THE POLICE AND NOW BEFUDDLES IT.
LET US GLANCE AT THE BUTCHERY ITSELF. HERE IS A WOMAN STRANGLED TO DEATH BY MANUAL STRENGTH, AND THRUST UP A CHIMNEY, HEAD DOWNWARD. YOU WILL ADMIT THAT THERE WAS SOMETHING EXCESSIVELY OUTRÉ ABOUT THIS.
AT THE VERY LEAST, YES.
IT IS ALTOGETHER IRRECONCILABLE WITH OUR COMMON NOTIONS OF HUMAN ACTION, EVEN WHEN WE SUPPOSE THE ACTORS THE MOST DEPRAVED OF MEN. AND NO ONE IS SUFFICIENTLY STRONG EITHER TO HAVE THRUST THE BODY UP SUCH AN APERTURE...
...OR TO HAVE TORN OUT VERY THICK TRESSES BY THE ROOTS.
THERE WERE PERHAPS HALF A MILLION OF HAIRS AT A TIME, WITH FRAGMENTS OF THE FLESH OF THE SCALP.
IN ADDITION TO THE GROTESQUERIE IN HORROR, THE ODD DISORDER OF THE CHAMBER, AND A VOICE DEVOID OF ALL DISTINCT OR INTELLIGIBLE SYLLABIFICATION.
WHAT RESULT, THEN, HAS ENSUED?
A MADMAN!

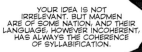

YOUR IDEA IS NOT IRRELEVANT. BUT MADMEN ARE OF SOME NATION, AND THEIR LANGUAGE, HOWEVER INCOHERENT, HAS ALWAYS THE COHERENCE OF SYLLABIFICATION.

DUPIN, WHY THESE HAIRS...

TO HELP YOU, I DISENTANGLED THIS LITTLE TUFT FROM THE RIGIDLY CLUTCHED FINGERS OF MADAME L'ESPANAYE.

OF COURSE, SOME RAVING MANIAC, ESCAPED FROM A NEIGHBORING MAISON DE SANTÉ.*

THIS IS NO HUMAN HAIR!

I HAVE NOT ASSERTED THAT IT IS.

I WISH YOU TO GLANCE AT THE LITTLE SKETCH.

WHAT IS IT?

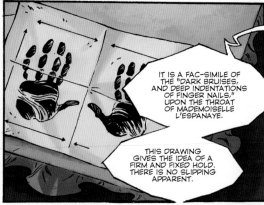

IT IS A FAC-SIMILE OF THE "DARK BRUISES, AND DEEP INDENTATIONS OF FINGER NAILS," UPON THE THROAT OF MADEMOISELLE L'ESPANAYE.

THIS DRAWING GIVES THE IDEA OF A FIRM AND FIXED HOLD. THERE IS NO SLIPPING APPARENT.

ATTEMPT, NOW, TO PLACE ALL YOUR FINGERS, AT THE SAME TIME, IN THE RESPECTIVE IMPRESSIONS AS YOU SEE THEM.

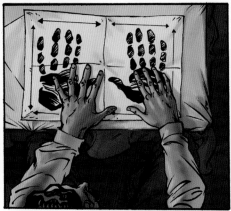

IMPOSSIBLE.

THIS IS THE MARK OF NO HUMAN HAND.

*"MENTAL HOME"

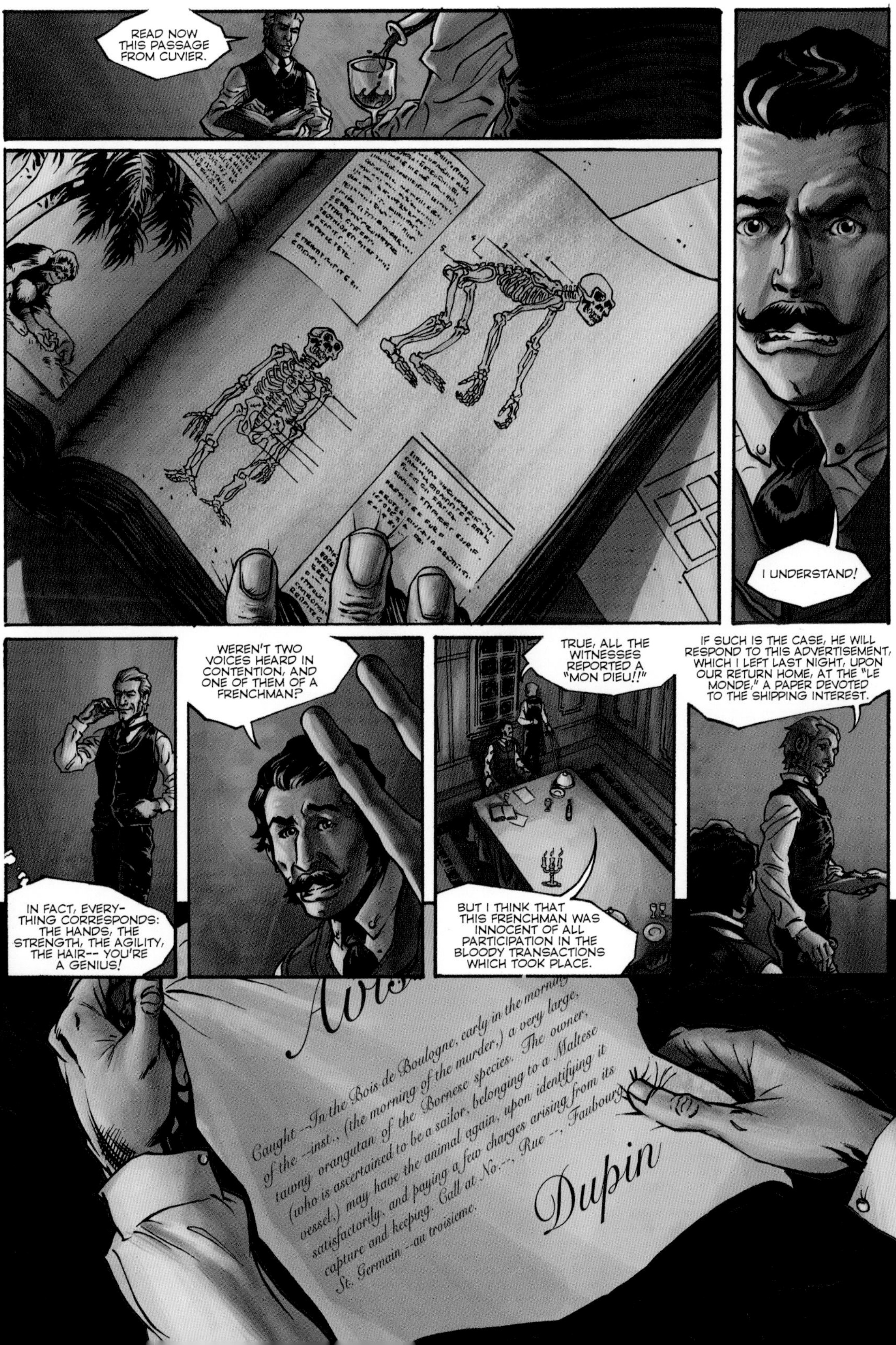
READ NOW THIS PASSAGE FROM CUVIER.
I UNDERSTAND!
IN FACT, EVERYTHING CORRESPONDS: THE HANDS, THE STRENGTH, THE AGILITY, THE HAIR-- YOU'RE A GENIUS!
WEREN'T TWO VOICES HEARD IN CONTENTION, AND ONE OF THEM OF A FRENCHMAN?
TRUE, ALL THE WITNESSES REPORTED A "MON DIEU!!"
BUT I THINK THAT THIS FRENCHMAN WAS INNOCENT OF ALL PARTICIPATION IN THE BLOODY TRANSACTIONS WHICH TOOK PLACE.
IF SUCH IS THE CASE, HE WILL RESPOND TO THIS ADVERTISEMENT, WHICH I LEFT LAST NIGHT, UPON OUR RETURN HOME, AT THE "LE MONDE," A PAPER DEVOTED TO THE SHIPPING INTEREST.
Caught --In the Bois de Boulogne, early in the morning of the --inst., (the morning of the murder,) a very large, tawny orangutan of the Bornese species. The owner, (who is ascertained to be a sailor, belonging to a Maltese vessel,) may have the animal again, upon identifying it satisfactorily, and paying a few charges arising from its capture and keeping. Call at No.--, Rue --, Faubourg St. Germain --au troisieme.
Dupin

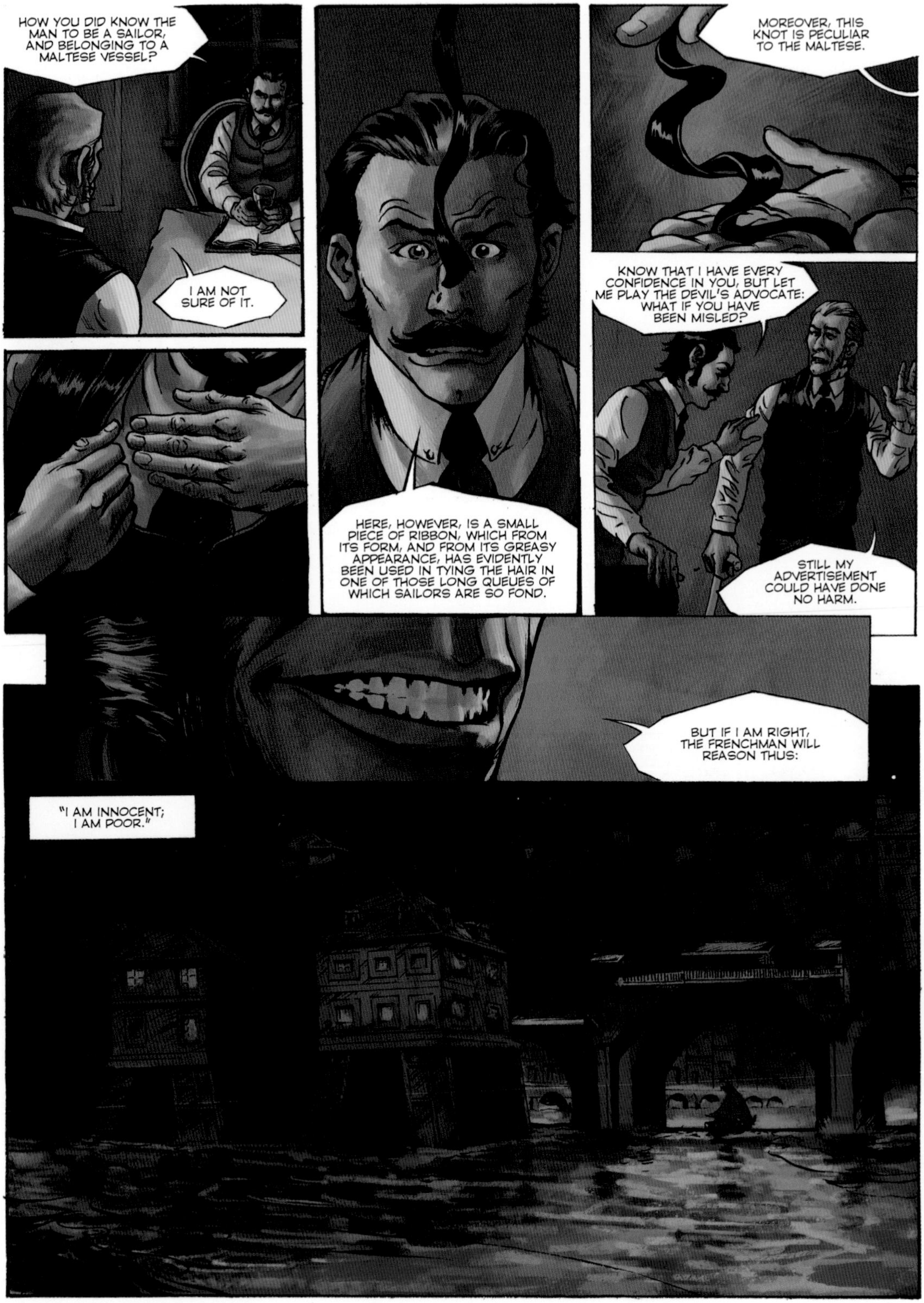
HOW YOU DID KNOW THE MAN TO BE A SAILOR, AND BELONGING TO A MALTESE VESSEL?
I AM NOT SURE OF IT.
HERE, HOWEVER, IS A SMALL PIECE OF RIBBON, WHICH FROM ITS FORM, AND FROM ITS GREASY APPEARANCE, HAS EVIDENTLY BEEN USED IN TYING THE HAIR IN ONE OF THOSE LONG QUEUES OF WHICH SAILORS ARE SO FOND.
MOREOVER, THIS KNOT IS PECULIAR TO THE MALTESE.
KNOW THAT I HAVE EVERY CONFIDENCE IN YOU, BUT LET ME PLAY THE DEVIL'S ADVOCATE: WHAT IF YOU HAVE BEEN MISLED?
STILL MY ADVERTISEMENT COULD HAVE DONE NO HARM.
BUT IF I AM RIGHT, THE FRENCHMAN WILL REASON THUS:
"I AM INNOCENT; I AM POOR."

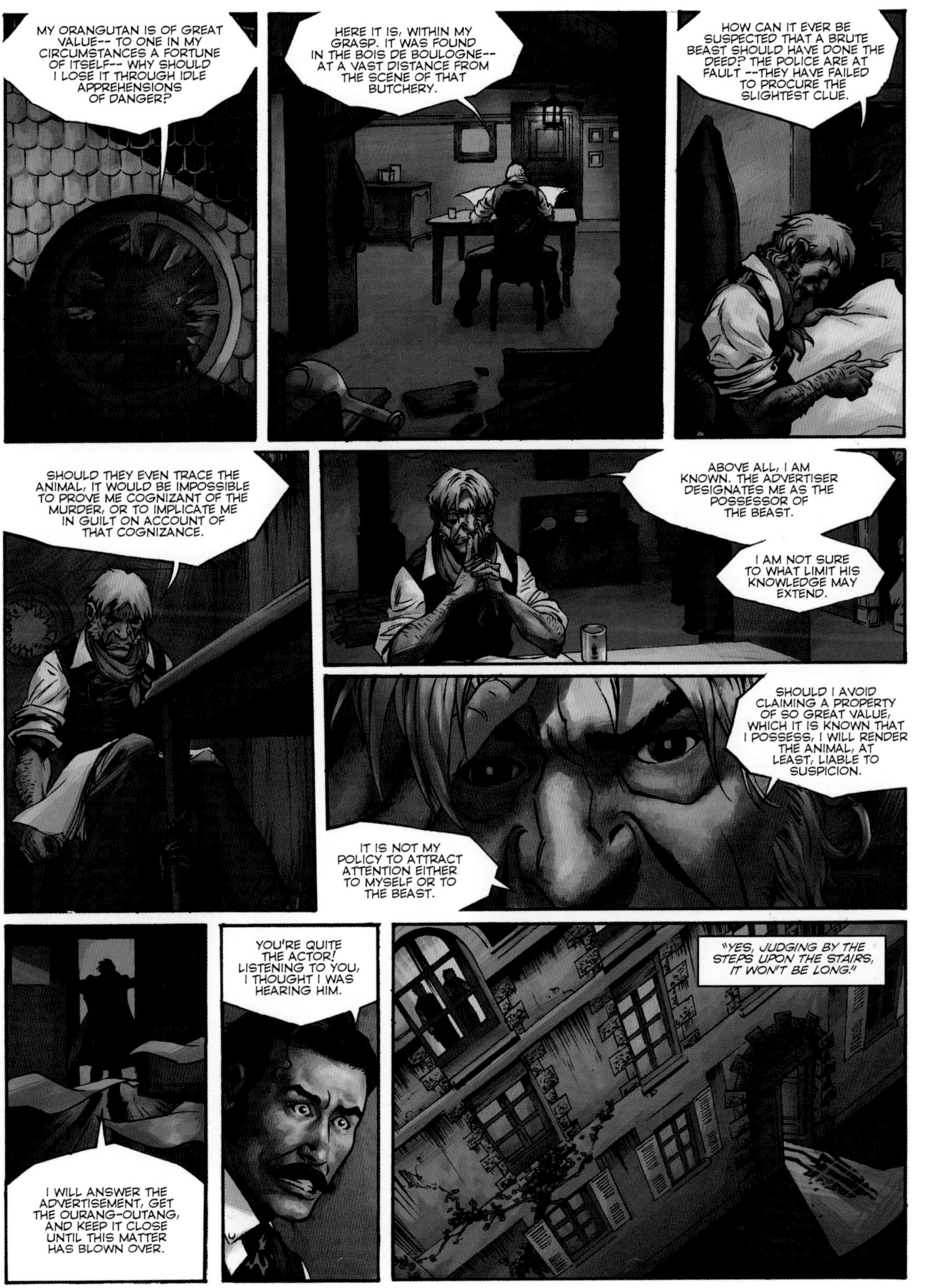
MY ORANGUTAN IS OF GREAT VALUE-- TO ONE IN MY CIRCUMSTANCES A FORTUNE OF ITSELF-- WHY SHOULD I LOSE IT THROUGH IDLE APPREHENSIONS OF DANGER?
HERE IT IS, WITHIN MY GRASP. IT WAS FOUND IN THE BOIS DE BOULOGNE-- AT A VAST DISTANCE FROM THE SCENE OF THAT BUTCHERY.
HOW CAN IT EVER BE SUSPECTED THAT A BRUTE BEAST SHOULD HAVE DONE THE DEED? THE POLICE ARE AT FAULT --THEY HAVE FAILED TO PROCURE THE SLIGHTEST CLUE.
SHOULD THEY EVEN TRACE THE ANIMAL, IT WOULD BE IMPOSSIBLE TO PROVE ME COGNIZANT OF THE MURDER, OR TO IMPLICATE ME IN GUILT ON ACCOUNT OF THAT COGNIZANCE.
ABOVE ALL, I AM KNOWN. THE ADVERTISER DESIGNATES ME AS THE POSSESSOR OF THE BEAST.
I AM NOT SURE TO WHAT LIMIT HIS KNOWLEDGE MAY EXTEND.
SHOULD I AVOID CLAIMING A PROPERTY OF SO GREAT VALUE, WHICH IT IS KNOWN THAT I POSSESS, I WILL RENDER THE ANIMAL, AT LEAST, LIABLE TO SUSPICION.
IT IS NOT MY POLICY TO ATTRACT ATTENTION EITHER TO MYSELF OR TO THE BEAST.
I WILL ANSWER THE ADVERTISEMENT, GET THE OURANG-OUTANG, AND KEEP IT CLOSE UNTIL THIS MATTER HAS BLOWN OVER.
YOU'RE QUITE THE ACTOR! LISTENING TO YOU, I THOUGHT I WAS HEARING HIM.
"YES, JUDGING BY THE STEPS UPON THE STAIRS, IT WON'T BE LONG."

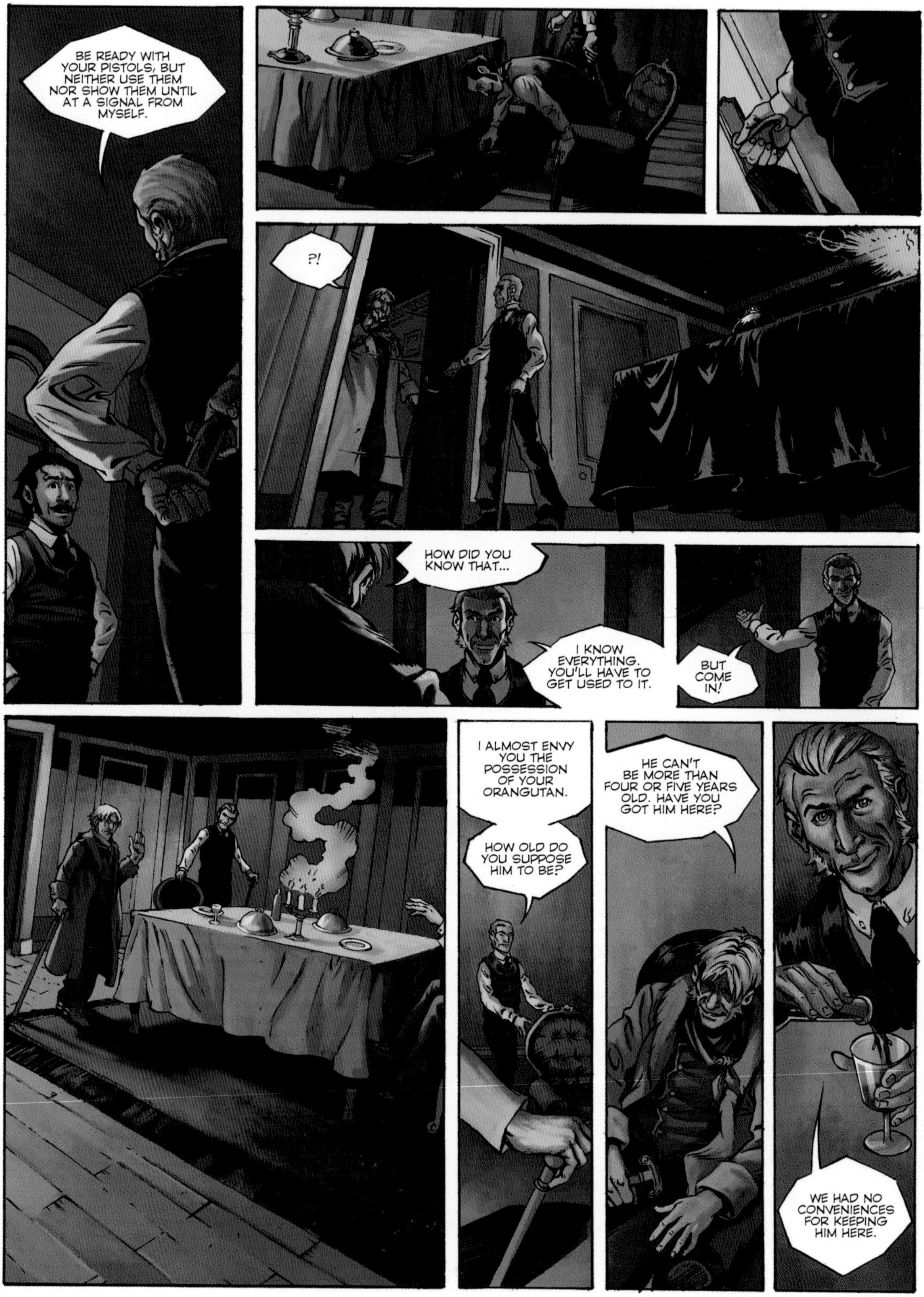
BE READY WITH YOUR PISTOLS, BUT NEITHER USE THEM NOR SHOW THEM UNTIL AT A SIGNAL FROM MYSELF.
?!
HOW DID YOU KNOW THAT...
I KNOW EVERYTHING. YOU'LL HAVE TO GET USED TO IT.
BUT COME IN!
I ALMOST ENVY YOU THE POSSESSION OF YOUR ORANGUTAN.
HOW OLD DO YOU SUPPOSE HIM TO BE?
HE CAN'T BE MORE THAN FOUR OR FIVE YEARS OLD. HAVE YOU GOT HIM HERE?
WE HAD NO CONVENIENCES FOR KEEPING HIM HERE.

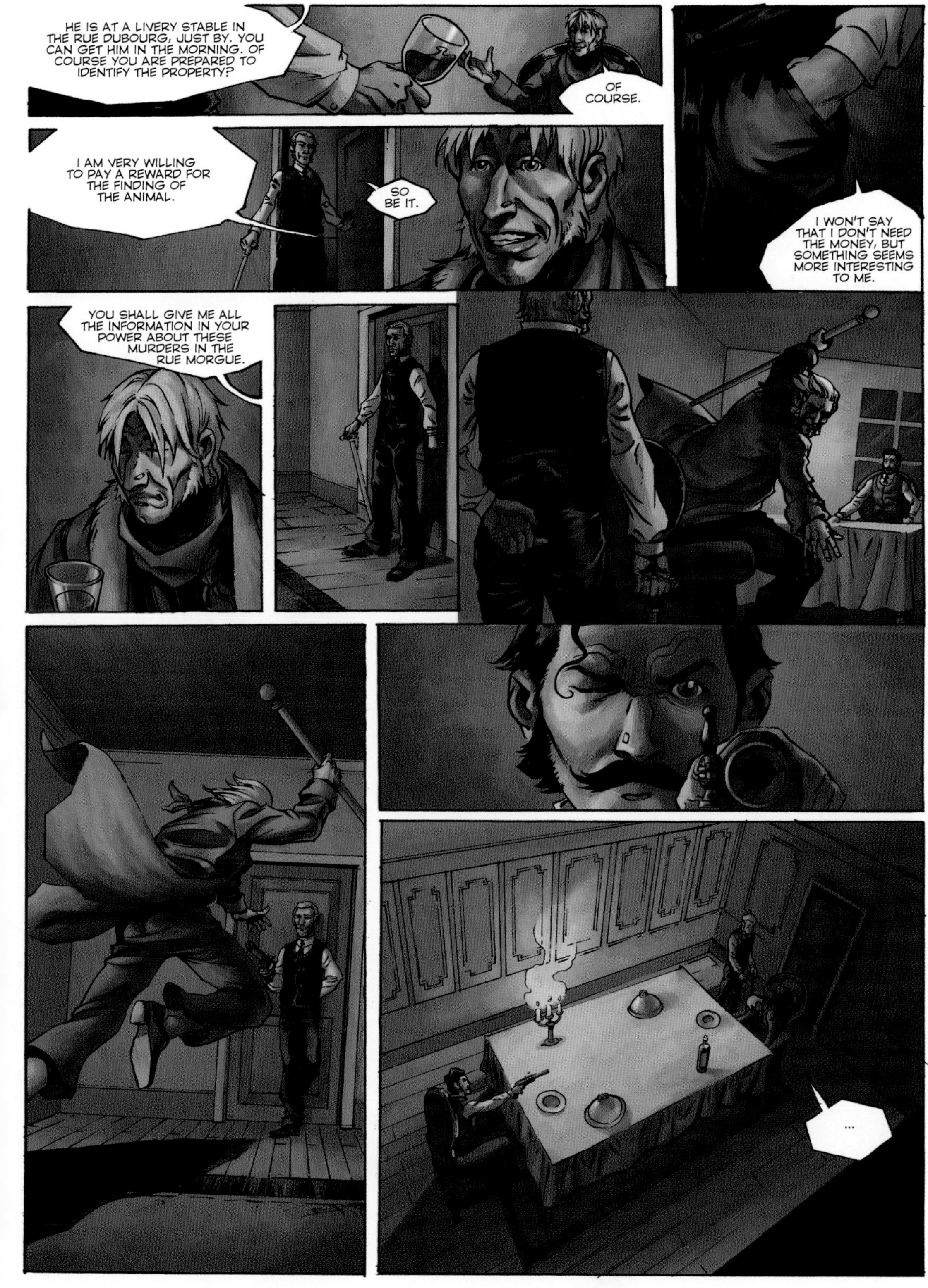
HE IS AT A LIVERY STABLE IN THE RUE DUBOURG, JUST BY. YOU CAN GET HIM IN THE MORNING. OF COURSE YOU ARE PREPARED TO IDENTIFY THE PROPERTY?
OF COURSE.
I AM VERY WILLING TO PAY A REWARD FOR THE FINDING OF THE ANIMAL.
SO BE IT.
I WON'T SAY THAT I DON'T NEED THE MONEY, BUT SOMETHING SEEMS MORE INTERESTING TO ME.
YOU SHALL GIVE ME ALL THE INFORMATION IN YOUR POWER ABOUT THESE MURDERS IN THE RUE MORGUE.
...

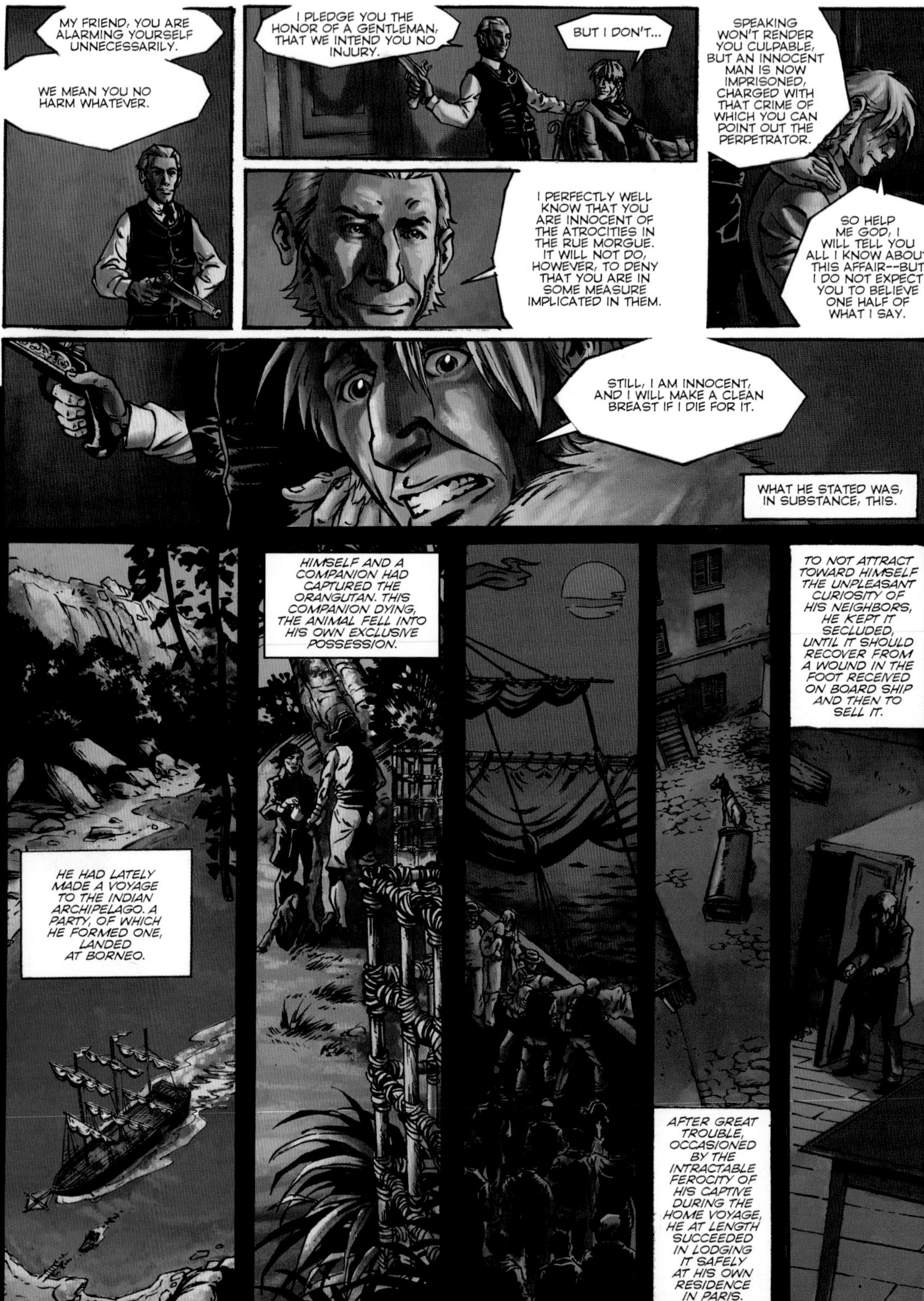
MY FRIEND, YOU ARE ALARMING YOURSELF UNNECESSARILY.
WE MEAN YOU NO HARM WHATEVER.
I PLEDGE YOU THE HONOR OF A GENTLEMAN, THAT WE INTEND YOU NO INJURY.
BUT I DON'T...
I PERFECTLY WELL KNOW THAT YOU ARE INNOCENT OF THE ATROCITIES IN THE RUE MORGUE. IT WILL NOT DO, HOWEVER, TO DENY THAT YOU ARE IN SOME MEASURE IMPLICATED IN THEM.
SPEAKING WON'T RENDER YOU CULPABLE, BUT AN INNOCENT MAN IS NOW IMPRISONED, CHARGED WITH THAT CRIME OF WHICH YOU CAN POINT OUT THE PERPETRATOR.
SO HELP ME GOD, I WILL TELL YOU ALL I KNOW ABOUT THIS AFFAIR--BUT I DO NOT EXPECT YOU TO BELIEVE ONE HALF OF WHAT I SAY.
STILL, I AM INNOCENT, AND I WILL MAKE A CLEAN BREAST IF I DIE FOR IT.
WHAT HE STATED WAS, IN SUBSTANCE, THIS.
HE HAD LATELY MADE A VOYAGE TO THE INDIAN ARCHIPELAGO. A PARTY, OF WHICH HE FORMED ONE, LANDED AT BORNEO.
HIMSELF AND A COMPANION HAD CAPTURED THE ORANGUTAN. THIS COMPANION DYING, THE ANIMAL FELL INTO HIS OWN EXCLUSIVE POSSESSION.
AFTER GREAT TROUBLE, OCCASIONED BY THE INTRACTABLE FEROCITY OF HIS CAPTIVE DURING THE HOME VOYAGE, HE AT LENGTH SUCCEEDED IN LODGING IT SAFELY AT HIS OWN RESIDENCE IN PARIS.
TO NOT ATTRACT TOWARD HIMSELF THE UNPLEASANT CURIOSITY OF HIS NEIGHBORS, HE KEPT IT SECLUDED, UNTIL IT SHOULD RECOVER FROM A WOUND IN THE FOOT RECEIVED ON BOARD SHIP AND THEN TO SELL IT.

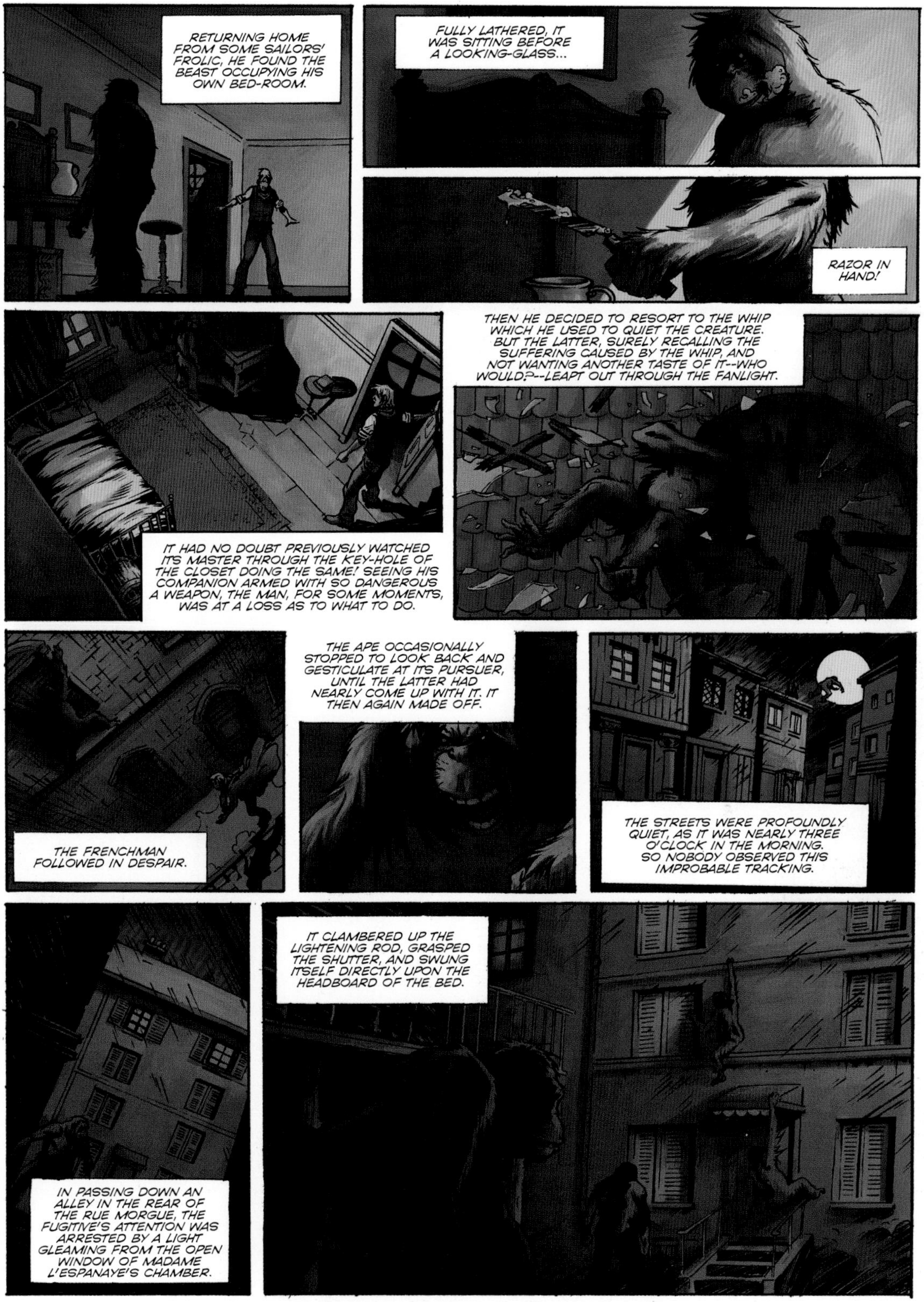
RETURNING HOME FROM SOME SAILORS' FROLIC, HE FOUND THE BEAST OCCUPYING HIS OWN BED-ROOM.
FULLY LATHERED, IT WAS SITTING BEFORE A LOOKING-GLASS...
RAZOR IN HAND!
IT HAD NO DOUBT PREVIOUSLY WATCHED ITS MASTER THROUGH THE KEY-HOLE OF THE CLOSET DOING THE SAME! SEEING HIS COMPANION ARMED WITH SO DANGEROUS A WEAPON, THE MAN, FOR SOME MOMENTS, WAS AT A LOSS AS TO WHAT TO DO.
THEN HE DECIDED TO RESORT TO THE WHIP WHICH HE USED TO QUIET THE CREATURE. BUT THE LATTER, SURELY RECALLING THE SUFFERING CAUSED BY THE WHIP, AND NOT WANTING ANOTHER TASTE OF IT--WHO WOULD?--LEAPT OUT THROUGH THE FANLIGHT.
THE FRENCHMAN FOLLOWED IN DESPAIR.
THE APE OCCASIONALLY STOPPED TO LOOK BACK AND GESTICULATE AT ITS PURSUER, UNTIL THE LATTER HAD NEARLY COME UP WITH IT. IT THEN AGAIN MADE OFF.
THE STREETS WERE PROFOUNDLY QUIET, AS IT WAS NEARLY THREE O'CLOCK IN THE MORNING. SO NOBODY OBSERVED THIS IMPROBABLE TRACKING.
IN PASSING DOWN AN ALLEY IN THE REAR OF THE RUE MORGUE, THE FUGITIVE'S ATTENTION WAS ARRESTED BY A LIGHT GLEAMING FROM THE OPEN WINDOW OF MADAME L'ESPANAYE'S CHAMBER.
IT CLAMBERED UP THE LIGHTENING ROD, GRASPED THE SHUTTER, AND SWUNG ITSELF DIRECTLY UPON THE HEADBOARD OF THE BED.

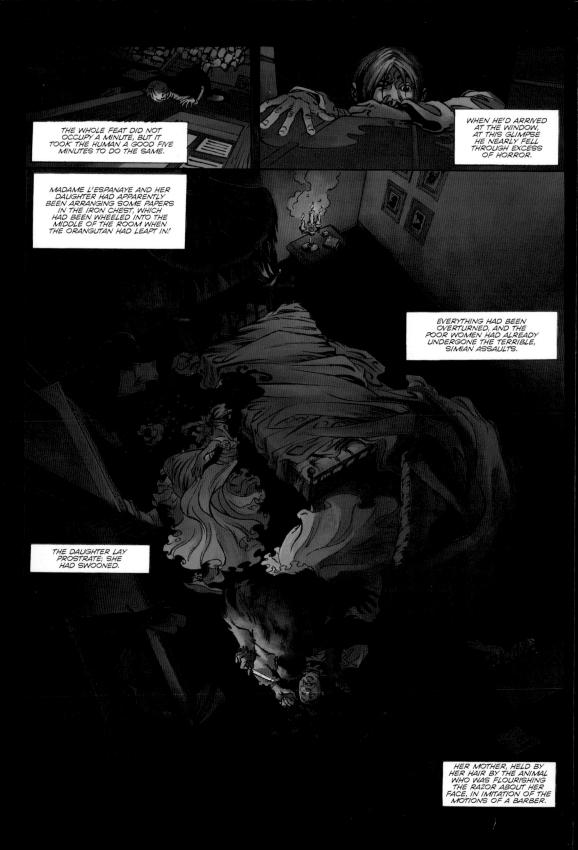

THE WHOLE FEAT DID NOT OCCUPY A MINUTE, BUT IT TOOK THE HUMAN A GOOD FIVE MINUTES TO DO THE SAME.

WHEN HE'D ARRIVED AT THE WINDOW, AT THIS GLIMPSE HE NEARLY FELL THROUGH EXCESS OF HORROR.

MADAME L'ESPANAYE AND HER DAUGHTER HAD APPARENTLY BEEN ARRANGING SOME PAPERS IN THE IRON CHEST, WHICH HAD BEEN WHEELED INTO THE MIDDLE OF THE ROOM WHEN THE ORANGUTAN HAD LEAPT IN!

EVERYTHING HAD BEEN OVERTURNED, AND THE POOR WOMEN HAD ALREADY UNDERGONE THE TERRIBLE, SIMIAN ASSAULTS.

THE DAUGHTER LAY PROSTRATE; SHE HAD SWOONED.

HER MOTHER, HELD BY HER HAIR BY THE ANIMAL WHO WAS FLOURISHING THE RAZOR ABOUT HER FACE, IN IMITATION OF THE MOTIONS OF A BARBER.

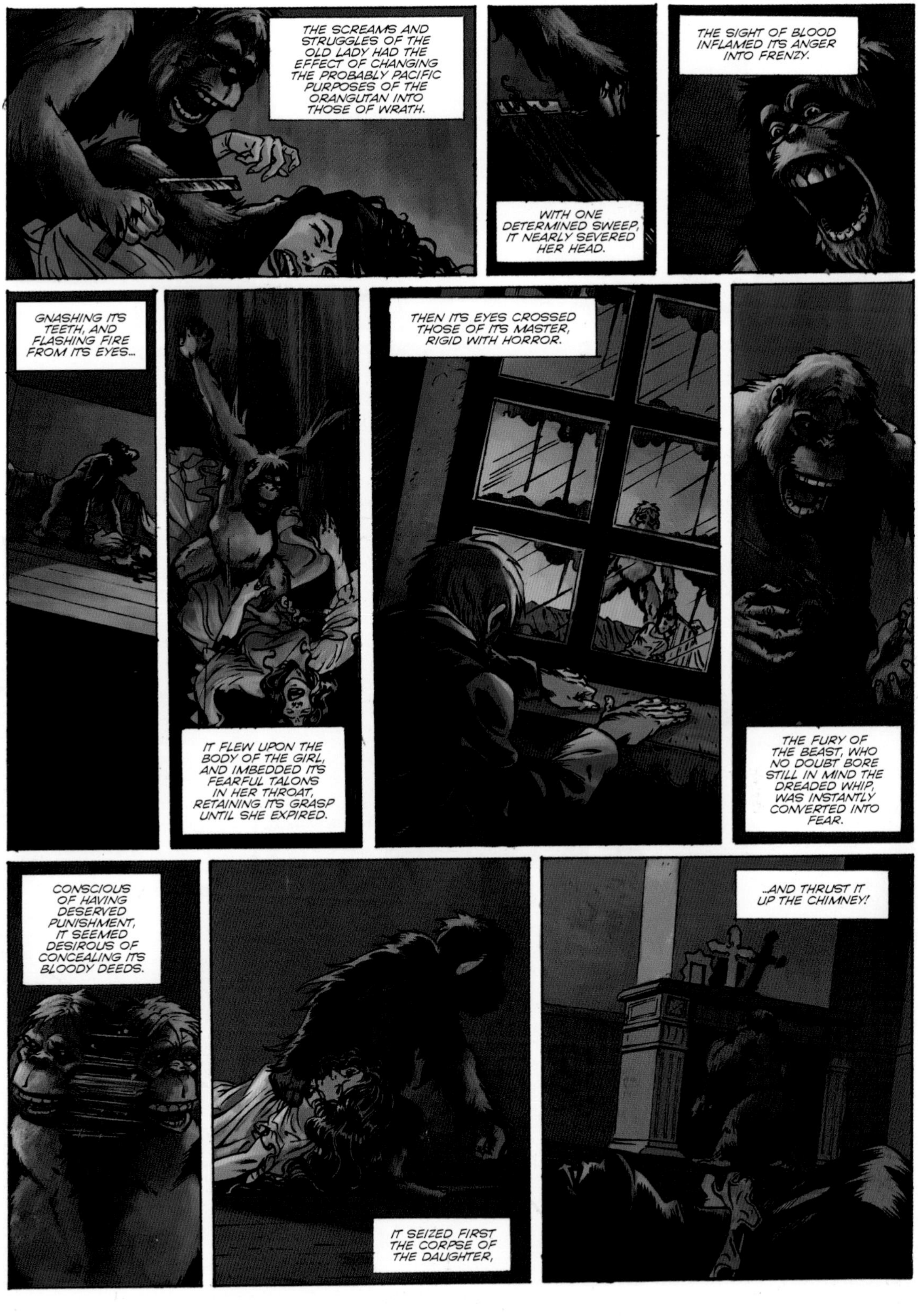
THE SCREAMS AND STRUGGLES OF THE OLD LADY HAD THE EFFECT OF CHANGING THE PROBABLY PACIFIC PURPOSES OF THE ORANGUTAN INTO THOSE OF WRATH.
WITH ONE DETERMINED SWEEP, IT NEARLY SEVERED HER HEAD.
THE SIGHT OF BLOOD INFLAMED ITS ANGER INTO FRENZY.
GNASHING ITS TEETH, AND FLASHING FIRE FROM ITS EYES...
IT FLEW UPON THE BODY OF THE GIRL, AND IMBEDDED ITS FEARFUL TALONS IN HER THROAT, RETAINING ITS GRASP UNTIL SHE EXPIRED.
THEN ITS EYES CROSSED THOSE OF ITS MASTER, RIGID WITH HORROR.
THE FURY OF THE BEAST, WHO NO DOUBT BORE STILL IN MIND THE DREADED WHIP, WAS INSTANTLY CONVERTED INTO FEAR.
CONSCIOUS OF HAVING DESERVED PUNISHMENT, IT SEEMED DESIROUS OF CONCEALING ITS BLOODY DEEDS.
IT SEIZED FIRST THE CORPSE OF THE DAUGHTER,
...AND THRUST IT UP THE CHIMNEY!

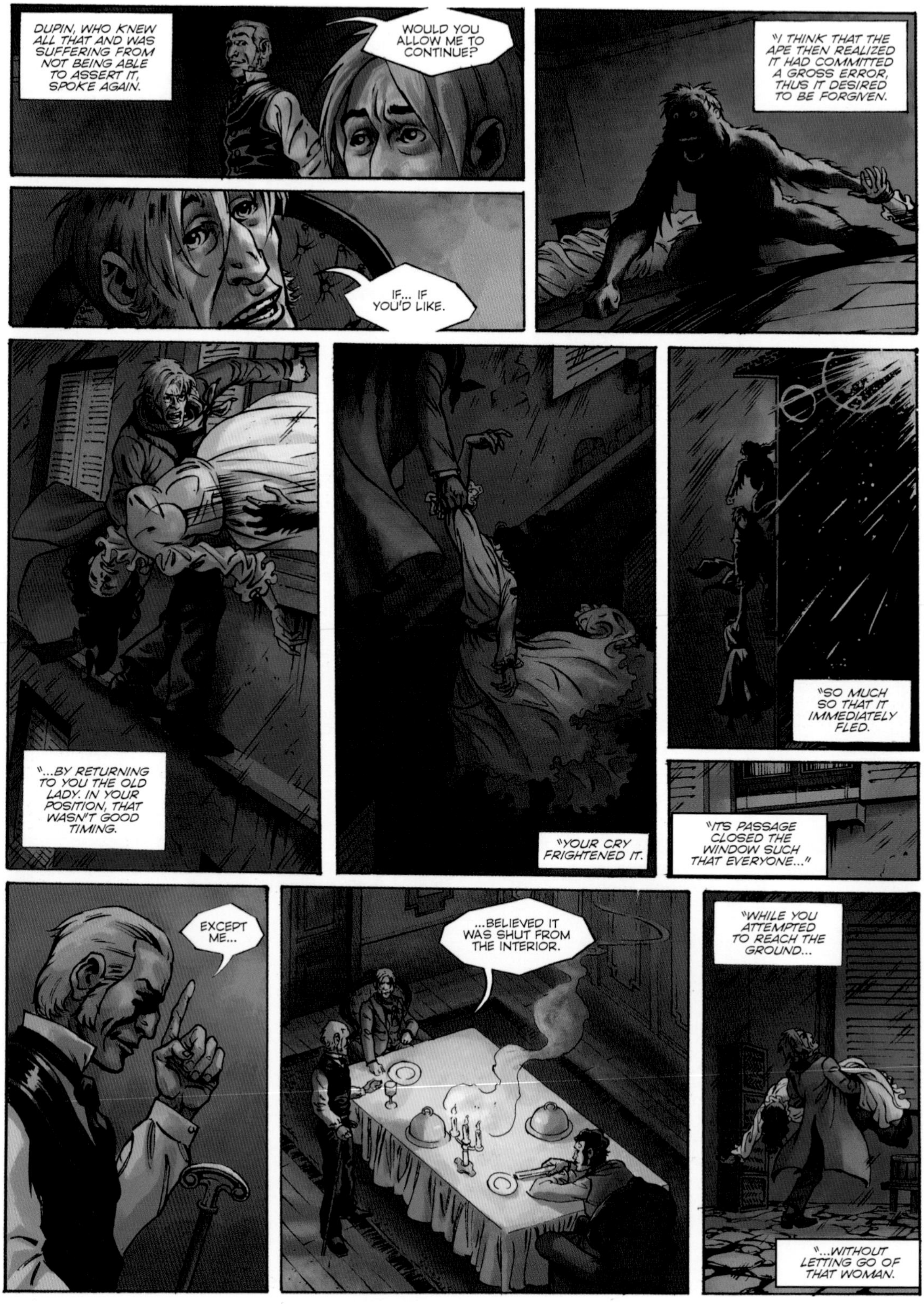
DUPIN, WHO KNEW ALL THAT AND WAS SUFFERING FROM NOT BEING ABLE TO ASSERT IT, SPOKE AGAIN.
WOULD YOU ALLOW ME TO CONTINUE?
IF... IF YOU'D LIKE.
"I THINK THAT THE APE THEN REALIZED IT HAD COMMITTED A GROSS ERROR, THUS IT DESIRED TO BE FORGIVEN.
"...BY RETURNING TO YOU THE OLD LADY. IN YOUR POSITION, THAT WASN'T GOOD TIMING.
"YOUR CRY FRIGHTENED IT.
"SO MUCH SO THAT IT IMMEDIATELY FLED.
"ITS PASSAGE CLOSED THE WINDOW SUCH THAT EVERYONE..."
EXCEPT ME...
...BELIEVED IT WAS SHUT FROM THE INTERIOR.
"WHILE YOU ATTEMPTED TO REACH THE GROUND...
"...WITHOUT LETTING GO OF THAT WOMAN.

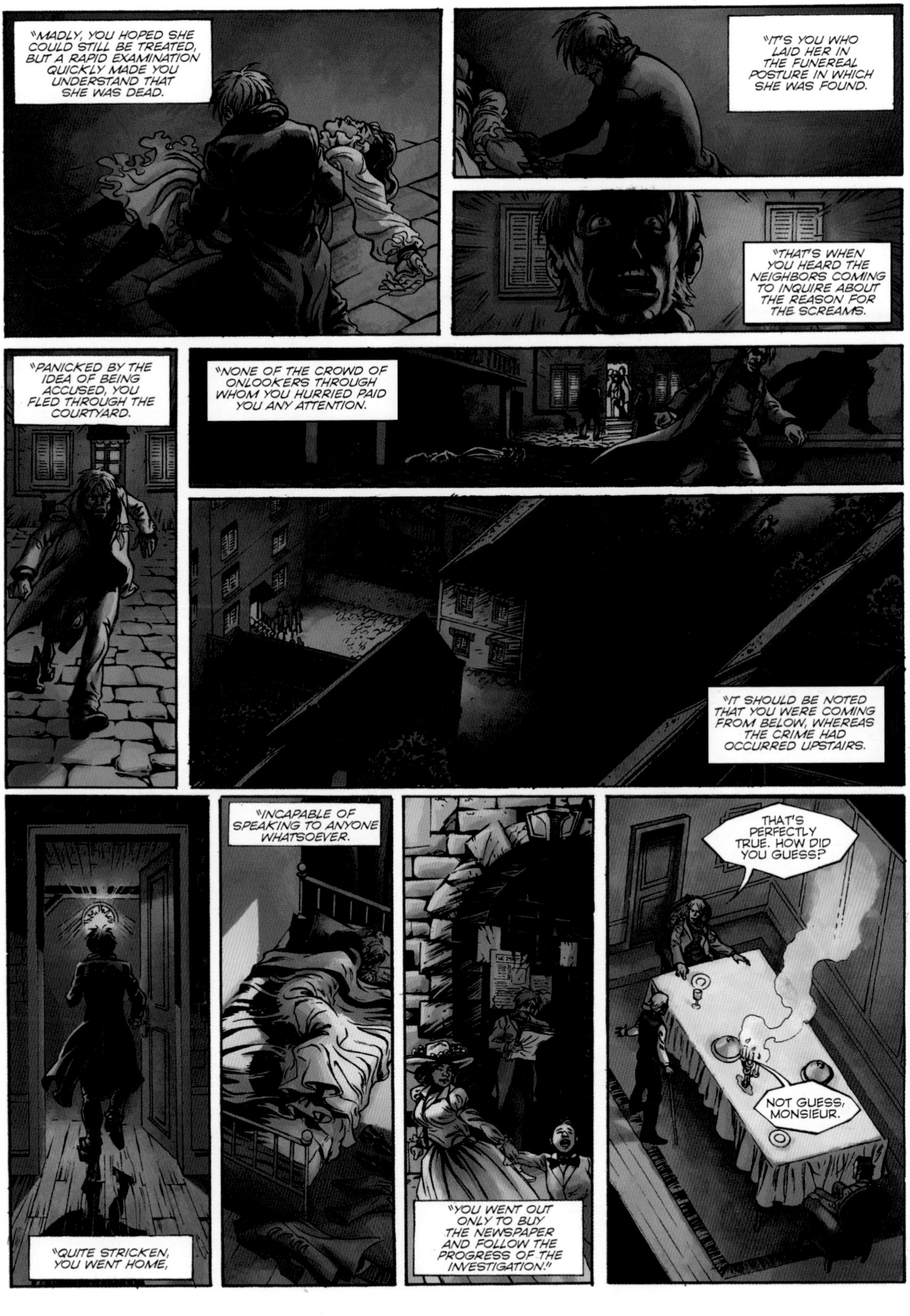
"MADLY, YOU HOPED SHE COULD STILL BE TREATED, BUT A RAPID EXAMINATION QUICKLY MADE YOU UNDERSTAND THAT SHE WAS DEAD.
"IT'S YOU WHO LAID HER IN THE FUNEREAL POSTURE IN WHICH SHE WAS FOUND.
"THAT'S WHEN YOU HEARD THE NEIGHBORS COMING TO INQUIRE ABOUT THE REASON FOR THE SCREAMS.
"PANICKED BY THE IDEA OF BEING ACCUSED, YOU FLED THROUGH THE COURTYARD.
"NONE OF THE CROWD OF ONLOOKERS THROUGH WHOM YOU HURRIED PAID YOU ANY ATTENTION.
"IT SHOULD BE NOTED THAT YOU WERE COMING FROM BELOW, WHEREAS THE CRIME HAD OCCURRED UPSTAIRS.
"QUITE STRICKEN, YOU WENT HOME,
"INCAPABLE OF SPEAKING TO ANYONE WHATSOEVER.
"YOU WENT OUT ONLY TO BUY THE NEWSPAPER AND FOLLOW THE PROGRESS OF THE INVESTIGATION."
THAT'S PERFECTLY TRUE. HOW DID YOU GUESS?
NOT GUESS, MONSIEUR.

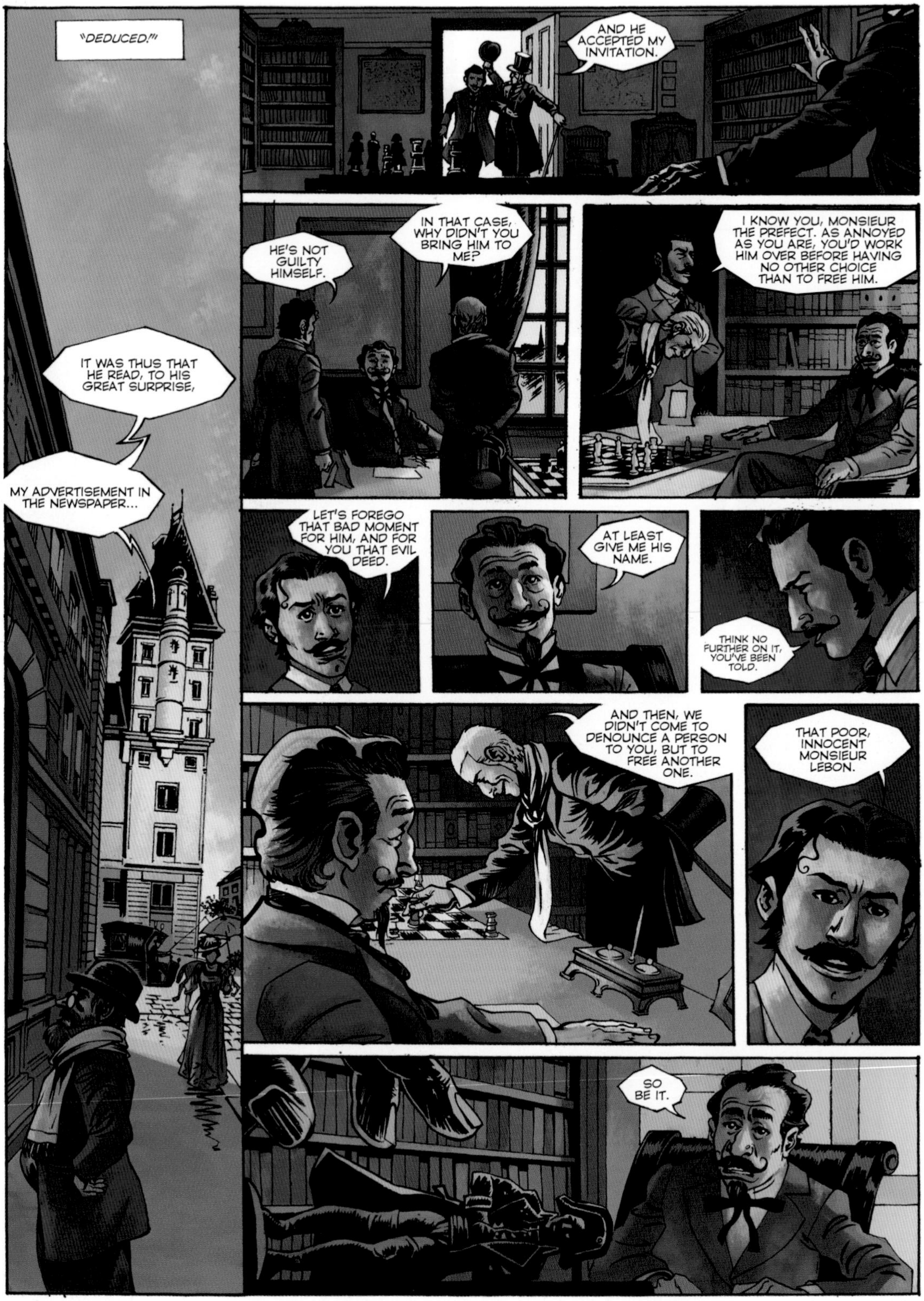
"DEDUCED!"
AND HE ACCEPTED MY INVITATION.
IT WAS THUS THAT HE READ, TO HIS GREAT SURPRISE,
MY ADVERTISEMENT IN THE NEWSPAPER...
HE'S NOT GUILTY HIMSELF.
IN THAT CASE, WHY DIDN'T YOU BRING HIM TO ME?
I KNOW YOU, MONSIEUR THE PREFECT. AS ANNOYED AS YOU ARE, YOU'D WORK HIM OVER BEFORE HAVING NO OTHER CHOICE THAN TO FREE HIM.
LET'S FOREGO THAT BAD MOMENT FOR HIM, AND FOR YOU THAT EVIL DEED.
AT LEAST GIVE ME HIS NAME.
THINK NO FURTHER ON IT, YOU'VE BEEN TOLD.
AND THEN, WE DIDN'T COME TO DENOUNCE A PERSON TO YOU, BUT TO FREE ANOTHER ONE.
THAT POOR, INNOCENT MONSIEUR LEBON.
SO BE IT.

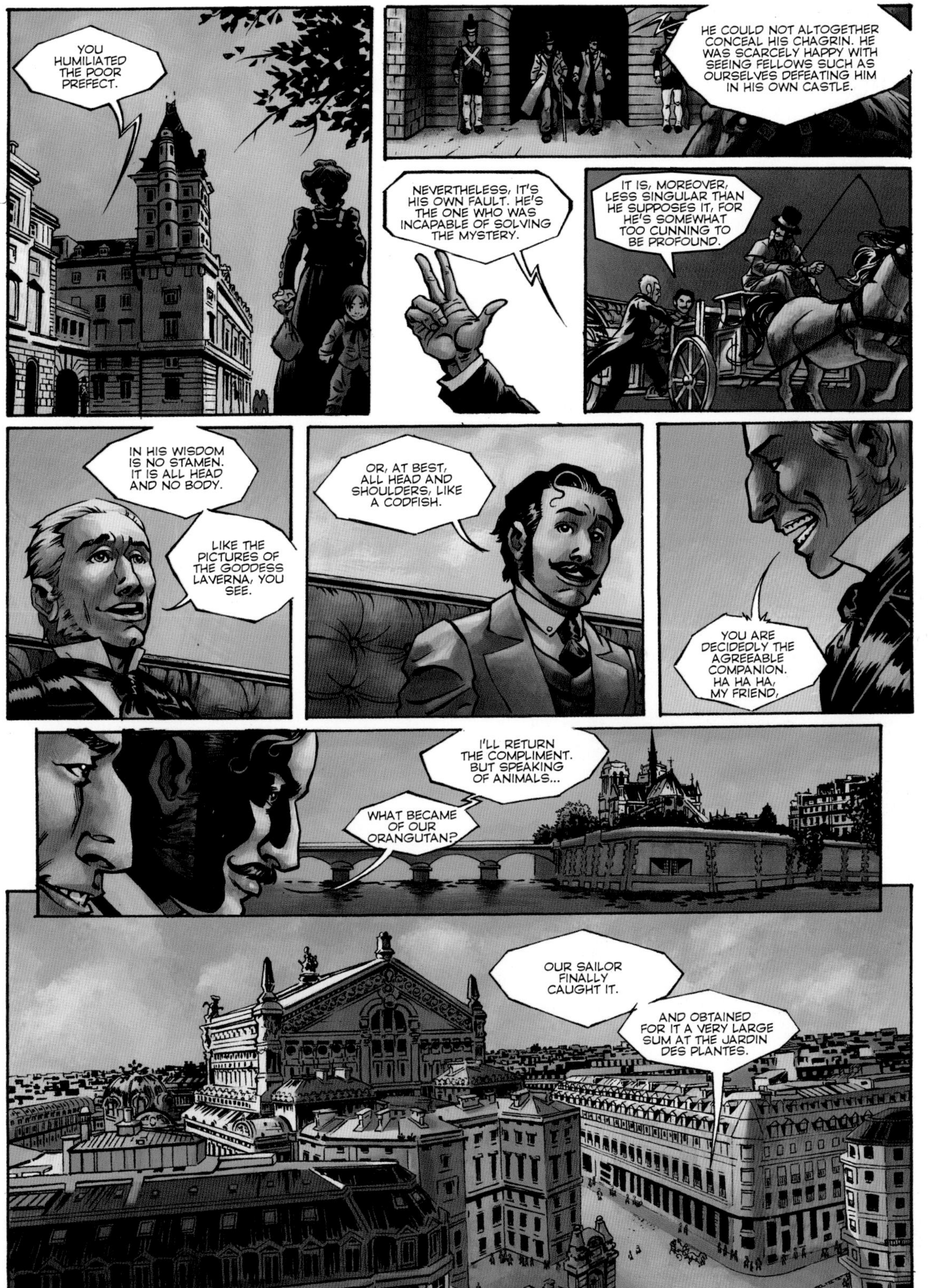
YOU HUMILIATED THE POOR PREFECT.
HE COULD NOT ALTOGETHER CONCEAL HIS CHAGRIN. HE WAS SCARCELY HAPPY WITH SEEING FELLOWS SUCH AS OURSELVES DEFEATING HIM IN HIS OWN CASTLE.
NEVERTHELESS, IT'S HIS OWN FAULT. HE'S THE ONE WHO WAS INCAPABLE OF SOLVING THE MYSTERY.
IT IS, MOREOVER, LESS SINGULAR THAN HE SUPPOSES IT, FOR HE'S SOMEWHAT TOO CUNNING TO BE PROFOUND.
IN HIS WISDOM IS NO STAMEN. IT IS ALL HEAD AND NO BODY.
LIKE THE PICTURES OF THE GODDESS LAVERNA, YOU SEE.
OR, AT BEST, ALL HEAD AND SHOULDERS, LIKE A CODFISH.
YOU ARE DECIDEDLY THE AGREEABLE COMPANION. HA HA HA, MY FRIEND,
I'LL RETURN THE COMPLIMENT. BUT SPEAKING OF ANIMALS...
WHAT BECAME OF OUR ORANGUTAN?
OUR SAILOR FINALLY CAUGHT IT.
AND OBTAINED FOR IT A VERY LARGE SUM AT THE JARDIN DES PLANTES.

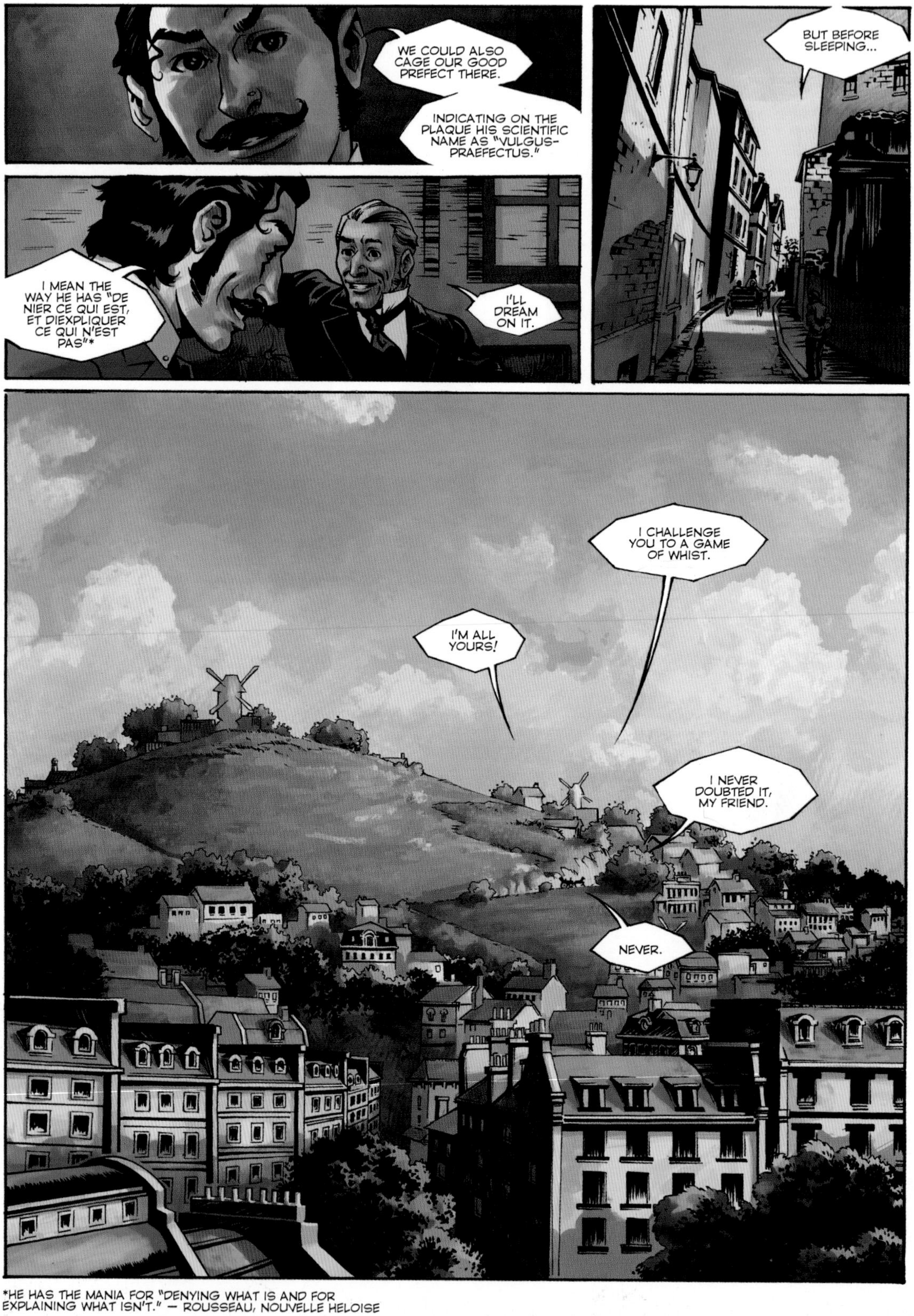
WE COULD ALSO CAGE OUR GOOD PREFECT THERE.
INDICATING ON THE PLAQUE HIS SCIENTIFIC NAME AS "VULGUS-PRAEFECTUS."
I MEAN THE WAY HE HAS "DE NIER CE QUI EST, ET DIEXPLIQUER CE QUI N'EST PAS"*
I'LL DREAM ON IT.
BUT BEFORE SLEEPING...
I CHALLENGE YOU TO A GAME OF WHIST.
I'M ALL YOURS!
I NEVER DOUBTED IT, MY FRIEND.
NEVER.

*HE HAS THE MANIA FOR "DENYING WHAT IS AND FOR EXPLAINING WHAT ISN'T." — ROUSSEAU, NOUVELLE HELOISE

MANY YEARS AGO, I CONTRACTED AN INTIMACY WITH A MR. WILLIAM LEGRAND.

HE WAS OF AN ANCIENT HUGUENOT FAMILY, AND HAD ONCE BEEN WEALTHY, BUT A SERIES OF MISFORTUNES HAD REDUCED HIM TO WANT.

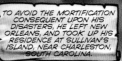
TO AVOID THE MORTIFICATION CONSEQUENT UPON HIS DISASTERS, HE LEFT NEW ORLEANS, AND TOOK UP HIS RESIDENCE AT SULLIVAN'S ISLAND, NEAR CHARLESTON, SOUTH CAROLINA.

CONSISTING OF LITTLE ELSE THAN THE SEA SAND, THE ISLAND OFFERS TO THE VISITOR'S GAZE SEVERAL TRAGIC ASPECTS.

SEPARATED FROM THE MAINLAND BY A SCARCELY PERCEPTIBLE CREEK, SURROUNDED BY REEDS, COVERED IN SCRUB AND BUSHES, THIS MOURNFUL SPACE IS SCARCELY THREE MILES LONG. ITS BREADTH AT NO POINT EXCEEDS A QUARTER OF A MILE.

NEAR THE WESTERN EXTREMITY ARE SOME MISERABLE FRAME BUILDINGS, TENANTED, DURING THE SUMMER, BY THE FUGITIVES FROM CHARLESTON DUST AND FEVER.

IN THE INMOST RECESSES OF THE COPPICE, NOT FAR FROM THE EASTERN END OF THE ISLAND, LEGRAND HAD BUILT HIMSELF A SMALL HUT.

# The Gold-Bug

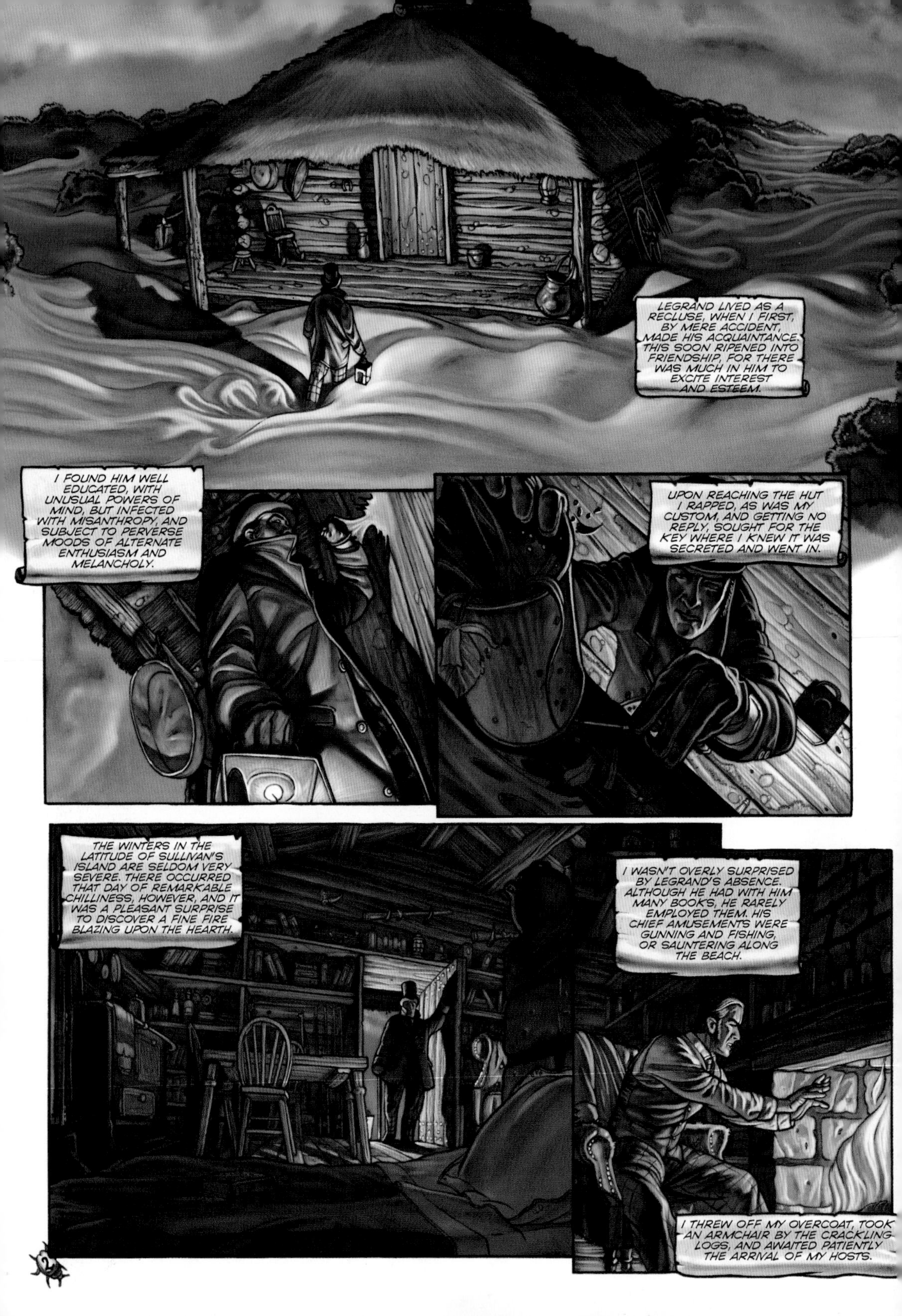
LEGRAND LIVED AS A RECLUSE, WHEN I FIRST, BY MERE ACCIDENT, MADE HIS ACQUAINTANCE. THIS SOON RIPENED INTO FRIENDSHIP, FOR THERE WAS MUCH IN HIM TO EXCITE INTEREST AND ESTEEM.
I FOUND HIM WELL EDUCATED, WITH UNUSUAL POWERS OF MIND, BUT INFECTED WITH MISANTHROPY, AND SUBJECT TO PERVERSE MOODS OF ALTERNATE ENTHUSIASM AND MELANCHOLY.
UPON REACHING THE HUT I RAPPED, AS WAS MY CUSTOM, AND GETTING NO REPLY, SOUGHT FOR THE KEY WHERE I KNEW IT WAS SECRETED AND WENT IN.
THE WINTERS IN THE LATITUDE OF SULLIVAN'S ISLAND ARE SELDOM VERY SEVERE. THERE OCCURRED THAT DAY OF REMARKABLE CHILLINESS, HOWEVER, AND IT WAS A PLEASANT SURPRISE TO DISCOVER A FINE FIRE BLAZING UPON THE HEARTH.
I WASN'T OVERLY SURPRISED BY LEGRAND'S ABSENCE. ALTHOUGH HE HAD WITH HIM MANY BOOKS, HE RARELY EMPLOYED THEM. HIS CHIEF AMUSEMENTS WERE GUNNING AND FISHING, OR SAUNTERING ALONG THE BEACH.
I THREW OFF MY OVERCOAT, TOOK AN ARMCHAIR BY THE CRACKLING LOGS, AND AWAITED PATIENTLY THE ARRIVAL OF MY HOSTS.

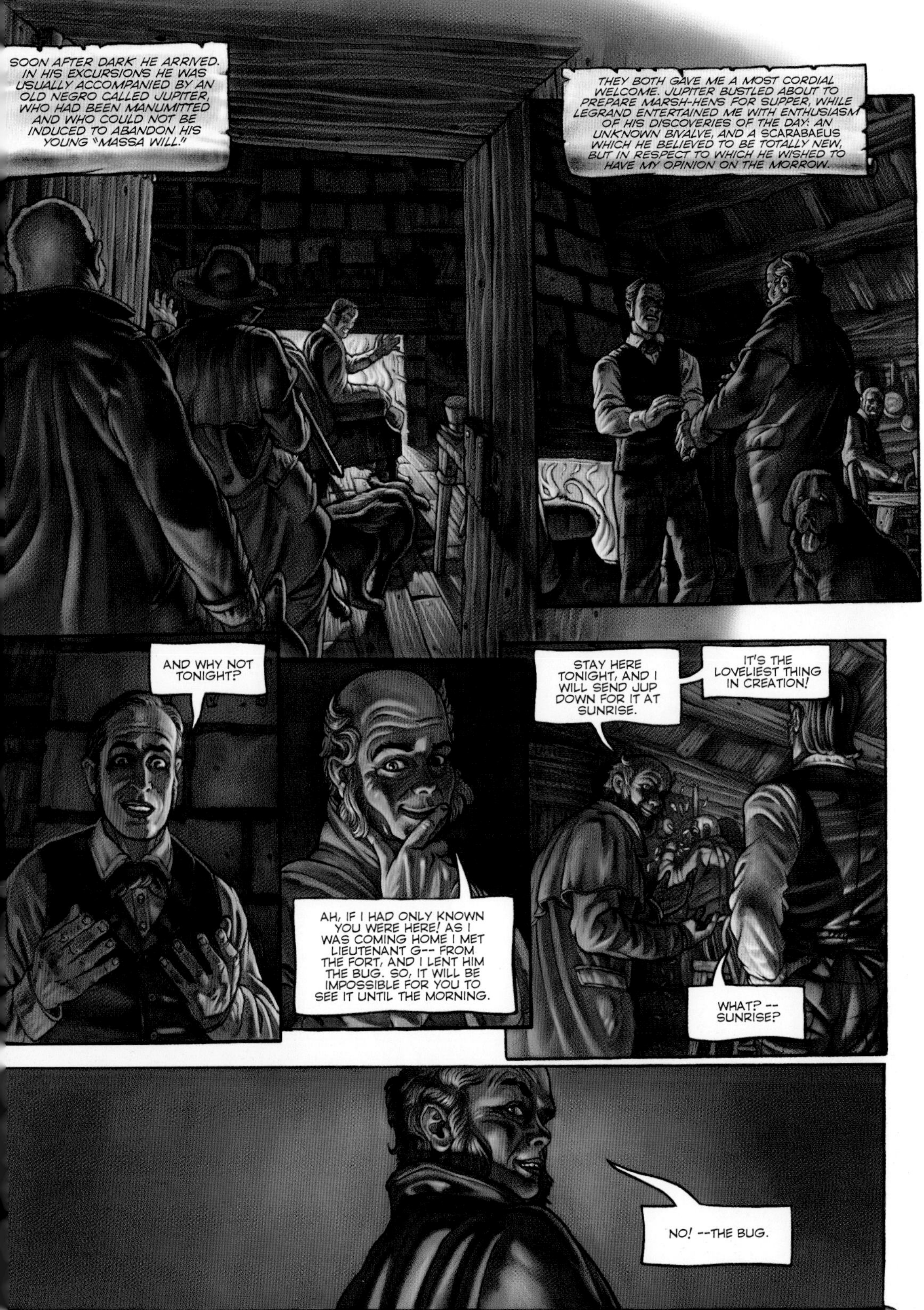
SOON AFTER DARK HE ARRIVED. IN HIS EXCURSIONS HE WAS USUALLY ACCOMPANIED BY AN OLD NEGRO CALLED JUPITER, WHO HAD BEEN MANUMITTED AND WHO COULD NOT BE INDUCED TO ABANDON HIS YOUNG "MASSA WILL."
THEY BOTH GAVE ME A MOST CORDIAL WELCOME. JUPITER BUSTLED ABOUT TO PREPARE MARSH-HENS FOR SUPPER, WHILE LEGRAND ENTERTAINED ME WITH ENTHUSIASM OF HIS DISCOVERIES OF THE DAY: AN UNKNOWN BIVALVE, AND A SCARABAEUS WHICH HE BELIEVED TO BE TOTALLY NEW, BUT IN RESPECT TO WHICH HE WISHED TO HAVE MY OPINION ON THE MORROW.
AND WHY NOT TONIGHT?
AH, IF I HAD ONLY KNOWN YOU WERE HERE! AS I WAS COMING HOME I MET LIEUTENANT G-- FROM THE FORT, AND I LENT HIM THE BUG. SO, IT WILL BE IMPOSSIBLE FOR YOU TO SEE IT UNTIL THE MORNING.
STAY HERE TONIGHT, AND I WILL SEND JUP DOWN FOR IT AT SUNRISE.
IT'S THE LOVELIEST THING IN CREATION!
WHAT? --SUNRISE?
NO! --THE BUG.

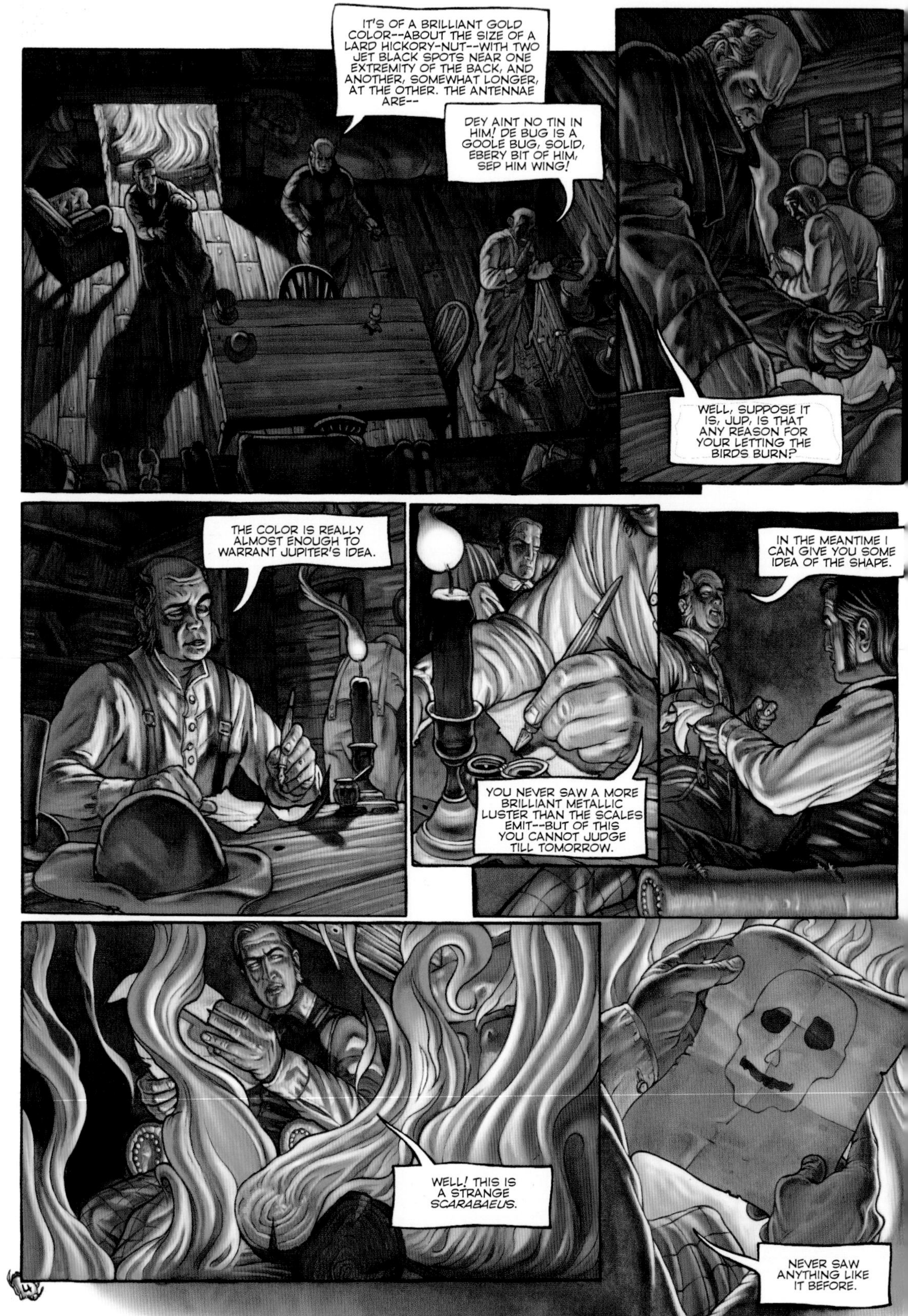
IT'S OF A BRILLIANT GOLD COLOR--ABOUT THE SIZE OF A LARD HICKORY-NUT--WITH TWO JET BLACK SPOTS NEAR ONE EXTREMITY OF THE BACK, AND ANOTHER, SOMEWHAT LONGER, AT THE OTHER. THE ANTENNAE ARE--
DEY AINT NO TIN IN HIM! DE BUG IS A GOOLE BUG, SOLID, EBERY BIT OF HIM, SEP HIM WING!
WELL, SUPPOSE IT IS, JUP, IS THAT ANY REASON FOR YOUR LETTING THE BIRDS BURN?
THE COLOR IS REALLY ALMOST ENOUGH TO WARRANT JUPITER'S IDEA.
YOU NEVER SAW A MORE BRILLIANT METALLIC LUSTER THAN THE SCALES EMIT--BUT OF THIS YOU CANNOT JUDGE TILL TOMORROW.
IN THE MEANTIME I CAN GIVE YOU SOME IDEA OF THE SHAPE.
WELL! THIS IS A STRANGE *SCARABAEUS*.
NEVER SAW ANYTHING LIKE IT BEFORE.
4

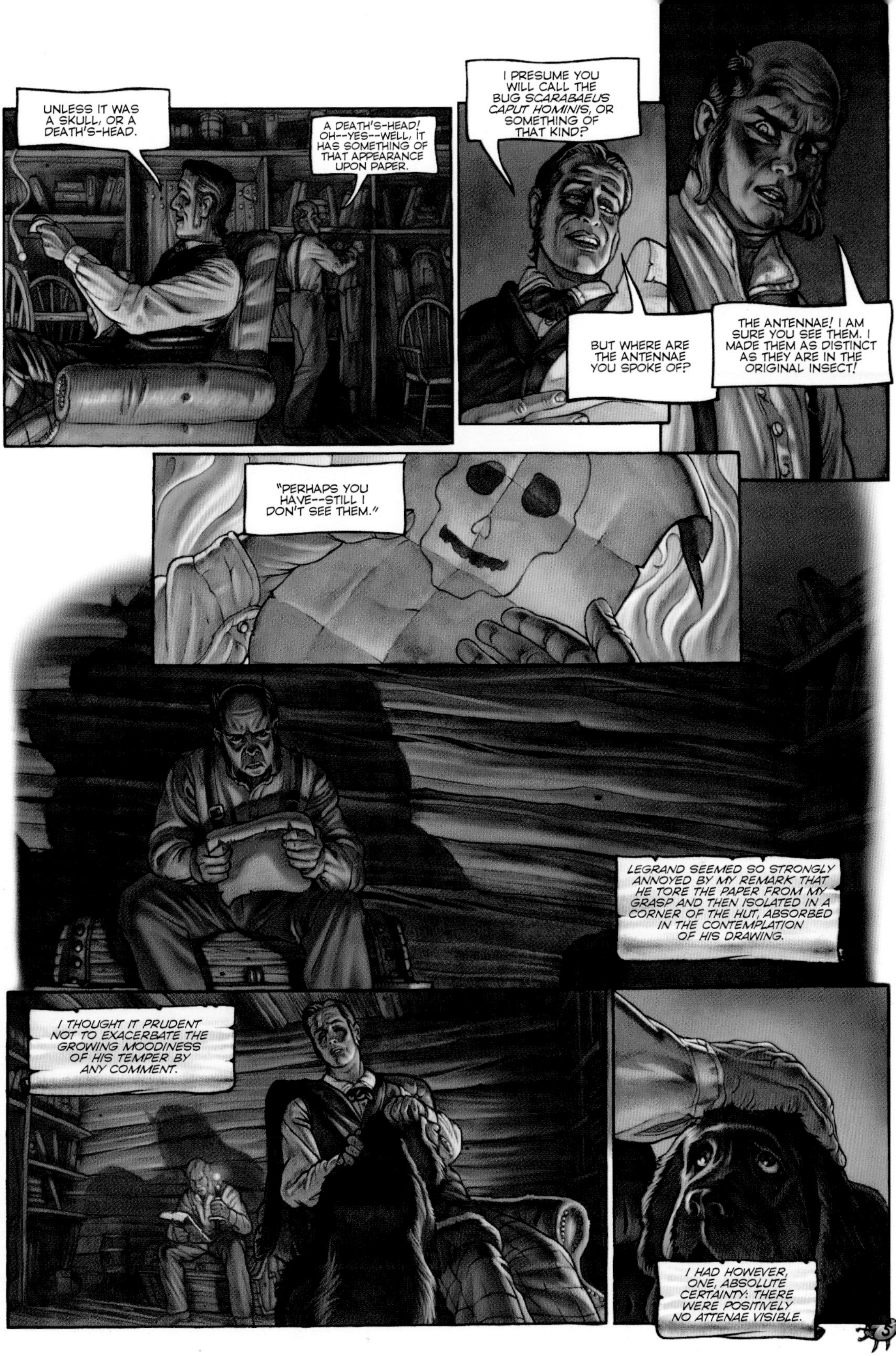
UNLESS IT WAS A SKULL, OR A DEATH'S-HEAD.
A DEATH'S-HEAD! OH--YES--WELL, IT HAS SOMETHING OF THAT APPEARANCE UPON PAPER.
I PRESUME YOU WILL CALL THE BUG *SCARABAEUS CAPUT HOMINIS*, OR SOMETHING OF THAT KIND?
BUT WHERE ARE THE ANTENNAE YOU SPOKE OF?
THE ANTENNAE! I AM SURE YOU SEE THEM. I MADE THEM AS DISTINCT AS THEY ARE IN THE ORIGINAL INSECT!
"PERHAPS YOU HAVE--STILL I DON'T SEE THEM."
*LEGRAND SEEMED SO STRONGLY ANNOYED BY MY REMARK THAT HE TORE THE PAPER FROM MY GRASP AND THEN ISOLATED IN A CORNER OF THE HUT, ABSORBED IN THE CONTEMPLATION OF HIS DRAWING.*
*I THOUGHT IT PRUDENT NOT TO EXACERBATE THE GROWING MOODINESS OF HIS TEMPER BY ANY COMMENT.*
*I HAD HOWEVER, ONE, ABSOLUTE CERTAINTY: THERE WERE POSITIVELY NO ATTENAE VISIBLE.*

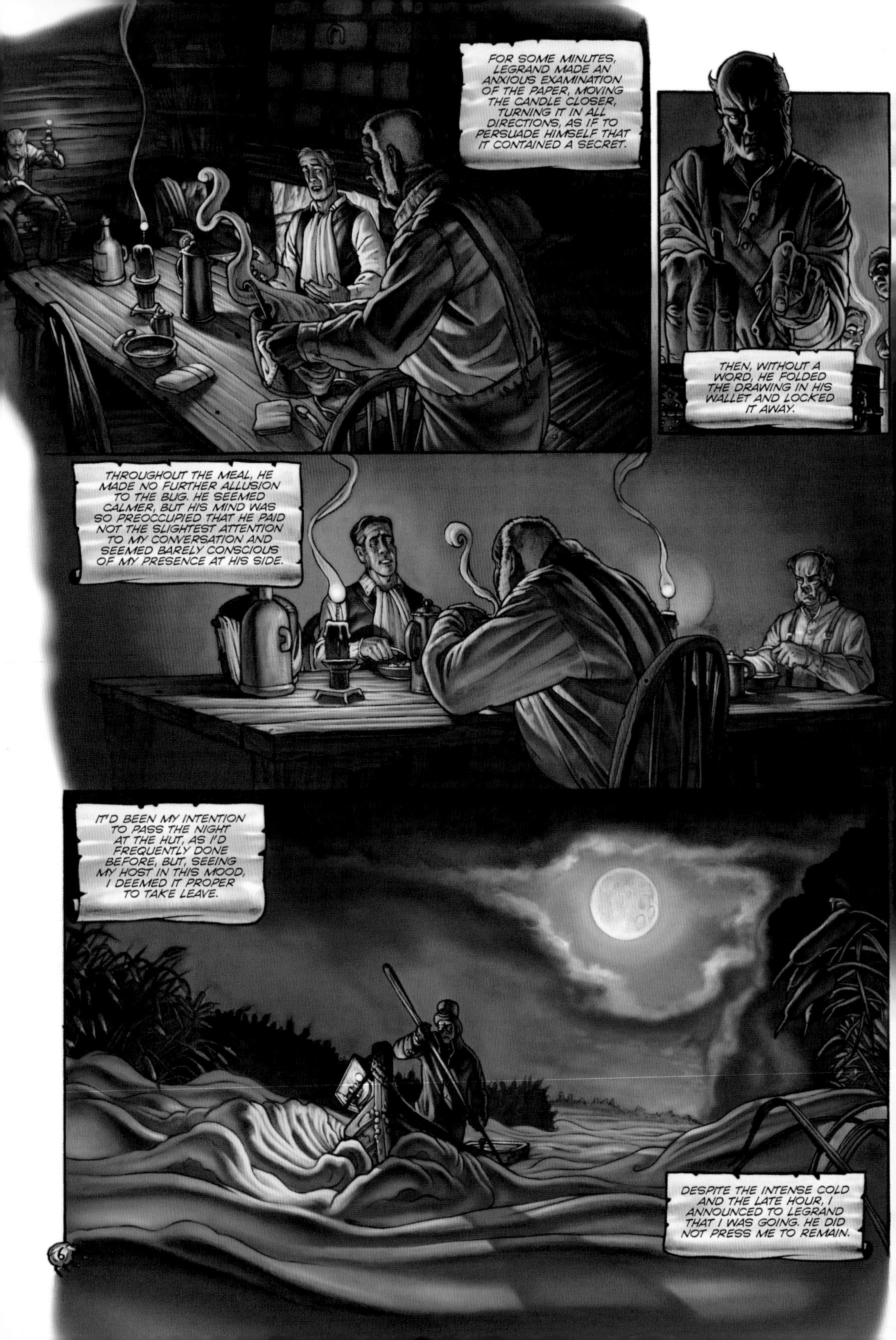
FOR SOME MINUTES, LEGRAND MADE AN ANXIOUS EXAMINATION OF THE PAPER, MOVING THE CANDLE CLOSER, TURNING IT IN ALL DIRECTIONS, AS IF TO PERSUADE HIMSELF THAT IT CONTAINED A SECRET.
THEN, WITHOUT A WORD, HE FOLDED THE DRAWING IN HIS WALLET AND LOCKED IT AWAY.
THROUGHOUT THE MEAL, HE MADE NO FURTHER ALLUSION TO THE BUG. HE SEEMED CALMER, BUT HIS MIND WAS SO PREOCCUPIED THAT HE PAID NOT THE SLIGHTEST ATTENTION TO MY CONVERSATION AND SEEMED BARELY CONSCIOUS OF MY PRESENCE AT HIS SIDE.
IT'D BEEN MY INTENTION TO PASS THE NIGHT AT THE HUT, AS I'D FREQUENTLY DONE BEFORE, BUT, SEEING MY HOST IN THIS MOOD, I DEEMED IT PROPER TO TAKE LEAVE.
DESPITE THE INTENSE COLD AND THE LATE HOUR, I ANNOUNCED TO LEGRAND THAT I WAS GOING. HE DID NOT PRESS ME TO REMAIN.

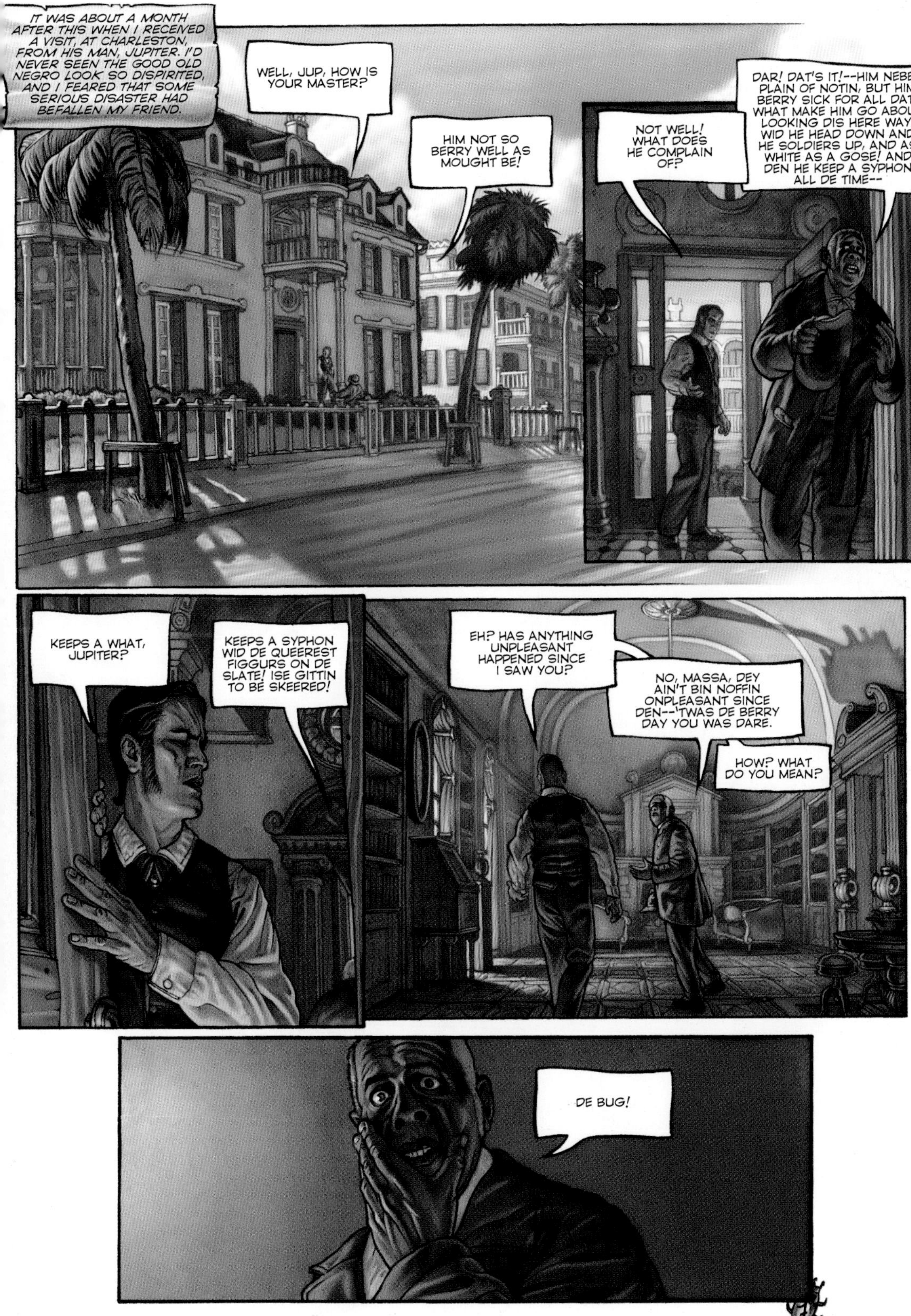
IT WAS ABOUT A MONTH AFTER THIS WHEN I RECEIVED A VISIT, AT CHARLESTON, FROM HIS MAN, JUPITER. I'D NEVER SEEN THE GOOD OLD NEGRO LOOK SO DISPIRITED, AND I FEARED THAT SOME SERIOUS DISASTER HAD BEFALLEN MY FRIEND.
WELL, JUP, HOW IS YOUR MASTER?
HIM NOT SO BERRY WELL AS MOUGHT BE!
NOT WELL! WHAT DOES HE COMPLAIN OF?
DAR! DAT'S IT!--HIM NEBER PLAIN OF NOTIN, BUT HIM BERRY SICK FOR ALL DAT. WHAT MAKE HIM GO ABOUT LOOKING DIS HERE WAY, WID HE HEAD DOWN AND HE SOLDIERS UP, AND AS WHITE AS A GOSE! AND DEN HE KEEP A SYPHON ALL DE TIME--
KEEPS A WHAT, JUPITER?
KEEPS A SYPHON WID DE QUEEREST FIGGURS ON DE SLATE! ISE GITTIN TO BE SKEERED!
EH? HAS ANYTHING UNPLEASANT HAPPENED SINCE I SAW YOU?
NO, MASSA, DEY AIN'T BIN NOFFIN ONPLEASANT SINCE DEN--'TWAS DE BERRY DAY YOU WAS DARE.
HOW? WHAT DO YOU MEAN?
DE BUG!

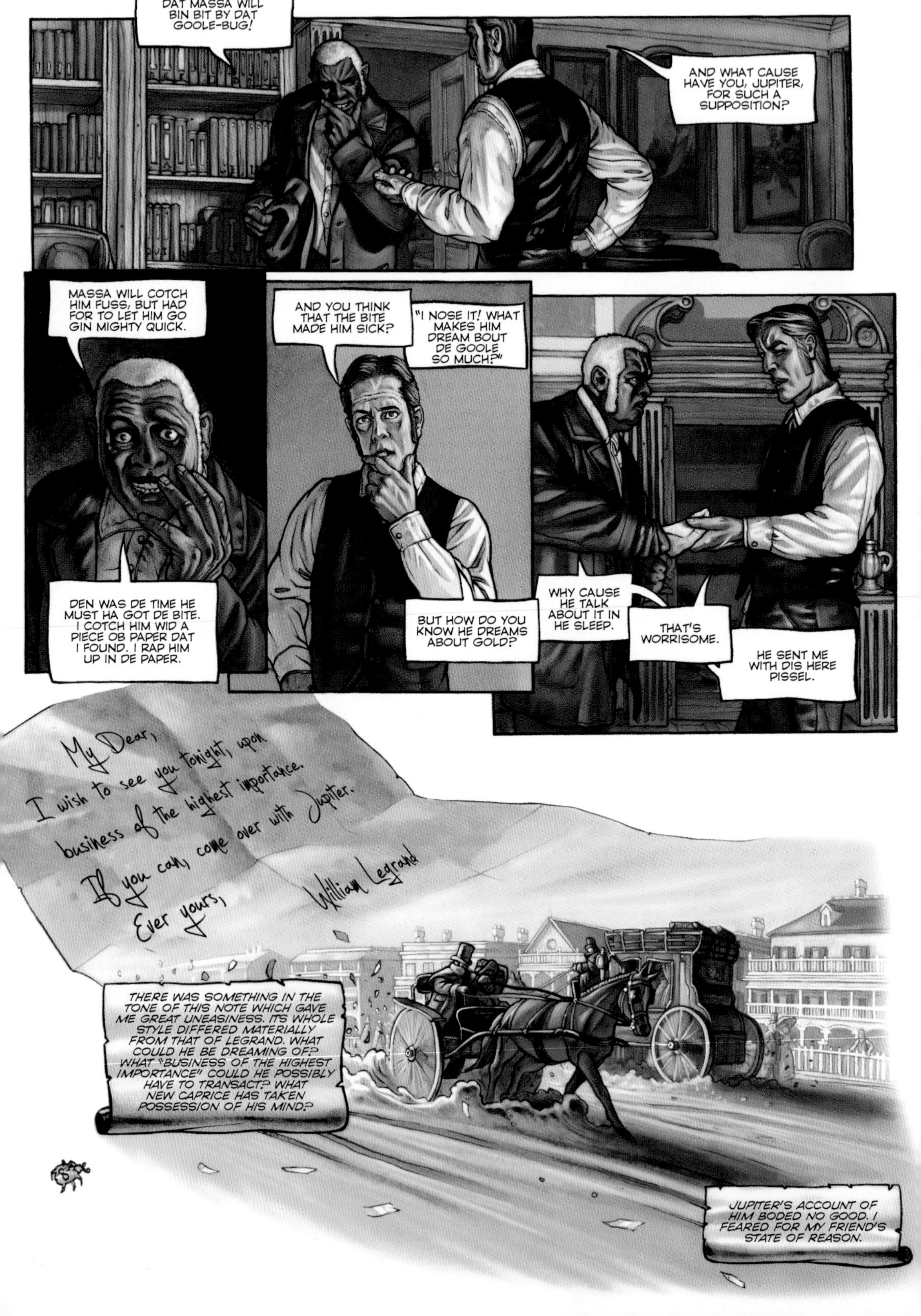
I'M BERRY SARTAIN DAT MASSA WILL BIN BIT BY DAT GOOLE-BUG!
AND WHAT CAUSE HAVE YOU, JUPITER, FOR SUCH A SUPPOSITION?
MASSA WILL COTCH HIM FUSS, BUT HAD FOR TO LET HIM GO GIN MIGHTY QUICK.
DEN WAS DE TIME HE MUST HA GOT DE BITE. I COTCH HIM WID A PIECE OB PAPER DAT I FOUND. I RAP HIM UP IN DE PAPER.
AND YOU THINK THAT THE BITE MADE HIM SICK?
"I NOSE IT! WHAT MAKES HIM DREAM BOUT DE GOOLE SO MUCH?"
BUT HOW DO YOU KNOW HE DREAMS ABOUT GOLD?
WHY CAUSE HE TALK ABOUT IT IN HE SLEEP.
THAT'S WORRISOME.
HE SENT ME WITH DIS HERE PISSEL.
My Dear,
I wish to see you tonight, upon business of the highest importance.
If you can, come over with Jupiter.
Ever yours,
William Legrand
THERE WAS SOMETHING IN THE TONE OF THIS NOTE WHICH GAVE ME GREAT UNEASINESS. ITS WHOLE STYLE DIFFERED MATERIALLY FROM THAT OF LEGRAND. WHAT COULD HE BE DREAMING OF? WHAT "BUSINESS OF THE HIGHEST IMPORTANCE" COULD HE POSSIBLY HAVE TO TRANSACT? WHAT NEW CAPRICE HAS TAKEN POSSESSION OF HIS MIND?
JUPITER'S ACCOUNT OF HIM BODED NO GOOD. I FEARED FOR MY FRIEND'S STATE OF REASON.

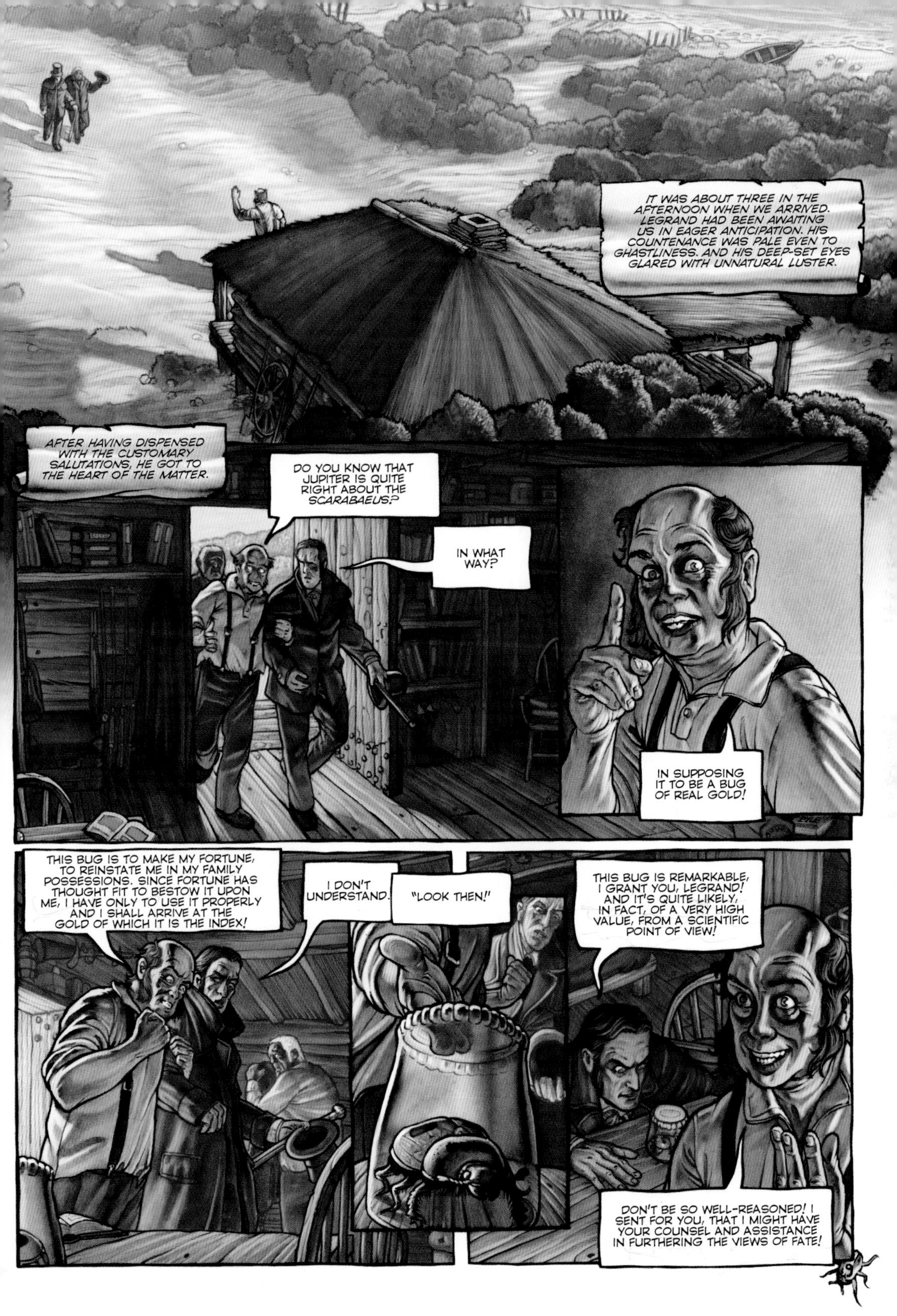

IT WAS ABOUT THREE IN THE AFTERNOON WHEN WE ARRIVED. LEGRAND HAD BEEN AWAITING US IN EAGER ANTICIPATION. HIS COUNTENANCE WAS PALE EVEN TO GHASTLINESS, AND HIS DEEP-SET EYES GLARED WITH UNNATURAL LUSTER.
AFTER HAVING DISPENSED WITH THE CUSTOMARY SALUTATIONS, HE GOT TO THE HEART OF THE MATTER.
DO YOU KNOW THAT JUPITER IS QUITE RIGHT ABOUT THE SCARABAEUS?
IN WHAT WAY?
IN SUPPOSING IT TO BE A BUG OF REAL GOLD!
THIS BUG IS TO MAKE MY FORTUNE, TO REINSTATE ME IN MY FAMILY POSSESSIONS. SINCE FORTUNE HAS THOUGHT FIT TO BESTOW IT UPON ME, I HAVE ONLY TO USE IT PROPERLY AND I SHALL ARRIVE AT THE GOLD OF WHICH IT IS THE INDEX!
I DON'T UNDERSTAND.
"LOOK THEN!"
THIS BUG IS REMARKABLE, I GRANT YOU, LEGRAND! AND IT'S QUITE LIKELY, IN FACT, OF A VERY HIGH VALUE, FROM A SCIENTIFIC POINT OF VIEW!
DON'T BE SO WELL-REASONED! I SENT FOR YOU, THAT I MIGHT HAVE YOUR COUNSEL AND ASSISTANCE IN FURTHERING THE VIEWS OF FATE!

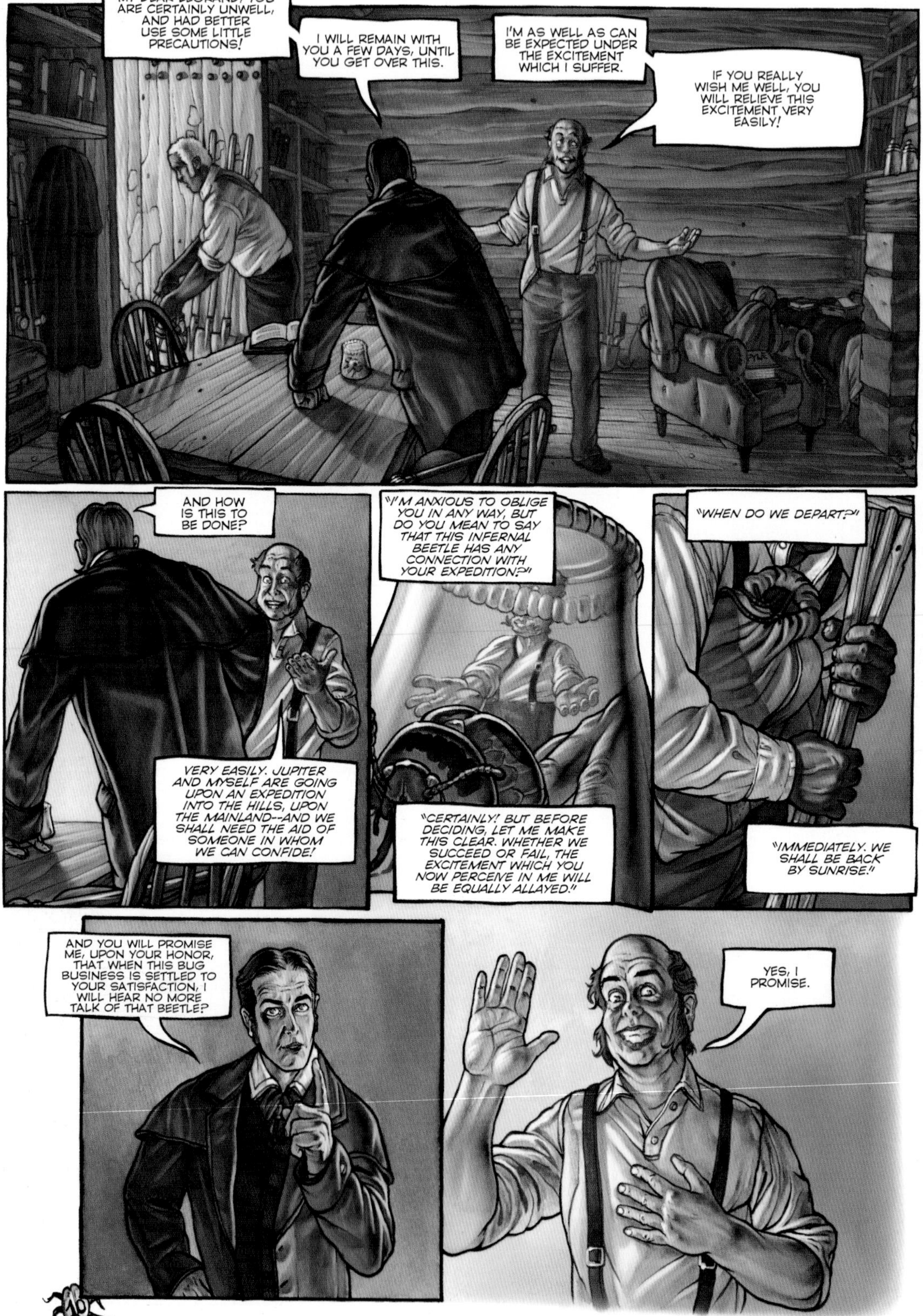

MY DEAR LEGRAND, YOU ARE CERTAINLY UNWELL, AND HAD BETTER USE SOME LITTLE PRECAUTIONS!
I WILL REMAIN WITH YOU A FEW DAYS, UNTIL YOU GET OVER THIS.
I'M AS WELL AS CAN BE EXPECTED UNDER THE EXCITEMENT WHICH I SUFFER.
IF YOU REALLY WISH ME WELL, YOU WILL RELIEVE THIS EXCITEMENT VERY EASILY!
AND HOW IS THIS TO BE DONE?
VERY EASILY. JUPITER AND MYSELF ARE GOING UPON AN EXPEDITION INTO THE HILLS, UPON THE MAINLAND--AND WE SHALL NEED THE AID OF SOMEONE IN WHOM WE CAN CONFIDE!
"I'M ANXIOUS TO OBLIGE YOU IN ANY WAY, BUT DO YOU MEAN TO SAY THAT THIS INFERNAL BEETLE HAS ANY CONNECTION WITH YOUR EXPEDITION?"
"CERTAINLY! BUT BEFORE DECIDING, LET ME MAKE THIS CLEAR. WHETHER WE SUCCEED OR FAIL, THE EXCITEMENT WHICH YOU NOW PERCEIVE IN ME WILL BE EQUALLY ALLAYED."
"WHEN DO WE DEPART?"
"IMMEDIATELY. WE SHALL BE BACK BY SUNRISE."
AND YOU WILL PROMISE ME, UPON YOUR HONOR, THAT WHEN THIS BUG BUSINESS IS SETTLED TO YOUR SATISFACTION, I WILL HEAR NO MORE TALK OF THAT BEETLE?
YES, I PROMISE.

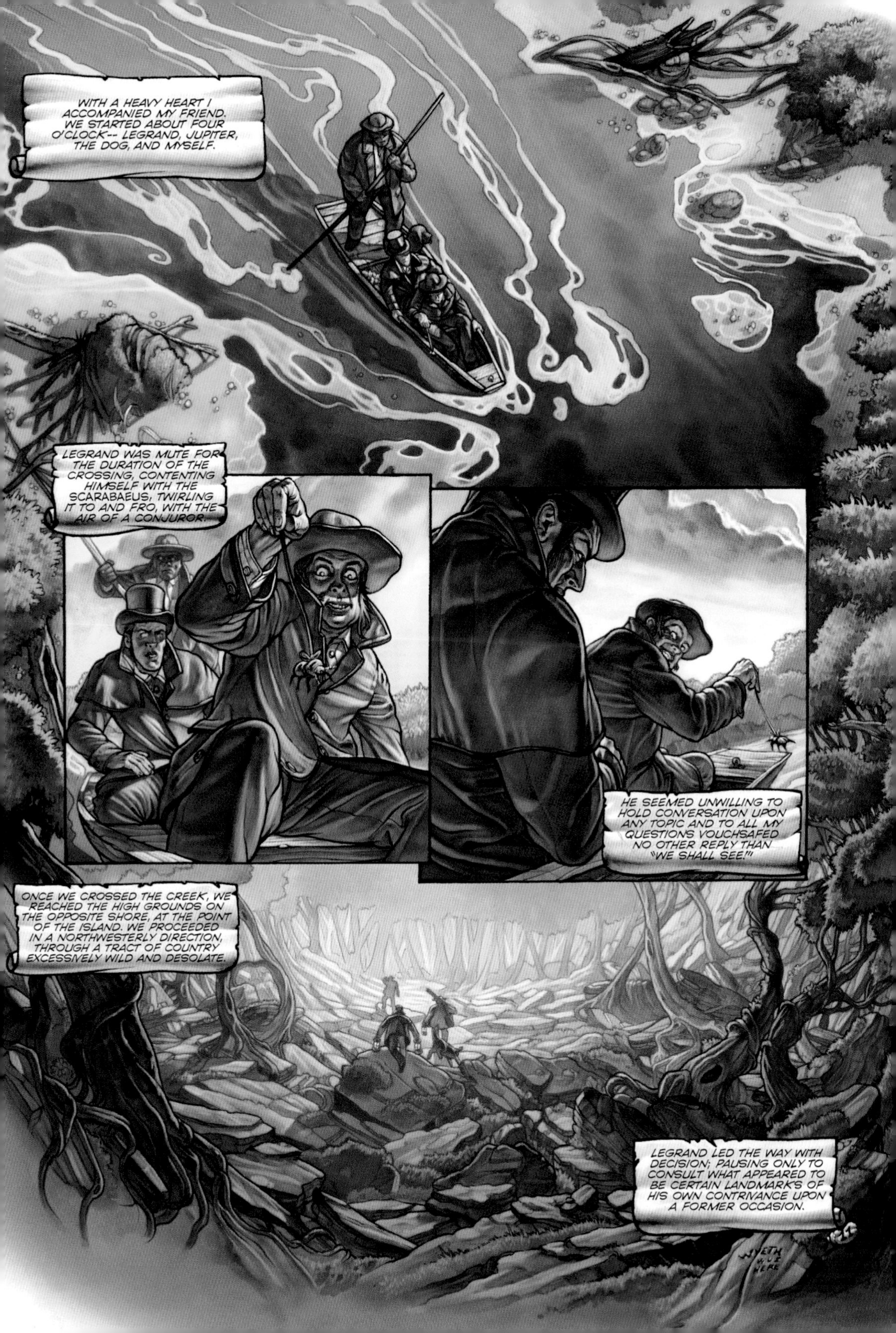
WITH A HEAVY HEART I ACCOMPANIED MY FRIEND. WE STARTED ABOUT FOUR O'CLOCK-- LEGRAND, JUPITER, THE DOG, AND MYSELF.
LEGRAND WAS MUTE FOR THE DURATION OF THE CROSSING, CONTENTING HIMSELF WITH THE SCARABAEUS, TWIRLING IT TO AND FRO, WITH THE AIR OF A CONJUROR.
HE SEEMED UNWILLING TO HOLD CONVERSATION UPON ANY TOPIC AND TO ALL MY QUESTIONS VOUCHSAFED NO OTHER REPLY THAN "WE SHALL SEE!"
ONCE WE CROSSED THE CREEK, WE REACHED THE HIGH GROUNDS ON THE OPPOSITE SHORE, AT THE POINT OF THE ISLAND. WE PROCEEDED IN A NORTHWESTERLY DIRECTION, THROUGH A TRACT OF COUNTRY EXCESSIVELY WILD AND DESOLATE.
LEGRAND LED THE WAY WITH DECISION; PAUSING ONLY TO CONSULT WHAT APPEARED TO BE CERTAIN LANDMARKS OF HIS OWN CONTRIVANCE UPON A FORMER OCCASION.

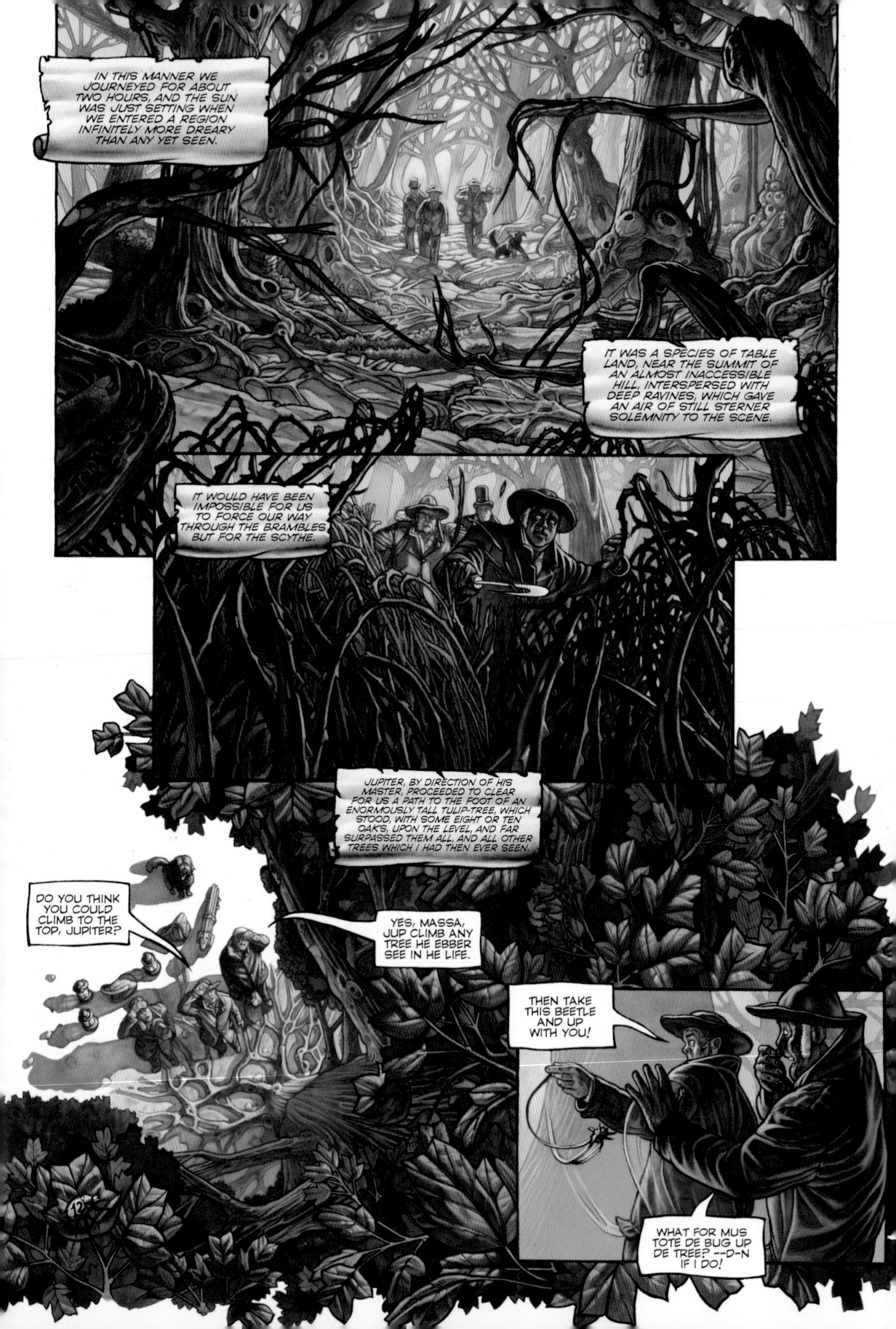
IN THIS MANNER WE JOURNEYED FOR ABOUT TWO HOURS, AND THE SUN WAS JUST SETTING WHEN WE ENTERED A REGION INFINITELY MORE DREARY THAN ANY YET SEEN.
IT WAS A SPECIES OF TABLE LAND, NEAR THE SUMMIT OF AN ALMOST INACCESSIBLE HILL, INTERSPERSED WITH DEEP RAVINES, WHICH GAVE AN AIR OF STILL STERNER SOLEMNITY TO THE SCENE.
IT WOULD HAVE BEEN IMPOSSIBLE FOR US TO FORCE OUR WAY THROUGH THE BRAMBLES BUT FOR THE SCYTHE.
JUPITER, BY DIRECTION OF HIS MASTER, PROCEEDED TO CLEAR FOR US A PATH TO THE FOOT OF AN ENORMOUSLY TALL TULIP-TREE, WHICH STOOD, WITH SOME EIGHT OR TEN OAKS, UPON THE LEVEL, AND FAR SURPASSED THEM ALL, AND ALL OTHER TREES WHICH I HAD THEN EVER SEEN.
DO YOU THINK YOU COULD CLIMB TO THE TOP, JUPITER?
YES, MASSA, JUP CLIMB ANY TREE HE EBBER SEE IN HE LIFE.
THEN TAKE THIS BEETLE AND UP WITH YOU!
WHAT FOR MUS TOTE DE BUG UP DE TREE? --D-N IF I DO!
12

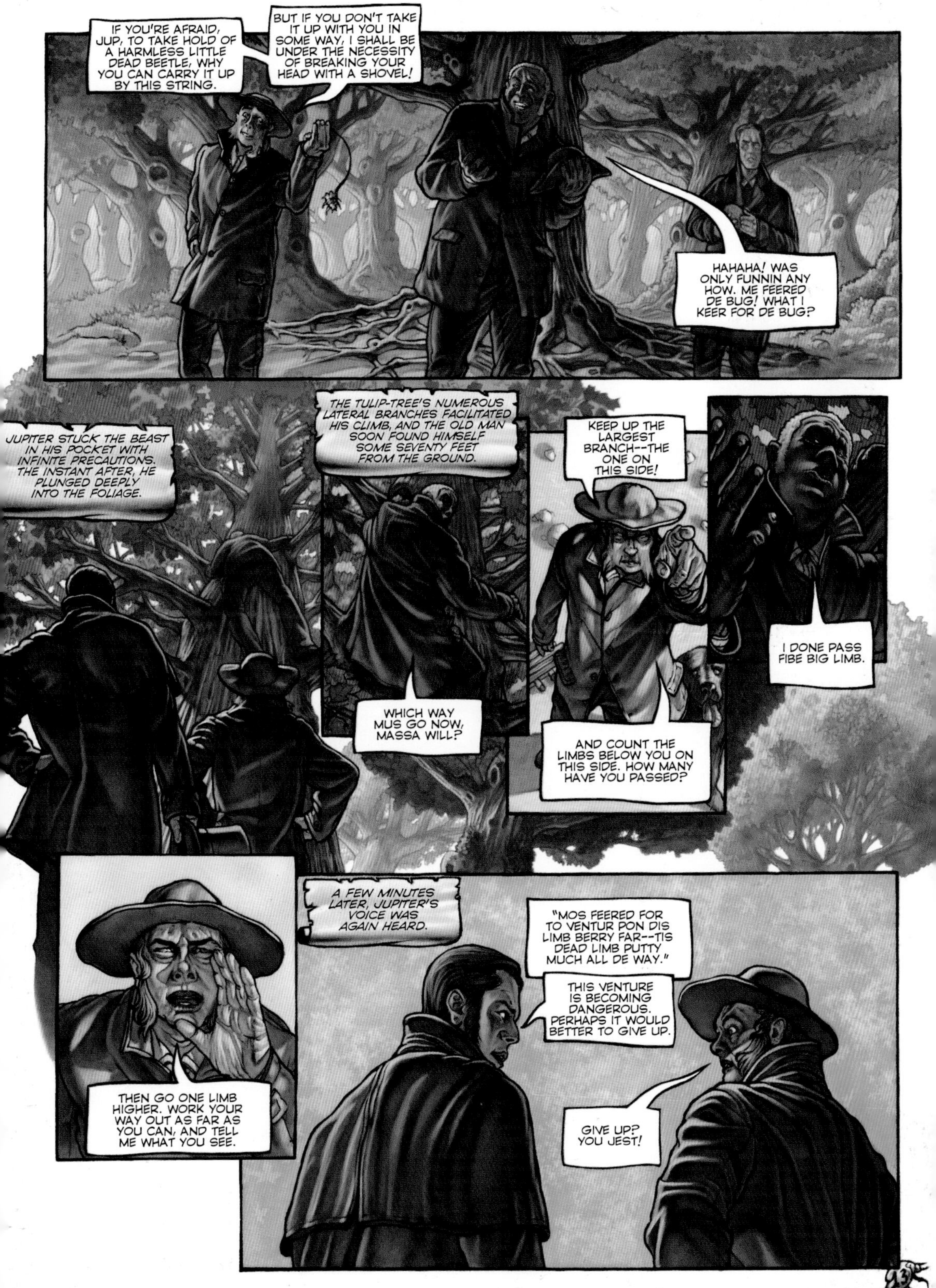

IF YOU'RE AFRAID, JUP, TO TAKE HOLD OF A HARMLESS LITTLE DEAD BEETLE, WHY YOU CAN CARRY IT UP BY THIS STRING.
BUT IF YOU DON'T TAKE IT UP WITH YOU IN SOME WAY, I SHALL BE UNDER THE NECESSITY OF BREAKING YOUR HEAD WITH A SHOVEL!
HAHAHA! WAS ONLY FUNNIN ANY HOW. ME FEERED DE BUG! WHAT I KEER FOR DE BUG?
JUPITER STUCK THE BEAST IN HIS POCKET WITH INFINITE PRECAUTIONS. THE INSTANT AFTER, HE PLUNGED DEEPLY INTO THE FOLIAGE.
THE TULIP-TREE'S NUMEROUS LATERAL BRANCHES FACILITATED HIS CLIMB, AND THE OLD MAN SOON FOUND HIMSELF SOME SEVENTY FEET FROM THE GROUND.
WHICH WAY MUS GO NOW, MASSA WILL?
KEEP UP THE LARGEST BRANCH--THE ONE ON THIS SIDE!
AND COUNT THE LIMBS BELOW YOU ON THIS SIDE. HOW MANY HAVE YOU PASSED?
I DONE PASS FIBE BIG LIMB.
THEN GO ONE LIMB HIGHER. WORK YOUR WAY OUT AS FAR AS YOU CAN, AND TELL ME WHAT YOU SEE.
A FEW MINUTES LATER, JUPITER'S VOICE WAS AGAIN HEARD.
"MOS FEERED FOR TO VENTUR PON DIS LIMB BERRY FAR--TIS DEAD LIMB PUTTY MUCH ALL DE WAY."
THIS VENTURE IS BECOMING DANGEROUS. PERHAPS IT WOULD BETTER TO GIVE UP.
GIVE UP? YOU JEST!

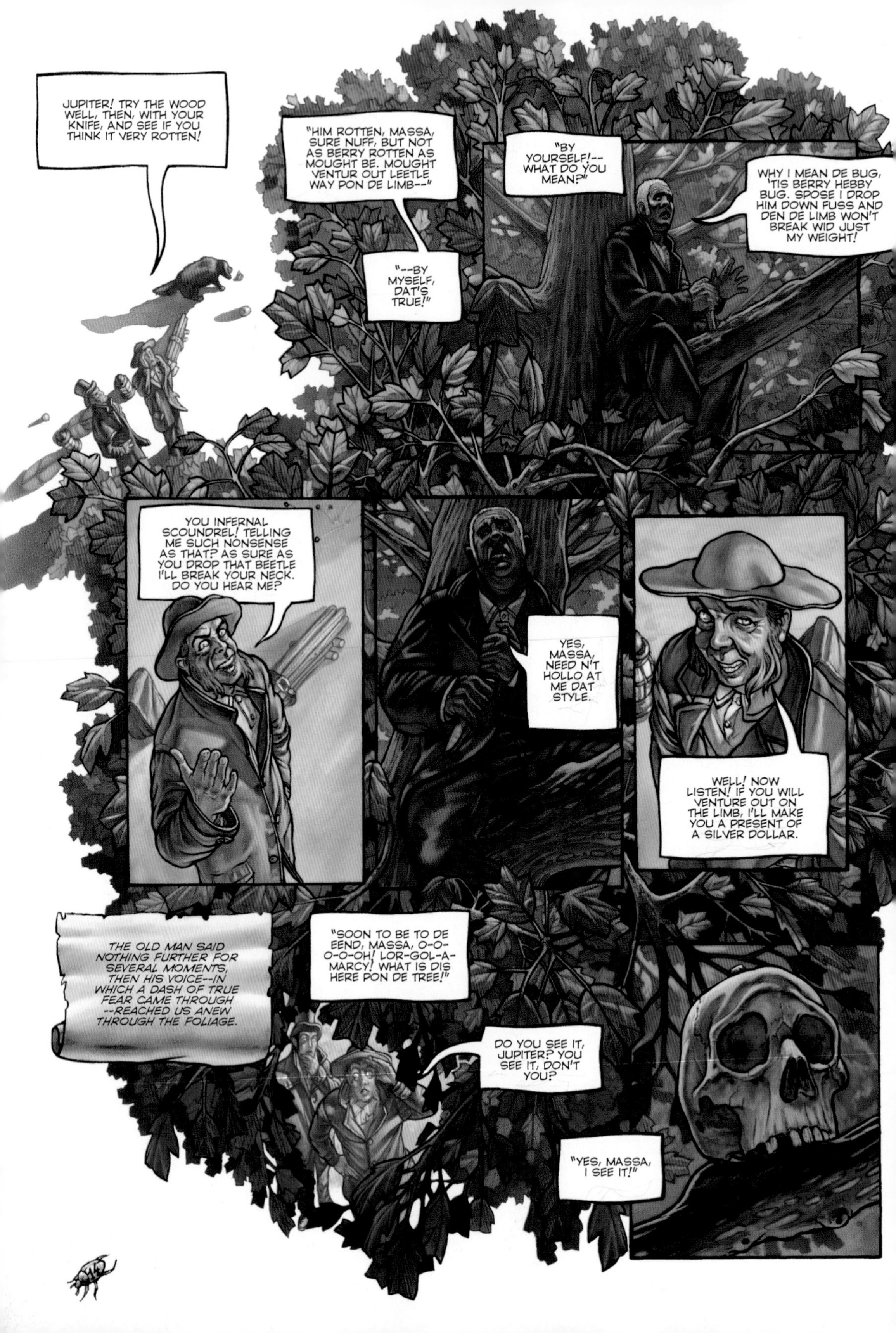
JUPITER! TRY THE WOOD WELL, THEN, WITH YOUR KNIFE, AND SEE IF YOU THINK IT VERY ROTTEN!
"HIM ROTTEN, MASSA, SURE NUFF, BUT NOT AS BERRY ROTTEN AS MOUGHT BE. MOUGHT VENTUR OUT LEETLE WAY PON DE LIMB--"
"--BY MYSELF, DAT'S TRUE!"
"BY YOURSELF!--WHAT DO YOU MEAN?"
WHY I MEAN DE BUG, 'TIS BERRY HEBBY BUG. SPOSE I DROP HIM DOWN FUSS AND DEN DE LIMB WON'T BREAK WID JUST MY WEIGHT!
YOU INFERNAL SCOUNDREL! TELLING ME SUCH NONSENSE AS THAT? AS SURE AS YOU DROP THAT BEETLE I'LL BREAK YOUR NECK. DO YOU HEAR ME?
YES, MASSA, NEED N'T HOLLO AT ME DAT STYLE.
WELL! NOW LISTEN! IF YOU WILL VENTURE OUT ON THE LIMB, I'LL MAKE YOU A PRESENT OF A SILVER DOLLAR.
THE OLD MAN SAID NOTHING FURTHER FOR SEVERAL MOMENTS, THEN HIS VOICE--IN WHICH A DASH OF TRUE FEAR CAME THROUGH--REACHED US ANEW THROUGH THE FOLIAGE.
"SOON TO BE TO DE EEND, MASSA, O-O-O-O-OH! LOR-GOL-A-MARCY! WHAT IS DIS HERE PON DE TREE!"
DO YOU SEE IT, JUPITER? YOU SEE IT, DON'T YOU?
"YES, MASSA, I SEE IT!"

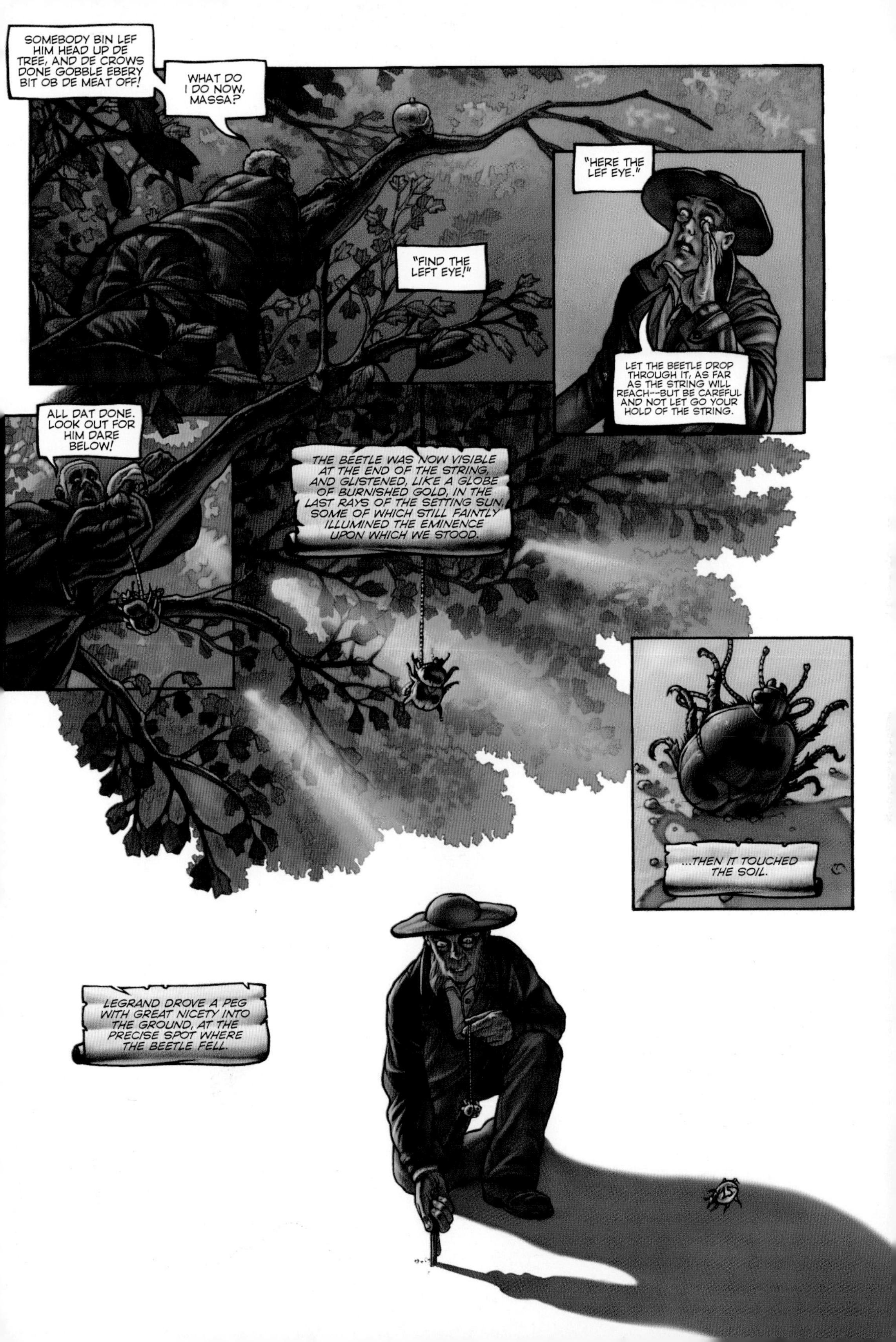
SOMEBODY BIN LEF HIM HEAD UP DE TREE, AND DE CROWS DONE GOBBLE EBERY BIT OB DE MEAT OFF!
WHAT DO I DO NOW, MASSA?
"FIND THE LEFT EYE!"
"HERE THE LEF EYE."
LET THE BEETLE DROP THROUGH IT, AS FAR AS THE STRING WILL REACH--BUT BE CAREFUL AND NOT LET GO YOUR HOLD OF THE STRING.
ALL DAT DONE. LOOK OUT FOR HIM DARE BELOW!
THE BEETLE WAS NOW VISIBLE AT THE END OF THE STRING, AND GLISTENED, LIKE A GLOBE OF BURNISHED GOLD, IN THE LAST RAYS OF THE SETTING SUN, SOME OF WHICH STILL FAINTLY ILLUMINED THE EMINENCE UPON WHICH WE STOOD.
...THEN IT TOUCHED THE SOIL.
LEGRAND DROVE A PEG WITH GREAT NICETY INTO THE GROUND, AT THE PRECISE SPOT WHERE THE BEETLE FELL.
15

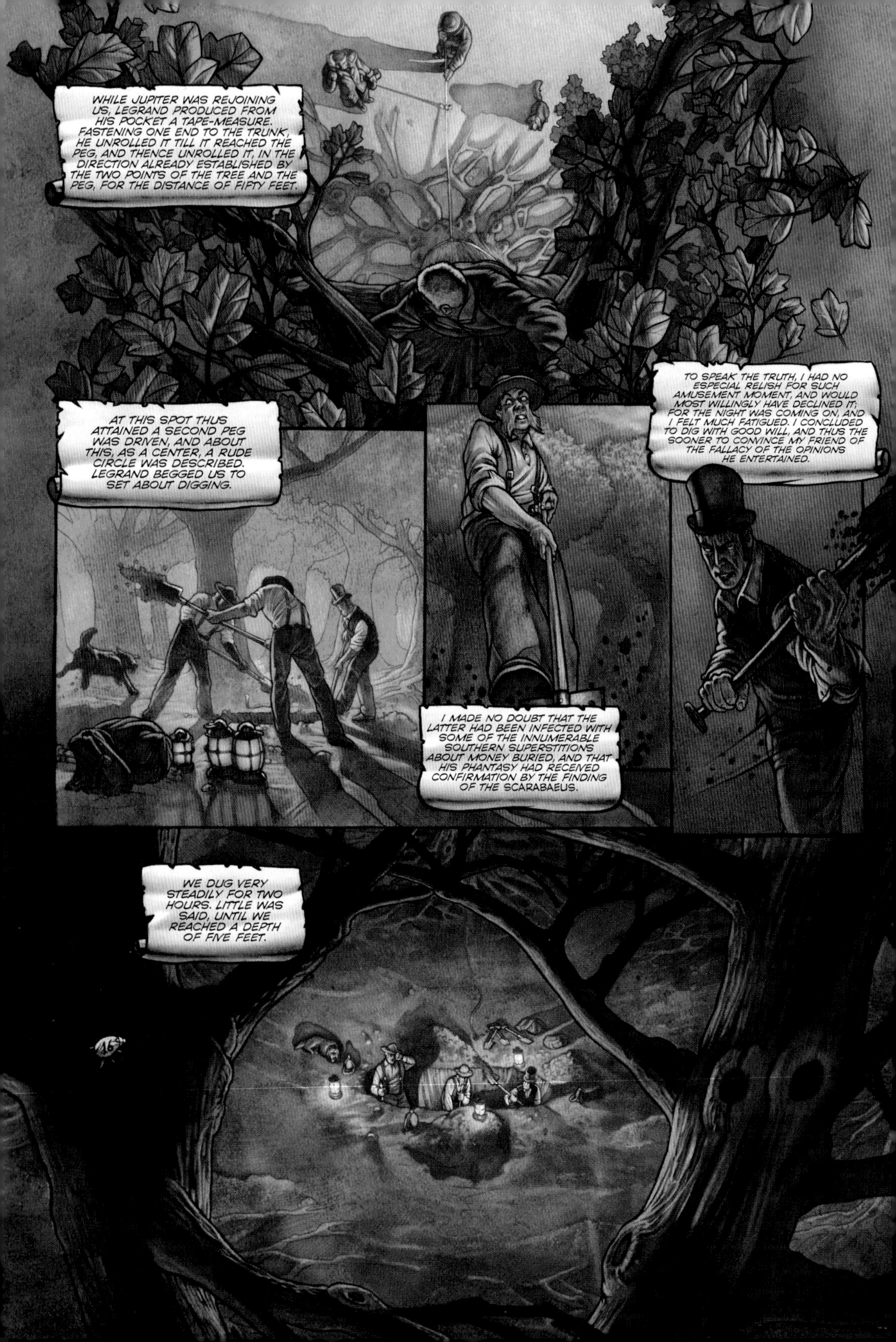
WHILE JUPITER WAS REJOINING US, LEGRAND PRODUCED FROM HIS POCKET A TAPE-MEASURE. FASTENING ONE END TO THE TRUNK, HE UNROLLED IT TILL IT REACHED THE PEG, AND THENCE UNROLLED IT, IN THE DIRECTION ALREADY ESTABLISHED BY THE TWO POINTS OF THE TREE AND THE PEG, FOR THE DISTANCE OF FIFTY FEET.
AT THIS SPOT THUS ATTAINED A SECOND PEG WAS DRIVEN, AND ABOUT THIS, AS A CENTER, A RUDE CIRCLE WAS DESCRIBED. LEGRAND BEGGED US TO SET ABOUT DIGGING.
I MADE NO DOUBT THAT THE LATTER HAD BEEN INFECTED WITH SOME OF THE INNUMERABLE SOUTHERN SUPERSTITIONS ABOUT MONEY BURIED, AND THAT HIS PHANTASY HAD RECEIVED CONFIRMATION BY THE FINDING OF THE SCARABAEUS.
TO SPEAK THE TRUTH, I HAD NO ESPECIAL RELISH FOR SUCH AMUSEMENT MOMENT, AND WOULD MOST WILLINGLY HAVE DECLINED IT; FOR THE NIGHT WAS COMING ON, AND I FELT MUCH FATIGUED. I CONCLUDED TO DIG WITH GOOD WILL, AND THUS THE SOONER TO CONVINCE MY FRIEND OF THE FALLACY OF THE OPINIONS HE ENTERTAINED.
WE DUG VERY STEADILY FOR TWO HOURS. LITTLE WAS SAID, UNTIL WE REACHED A DEPTH OF FIVE FEET.

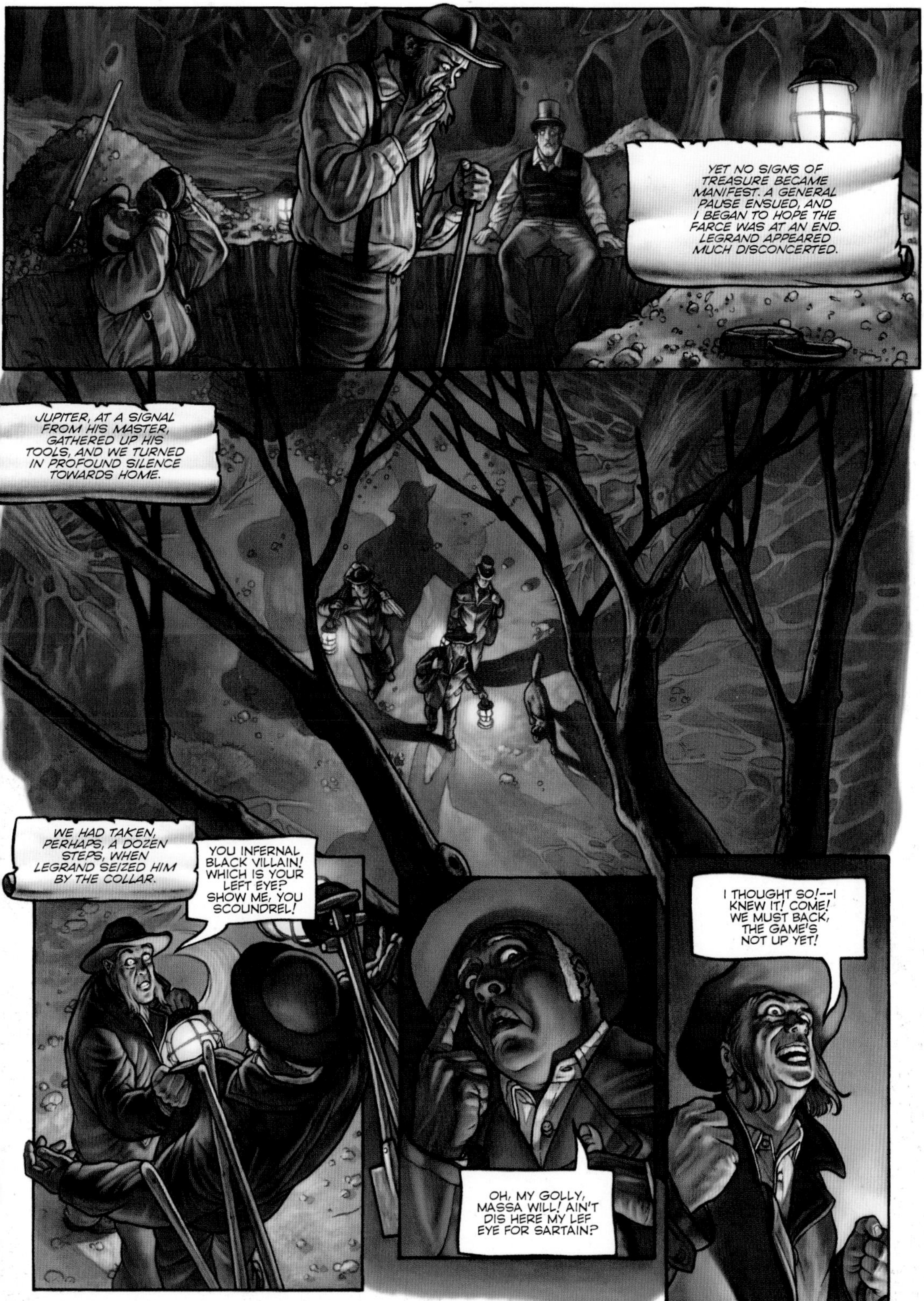
YET NO SIGNS OF TREASURE BECAME MANIFEST. A GENERAL PAUSE ENSUED, AND I BEGAN TO HOPE THE FARCE WAS AT AN END. LEGRAND APPEARED MUCH DISCONCERTED.
JUPITER, AT A SIGNAL FROM HIS MASTER, GATHERED UP HIS TOOLS, AND WE TURNED IN PROFOUND SILENCE TOWARDS HOME.
WE HAD TAKEN, PERHAPS, A DOZEN STEPS, WHEN LEGRAND SEIZED HIM BY THE COLLAR.
YOU INFERNAL BLACK VILLAIN! WHICH IS YOUR LEFT EYE? SHOW ME, YOU SCOUNDREL!
OH, MY GOLLY, MASSA WILL! AIN'T DIS HERE MY LEF EYE FOR SARTAIN?
I THOUGHT SO!--I KNEW IT! COME! WE MUST BACK, THE GAME'S NOT UP YET!

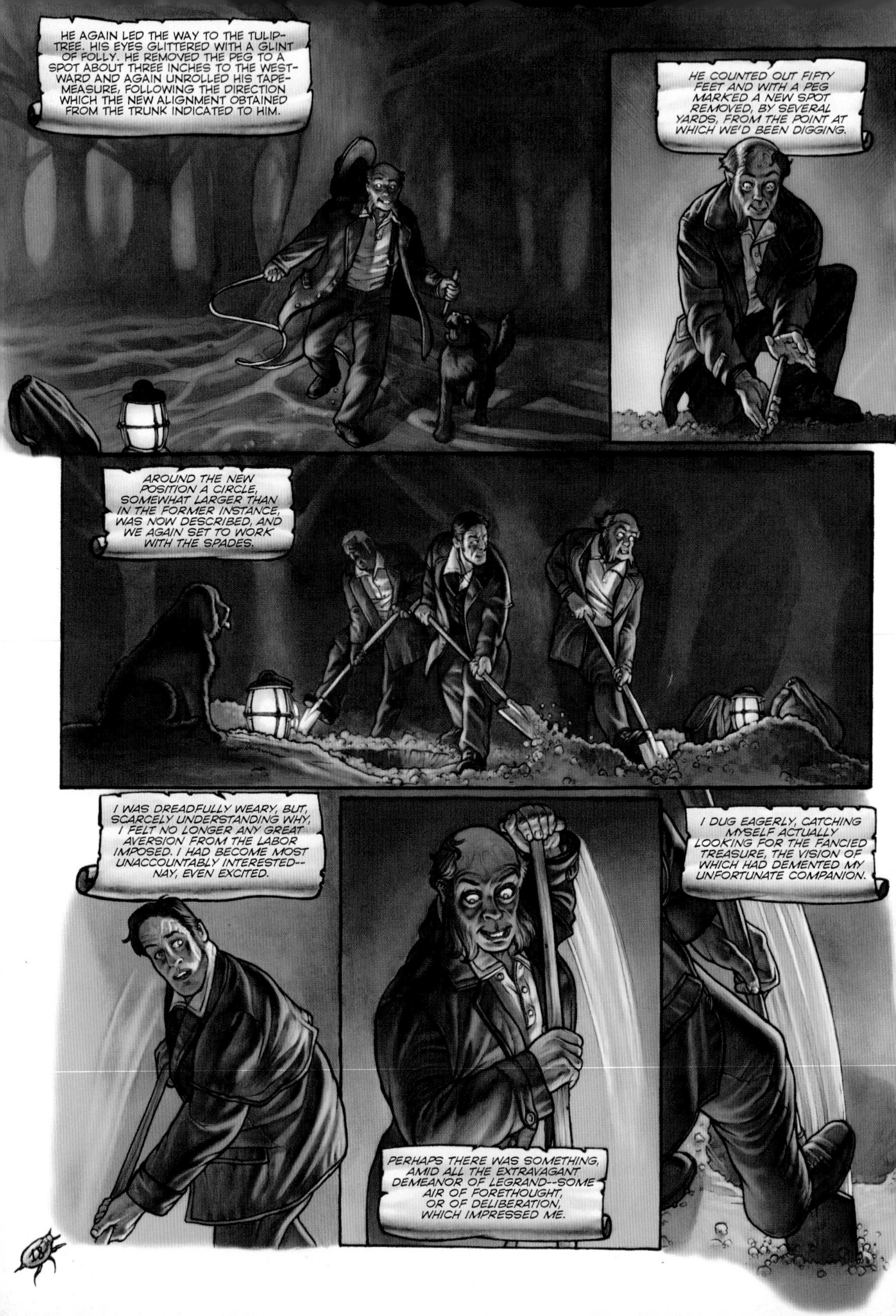
HE AGAIN LED THE WAY TO THE TULIP-TREE. HIS EYES GLITTERED WITH A GLINT OF FOLLY. HE REMOVED THE PEG TO A SPOT ABOUT THREE INCHES TO THE WESTWARD AND AGAIN UNROLLED HIS TAPE-MEASURE, FOLLOWING THE DIRECTION WHICH THE NEW ALIGNMENT OBTAINED FROM THE TRUNK INDICATED TO HIM.
HE COUNTED OUT FIFTY FEET AND WITH A PEG MARKED A NEW SPOT REMOVED, BY SEVERAL YARDS, FROM THE POINT AT WHICH WE'D BEEN DIGGING.
AROUND THE NEW POSITION A CIRCLE, SOMEWHAT LARGER THAN IN THE FORMER INSTANCE, WAS NOW DESCRIBED, AND WE AGAIN SET TO WORK WITH THE SPADES.
I WAS DREADFULLY WEARY, BUT, SCARCELY UNDERSTANDING WHY, I FELT NO LONGER ANY GREAT AVERSION FROM THE LABOR IMPOSED. I HAD BECOME MOST UNACCOUNTABLY INTERESTED--NAY, EVEN EXCITED.
PERHAPS THERE WAS SOMETHING, AMID ALL THE EXTRAVAGANT DEMEANOR OF LEGRAND--SOME AIR OF FORETHOUGHT, OR OF DELIBERATION, WHICH IMPRESSED ME.
I DUG EAGERLY, CATCHING MYSELF ACTUALLY LOOKING FOR THE FANCIED TREASURE, THE VISION OF WHICH HAD DEMENTED MY UNFORTUNATE COMPANION.

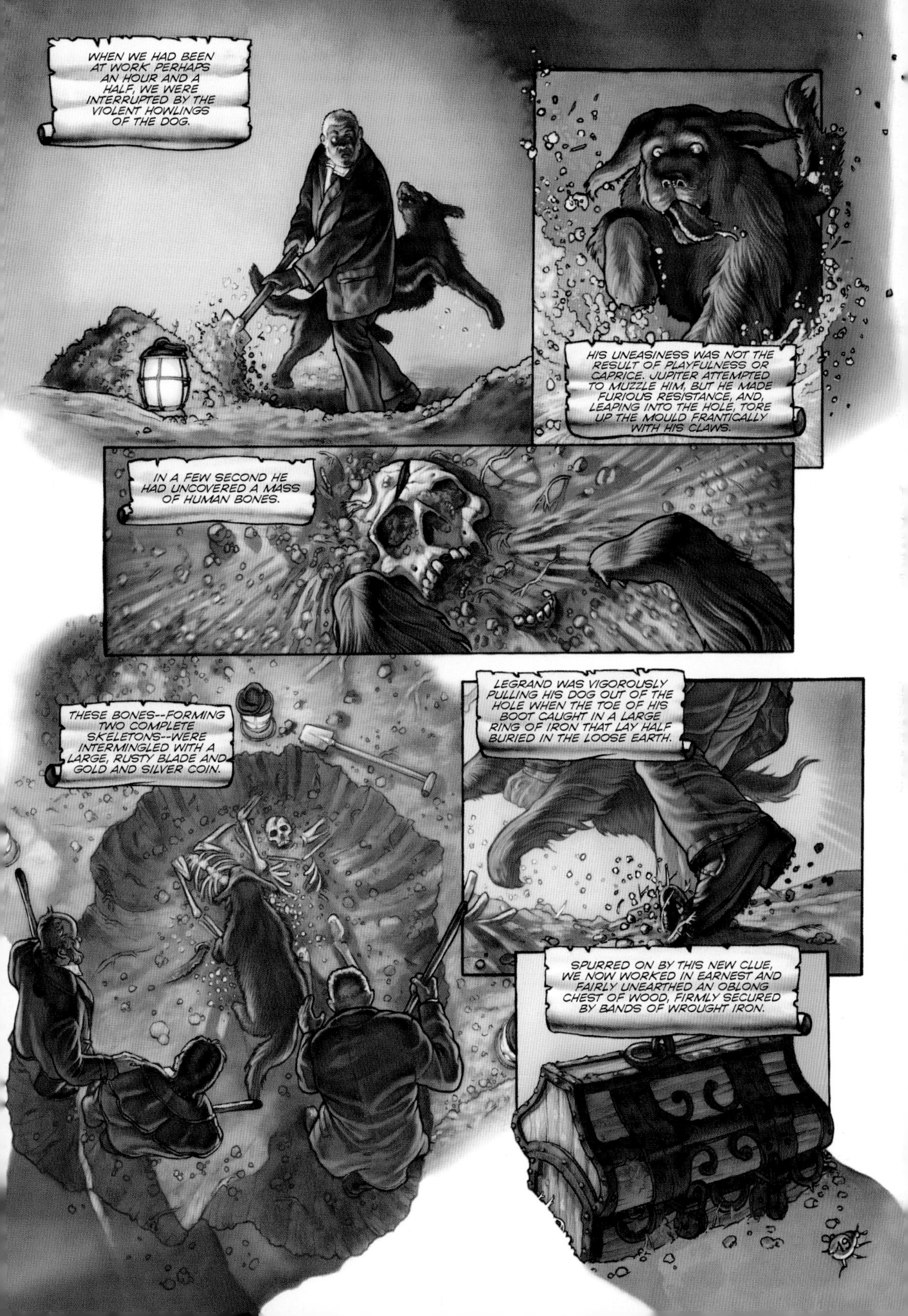
WHEN WE HAD BEEN AT WORK PERHAPS AN HOUR AND A HALF, WE WERE INTERRUPTED BY THE VIOLENT HOWLINGS OF THE DOG.
HIS UNEASINESS WAS NOT THE RESULT OF PLAYFULNESS OR CAPRICE. JUPITER ATTEMPTED TO MUZZLE HIM, BUT HE MADE FURIOUS RESISTANCE, AND, LEAPING INTO THE HOLE, TORE UP THE MOULD FRANTICALLY WITH HIS CLAWS.
IN A FEW SECOND HE HAD UNCOVERED A MASS OF HUMAN BONES.
THESE BONES--FORMING TWO COMPLETE SKELETONS--WERE INTERMINGLED WITH A LARGE, RUSTY BLADE AND GOLD AND SILVER COIN.
LEGRAND WAS VIGOROUSLY PULLING HIS DOG OUT OF THE HOLE WHEN THE TOE OF HIS BOOT CAUGHT IN A LARGE RING OF IRON THAT LAY HALF BURIED IN THE LOOSE EARTH.
SPURRED ON BY THIS NEW CLUE, WE NOW WORKED IN EARNEST AND FAIRLY UNEARTHED AN OBLONG CHEST OF WOOD, FIRMLY SECURED BY BANDS OF WROUGHT IRON.

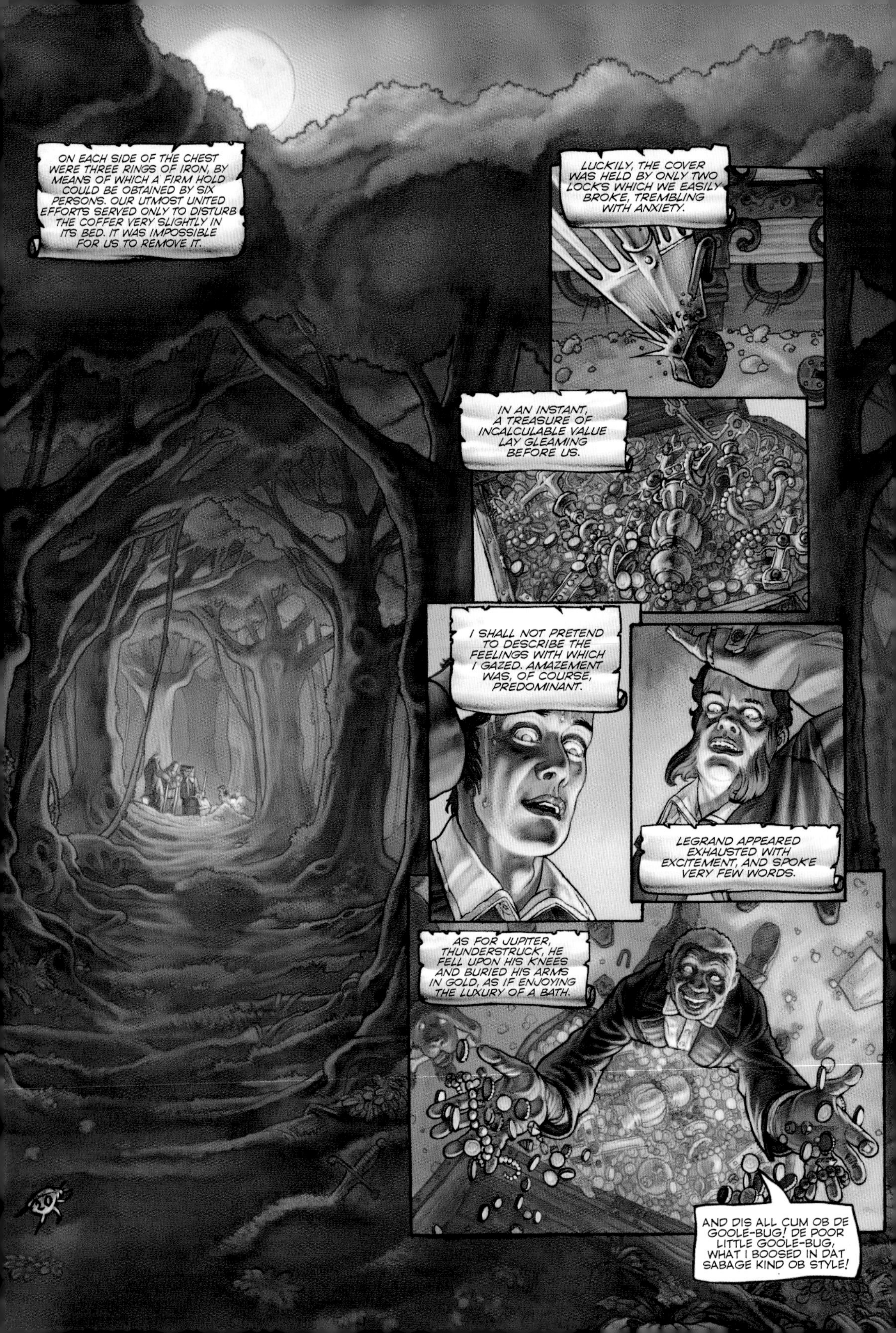

ON EACH SIDE OF THE CHEST WERE THREE RINGS OF IRON, BY MEANS OF WHICH A FIRM HOLD COULD BE OBTAINED BY SIX PERSONS. OUR UTMOST UNITED EFFORTS SERVED ONLY TO DISTURB THE COFFER VERY SLIGHTLY IN ITS BED. IT WAS IMPOSSIBLE FOR US TO REMOVE IT.
LUCKILY, THE COVER WAS HELD BY ONLY TWO LOCKS WHICH WE EASILY BROKE, TREMBLING WITH ANXIETY.
IN AN INSTANT, A TREASURE OF INCALCULABLE VALUE LAY GLEAMING BEFORE US.
I SHALL NOT PRETEND TO DESCRIBE THE FEELINGS WITH WHICH I GAZED. AMAZEMENT WAS, OF COURSE, PREDOMINANT.
LEGRAND APPEARED EXHAUSTED WITH EXCITEMENT, AND SPOKE VERY FEW WORDS.
AS FOR JUPITER, THUNDERSTRUCK, HE FELL UPON HIS KNEES AND BURIED HIS ARMS IN GOLD, AS IF ENJOYING THE LUXURY OF A BATH.
AND DIS ALL CUM OB DE GOOLE-BUG! DE POOR LITTLE GOOLE-BUG, WHAT I BOOSED IN DAT SABAGE KIND OB STYLE!

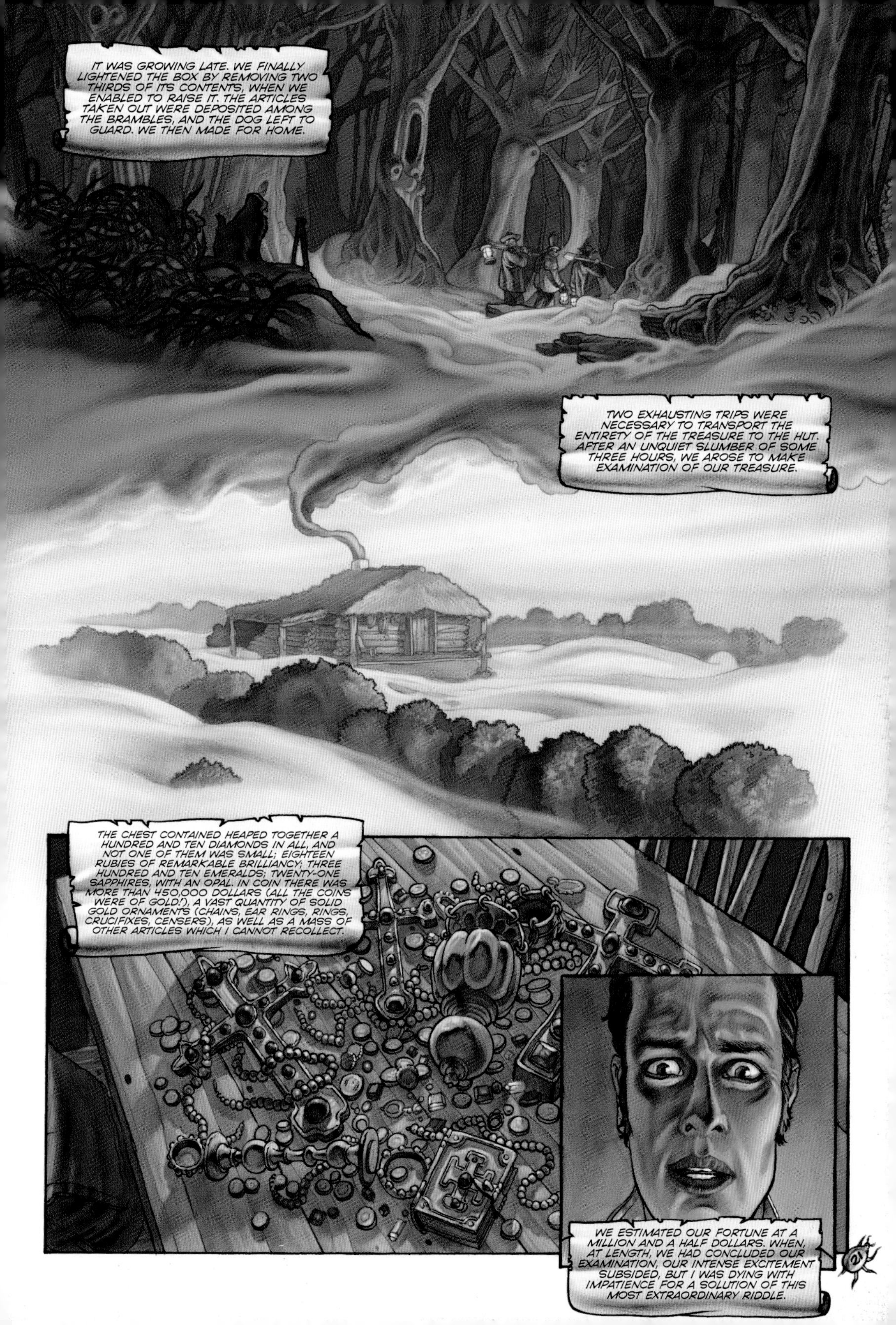
IT WAS GROWING LATE. WE FINALLY LIGHTENED THE BOX BY REMOVING TWO THIRDS OF ITS CONTENTS, WHEN WE ENABLED TO RAISE IT. THE ARTICLES TAKEN OUT WERE DEPOSITED AMONG THE BRAMBLES, AND THE DOG LEFT TO GUARD. WE THEN MADE FOR HOME.
TWO EXHAUSTING TRIPS WERE NECESSARY TO TRANSPORT THE ENTIRETY OF THE TREASURE TO THE HUT. AFTER AN UNQUIET SLUMBER OF SOME THREE HOURS, WE AROSE TO MAKE EXAMINATION OF OUR TREASURE.
THE CHEST CONTAINED HEAPED TOGETHER A HUNDRED AND TEN DIAMONDS IN ALL, AND NOT ONE OF THEM WAS SMALL; EIGHTEEN RUBIES OF REMARKABLE BRILLIANCY; THREE HUNDRED AND TEN EMERALDS; TWENTY-ONE SAPPHIRES, WITH AN OPAL. IN COIN THERE WAS MORE THAN 450,000 DOLLARS (ALL THE COINS WERE OF GOLD!), A VAST QUANTITY OF SOLID GOLD ORNAMENTS (CHAINS, EAR RINGS, RINGS, CRUCIFIXES, CENSERS), AS WELL AS A MASS OF OTHER ARTICLES WHICH I CANNOT RECOLLECT.
WE ESTIMATED OUR FORTUNE AT A MILLION AND A HALF DOLLARS. WHEN, AT LENGTH, WE HAD CONCLUDED OUR EXAMINATION, OUR INTENSE EXCITEMENT SUBSIDED, BUT I WAS DYING WITH IMPATIENCE FOR A SOLUTION OF THIS MOST EXTRAORDINARY RIDDLE.

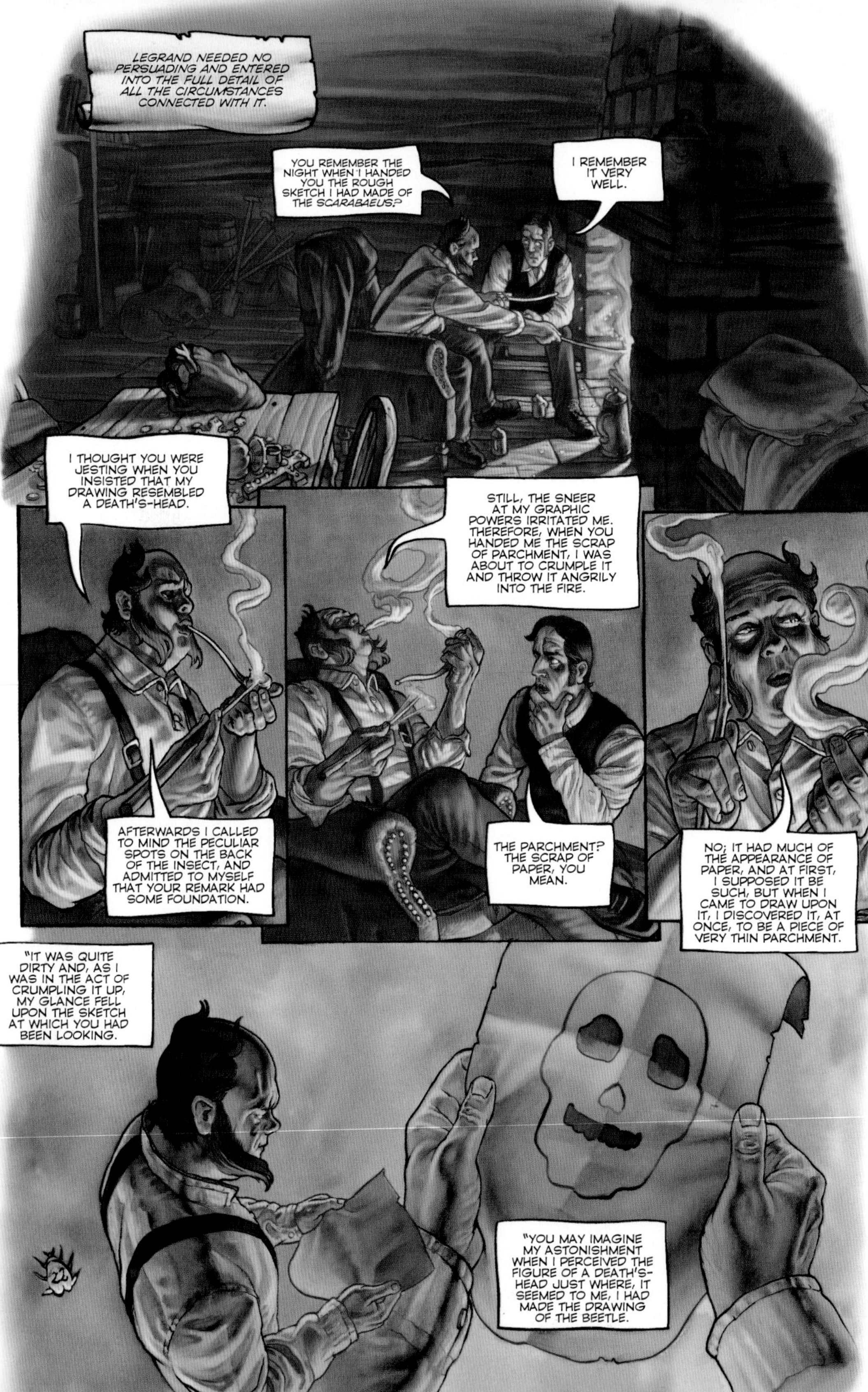
LEGRAND NEEDED NO PERSUADING AND ENTERED INTO THE FULL DETAIL OF ALL THE CIRCUMSTANCES CONNECTED WITH IT.
YOU REMEMBER THE NIGHT WHEN I HANDED YOU THE ROUGH SKETCH I HAD MADE OF THE SCARABAEUS?
I REMEMBER IT VERY WELL.
I THOUGHT YOU WERE JESTING WHEN YOU INSISTED THAT MY DRAWING RESEMBLED A DEATH'S-HEAD.
AFTERWARDS I CALLED TO MIND THE PECULIAR SPOTS ON THE BACK OF THE INSECT, AND ADMITTED TO MYSELF THAT YOUR REMARK HAD SOME FOUNDATION.
STILL, THE SNEER AT MY GRAPHIC POWERS IRRITATED ME. THEREFORE, WHEN YOU HANDED ME THE SCRAP OF PARCHMENT, I WAS ABOUT TO CRUMPLE IT AND THROW IT ANGRILY INTO THE FIRE.
THE PARCHMENT? THE SCRAP OF PAPER, YOU MEAN.
NO; IT HAD MUCH OF THE APPEARANCE OF PAPER, AND AT FIRST, I SUPPOSED IT BE SUCH, BUT WHEN I CAME TO DRAW UPON IT, I DISCOVERED IT, AT ONCE, TO BE A PIECE OF VERY THIN PARCHMENT.
"IT WAS QUITE DIRTY AND, AS I WAS IN THE ACT OF CRUMPLING IT UP, MY GLANCE FELL UPON THE SKETCH AT WHICH YOU HAD BEEN LOOKING.
"YOU MAY IMAGINE MY ASTONISHMENT WHEN I PERCEIVED THE FIGURE OF A DEATH'S-HEAD JUST WHERE, IT SEEMED TO ME, I HAD MADE THE DRAWING OF THE BEETLE.

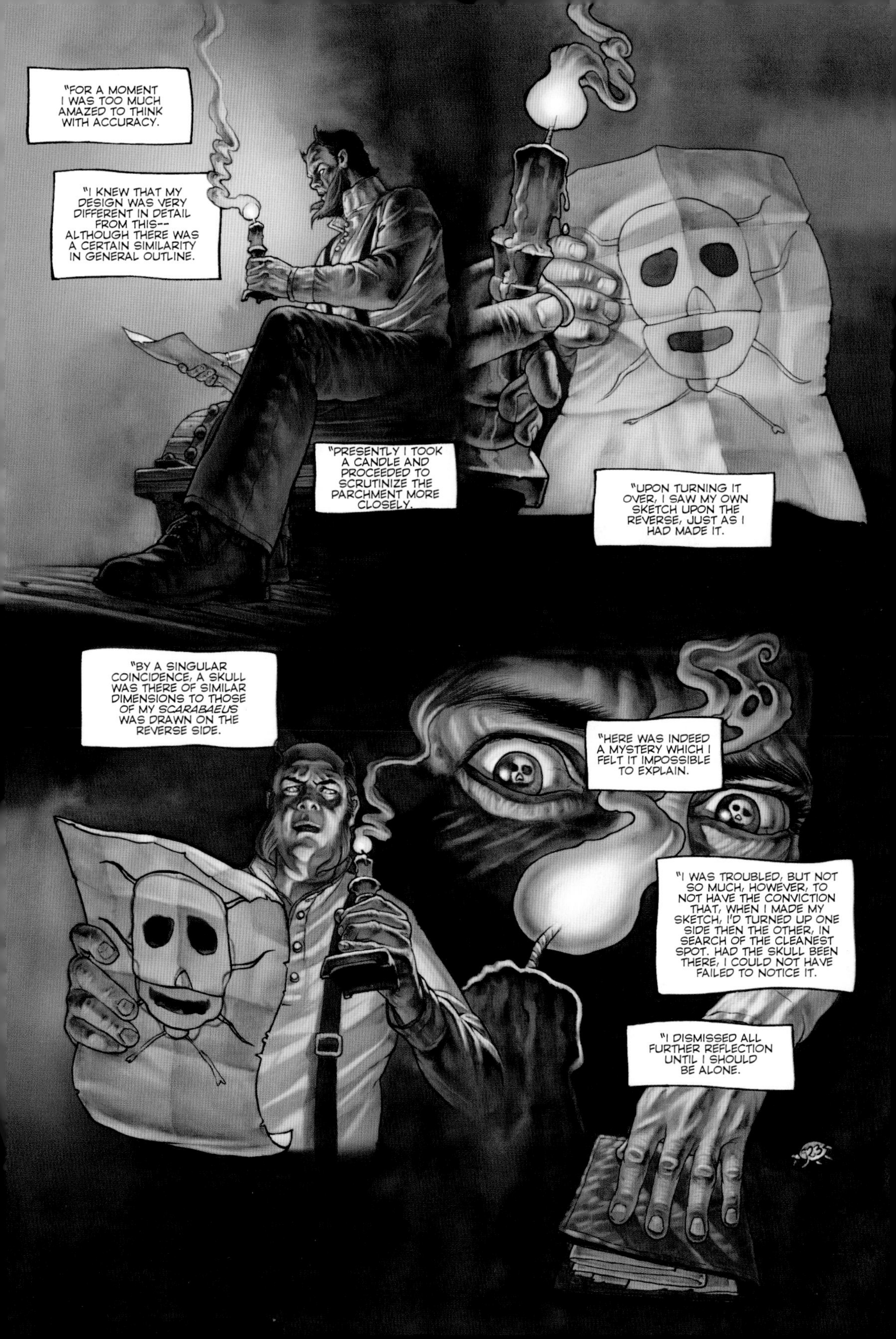
"FOR A MOMENT I WAS TOO MUCH AMAZED TO THINK WITH ACCURACY.
"I KNEW THAT MY DESIGN WAS VERY DIFFERENT IN DETAIL FROM THIS--ALTHOUGH THERE WAS A CERTAIN SIMILARITY IN GENERAL OUTLINE.
"PRESENTLY I TOOK A CANDLE AND PROCEEDED TO SCRUTINIZE THE PARCHMENT MORE CLOSELY.
"UPON TURNING IT OVER, I SAW MY OWN SKETCH UPON THE REVERSE, JUST AS I HAD MADE IT.
"BY A SINGULAR COINCIDENCE, A SKULL WAS THERE OF SIMILAR DIMENSIONS TO THOSE OF MY *SCARABAEUS* WAS DRAWN ON THE REVERSE SIDE.
"HERE WAS INDEED A MYSTERY WHICH I FELT IT IMPOSSIBLE TO EXPLAIN.
"I WAS TROUBLED, BUT NOT SO MUCH, HOWEVER, TO NOT HAVE THE CONVICTION THAT, WHEN I MADE MY SKETCH, I'D TURNED UP ONE SIDE THEN THE OTHER, IN SEARCH OF THE CLEANEST SPOT. HAD THE SKULL BEEN THERE, I COULD NOT HAVE FAILED TO NOTICE IT.
"I DISMISSED ALL FURTHER REFLECTION UNTIL I SHOULD BE ALONE.

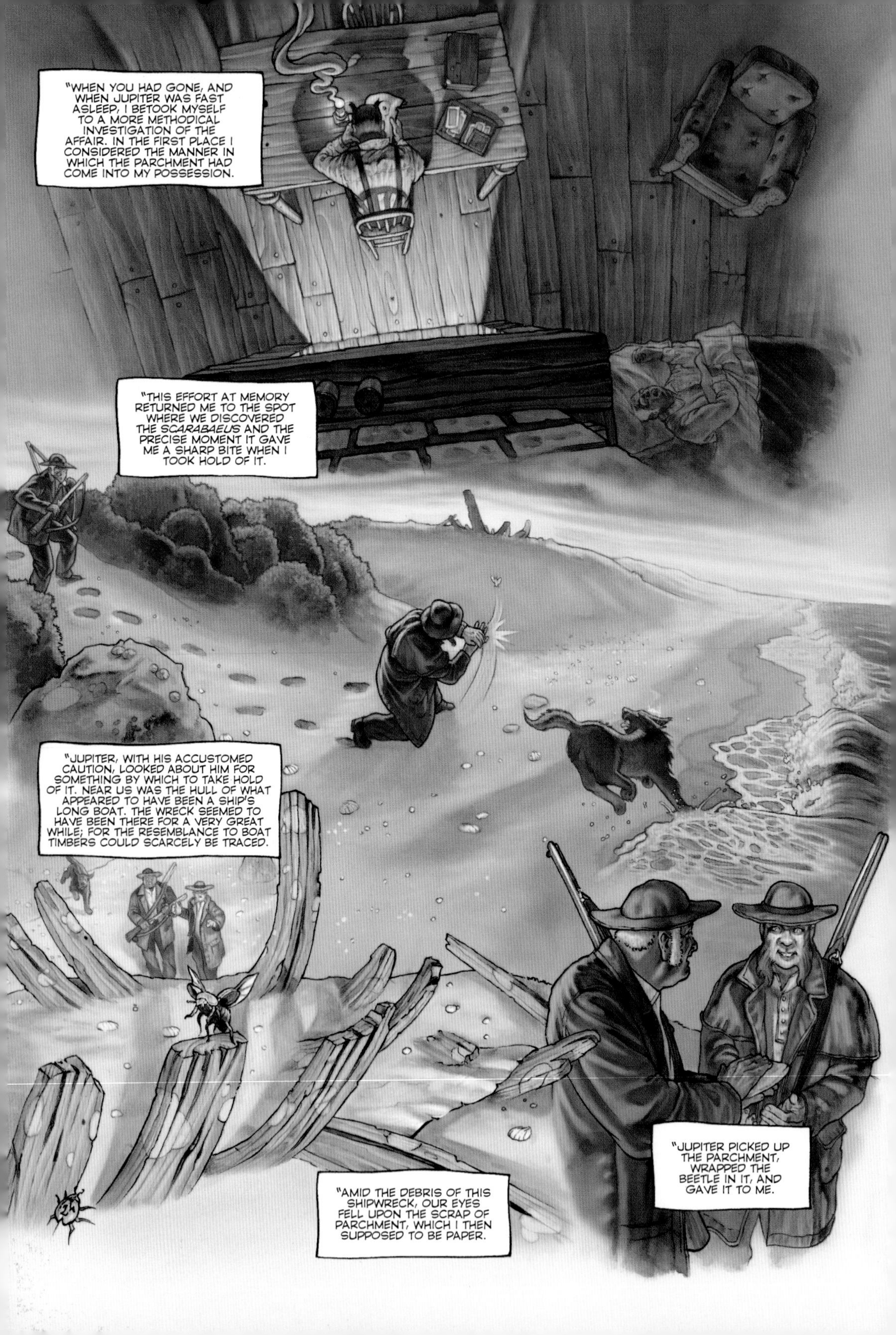
"WHEN YOU HAD GONE, AND WHEN JUPITER WAS FAST ASLEEP, I BETOOK MYSELF TO A MORE METHODICAL INVESTIGATION OF THE AFFAIR. IN THE FIRST PLACE I CONSIDERED THE MANNER IN WHICH THE PARCHMENT HAD COME INTO MY POSSESSION.
"THIS EFFORT AT MEMORY RETURNED ME TO THE SPOT WHERE WE DISCOVERED THE *SCARABAEUS* AND THE PRECISE MOMENT IT GAVE ME A SHARP BITE WHEN I TOOK HOLD OF IT.
"JUPITER, WITH HIS ACCUSTOMED CAUTION, LOOKED ABOUT HIM FOR SOMETHING BY WHICH TO TAKE HOLD OF IT. NEAR US WAS THE HULL OF WHAT APPEARED TO HAVE BEEN A SHIP'S LONG BOAT. THE WRECK SEEMED TO HAVE BEEN THERE FOR A VERY GREAT WHILE; FOR THE RESEMBLANCE TO BOAT TIMBERS COULD SCARCELY BE TRACED.
"AMID THE DEBRIS OF THIS SHIPWRECK, OUR EYES FELL UPON THE SCRAP OF PARCHMENT, WHICH I THEN SUPPOSED TO BE PAPER.
"JUPITER PICKED UP THE PARCHMENT, WRAPPED THE BEETLE IN IT, AND GAVE IT TO ME.

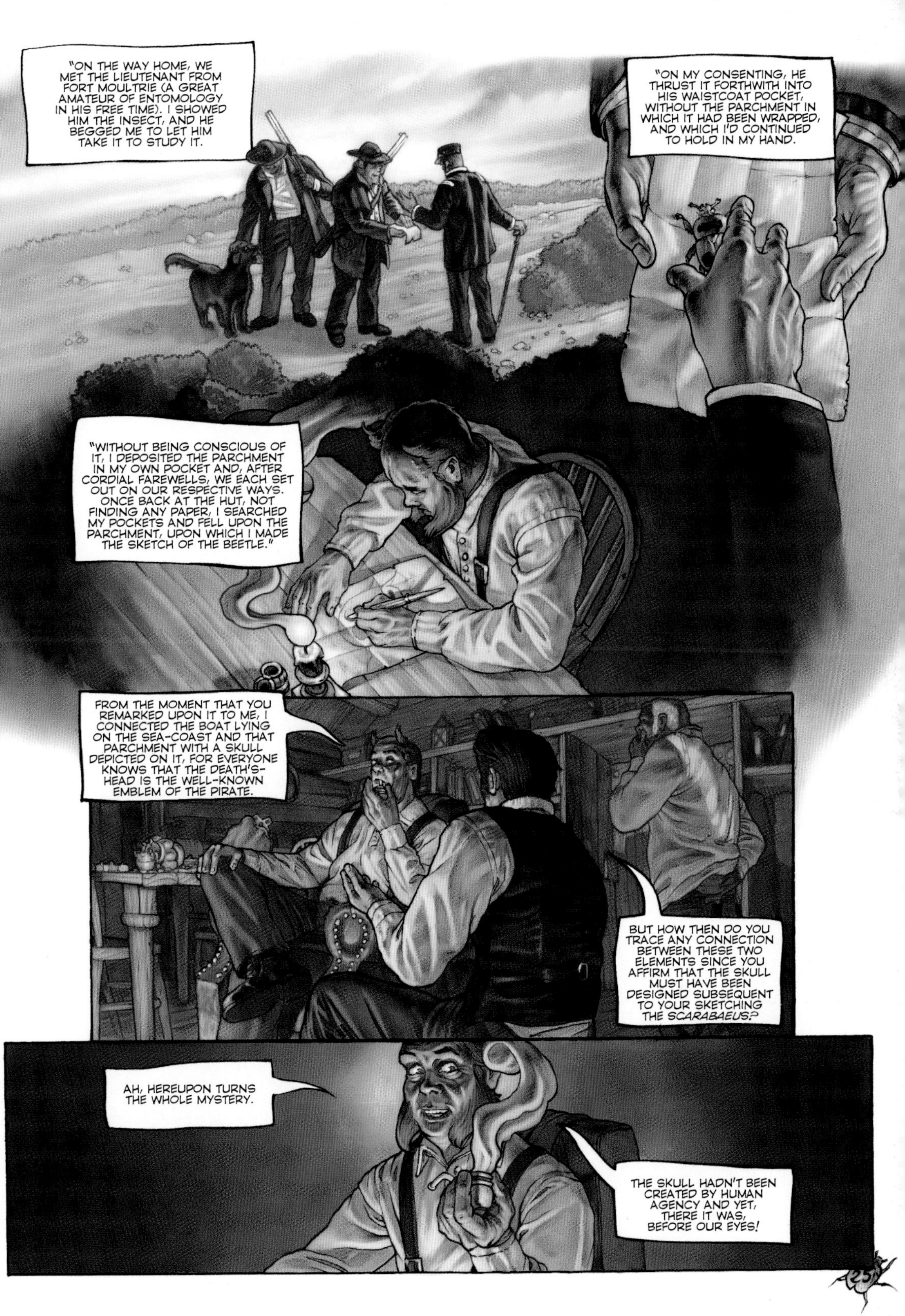
"ON THE WAY HOME, WE MET THE LIEUTENANT FROM FORT MOULTRIE (A GREAT AMATEUR OF ENTOMOLOGY IN HIS FREE TIME). I SHOWED HIM THE INSECT, AND HE BEGGED ME TO LET HIM TAKE IT TO STUDY IT.
"ON MY CONSENTING, HE THRUST IT FORTHWITH INTO HIS WAISTCOAT POCKET, WITHOUT THE PARCHMENT IN WHICH IT HAD BEEN WRAPPED, AND WHICH I'D CONTINUED TO HOLD IN MY HAND.
"WITHOUT BEING CONSCIOUS OF IT, I DEPOSITED THE PARCHMENT IN MY OWN POCKET AND, AFTER CORDIAL FAREWELLS, WE EACH SET OUT ON OUR RESPECTIVE WAYS. ONCE BACK AT THE HUT, NOT FINDING ANY PAPER, I SEARCHED MY POCKETS AND FELL UPON THE PARCHMENT, UPON WHICH I MADE THE SKETCH OF THE BEETLE."
FROM THE MOMENT THAT YOU REMARKED UPON IT TO ME, I CONNECTED THE BOAT LYING ON THE SEA-COAST AND THAT PARCHMENT WITH A SKULL DEPICTED ON IT, FOR EVERYONE KNOWS THAT THE DEATH'S-HEAD IS THE WELL-KNOWN EMBLEM OF THE PIRATE.
BUT HOW THEN DO YOU TRACE ANY CONNECTION BETWEEN THESE TWO ELEMENTS SINCE YOU AFFIRM THAT THE SKULL MUST HAVE BEEN DESIGNED SUBSEQUENT TO YOUR SKETCHING THE *SCARABAEUS*?
AH, HEREUPON TURNS THE WHOLE MYSTERY.
THE SKULL HADN'T BEEN CREATED BY HUMAN AGENCY AND YET, THERE IT WAS, BEFORE OUR EYES!

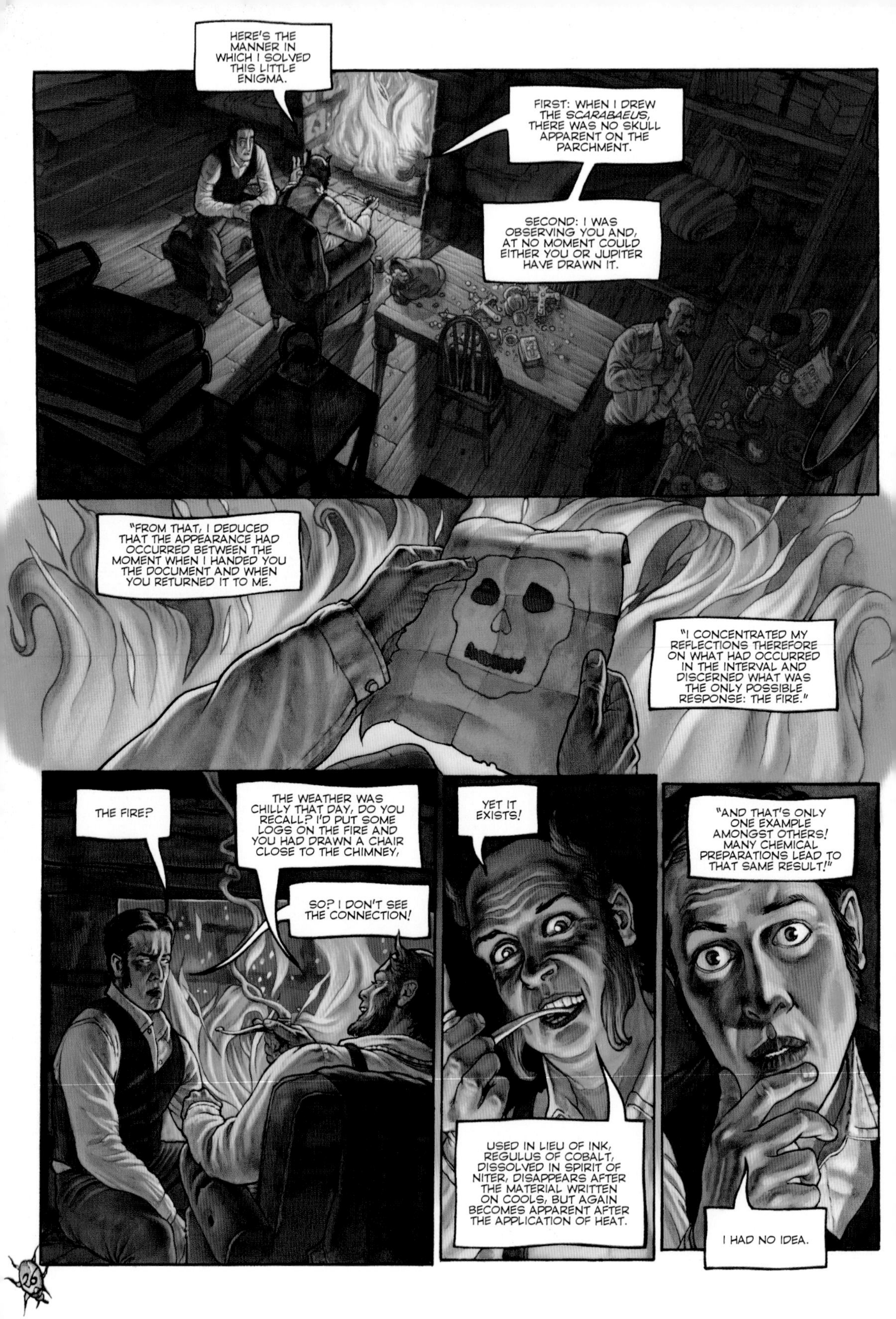
HERE'S THE MANNER IN WHICH I SOLVED THIS LITTLE ENIGMA.
FIRST: WHEN I DREW THE *SCARABAEUS*, THERE WAS NO SKULL APPARENT ON THE PARCHMENT.
SECOND: I WAS OBSERVING YOU AND, AT NO MOMENT COULD EITHER YOU OR JUPITER HAVE DRAWN IT.
"FROM THAT, I DEDUCED THAT THE APPEARANCE HAD OCCURRED BETWEEN THE MOMENT WHEN I HANDED YOU THE DOCUMENT AND WHEN YOU RETURNED IT TO ME.
"I CONCENTRATED MY REFLECTIONS THEREFORE ON WHAT HAD OCCURRED IN THE INTERVAL AND DISCERNED WHAT WAS THE ONLY POSSIBLE RESPONSE: THE FIRE."
THE FIRE?
THE WEATHER WAS CHILLY THAT DAY, DO YOU RECALL? I'D PUT SOME LOGS ON THE FIRE AND YOU HAD DRAWN A CHAIR CLOSE TO THE CHIMNEY,
SO? I DON'T SEE THE CONNECTION!
YET IT EXISTS!
USED IN LIEU OF INK, REGULUS OF COBALT, DISSOLVED IN SPIRIT OF NITER, DISAPPEARS AFTER THE MATERIAL WRITTEN ON COOLS, BUT AGAIN BECOMES APPARENT AFTER THE APPLICATION OF HEAT.
"AND THAT'S ONLY ONE EXAMPLE AMONGST OTHERS! MANY CHEMICAL PREPARATIONS LEAD TO THAT SAME RESULT!"
I HAD NO IDEA.

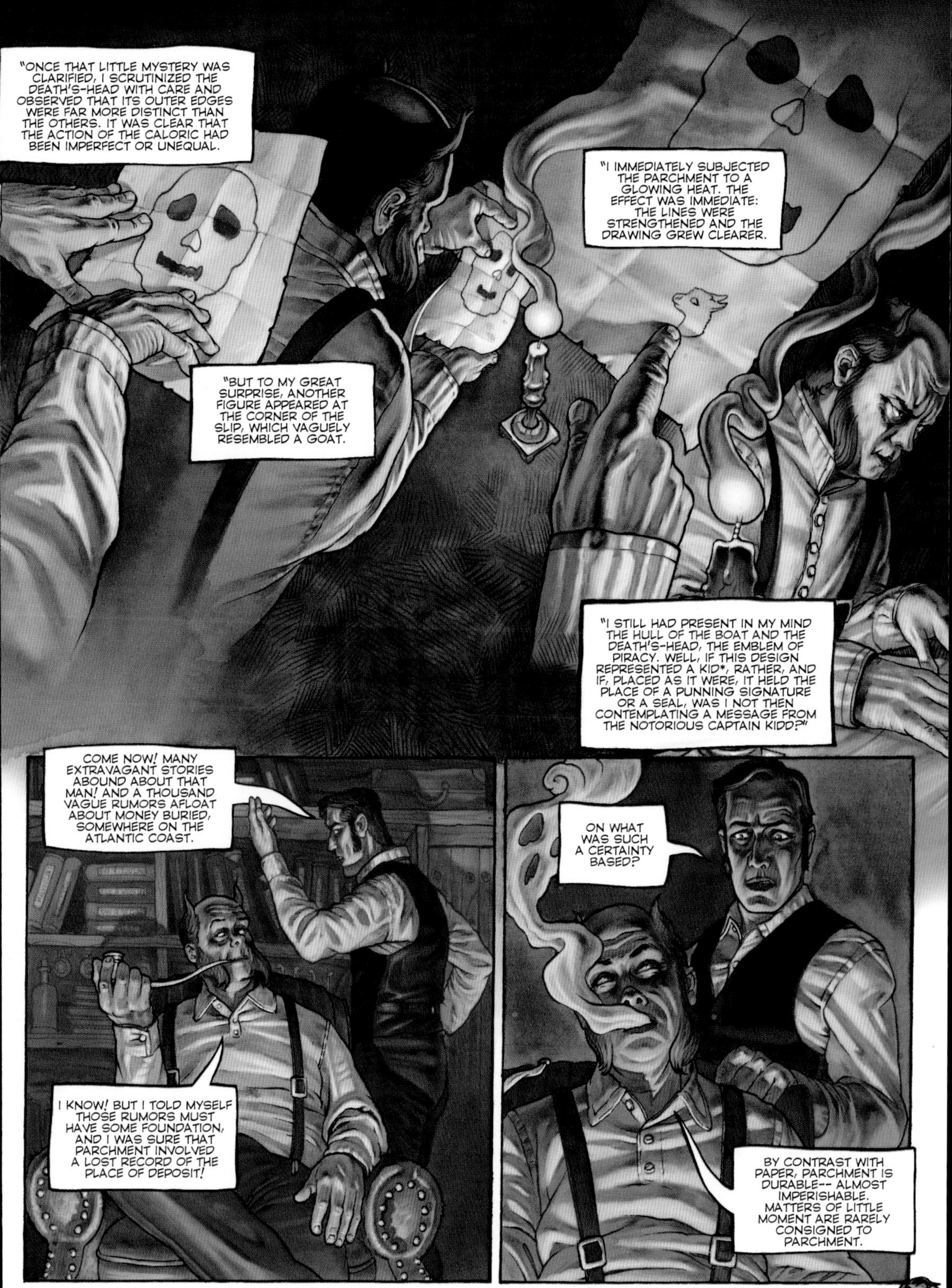
"ONCE THAT LITTLE MYSTERY WAS CLARIFIED, I SCRUTINIZED THE DEATH'S-HEAD WITH CARE AND OBSERVED THAT ITS OUTER EDGES WERE FAR MORE DISTINCT THAN THE OTHERS. IT WAS CLEAR THAT THE ACTION OF THE CALORIC HAD BEEN IMPERFECT OR UNEQUAL.
"I IMMEDIATELY SUBJECTED THE PARCHMENT TO A GLOWING HEAT. THE EFFECT WAS IMMEDIATE: THE LINES WERE STRENGTHENED AND THE DRAWING GREW CLEARER.
"BUT TO MY GREAT SURPRISE, ANOTHER FIGURE APPEARED AT THE CORNER OF THE SLIP, WHICH VAGUELY RESEMBLED A GOAT.
"I STILL HAD PRESENT IN MY MIND THE HULL OF THE BOAT AND THE DEATH'S-HEAD, THE EMBLEM OF PIRACY. WELL, IF THIS DESIGN REPRESENTED A KID*, RATHER, AND IF, PLACED AS IT WERE, IT HELD THE PLACE OF A PUNNING SIGNATURE OR A SEAL, WAS I NOT THEN CONTEMPLATING A MESSAGE FROM THE NOTORIOUS CAPTAIN KIDD?"
COME NOW! MANY EXTRAVAGANT STORIES ABOUND ABOUT THAT MAN! AND A THOUSAND VAGUE RUMORS AFLOAT ABOUT MONEY BURIED, SOMEWHERE ON THE ATLANTIC COAST.
I KNOW! BUT I TOLD MYSELF THOSE RUMORS MUST HAVE SOME FOUNDATION, AND I WAS SURE THAT PARCHMENT INVOLVED A LOST RECORD OF THE PLACE OF DEPOSIT!
ON WHAT WAS SUCH A CERTAINTY BASED?
BY CONTRAST WITH PAPER, PARCHMENT IS DURABLE-- ALMOST IMPERISHABLE. MATTERS OF LITTLE MOMENT ARE RARELY CONSIGNED TO PARCHMENT.

*AN ADOLESCENT GOAT

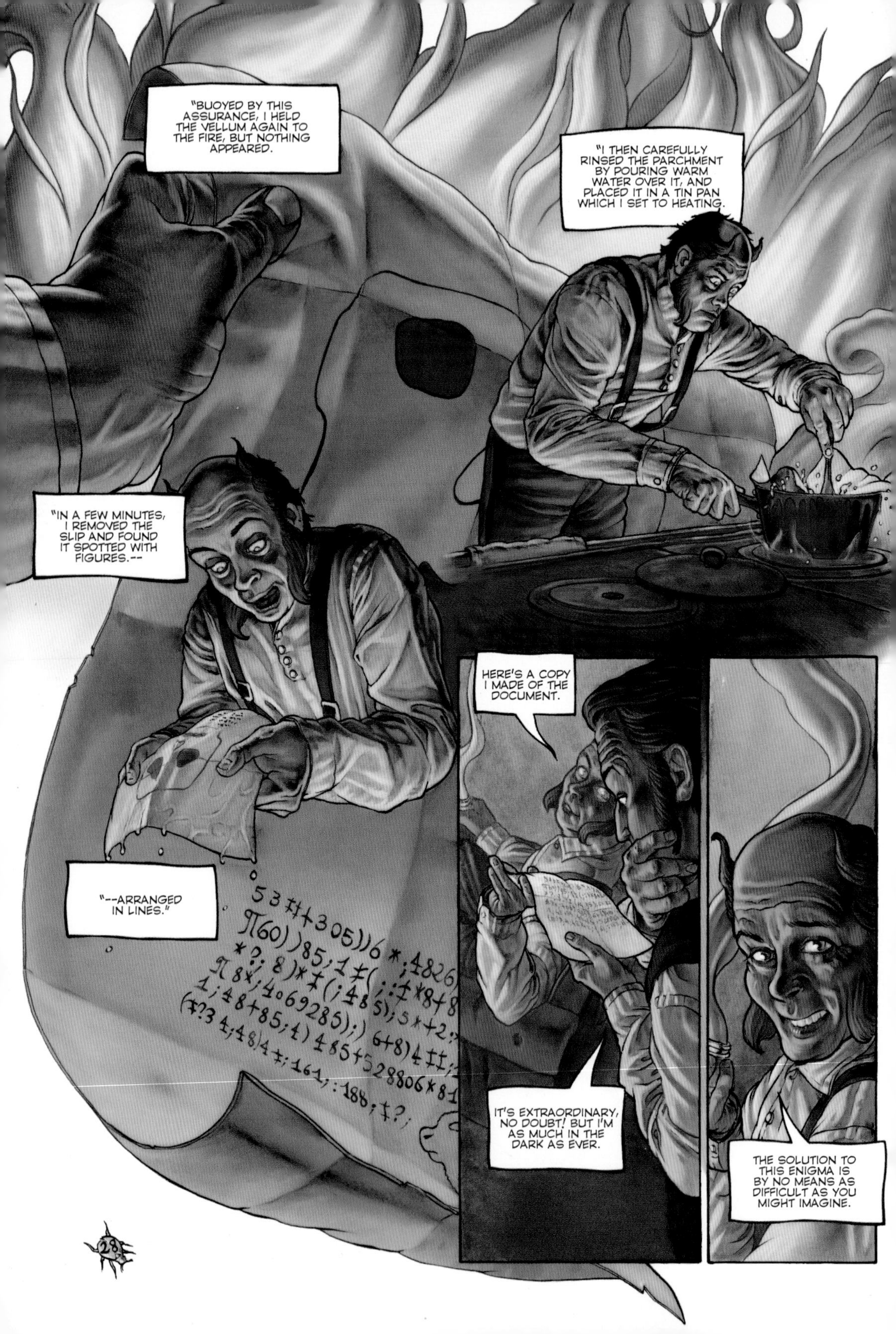
"BUOYED BY THIS ASSURANCE, I HELD THE VELLUM AGAIN TO THE FIRE, BUT NOTHING APPEARED.
"I THEN CAREFULLY RINSED THE PARCHMENT BY POURING WARM WATER OVER IT, AND PLACED IT IN A TIN PAN WHICH I SET TO HEATING.
"IN A FEW MINUTES, I REMOVED THE SLIP AND FOUND IT SPOTTED WITH FIGURES.--
"--ARRANGED IN LINES."
HERE'S A COPY I MADE OF THE DOCUMENT.
IT'S EXTRAORDINARY, NO DOUBT! BUT I'M AS MUCH IN THE DARK AS EVER.
THE SOLUTION TO THIS ENIGMA IS BY NO MEANS AS DIFFICULT AS YOU MIGHT IMAGINE.

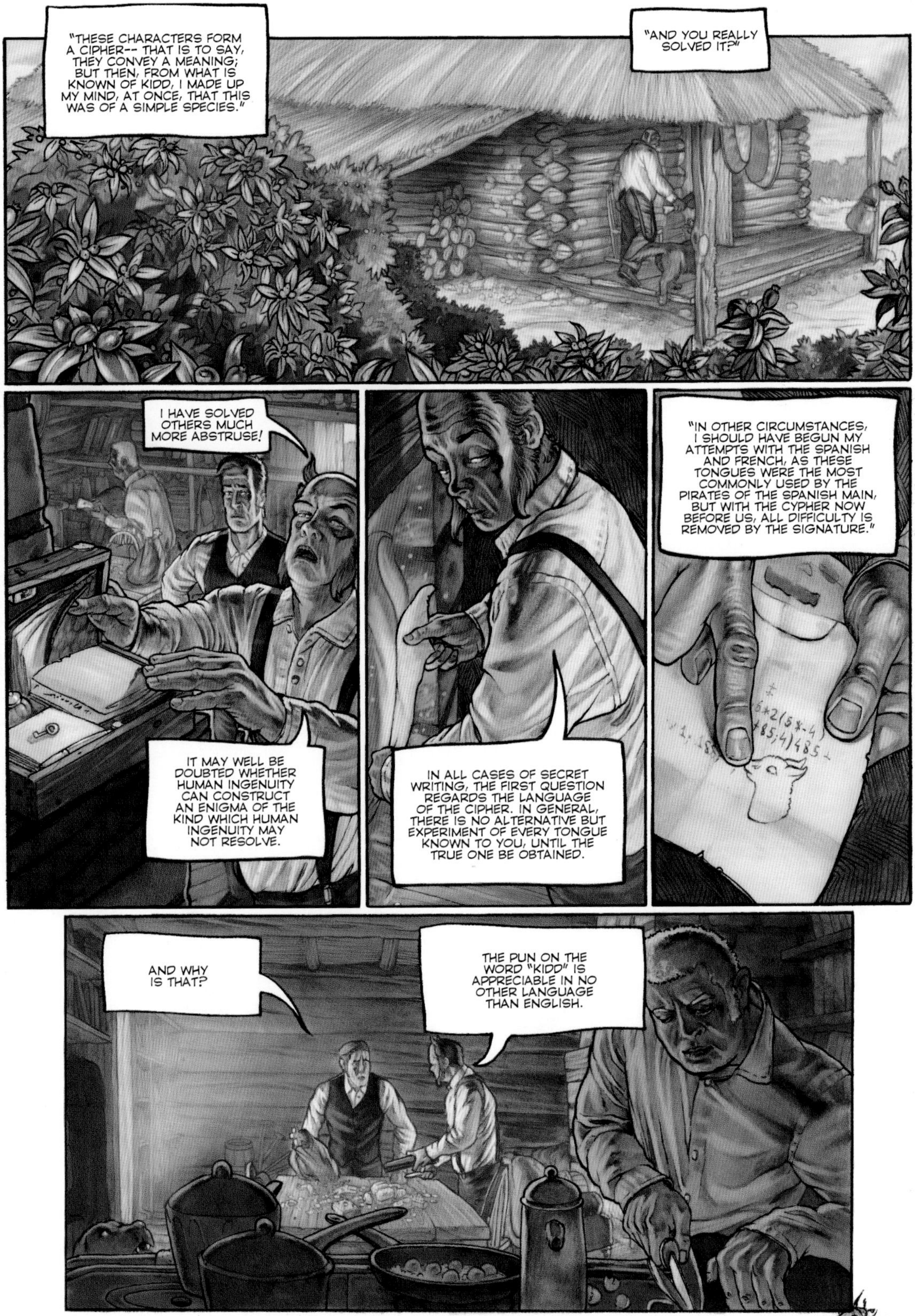
"THESE CHARACTERS FORM A CIPHER-- THAT IS TO SAY, THEY CONVEY A MEANING; BUT THEN, FROM WHAT IS KNOWN OF KIDD, I MADE UP MY MIND, AT ONCE, THAT THIS WAS OF A SIMPLE SPECIES."
"AND YOU REALLY SOLVED IT?"
I HAVE SOLVED OTHERS MUCH MORE ABSTRUSE!
IT MAY WELL BE DOUBTED WHETHER HUMAN INGENUITY CAN CONSTRUCT AN ENIGMA OF THE KIND WHICH HUMAN INGENUITY MAY NOT RESOLVE.
IN ALL CASES OF SECRET WRITING, THE FIRST QUESTION REGARDS THE LANGUAGE OF THE CIPHER. IN GENERAL, THERE IS NO ALTERNATIVE BUT EXPERIMENT OF EVERY TONGUE KNOWN TO YOU, UNTIL THE TRUE ONE BE OBTAINED.
"IN OTHER CIRCUMSTANCES, I SHOULD HAVE BEGUN MY ATTEMPTS WITH THE SPANISH AND FRENCH, AS THESE TONGUES WERE THE MOST COMMONLY USED BY THE PIRATES OF THE SPANISH MAIN, BUT WITH THE CYPHER NOW BEFORE US, ALL DIFFICULTY IS REMOVED BY THE SIGNATURE."
AND WHY IS THAT?
THE PUN ON THE WORD "KIDD" IS APPRECIABLE IN NO OTHER LANGUAGE THAN ENGLISH.

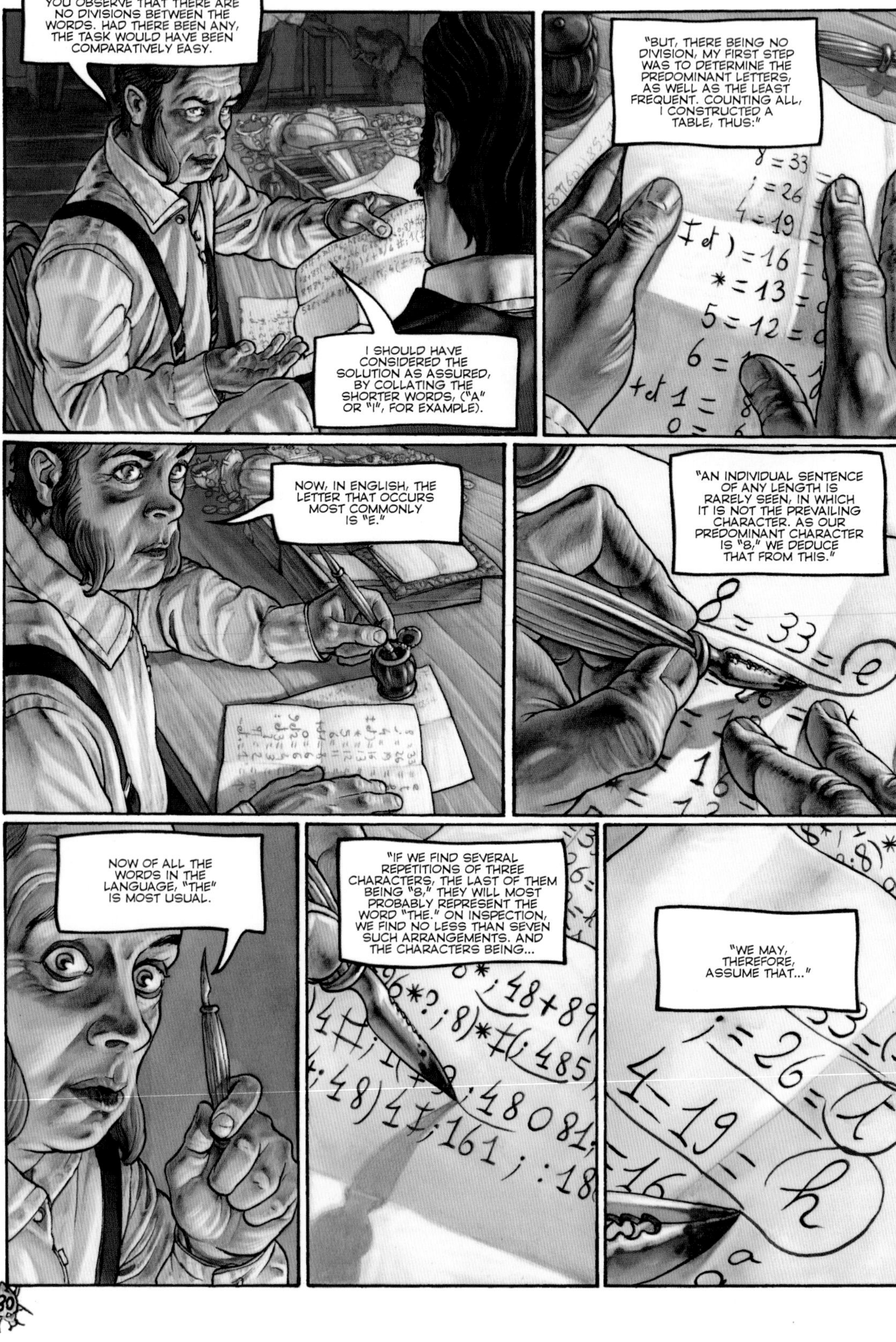

YOU OBSERVE THAT THERE ARE NO DIVISIONS BETWEEN THE WORDS. HAD THERE BEEN ANY, THE TASK WOULD HAVE BEEN COMPARATIVELY EASY.
I SHOULD HAVE CONSIDERED THE SOLUTION AS ASSURED, BY COLLATING THE SHORTER WORDS, ("A" OR "I", FOR EXAMPLE).
"BUT, THERE BEING NO DIVISION, MY FIRST STEP WAS TO DETERMINE THE PREDOMINANT LETTERS, AS WELL AS THE LEAST FREQUENT. COUNTING ALL, I CONSTRUCTED A TABLE, THUS:"
8 = 33
; = 26
4 = 19
‡ et ) = 16
* = 13
5 = 12
NOW, IN ENGLISH, THE LETTER THAT OCCURS MOST COMMONLY IS "E."
"AN INDIVIDUAL SENTENCE OF ANY LENGTH IS RARELY SEEN, IN WHICH IT IS NOT THE PREVAILING CHARACTER. AS OUR PREDOMINANT CHARACTER IS "8," WE DEDUCE THAT FROM THIS."
8 = 33 = e
NOW OF ALL THE WORDS IN THE LANGUAGE, "THE" IS MOST USUAL.
"IF WE FIND SEVERAL REPETITIONS OF THREE CHARACTERS, THE LAST OF THEM BEING "8," THEY WILL MOST PROBABLY REPRESENT THE WORD "THE." ON INSPECTION, WE FIND NO LESS THAN SEVEN SUCH ARRANGEMENTS. AND THE CHARACTERS BEING...
"WE MAY, THEREFORE, ASSUME THAT..."
; = 26 = t
4 = 19 = h

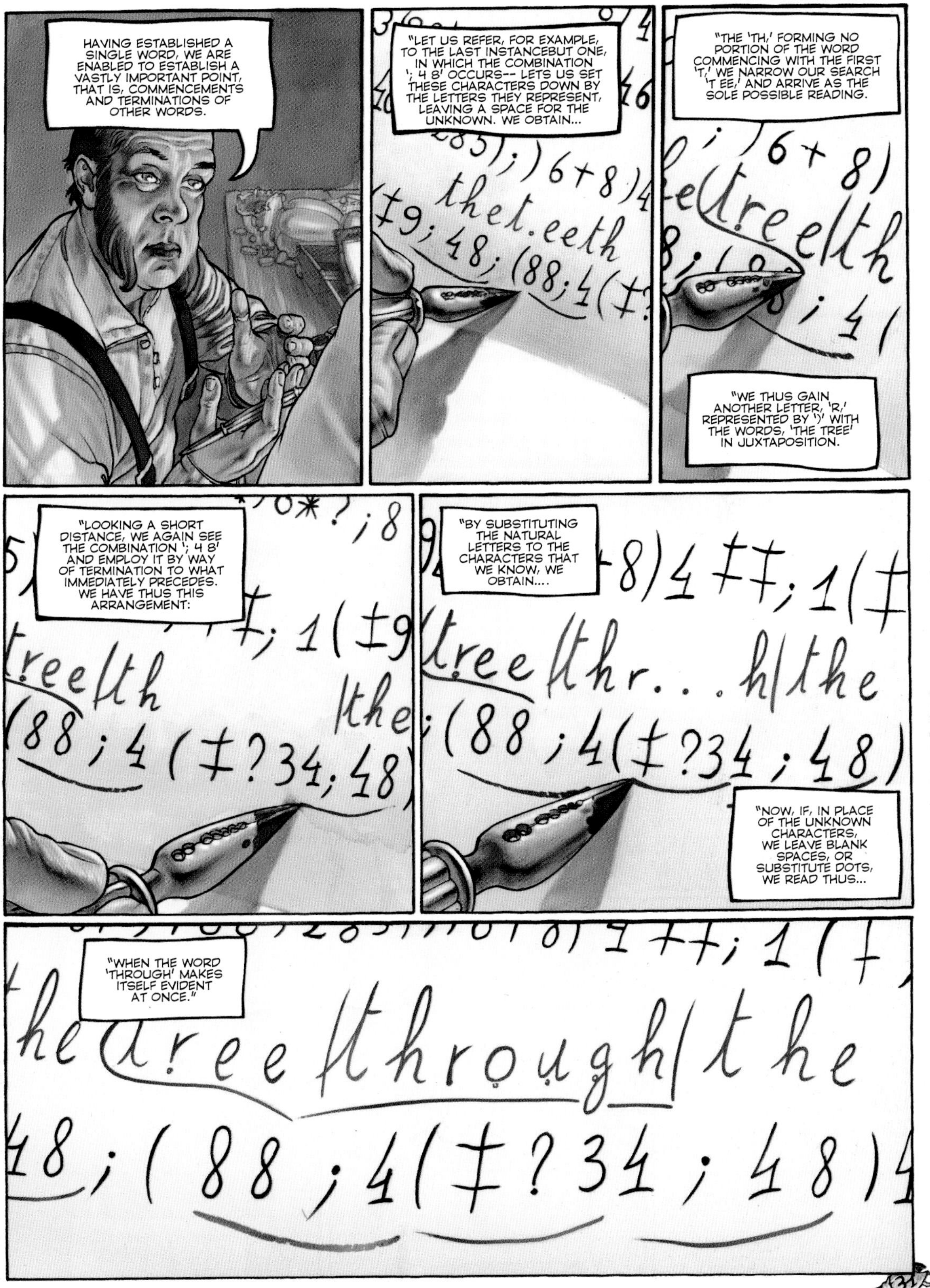
HAVING ESTABLISHED A SINGLE WORD, WE ARE ENABLED TO ESTABLISH A VASTLY IMPORTANT POINT, THAT IS, COMMENCEMENTS AND TERMINATIONS OF OTHER WORDS.
"LET US REFER, FOR EXAMPLE, TO THE LAST INSTANCEBUT ONE, IN WHICH THE COMBINATION '; 4 8' OCCURS-- LETS US SET THESE CHARACTERS DOWN BY THE LETTERS THEY REPRESENT, LEAVING A SPACE FOR THE UNKNOWN. WE OBTAIN...
thet.eeth
"THE 'TH,' FORMING NO PORTION OF THE WORD COMMENCING WITH THE FIRST 'T,' WE NARROW OUR SEARCH 'T EE,' AND ARRIVE AS THE SOLE POSSIBLE READING.
"WE THUS GAIN ANOTHER LETTER, 'R,' REPRESENTED BY ')' WITH THE WORDS, 'THE TREE' IN JUXTAPOSITION.
"LOOKING A SHORT DISTANCE, WE AGAIN SEE THE COMBINATION '; 4 8' AND EMPLOY IT BY WAY OF TERMINATION TO WHAT IMMEDIATELY PRECEDES. WE HAVE THUS THIS ARRANGEMENT:
"BY SUBSTITUTING THE NATURAL LETTERS TO THE CHARACTERS THAT WE KNOW, WE OBTAIN....
"NOW, IF, IN PLACE OF THE UNKNOWN CHARACTERS, WE LEAVE BLANK SPACES, OR SUBSTITUTE DOTS, WE READ THUS...
"WHEN THE WORD 'THROUGH' MAKES ITSELF EVIDENT AT ONCE."

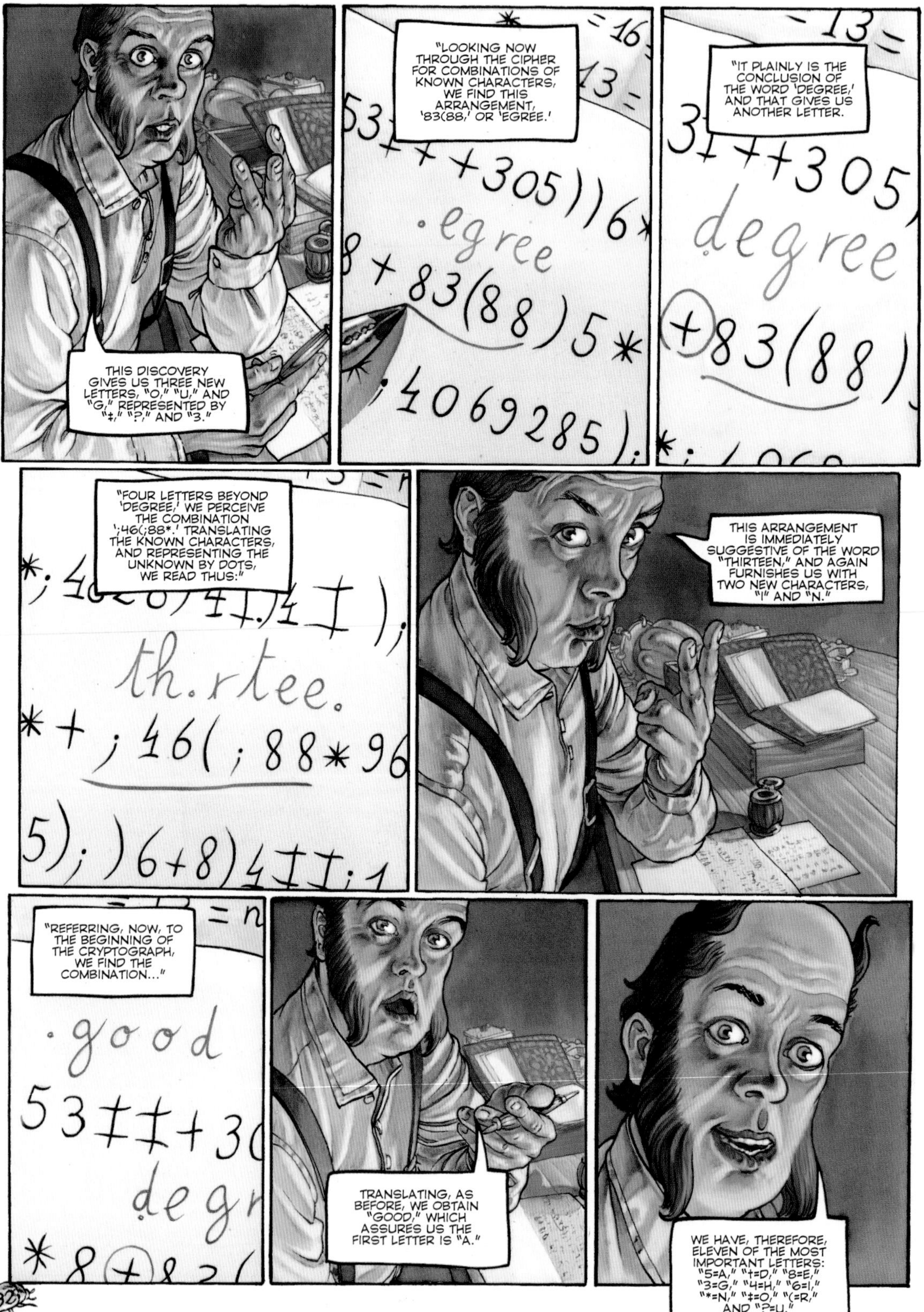
THIS DISCOVERY GIVES US THREE NEW LETTERS, "O," "U," AND "G," REPRESENTED BY "‡," "?," AND "3."
"LOOKING NOW THROUGH THE CIPHER FOR COMBINATIONS OF KNOWN CHARACTERS, WE FIND THIS ARRANGEMENT, '83(88,' OR 'EGREE.'
"IT PLAINLY IS THE CONCLUSION OF THE WORD 'DEGREE,' AND THAT GIVES US ANOTHER LETTER.
"FOUR LETTERS BEYOND 'DEGREE,' WE PERCEIVE THE COMBINATION ';46(;88*.' TRANSLATING THE KNOWN CHARACTERS, AND REPRESENTING THE UNKNOWN BY DOTS, WE READ THUS:"
THIS ARRANGEMENT IS IMMEDIATELY SUGGESTIVE OF THE WORD "THIRTEEN," AND AGAIN FURNISHES US WITH TWO NEW CHARACTERS, "I" AND "N."
"REFERRING, NOW, TO THE BEGINNING OF THE CRYPTOGRAPH, WE FIND THE COMBINATION..."
TRANSLATING, AS BEFORE, WE OBTAIN "GOOD," WHICH ASSURES US THE FIRST LETTER IS "A."
WE HAVE, THEREFORE, ELEVEN OF THE MOST IMPORTANT LETTERS: "5=A," "†=D," "8=E," "3=G," "4=H," "6=I," "*=N," "‡=O," "(=R," AND "?=U."

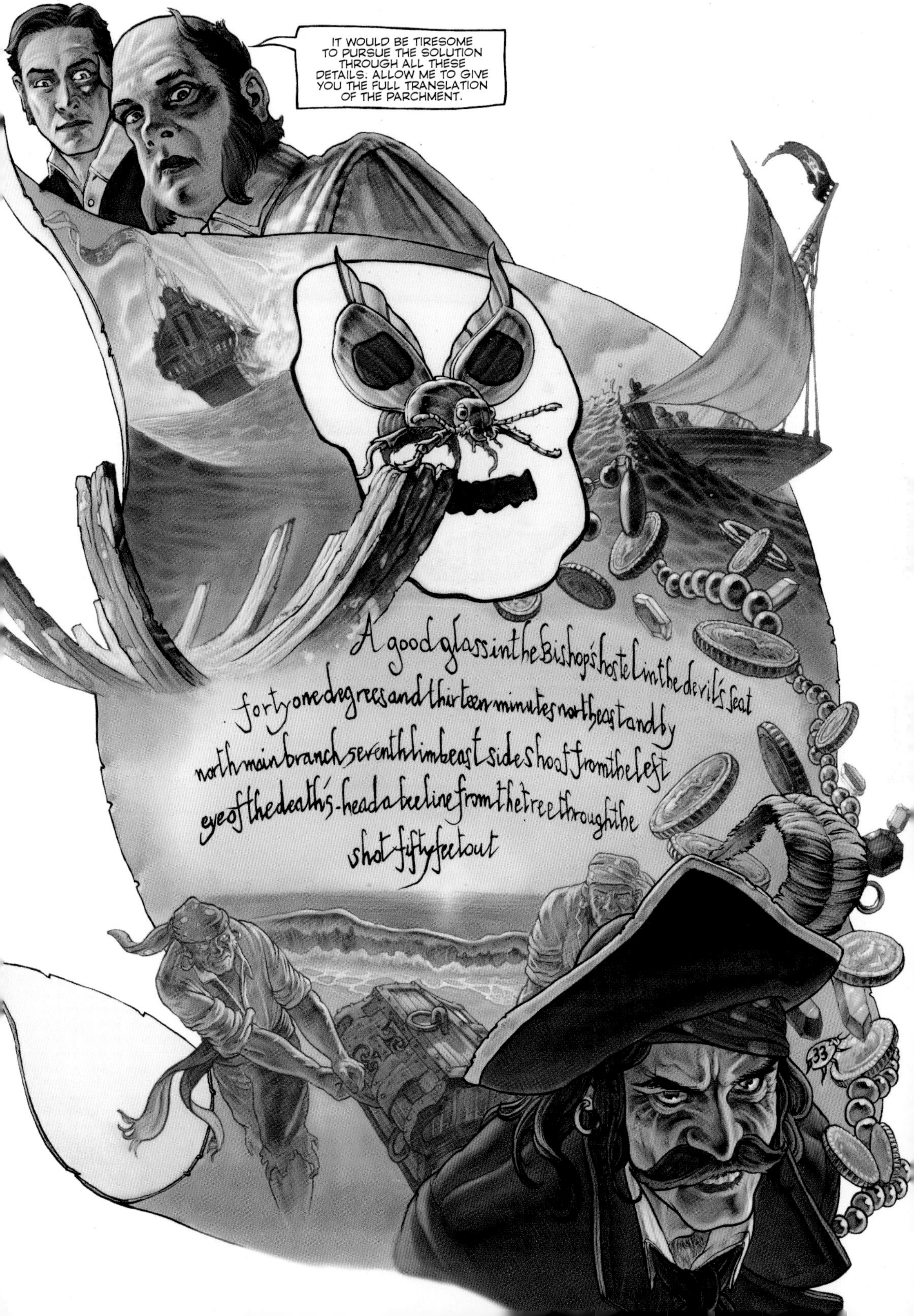
IT WOULD BE TIRESOME TO PURSUE THE SOLUTION THROUGH ALL THESE DETAILS. ALLOW ME TO GIVE YOU THE FULL TRANSLATION OF THE PARCHMENT.
A good glass in the Bishop's hostel in the devil's seat
forty one degrees and thirteen minutes northeast and by
north main branch seventh limb east side shoot from the left
eye of the death's-head a bee line from the tree through the
shot fifty feet out
33

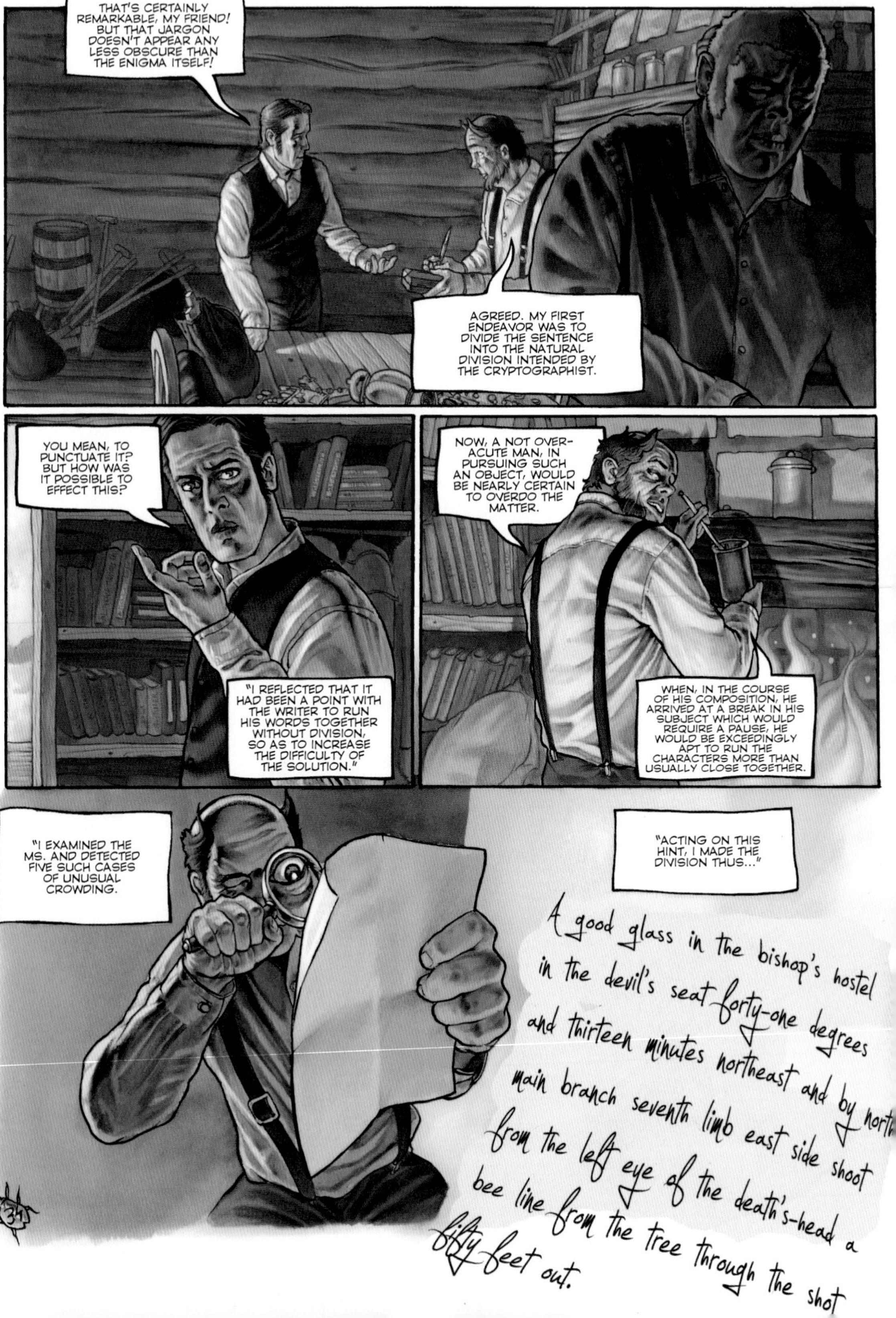
THAT'S CERTAINLY REMARKABLE, MY FRIEND! BUT THAT JARGON DOESN'T APPEAR ANY LESS OBSCURE THAN THE ENIGMA ITSELF!
AGREED. MY FIRST ENDEAVOR WAS TO DIVIDE THE SENTENCE INTO THE NATURAL DIVISION INTENDED BY THE CRYPTOGRAPHIST.
YOU MEAN, TO PUNCTUATE IT? BUT HOW WAS IT POSSIBLE TO EFFECT THIS?
"I REFLECTED THAT IT HAD BEEN A POINT WITH THE WRITER TO RUN HIS WORDS TOGETHER WITHOUT DIVISION, SO AS TO INCREASE THE DIFFICULTY OF THE SOLUTION."
NOW, A NOT OVER-ACUTE MAN, IN PURSUING SUCH AN OBJECT, WOULD BE NEARLY CERTAIN TO OVERDO THE MATTER.
WHEN, IN THE COURSE OF HIS COMPOSITION, HE ARRIVED AT A BREAK IN HIS SUBJECT WHICH WOULD REQUIRE A PAUSE, HE WOULD BE EXCEEDINGLY APT TO RUN THE CHARACTERS MORE THAN USUALLY CLOSE TOGETHER.
"I EXAMINED THE MS. AND DETECTED FIVE SUCH CASES OF UNUSUAL CROWDING.
"ACTING ON THIS HINT, I MADE THE DIVISION THUS..."
A good glass in the bishop's hostel
in the devil's seat forty-one degrees
and thirteen minutes northeast and by north
main branch seventh limb east side shoot
from the left eye of the death's-head a
bee line from the tree through the shot
fifty feet out.

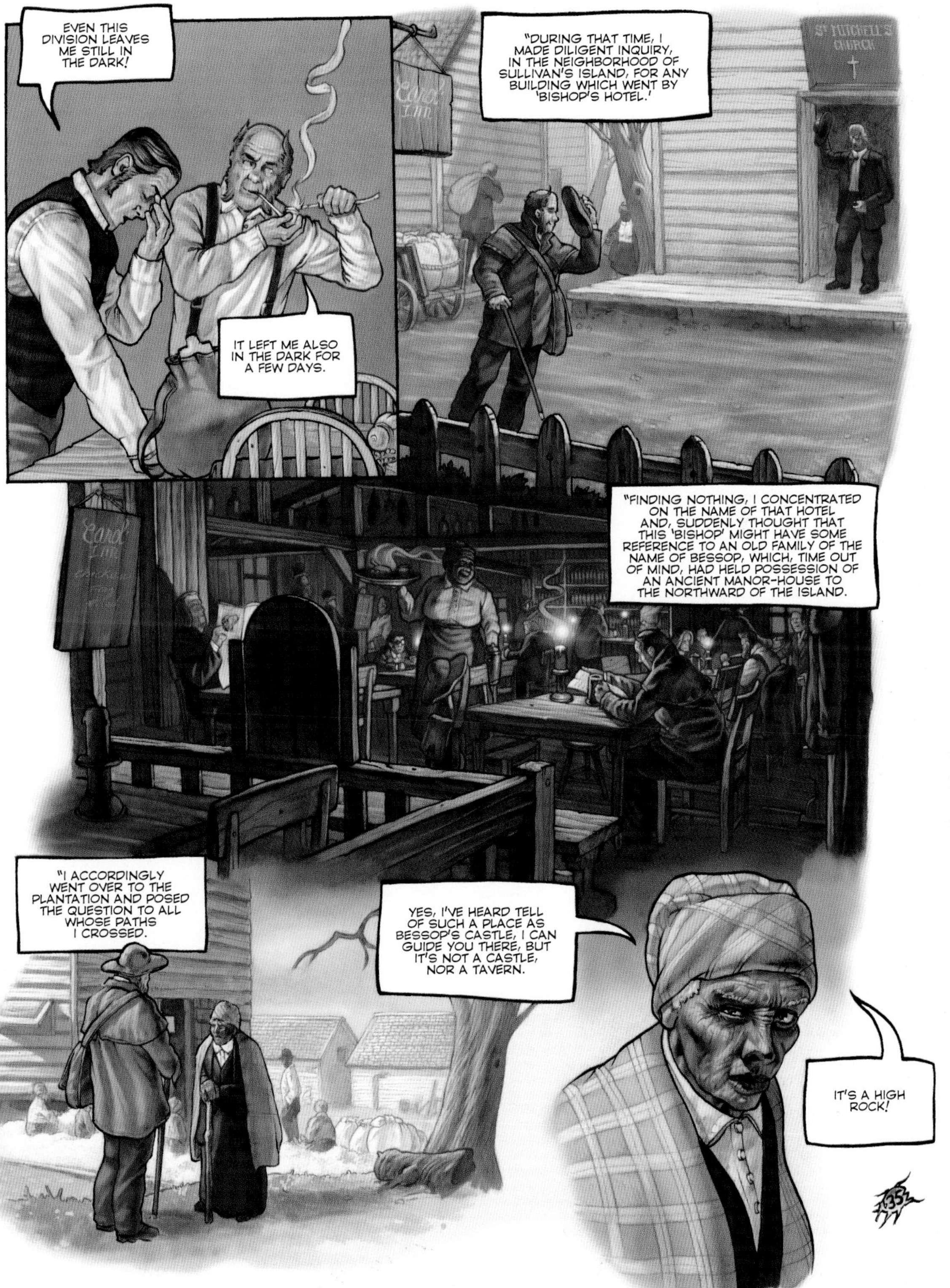

EVEN THIS DIVISION LEAVES ME STILL IN THE DARK!
IT LEFT ME ALSO IN THE DARK FOR A FEW DAYS.
"DURING THAT TIME, I MADE DILIGENT INQUIRY, IN THE NEIGHBORHOOD OF SULLIVAN'S ISLAND, FOR ANY BUILDING WHICH WENT BY 'BISHOP'S HOTEL.'
"FINDING NOTHING, I CONCENTRATED ON THE NAME OF THAT HOTEL AND, SUDDENLY THOUGHT THAT THIS 'BISHOP' MIGHT HAVE SOME REFERENCE TO AN OLD FAMILY OF THE NAME OF BESSOP, WHICH, TIME OUT OF MIND, HAD HELD POSSESSION OF AN ANCIENT MANOR-HOUSE TO THE NORTHWARD OF THE ISLAND.
"I ACCORDINGLY WENT OVER TO THE PLANTATION AND POSED THE QUESTION TO ALL WHOSE PATHS I CROSSED.
YES, I'VE HEARD TELL OF SUCH A PLACE AS BESSOP'S CASTLE, I CAN GUIDE YOU THERE, BUT IT'S NOT A CASTLE, NOR A TAVERN.
IT'S A HIGH ROCK!

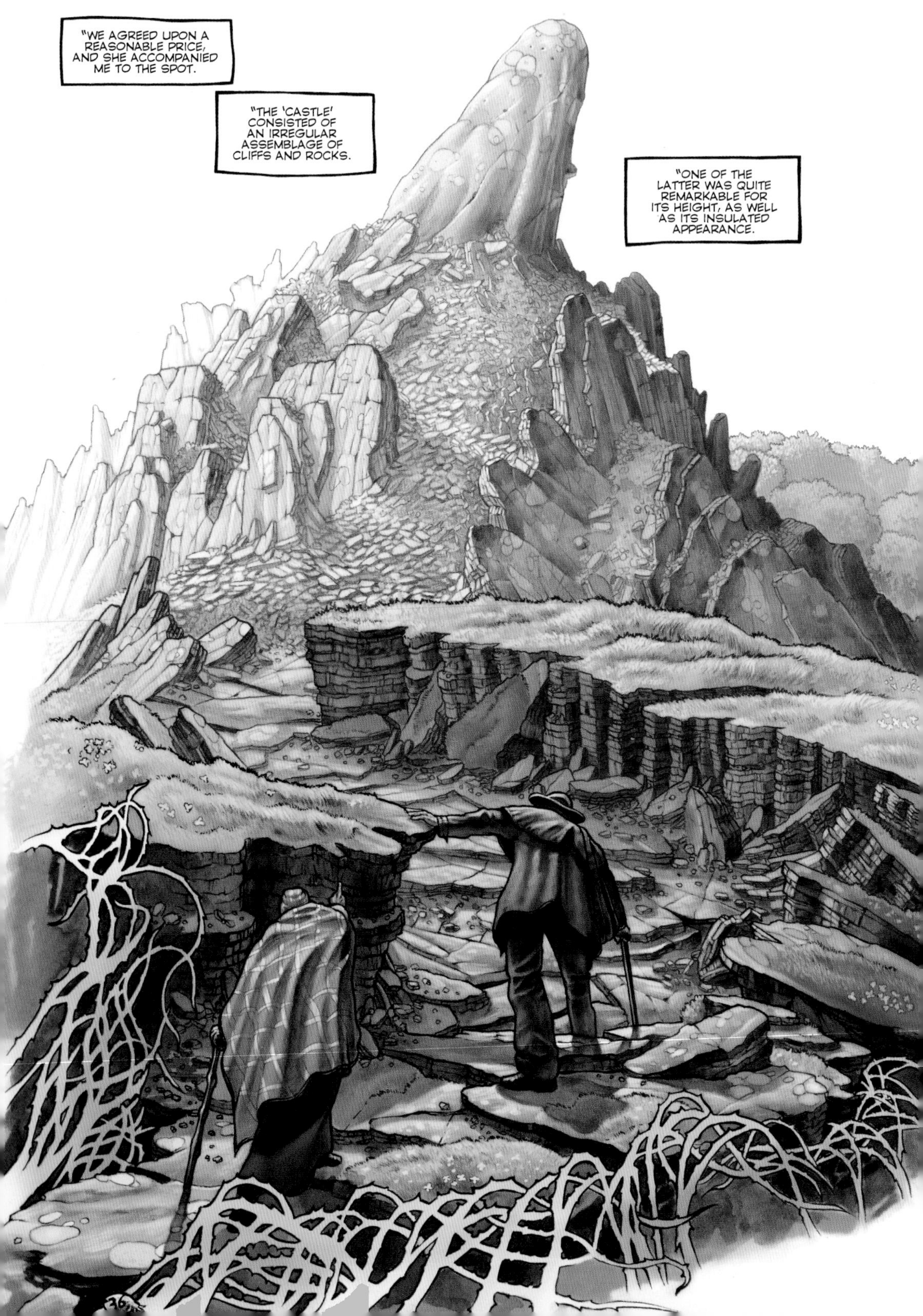
"WE AGREED UPON A REASONABLE PRICE, AND SHE ACCOMPANIED ME TO THE SPOT.
"THE 'CASTLE' CONSISTED OF AN IRREGULAR ASSEMBLAGE OF CLIFFS AND ROCKS.
"ONE OF THE LATTER WAS QUITE REMARKABLE FOR ITS HEIGHT, AS WELL AS ITS INSULATED APPEARANCE.

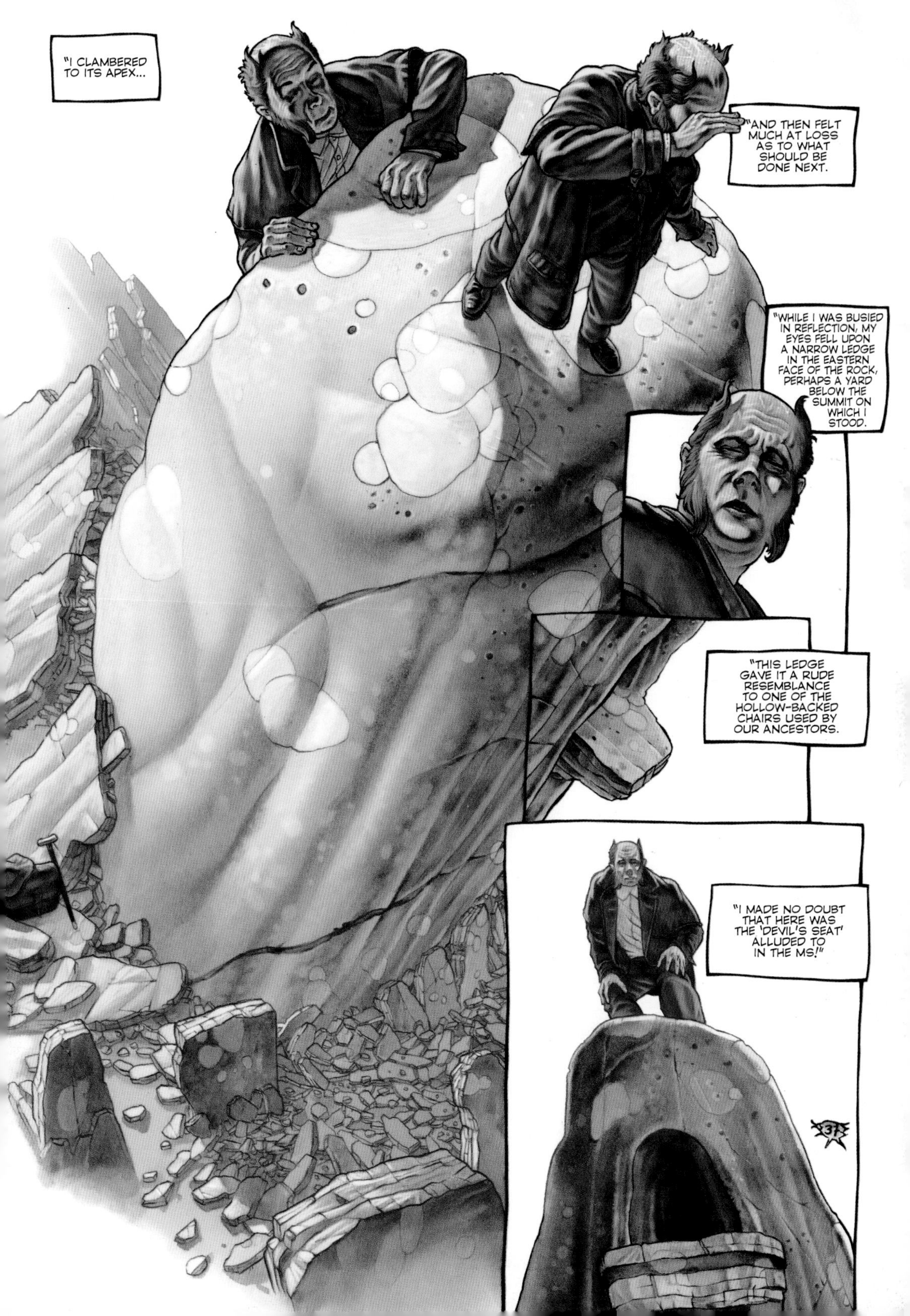
"I CLAMBERED TO ITS APEX...
"AND THEN FELT MUCH AT LOSS AS TO WHAT SHOULD BE DONE NEXT.
"WHILE I WAS BUSIED IN REFLECTION, MY EYES FELL UPON A NARROW LEDGE IN THE EASTERN FACE OF THE ROCK, PERHAPS A YARD BELOW THE SUMMIT ON WHICH I STOOD.
"THIS LEDGE GAVE IT A RUDE RESEMBLANCE TO ONE OF THE HOLLOW-BACKED CHAIRS USED BY OUR ANCESTORS.
"I MADE NO DOUBT THAT HERE WAS THE 'DEVIL'S SEAT' ALLUDED TO IN THE MS!"
31

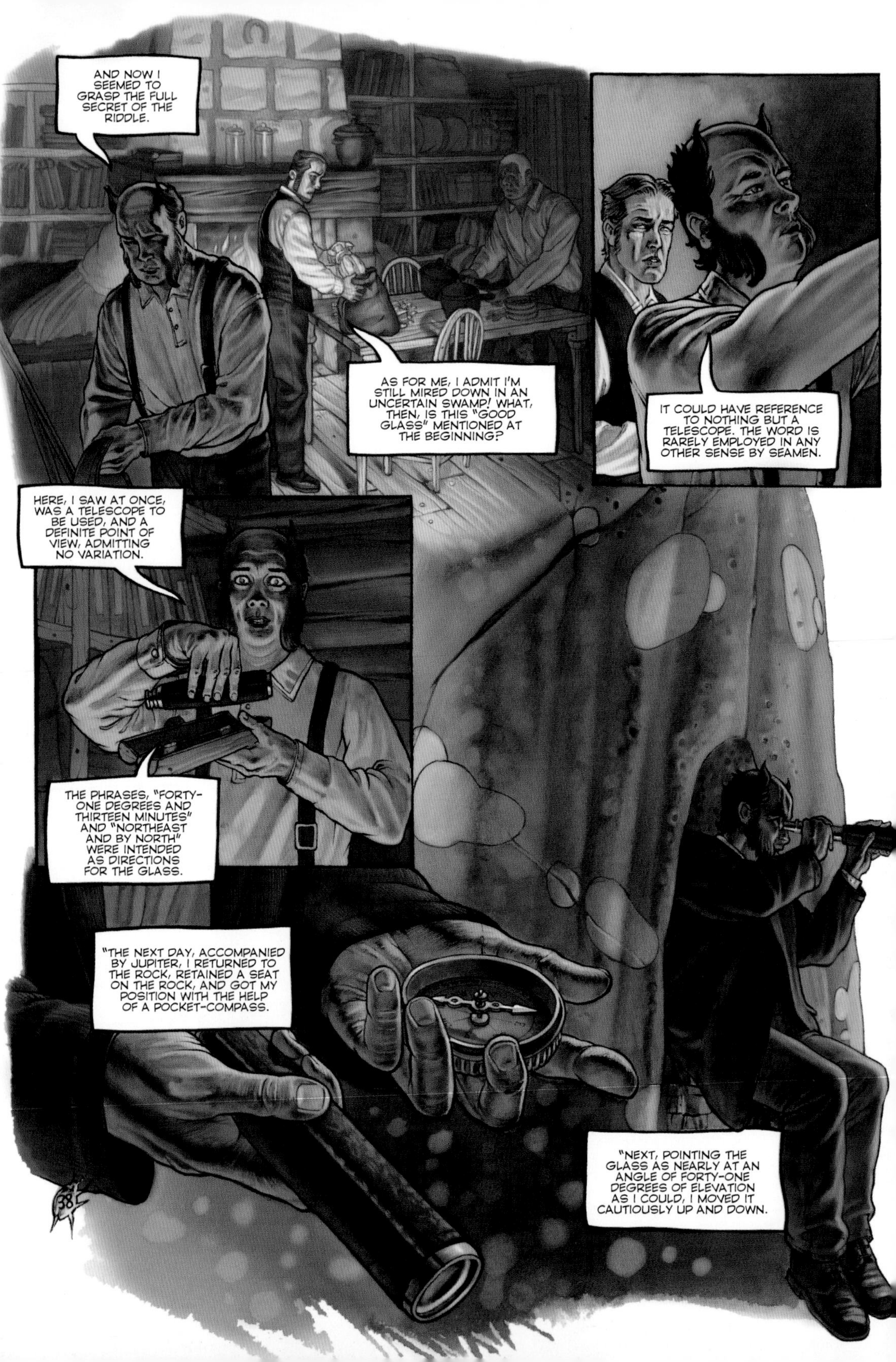
AND NOW I SEEMED TO GRASP THE FULL SECRET OF THE RIDDLE.
AS FOR ME, I ADMIT I'M STILL MIRED DOWN IN AN UNCERTAIN SWAMP! WHAT, THEN, IS THIS "GOOD GLASS" MENTIONED AT THE BEGINNING?
IT COULD HAVE REFERENCE TO NOTHING BUT A TELESCOPE. THE WORD IS RARELY EMPLOYED IN ANY OTHER SENSE BY SEAMEN.
HERE, I SAW AT ONCE, WAS A TELESCOPE TO BE USED, AND A DEFINITE POINT OF VIEW, ADMITTING NO VARIATION.
THE PHRASES, "FORTY-ONE DEGREES AND THIRTEEN MINUTES" AND "NORTHEAST AND BY NORTH" WERE INTENDED AS DIRECTIONS FOR THE GLASS.
"THE NEXT DAY, ACCOMPANIED BY JUPITER, I RETURNED TO THE ROCK, RETAINED A SEAT ON THE ROCK, AND GOT MY POSITION WITH THE HELP OF A POCKET-COMPASS.
"NEXT, POINTING THE GLASS AS NEARLY AT AN ANGLE OF FORTY-ONE DEGREES OF ELEVATION AS I COULD, I MOVED IT CAUTIOUSLY UP AND DOWN.

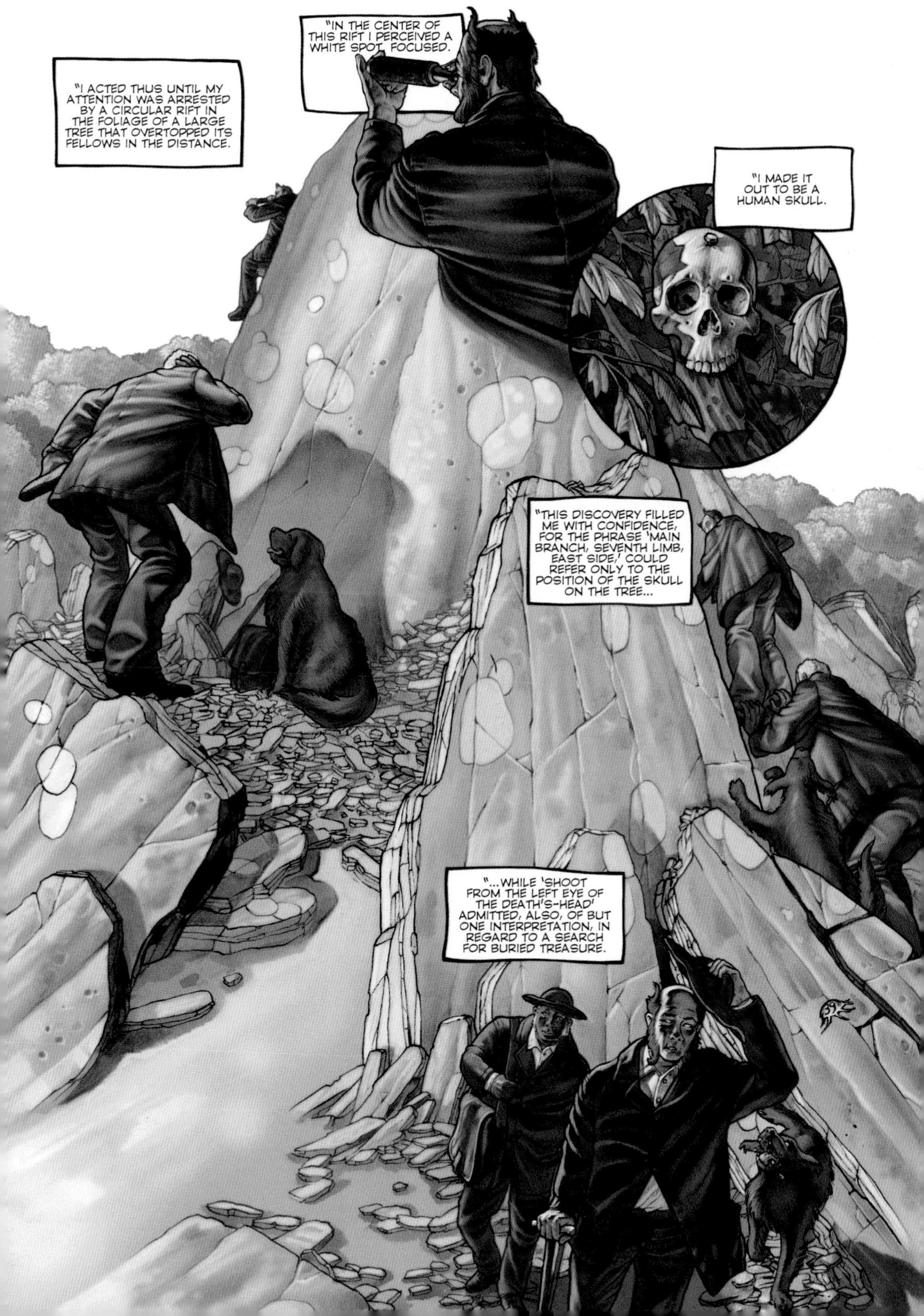
"I ACTED THUS UNTIL MY ATTENTION WAS ARRESTED BY A CIRCULAR RIFT IN THE FOLIAGE OF A LARGE TREE THAT OVERTOPPED ITS FELLOWS IN THE DISTANCE.
"IN THE CENTER OF THIS RIFT I PERCEIVED A WHITE SPOT, FOCUSED.
"I MADE IT OUT TO BE A HUMAN SKULL.
"THIS DISCOVERY FILLED ME WITH CONFIDENCE, FOR THE PHRASE 'MAIN BRANCH, SEVENTH LIMB, EAST SIDE,' COULD REFER ONLY TO THE POSITION OF THE SKULL ON THE TREE...
"...WHILE 'SHOOT FROM THE LEFT EYE OF THE DEATH'S-HEAD' ADMITTED, ALSO, OF BUT ONE INTERPRETATION, IN REGARD TO A SEARCH FOR BURIED TREASURE.

"I PERCEIVED THAT THE DESIGN WAS TO DROP A BULLET FROM THE LEFT EYE OF THE SKULL, AND THAT A BEE-LINE, OR, IN OTHER WORDS, A STRAIGHT LINE, DRAWN FROM THE NEAREST POINT OF THE TRUNK THROUGH 'THE SHOT,' (OR THE SPOT WHERE THE BULLET FELL,) WOULD INDICATE A DEFINITE POINT-- AND BENEATH THIS POINT I THOUGHT IT AT LEAST POSSIBLE THAT A DEPOSIT OF VALUE LAY CONCEALED."

ALL THIS IS EXCEEDINGLY CLEAR, AND, ALTHOUGH INGENIOUS, STILL SIMPLE AND EXPLICIT. WHEN YOU LEFT THE BISHOP'S HOTEL, WHAT THEN?

WHY, HAVING CAREFULLY TAKEN THE BEARINGS OF THE TREE, I TURNED HOMEWARDS.

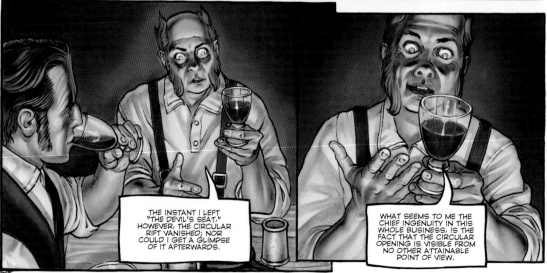

THE INSTANT I LEFT "THE DEVIL'S SEAT," HOWEVER, THE CIRCULAR RIFT VANISHED; NOR COULD I GET A GLIMPSE OF IT AFTERWARDS.

WHAT SEEMS TO ME THE CHIEF INGENUITY IN THIS WHOLE BUSINESS, IS THE FACT THAT THE CIRCULAR OPENING IS VISIBLE FROM NO OTHER ATTAINABLE POINT OF VIEW.

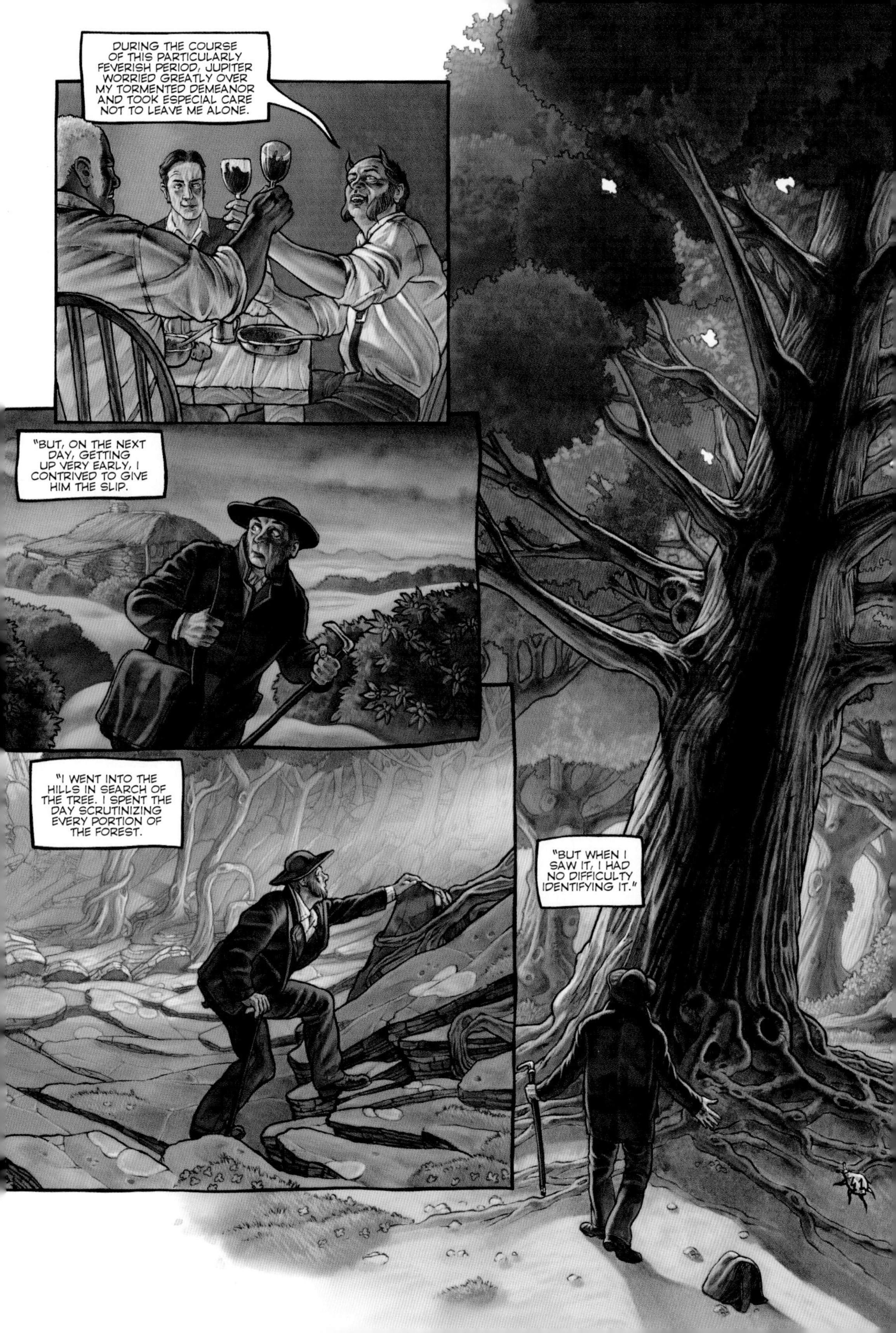
DURING THE COURSE OF THIS PARTICULARLY FEVERISH PERIOD, JUPITER WORRIED GREATLY OVER MY TORMENTED DEMEANOR AND TOOK ESPECIAL CARE NOT TO LEAVE ME ALONE.
"BUT, ON THE NEXT DAY, GETTING UP VERY EARLY, I CONTRIVED TO GIVE HIM THE SLIP.
"I WENT INTO THE HILLS IN SEARCH OF THE TREE. I SPENT THE DAY SCRUTINIZING EVERY PORTION OF THE FOREST.
"BUT WHEN I SAW IT, I HAD NO DIFFICULTY IDENTIFYING IT."

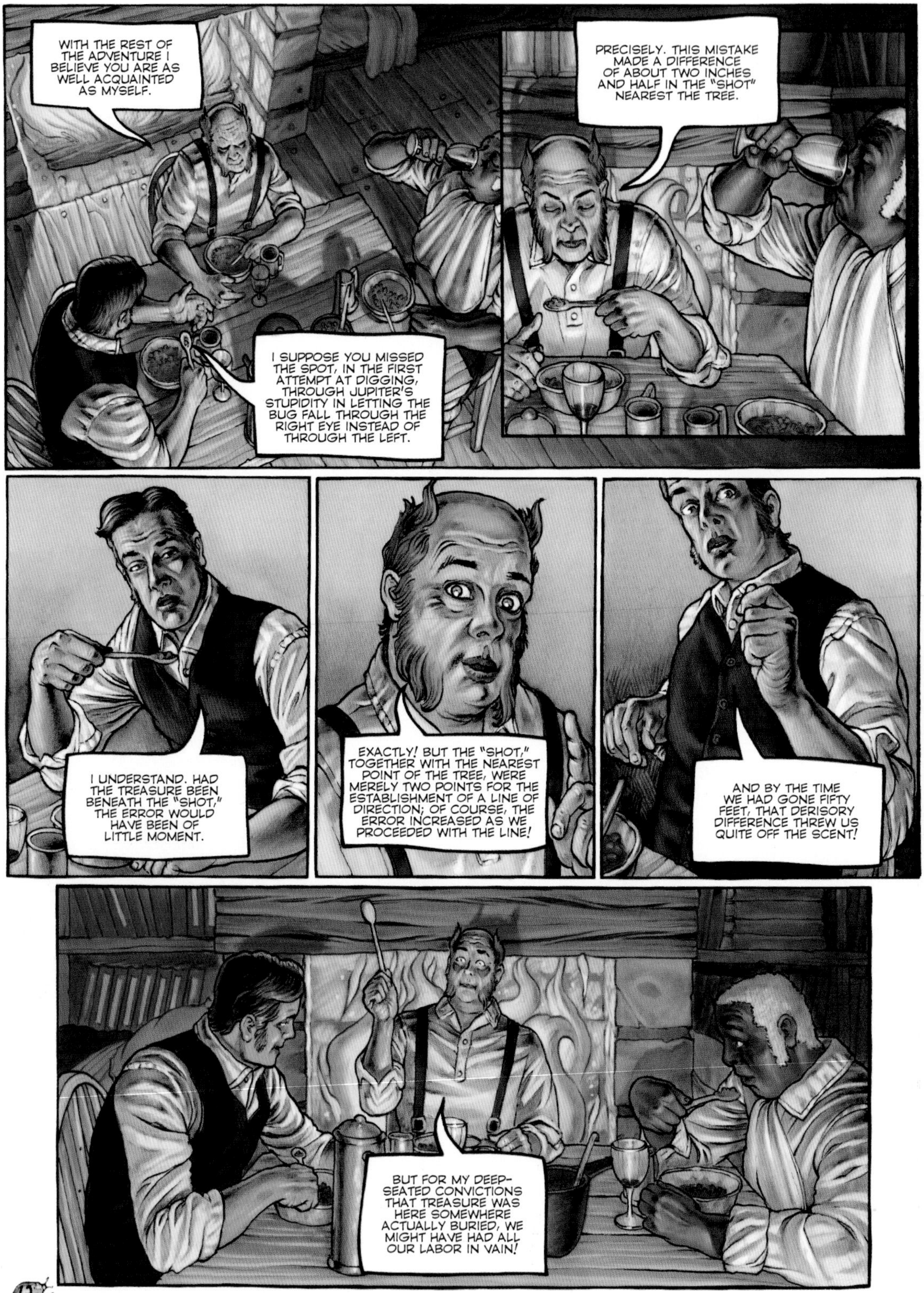

WITH THE REST OF THE ADVENTURE I BELIEVE YOU ARE AS WELL ACQUAINTED AS MYSELF.
I SUPPOSE YOU MISSED THE SPOT, IN THE FIRST ATTEMPT AT DIGGING, THROUGH JUPITER'S STUPIDITY IN LETTING THE BUG FALL THROUGH THE RIGHT EYE INSTEAD OF THROUGH THE LEFT.
PRECISELY. THIS MISTAKE MADE A DIFFERENCE OF ABOUT TWO INCHES AND HALF IN THE "SHOT" NEAREST THE TREE.
I UNDERSTAND. HAD THE TREASURE BEEN BENEATH THE "SHOT," THE ERROR WOULD HAVE BEEN OF LITTLE MOMENT.
EXACTLY! BUT THE "SHOT," TOGETHER WITH THE NEAREST POINT OF THE TREE, WERE MERELY TWO POINTS FOR THE ESTABLISHMENT OF A LINE OF DIRECTION; OF COURSE, THE ERROR INCREASED AS WE PROCEEDED WITH THE LINE!
AND BY THE TIME WE HAD GONE FIFTY FEET, THAT DERISORY DIFFERENCE THREW US QUITE OFF THE SCENT!
BUT FOR MY DEEP-SEATED CONVICTIONS THAT TREASURE WAS HERE SOMEWHERE ACTUALLY BURIED, WE MIGHT HAVE HAD ALL OUR LABOR IN VAIN!

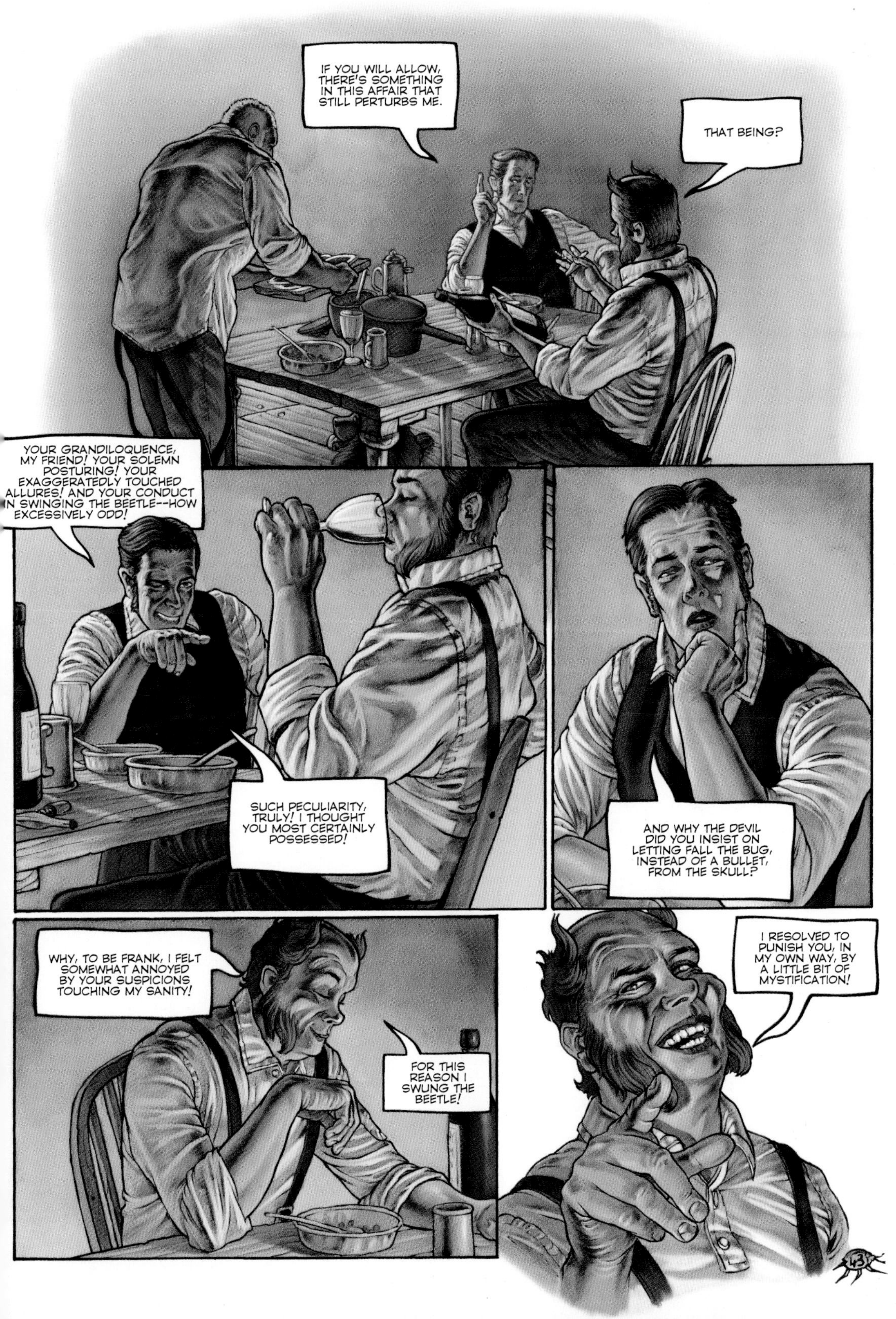
IF YOU WILL ALLOW, THERE'S SOMETHING IN THIS AFFAIR THAT STILL PERTURBS ME.
THAT BEING?
YOUR GRANDILOQUENCE, MY FRIEND! YOUR SOLEMN POSTURING! YOUR EXAGGERATEDLY TOUCHED ALLURES! AND YOUR CONDUCT IN SWINGING THE BEETLE--HOW EXCESSIVELY ODD!
SUCH PECULIARITY, TRULY! I THOUGHT YOU MOST CERTAINLY POSSESSED!
AND WHY THE DEVIL DID YOU INSIST ON LETTING FALL THE BUG, INSTEAD OF A BULLET, FROM THE SKULL?
WHY, TO BE FRANK, I FELT SOMEWHAT ANNOYED BY YOUR SUSPICIONS TOUCHING MY SANITY!
FOR THIS REASON I SWUNG THE BEETLE!
I RESOLVED TO PUNISH YOU, IN MY OWN WAY, BY A LITTLE BIT OF MYSTIFICATION!

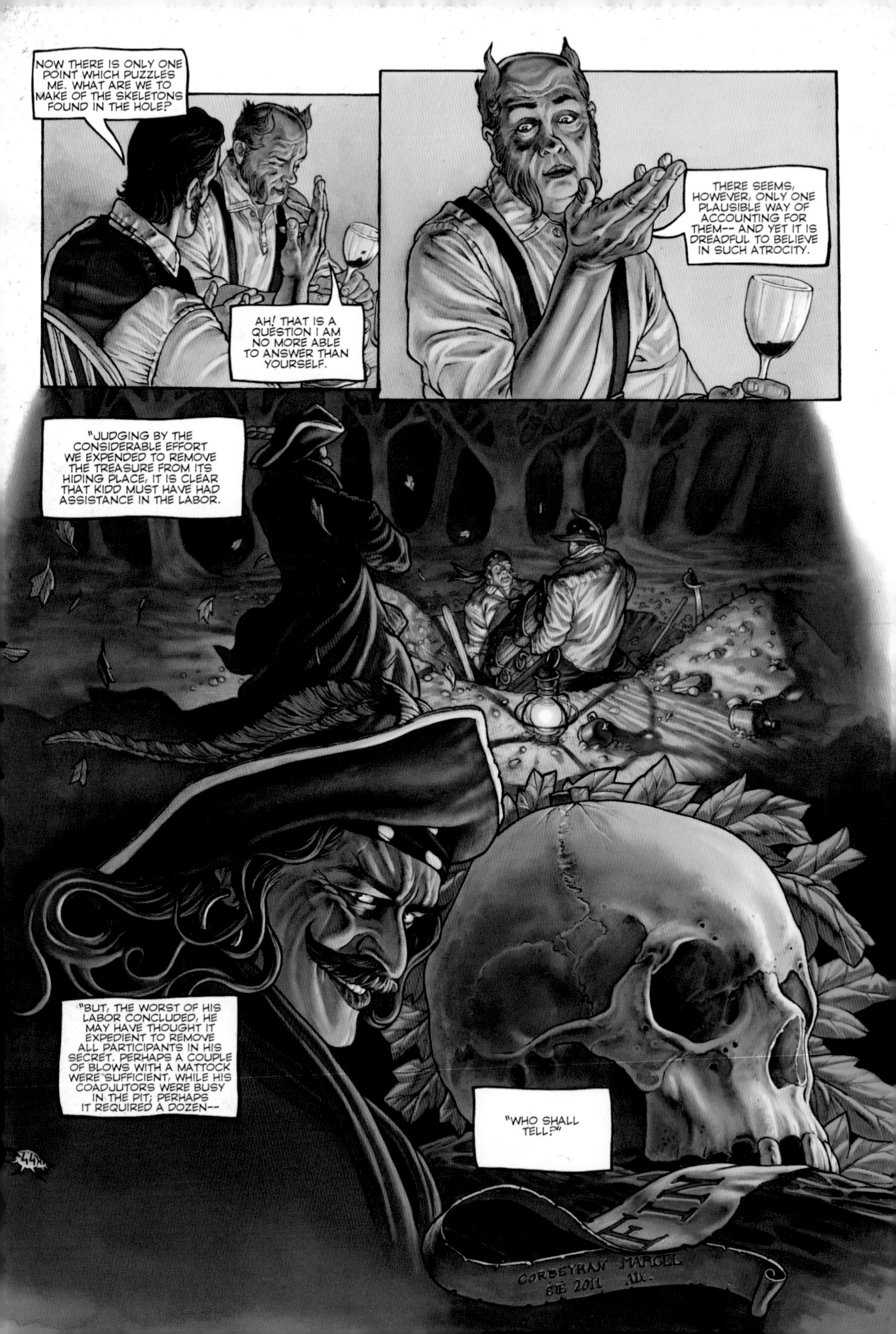
NOW THERE IS ONLY ONE POINT WHICH PUZZLES ME. WHAT ARE WE TO MAKE OF THE SKELETONS FOUND IN THE HOLE?
AH! THAT IS A QUESTION I AM NO MORE ABLE TO ANSWER THAN YOURSELF.
THERE SEEMS, HOWEVER, ONLY ONE PLAUSIBLE WAY OF ACCOUNTING FOR THEM-- AND YET IT IS DREADFUL TO BELIEVE IN SUCH ATROCITY.
"JUDGING BY THE CONSIDERABLE EFFORT WE EXPENDED TO REMOVE THE TREASURE FROM ITS HIDING PLACE, IT IS CLEAR THAT KIDD MUST HAVE HAD ASSISTANCE IN THE LABOR.
"BUT, THE WORST OF HIS LABOR CONCLUDED, HE MAY HAVE THOUGHT IT EXPEDIENT TO REMOVE ALL PARTICIPANTS IN HIS SECRET. PERHAPS A COUPLE OF BLOWS WITH A MATTOCK WERE SUFFICIENT, WHILE HIS COADJUTORS WERE BUSY IN THE PIT; PERHAPS IT REQUIRED A DOZEN--
"WHO SHALL TELL?"
CORBEYRAN MARCEL
ÉTÉ 2011 AIX.

# The Mystery of Marie Roget

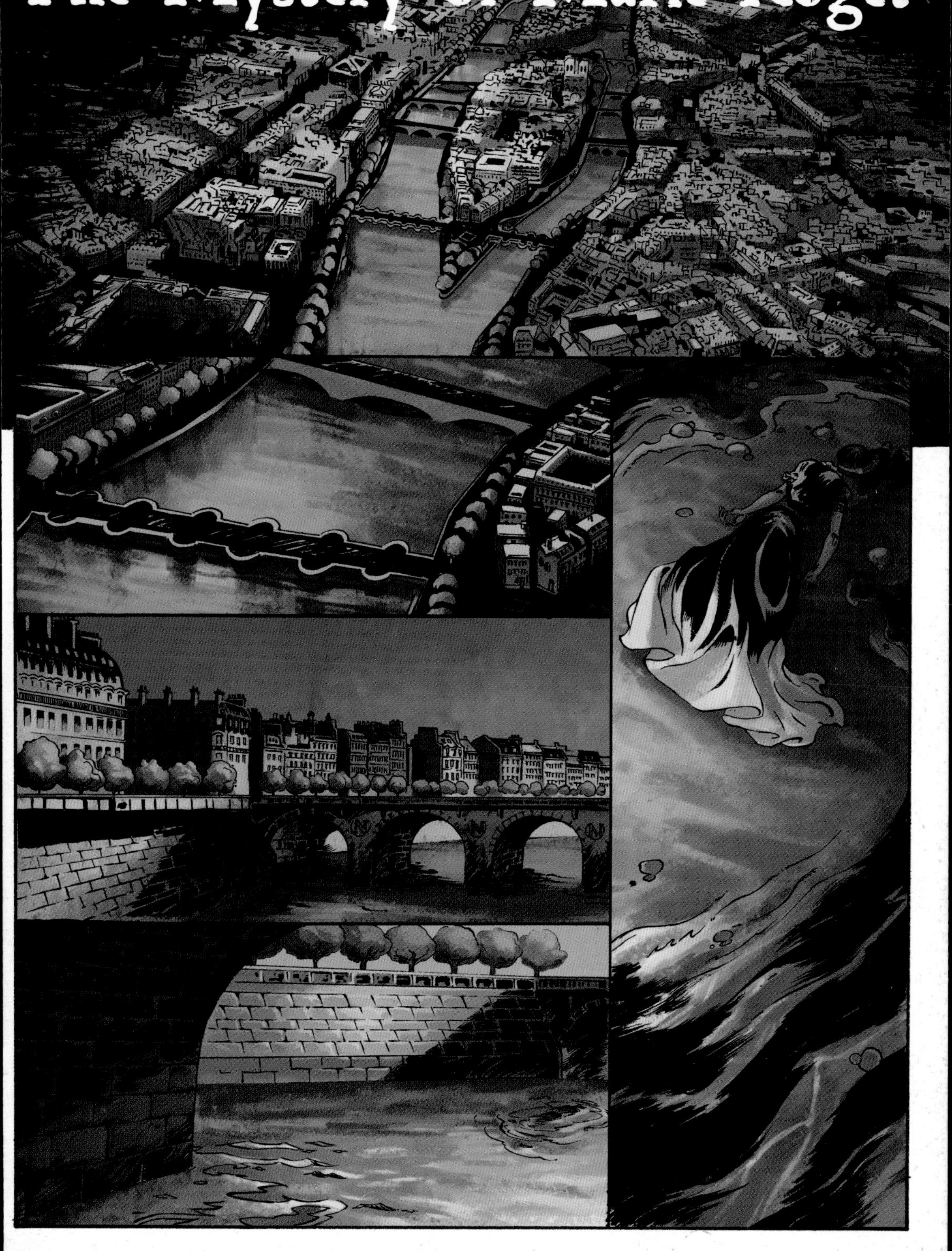

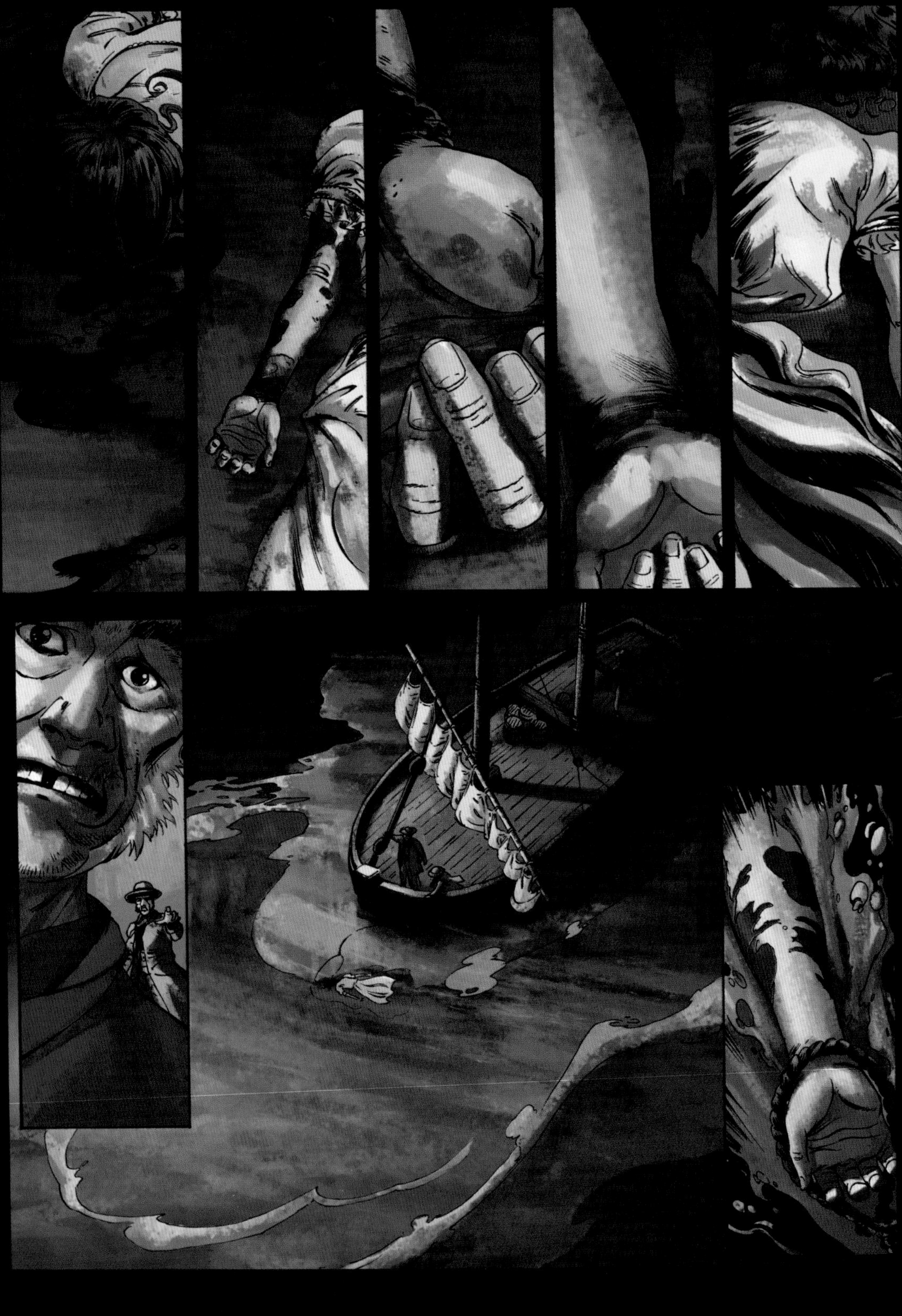

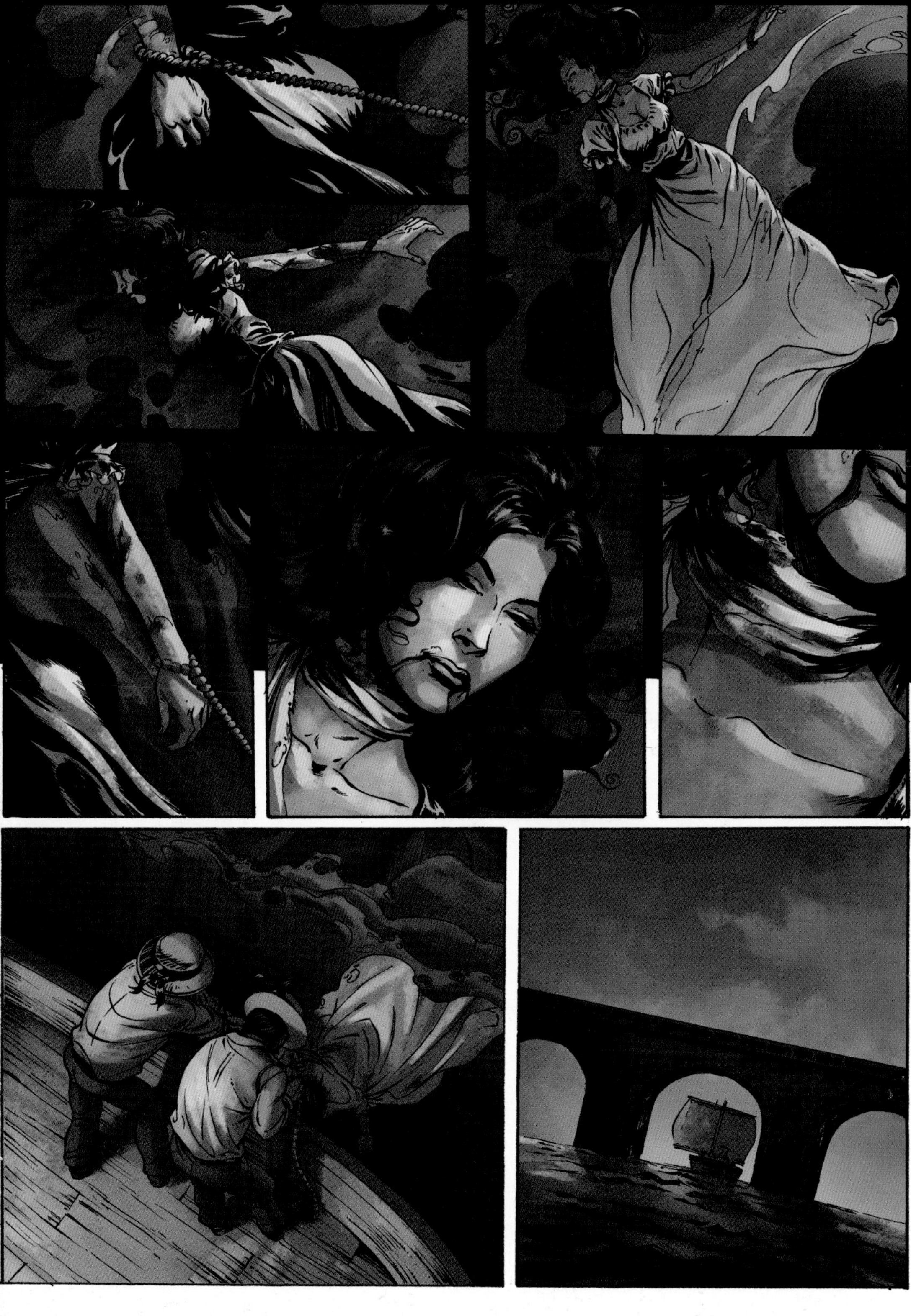

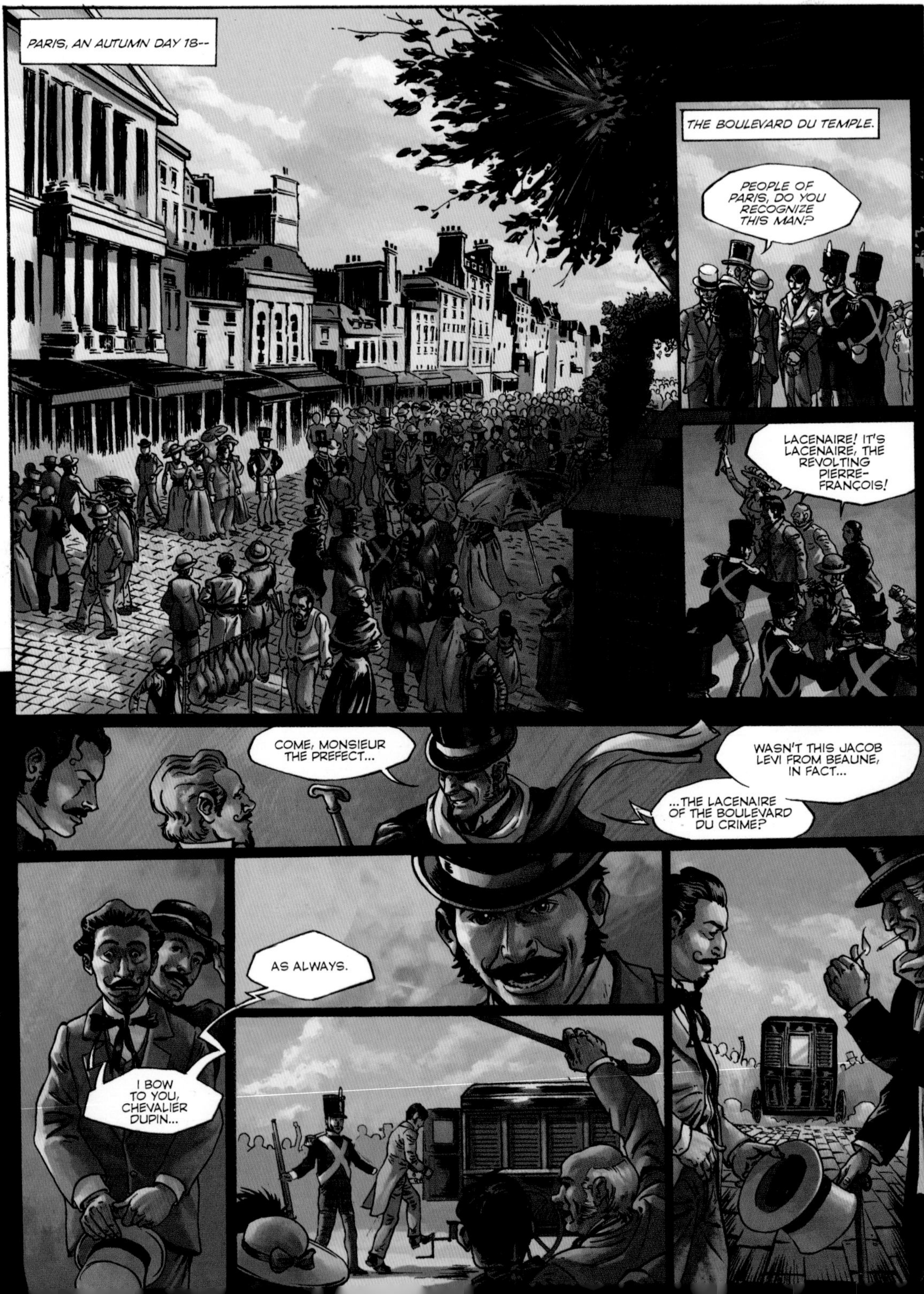
PARIS, AN AUTUMN DAY 18--
THE BOULEVARD DU TEMPLE.
PEOPLE OF PARIS, DO YOU RECOGNIZE THIS MAN?
LACENAIRE! IT'S LACENAIRE, THE REVOLTING PIERRE-FRANÇOIS!
COME, MONSIEUR THE PREFECT...
WASN'T THIS JACOB LEVI FROM BEAUNE, IN FACT...
...THE LACENAIRE OF THE BOULEVARD DU CRIME?
AS ALWAYS.
I BOW TO YOU, CHEVALIER DUPIN...

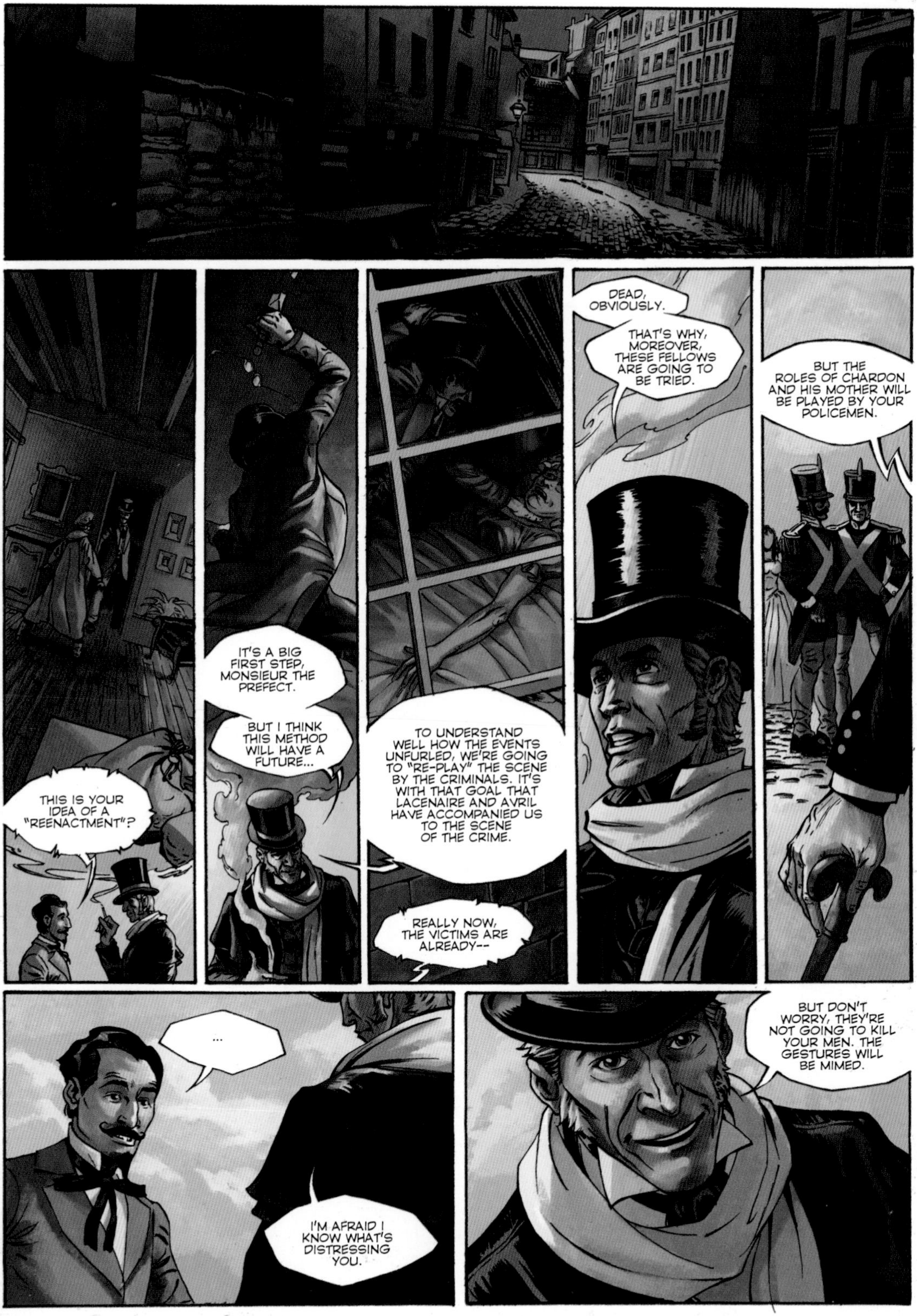
THIRD ARRONDISSEMENT: PASSAGE DU CHEVAL-ROUGE.
THIS IS YOUR IDEA OF A "REENACTMENT"?
IT'S A BIG FIRST STEP, MONSIEUR THE PREFECT.
BUT I THINK THIS METHOD WILL HAVE A FUTURE...
TO UNDERSTAND WELL HOW THE EVENTS UNFURLED, WE'RE GOING TO "RE-PLAY" THE SCENE BY THE CRIMINALS. IT'S WITH THAT GOAL THAT LACENAIRE AND AVRIL HAVE ACCOMPANIED US TO THE SCENE OF THE CRIME.
REALLY NOW, THE VICTIMS ARE ALREADY--
DEAD, OBVIOUSLY.
THAT'S WHY, MOREOVER, THESE FELLOWS ARE GOING TO BE TRIED.
BUT THE ROLES OF CHARDON AND HIS MOTHER WILL BE PLAYED BY YOUR POLICEMEN.
...
I'M AFRAID I KNOW WHAT'S DISTRESSING YOU.
BUT DON'T WORRY, THEY'RE NOT GOING TO KILL YOUR MEN. THE GESTURES WILL BE MIMED.

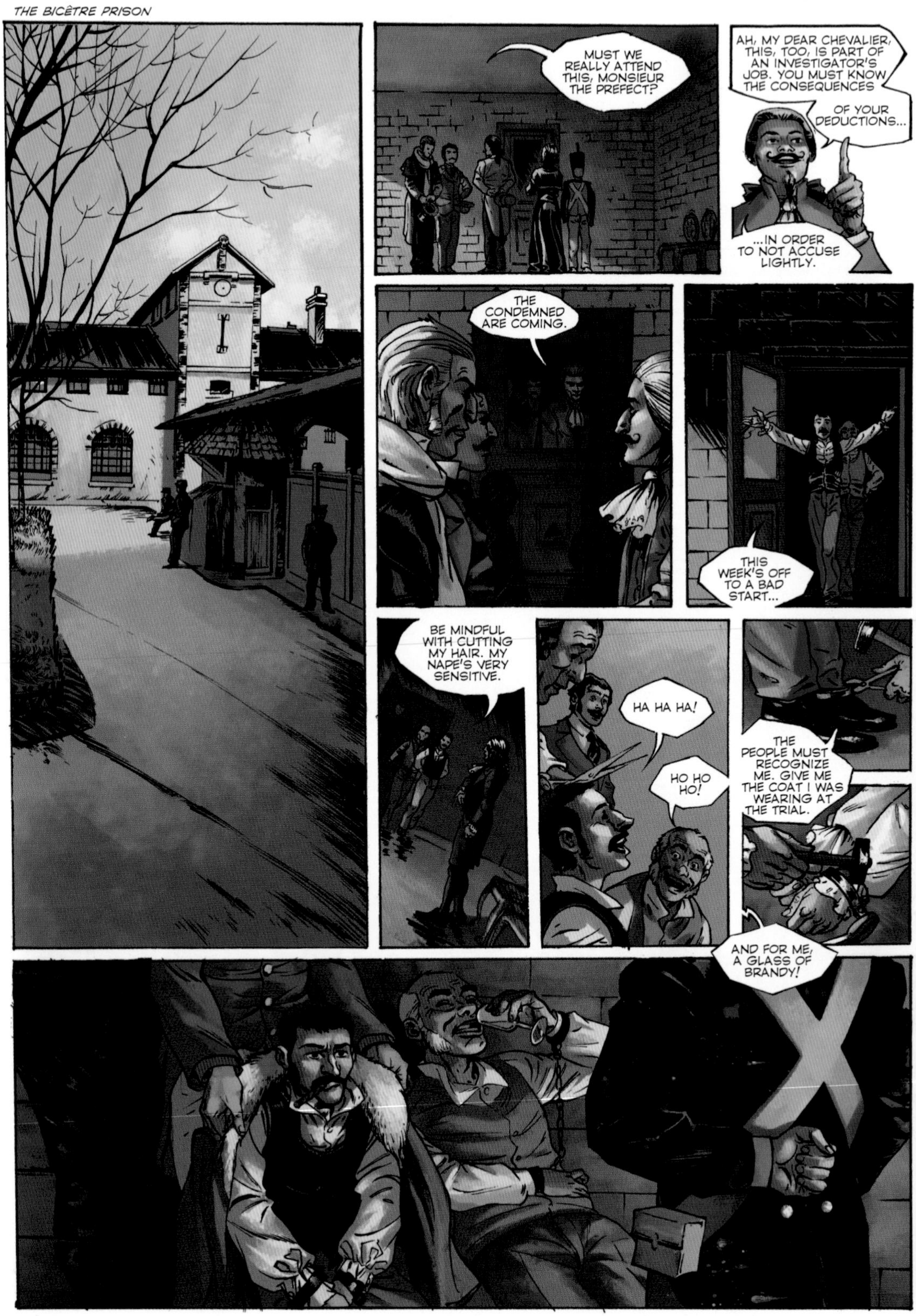
THE BICÊTRE PRISON
MUST WE REALLY ATTEND THIS, MONSIEUR THE PREFECT?
AH, MY DEAR CHEVALIER, THIS, TOO, IS PART OF AN INVESTIGATOR'S JOB. YOU MUST KNOW THE CONSEQUENCES
OF YOUR DEDUCTIONS...
...IN ORDER TO NOT ACCUSE LIGHTLY.
THE CONDEMNED ARE COMING.
THIS WEEK'S OFF TO A BAD START...
BE MINDFUL WITH CUTTING MY HAIR. MY NAPE'S VERY SENSITIVE.
HA HA HA!
HO HO HO!
THE PEOPLE MUST RECOGNIZE ME. GIVE ME THE COAT I WAS WEARING AT THE TRIAL.
AND FOR ME, A GLASS OF BRANDY!

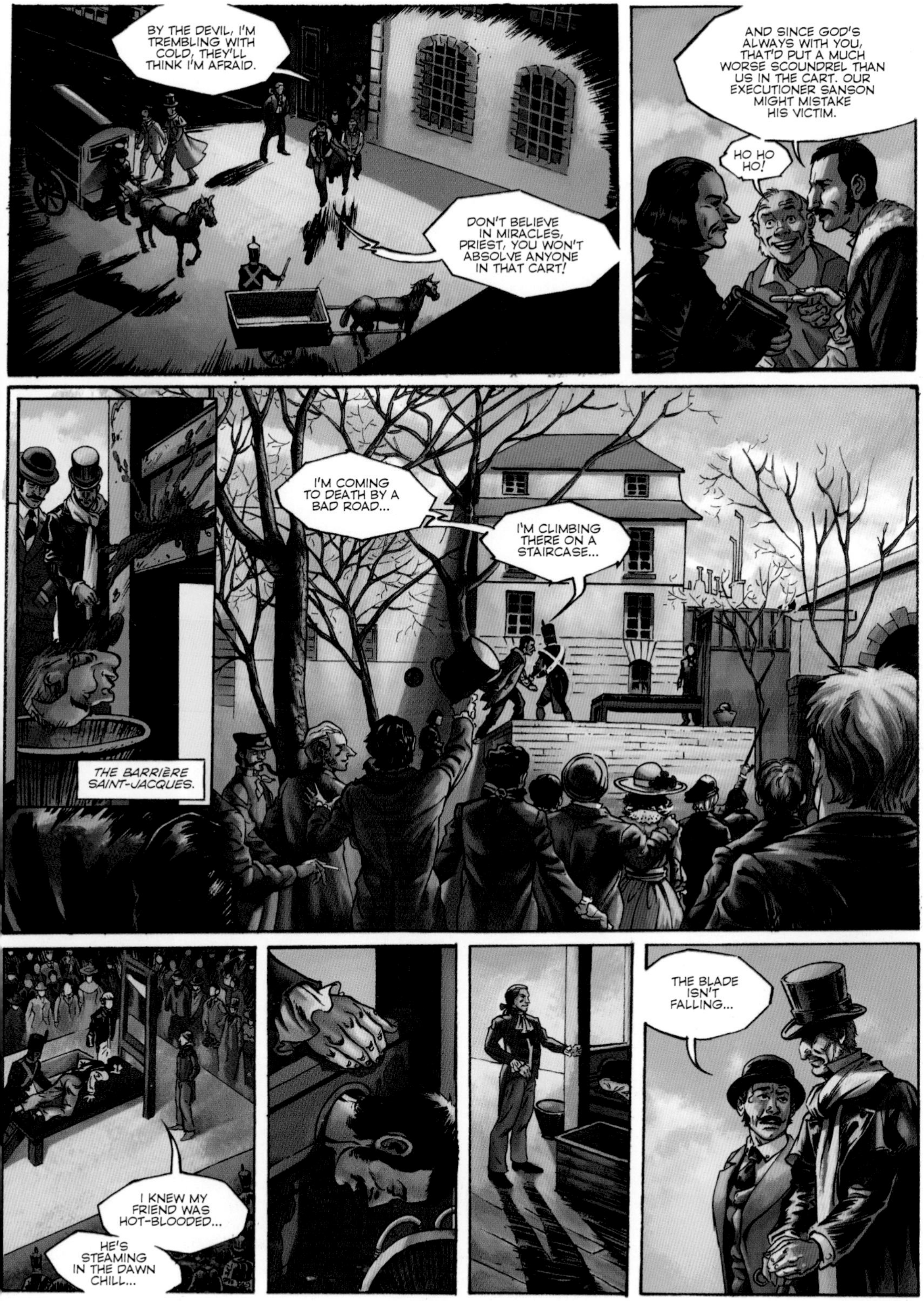
BY THE DEVIL, I'M TREMBLING WITH COLD, THEY'LL THINK I'M AFRAID.
DON'T BELIEVE IN MIRACLES, PRIEST, YOU WON'T ABSOLVE ANYONE IN THAT CART!
AND SINCE GOD'S ALWAYS WITH YOU, THAT'D PUT A MUCH WORSE SCOUNDREL THAN US IN THE CART. OUR EXECUTIONER SANSON MIGHT MISTAKE HIS VICTIM.
HO HO HO!
THE BARRIÈRE SAINT-JACQUES.
I'M COMING TO DEATH BY A BAD ROAD...
I'M CLIMBING THERE ON A STAIRCASE...
I KNEW MY FRIEND WAS HOT-BLOODED...
HE'S STEAMING IN THE DAWN CHILL...
THE BLADE ISN'T FALLING...

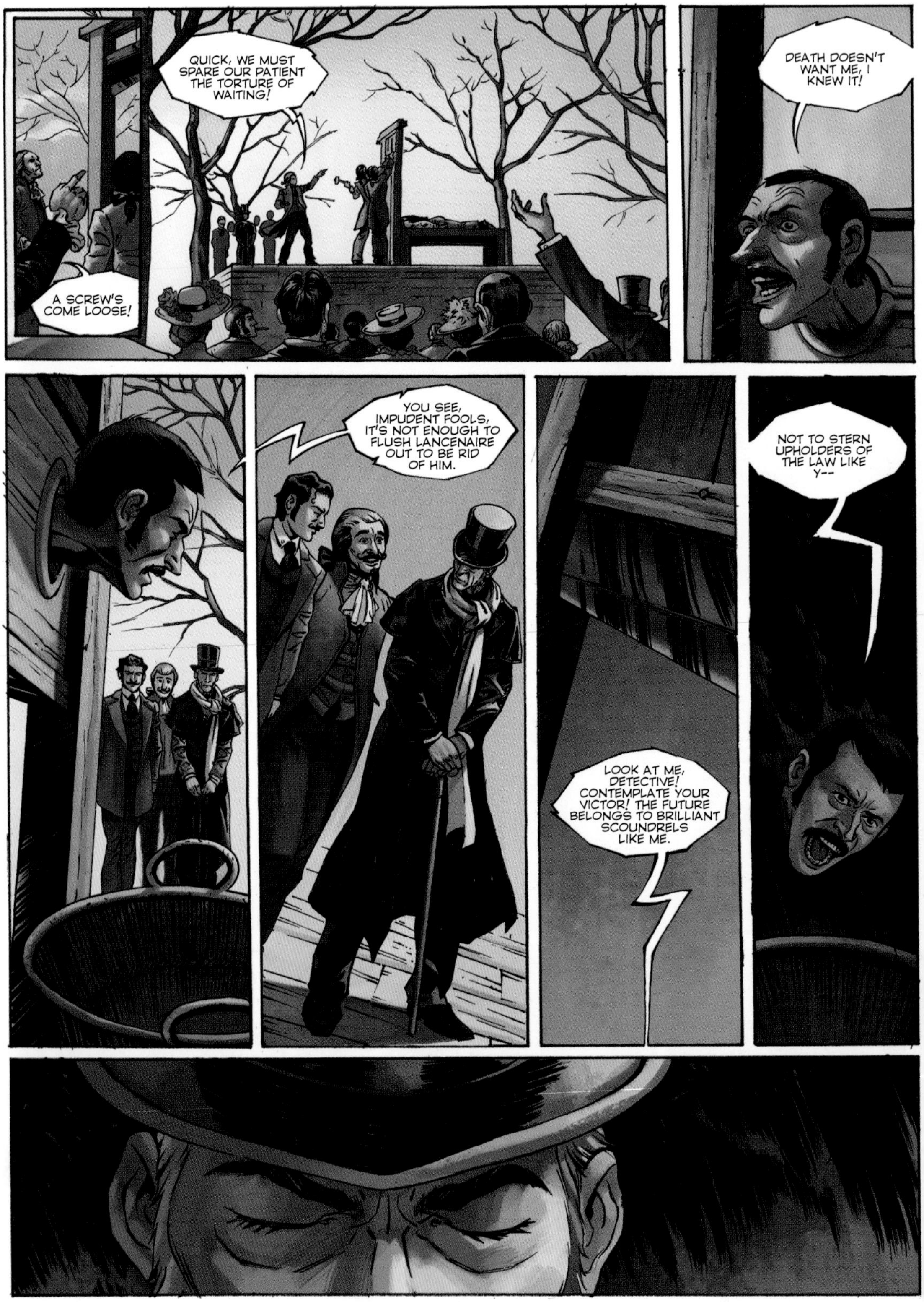
QUICK, WE MUST SPARE OUR PATIENT THE TORTURE OF WAITING!
A SCREW'S COME LOOSE!
DEATH DOESN'T WANT ME, I KNEW IT!
YOU SEE, IMPUDENT FOOLS, IT'S NOT ENOUGH TO FLUSH LANCENAIRE OUT TO BE RID OF HIM.
LOOK AT ME, DETECTIVE! CONTEMPLATE YOUR VICTOR! THE FUTURE BELONGS TO BRILLIANT SCOUNDRELS LIKE ME.
NOT TO STERN UPHOLDERS OF THE LAW LIKE Y--

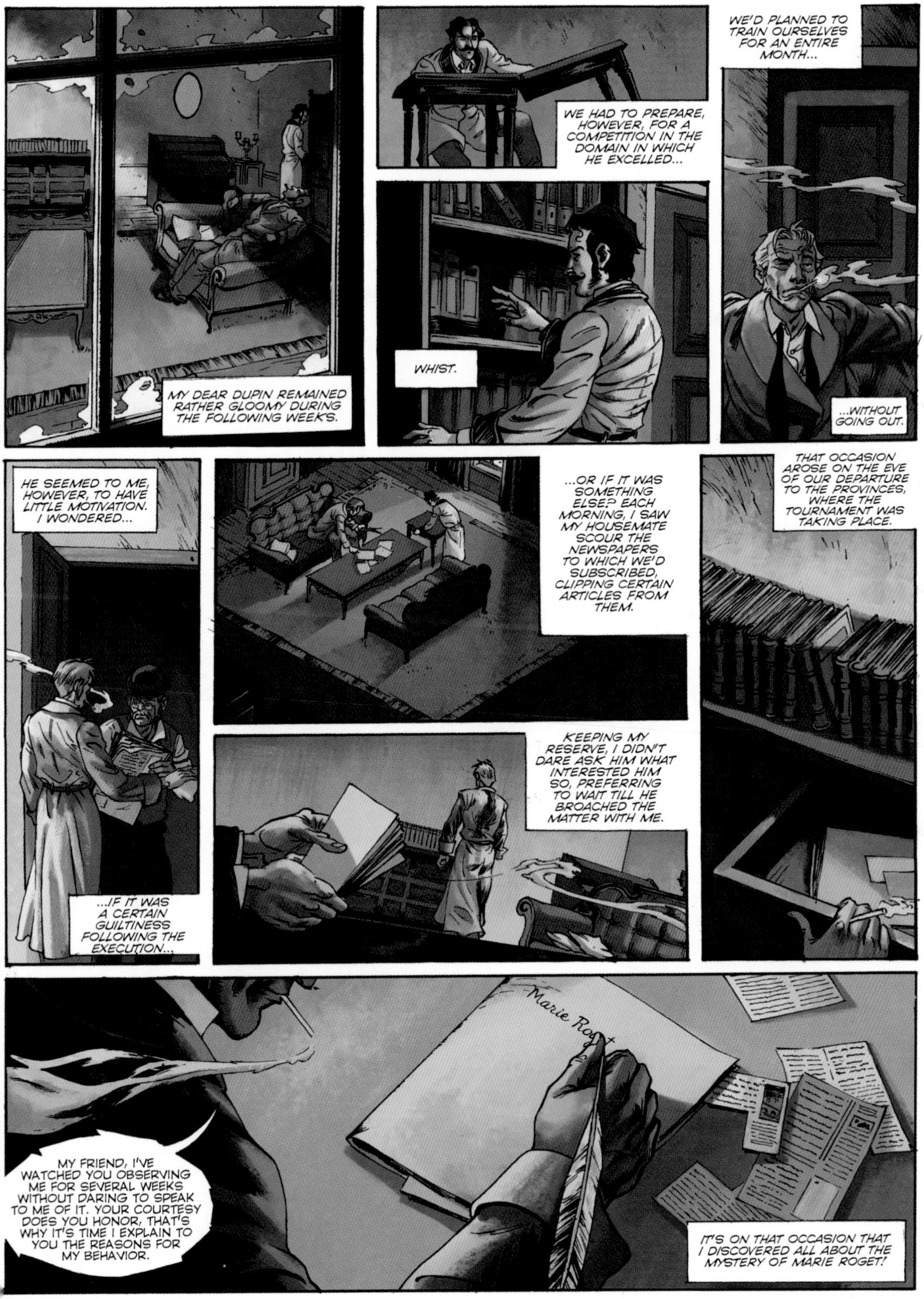
MY DEAR DUPIN REMAINED RATHER GLOOMY DURING THE FOLLOWING WEEKS.
WE HAD TO PREPARE, HOWEVER, FOR A COMPETITION IN THE DOMAIN IN WHICH HE EXCELLED...
WHIST.
WE'D PLANNED TO TRAIN OURSELVES FOR AN ENTIRE MONTH...
...WITHOUT GOING OUT.
HE SEEMED TO ME, HOWEVER, TO HAVE LITTLE MOTIVATION. I WONDERED...
...IF IT WAS A CERTAIN GUILTINESS FOLLOWING THE EXECUTION...
...OR IF IT WAS SOMETHING ELSE? EACH MORNING, I SAW MY HOUSEMATE SCOUR THE NEWSPAPERS TO WHICH WE'D SUBSCRIBED, CLIPPING CERTAIN ARTICLES FROM THEM.
KEEPING MY RESERVE, I DIDN'T DARE ASK HIM WHAT INTERESTED HIM SO, PREFERRING TO WAIT TILL HE BROACHED THE MATTER WITH ME.
THAT OCCASION AROSE ON THE EVE OF OUR DEPARTURE TO THE PROVINCES, WHERE THE TOURNAMENT WAS TAKING PLACE.
Marie Roget
MY FRIEND, I'VE WATCHED YOU OBSERVING ME FOR SEVERAL WEEKS WITHOUT DARING TO SPEAK TO ME OF IT. YOUR COURTESY DOES YOU HONOR, THAT'S WHY IT'S TIME I EXPLAIN TO YOU THE REASONS FOR MY BEHAVIOR.
IT'S ON THAT OCCASION THAT I DISCOVERED ALL ABOUT THE MYSTERY OF MARIE ROGET!

THE FIRST NEWS BRIEF ABOUT THAT YOUNG WOMAN APPEARED AFTER THE BEGINNING OF OUR SECLUSION.

THE POOR GIRL WAS FOUND DROWNED IN THE SEINE.

I WILL GO OVER THE CRIME SCENE WITH YOU LATER.

"MARIE ROGET WAS THE ONLY DAUGHTER OF THE WIDOW ESTELLE ROGET. UNTIL 18 MONTHS BEFORE THE SUBJECT OF OUR NARRATIVE, SHE HAD ALWAYS DWELT IN THE BOURGEOIS PENSION OF HER MOTHER...

"...IN THE RUE PAVÉE SAINT ANDRÉ.

"AT 22 YEARS OF AGE, MARIE WAS A GREAT BEAUTY, SO MUCH SO THAT A PERFUMER IN THE PALAIS ROYAL HIRED HER TO GIVE ADDED EFFECT TO HIS SHOP.

"THE ANTICIPATIONS OF THE SHOPKEEPER WERE REALIZED, AND HIS ROOMS SOON BECAME NOTORIOUS THROUGH THE CHARMS OF THE SPRIGHTLY GRISETTE.

"SHE DISAPPEARED FOR A WEEK, CAUSING HER MOTHER GREAT ANXIETY AND AN UPROAR IN THE PRESS.

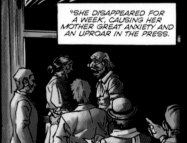

"SHE HAD BEEN IN HIS EMPLOY ABOUT A YEAR, WHEN HER ADMIRERS WERE THROWN INTO CONFUSION BY HER SUDDEN DISAPPEARANCE FROM THE SHOP.

"WHEN MARIE, IN GOOD HEALTH, MADE HER RE-APPEARANCE, ALL ANGUISH AND INQUIRY WERE IMMEDIATELY HUSHED.

"THE GIRL, OSTENSIBLY TO RELIEVE HERSELF FROM THE IMPERTINENCE OF CURIOSITY, SOON BADE A FINAL ADIEU TO THE PERFUMER, AND SOUGHT THE SHELTER OF HER MOTHER'S RESIDENCE IN THE RUE PAVÉE SAINT ANDRÉ."

IT WAS ABOUT FIVE MONTHS AFTER THIS RETURN HOME...

...THAT HER FRIENDS WERE ALARMED BY HER SUDDEN DISAPPEARANCE FOR THE SECOND TIME.

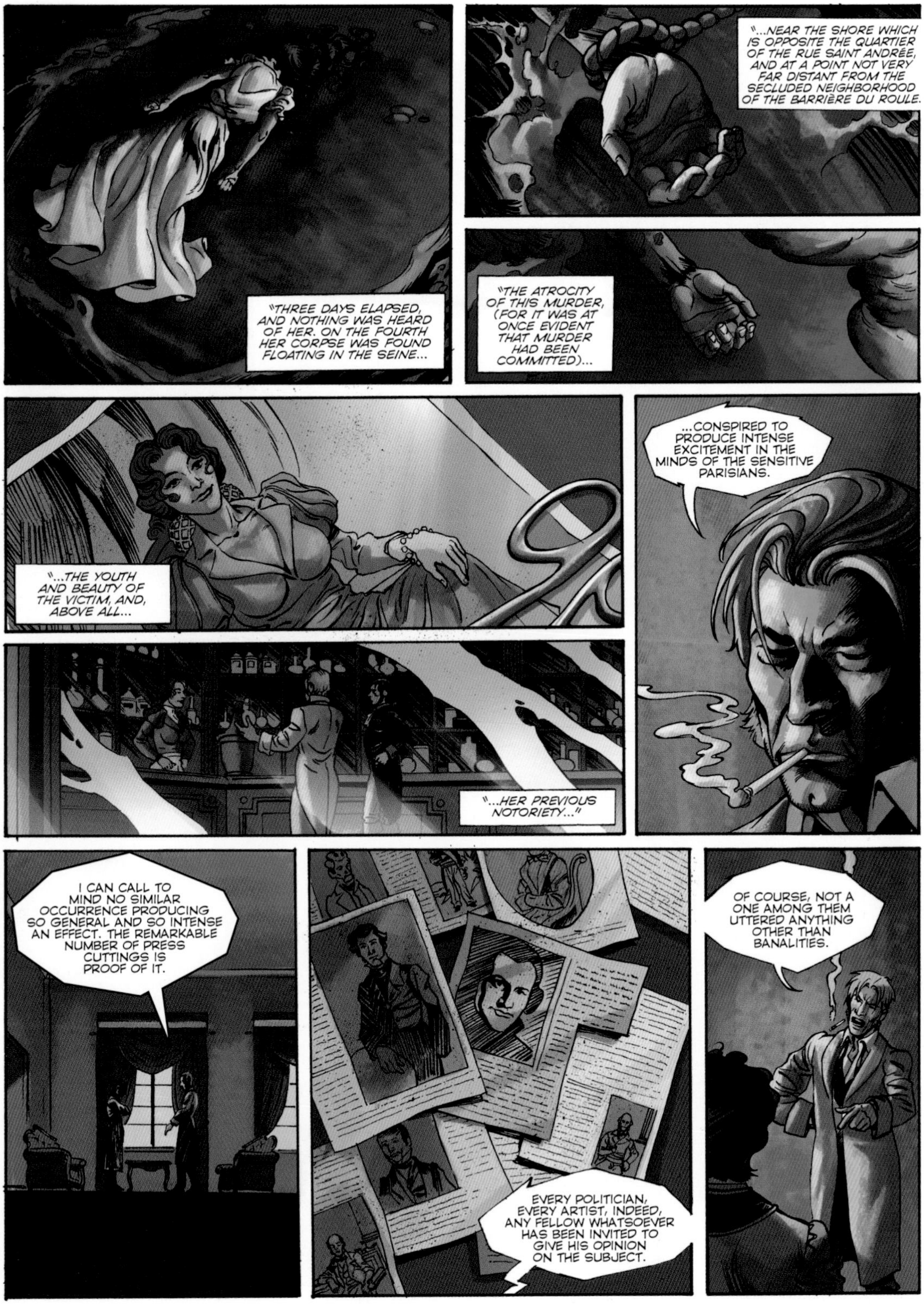
"THREE DAYS ELAPSED, AND NOTHING WAS HEARD OF HER. ON THE FOURTH HER CORPSE WAS FOUND FLOATING IN THE SEINE...
"...NEAR THE SHORE WHICH IS OPPOSITE THE QUARTIER OF THE RUE SAINT ANDRÉE, AND AT A POINT NOT VERY FAR DISTANT FROM THE SECLUDED NEIGHBORHOOD OF THE BARRIÈRE DU ROULE.
"THE ATROCITY OF THIS MURDER, (FOR IT WAS AT ONCE EVIDENT THAT MURDER HAD BEEN COMMITTED)...
"...THE YOUTH AND BEAUTY OF THE VICTIM, AND, ABOVE ALL...
"...HER PREVIOUS NOTORIETY..."
...CONSPIRED TO PRODUCE INTENSE EXCITEMENT IN THE MINDS OF THE SENSITIVE PARISIANS.
I CAN CALL TO MIND NO SIMILAR OCCURRENCE PRODUCING SO GENERAL AND SO INTENSE AN EFFECT. THE REMARKABLE NUMBER OF PRESS CUTTINGS IS PROOF OF IT.
EVERY POLITICIAN, EVERY ARTIST, INDEED, ANY FELLOW WHATSOEVER HAS BEEN INVITED TO GIVE HIS OPINION ON THE SUBJECT.
OF COURSE, NOT A ONE AMONG THEM UTTERED ANYTHING OTHER THAN BANALITIES.

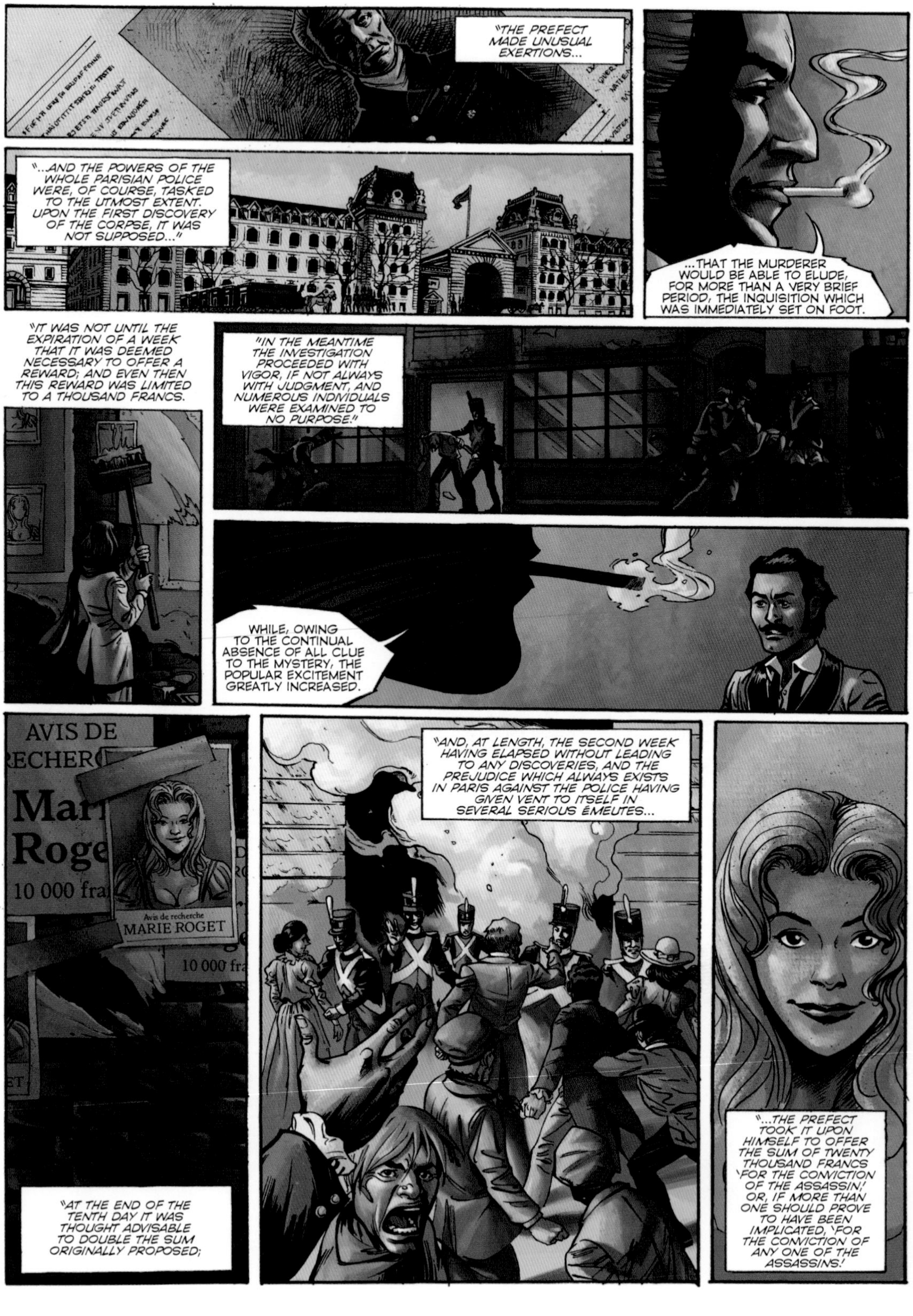

"THE PREFECT MADE UNUSUAL EXERTIONS...
"...AND THE POWERS OF THE WHOLE PARISIAN POLICE WERE, OF COURSE, TASKED TO THE UTMOST EXTENT. UPON THE FIRST DISCOVERY OF THE CORPSE, IT WAS NOT SUPPOSED..."
...THAT THE MURDERER WOULD BE ABLE TO ELUDE, FOR MORE THAN A VERY BRIEF PERIOD, THE INQUISITION WHICH WAS IMMEDIATELY SET ON FOOT.
"IT WAS NOT UNTIL THE EXPIRATION OF A WEEK THAT IT WAS DEEMED NECESSARY TO OFFER A REWARD; AND EVEN THEN THIS REWARD WAS LIMITED TO A THOUSAND FRANCS.
"IN THE MEANTIME THE INVESTIGATION PROCEEDED WITH VIGOR, IF NOT ALWAYS WITH JUDGMENT, AND NUMEROUS INDIVIDUALS WERE EXAMINED TO NO PURPOSE."
WHILE, OWING TO THE CONTINUAL ABSENCE OF ALL CLUE TO THE MYSTERY, THE POPULAR EXCITEMENT GREATLY INCREASED.
AVIS DE
Avis de recherche
MARIE ROGET
"AT THE END OF THE TENTH DAY IT WAS THOUGHT ADVISABLE TO DOUBLE THE SUM ORIGINALLY PROPOSED;
"AND, AT LENGTH, THE SECOND WEEK HAVING ELAPSED WITHOUT LEADING TO ANY DISCOVERIES, AND THE PREJUDICE WHICH ALWAYS EXISTS IN PARIS AGAINST THE POLICE HAVING GIVEN VENT TO ITSELF IN SEVERAL SERIOUS ÉMEUTES...
"...THE PREFECT TOOK IT UPON HIMSELF TO OFFER THE SUM OF TWENTY THOUSAND FRANCS 'FOR THE CONVICTION OF THE ASSASSIN,' OR, IF MORE THAN ONE SHOULD PROVE TO HAVE BEEN IMPLICATED, 'FOR THE CONVICTION OF ANY ONE OF THE ASSASSINS.'

"IN THE PROCLAMATION SETTING FORTH THIS REWARD, A FULL PARDON WAS PROMISED TO ANY ACCOMPLICE WHO SHOULD COME FORWARD IN EVIDENCE AGAINST HIS FELLOW.

THE ENTIRE REWARD THUS STOOD AT NO LESS THAN THIRTY THOUSAND FRANCS, WHICH WILL BE REGARDED AS AN EXTRAORDINARY SUM...

...WHEN WE CONSIDER THE HUMBLE CONDITION OF THE GIRL, AND THE GREAT FREQUENCY, IN LARGE CITIES, OF SUCH ATROCITIES AS THE ONE DESCRIBED.

"AND TO THE WHOLE WAS APPENDED, WHEREVER IT APPEARED, THE PRIVATE PLACARD OF A COMMITTEE OF CITIZENS, OFFERING TEN THOUSAND FRANCS, IN ADDITION TO THE AMOUNT PROPOSED BY THE PREFECTURE."

NO ONE, APART FROM ME, DOUBTED NOW THAT THE MYSTERY OF THIS MURDER WOULD BE IMMEDIATELY BROUGHT TO LIGHT.

"BUT ALTHOUGH, IN ONE OR TWO INSTANCES, ARRESTS WERE MADE WHICH PROMISED ELUCIDATION...

"...YET NOTHING WAS ELICITED WHICH COULD IMPLICATE THE PARTIES SUSPECTED; AND THEY WERE DISCHARGED FORTHWITH!"

STRANGE AS IT MAY APPEAR, THE THIRD WEEK FROM THE DISCOVERY OF THE BODY HAD PASSED, AND PASSED WITHOUT ANY LIGHT BEING THROWN UPON THE SUBJECT.

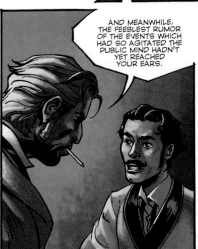

AND MEANWHILE, THE FEEBLEST RUMOR OF THE EVENTS WHICH HAD SO AGITATED THE PUBLIC MIND HADN'T YET REACHED YOUR EARS.

FOR YOU HAD AS YOUR SOLE PREOCCUPATION OUR WHIST COMPETITION.

FOR MY PART, I WAGERED WITH MYSELF THAT I COULD RESOLVE THE MATTER WITHOUT EVER LEAVING OUR APARTMENT.

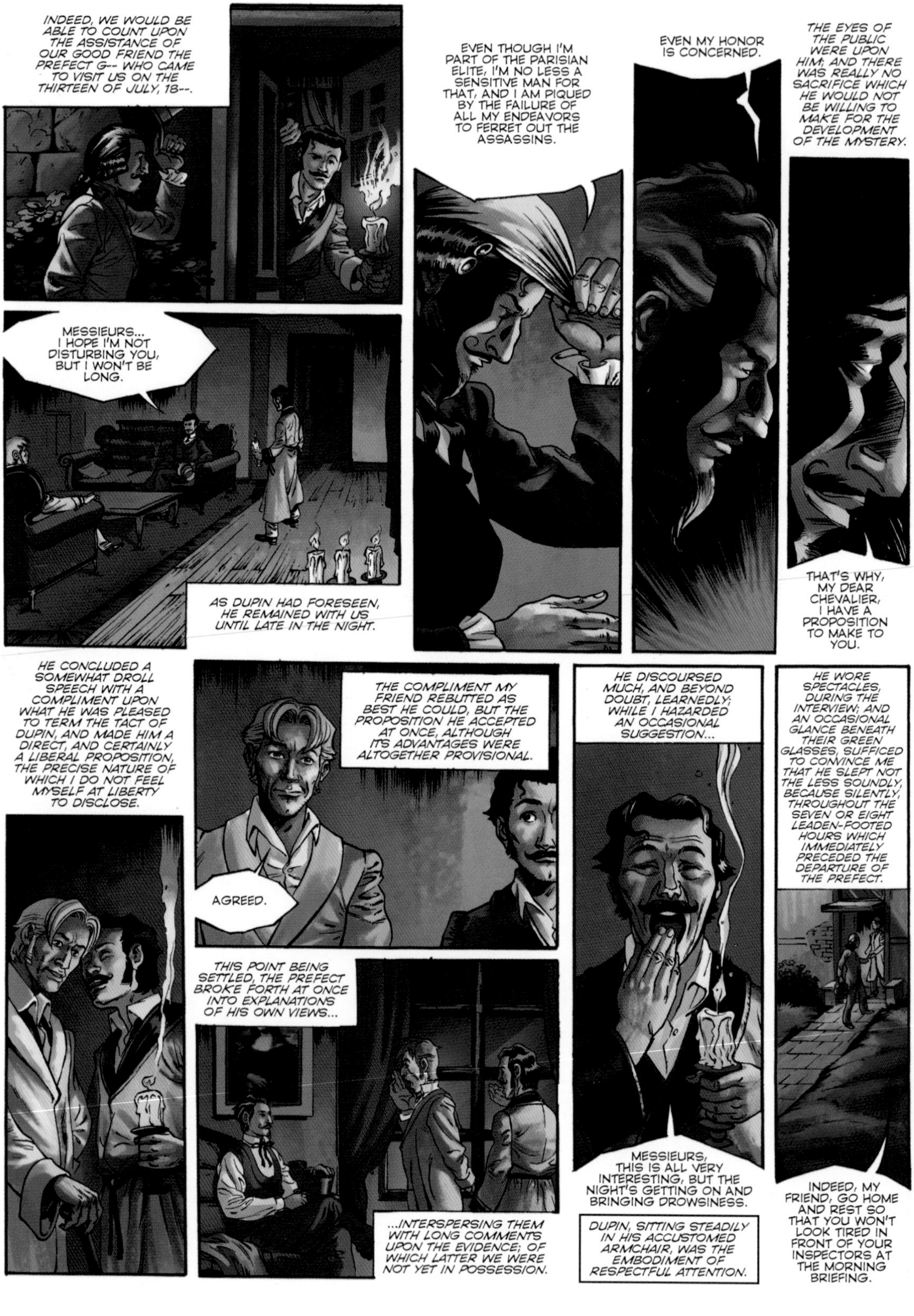

INDEED, WE WOULD BE ABLE TO COUNT UPON THE ASSISTANCE OF OUR GOOD FRIEND THE PREFECT G-- WHO CAME TO VISIT US ON THE THIRTEEN OF JULY, 18--.
MESSIEURS... I HOPE I'M NOT DISTURBING YOU, BUT I WON'T BE LONG.
AS DUPIN HAD FORESEEN, HE REMAINED WITH US UNTIL LATE IN THE NIGHT.
EVEN THOUGH I'M PART OF THE PARISIAN ELITE, I'M NO LESS A SENSITIVE MAN FOR THAT, AND I AM PIQUED BY THE FAILURE OF ALL MY ENDEAVORS TO FERRET OUT THE ASSASSINS.
EVEN MY HONOR IS CONCERNED.
THE EYES OF THE PUBLIC WERE UPON HIM; AND THERE WAS REALLY NO SACRIFICE WHICH HE WOULD NOT BE WILLING TO MAKE FOR THE DEVELOPMENT OF THE MYSTERY.
THAT'S WHY, MY DEAR CHEVALIER, I HAVE A PROPOSITION TO MAKE TO YOU.
HE CONCLUDED A SOMEWHAT DROLL SPEECH WITH A COMPLIMENT UPON WHAT HE WAS PLEASED TO TERM THE TACT OF DUPIN, AND MADE HIM A DIRECT, AND CERTAINLY A LIBERAL PROPOSITION, THE PRECISE NATURE OF WHICH I DO NOT FEEL MYSELF AT LIBERTY TO DISCLOSE.
THE COMPLIMENT MY FRIEND REBUTTED AS BEST HE COULD, BUT THE PROPOSITION HE ACCEPTED AT ONCE, ALTHOUGH ITS ADVANTAGES WERE ALTOGETHER PROVISIONAL.
AGREED.
THIS POINT BEING SETTLED, THE PREFECT BROKE FORTH AT ONCE INTO EXPLANATIONS OF HIS OWN VIEWS...
...INTERSPERSING THEM WITH LONG COMMENTS UPON THE EVIDENCE; OF WHICH LATTER WE WERE NOT YET IN POSSESSION.
HE DISCOURSED MUCH, AND BEYOND DOUBT, LEARNEDLY; WHILE I HAZARDED AN OCCASIONAL SUGGESTION...
MESSIEURS, THIS IS ALL VERY INTERESTING, BUT THE NIGHT'S GETTING ON AND BRINGING DROWSINESS.
DUPIN, SITTING STEADILY IN HIS ACCUSTOMED ARMCHAIR, WAS THE EMBODIMENT OF RESPECTFUL ATTENTION.
HE WORE SPECTACLES, DURING THE INTERVIEW; AND AN OCCASIONAL GLANCE BENEATH THEIR GREEN GLASSES, SUFFICED TO CONVINCE ME THAT HE SLEPT NOT THE LESS SOUNDLY, BECAUSE SILENTLY, THROUGHOUT THE SEVEN OR EIGHT LEADEN-FOOTED HOURS WHICH IMMEDIATELY PRECEDED THE DEPARTURE OF THE PREFECT.
INDEED, MY FRIEND, GO HOME AND REST SO THAT YOU WON'T LOOK TIRED IN FRONT OF YOUR INSPECTORS AT THE MORNING BRIEFING.

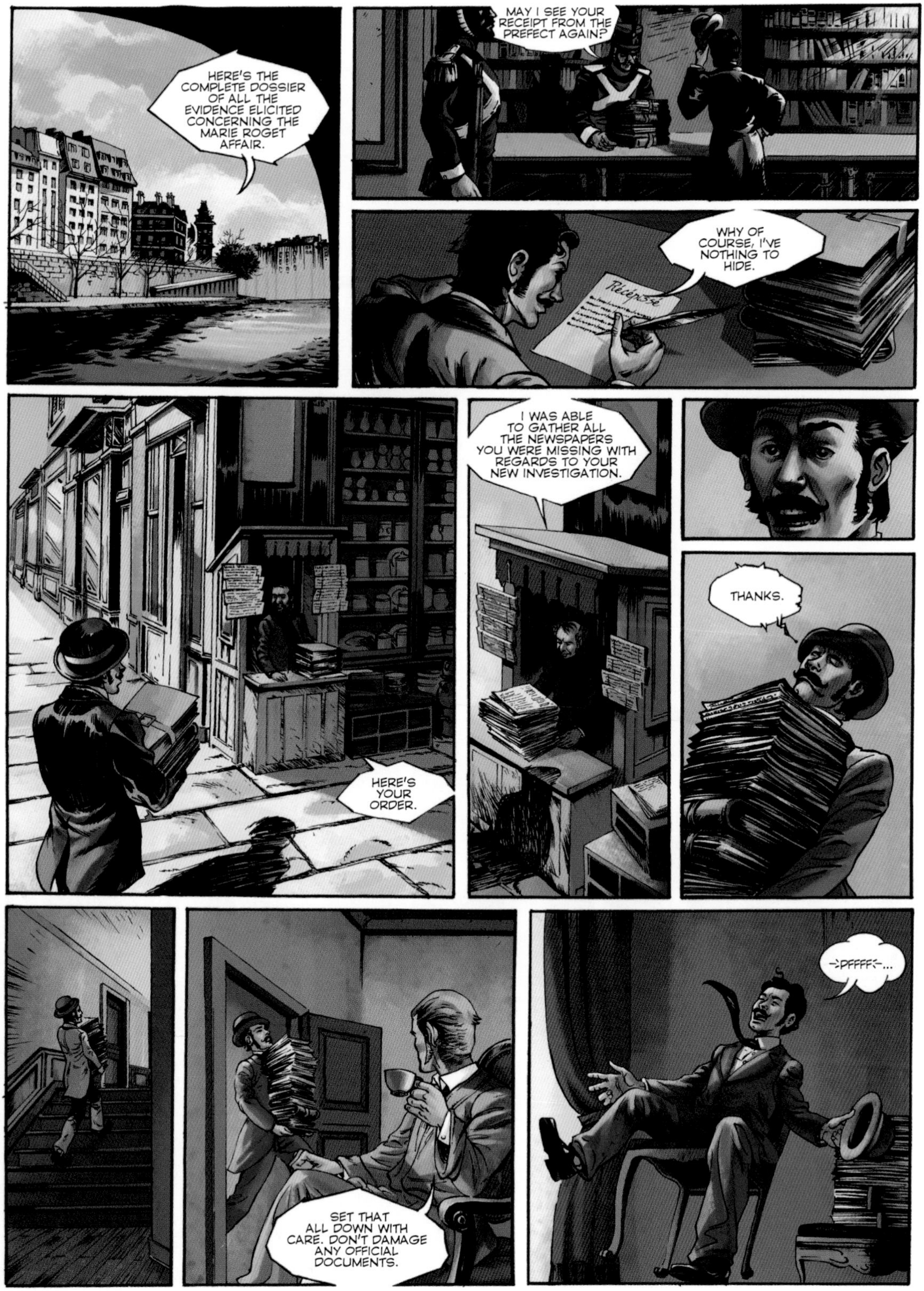
HERE'S THE COMPLETE DOSSIER OF ALL THE EVIDENCE ELICITED CONCERNING THE MARIE ROGET AFFAIR.
MAY I SEE YOUR RECEIPT FROM THE PREFECT AGAIN?
Récépissé
WHY OF COURSE, I'VE NOTHING TO HIDE.
HERE'S YOUR ORDER.
I WAS ABLE TO GATHER ALL THE NEWSPAPERS YOU WERE MISSING WITH REGARDS TO YOUR NEW INVESTIGATION.
THANKS.
SET THAT ALL DOWN WITH CARE. DON'T DAMAGE ANY OFFICIAL DOCUMENTS.
PFFFF...

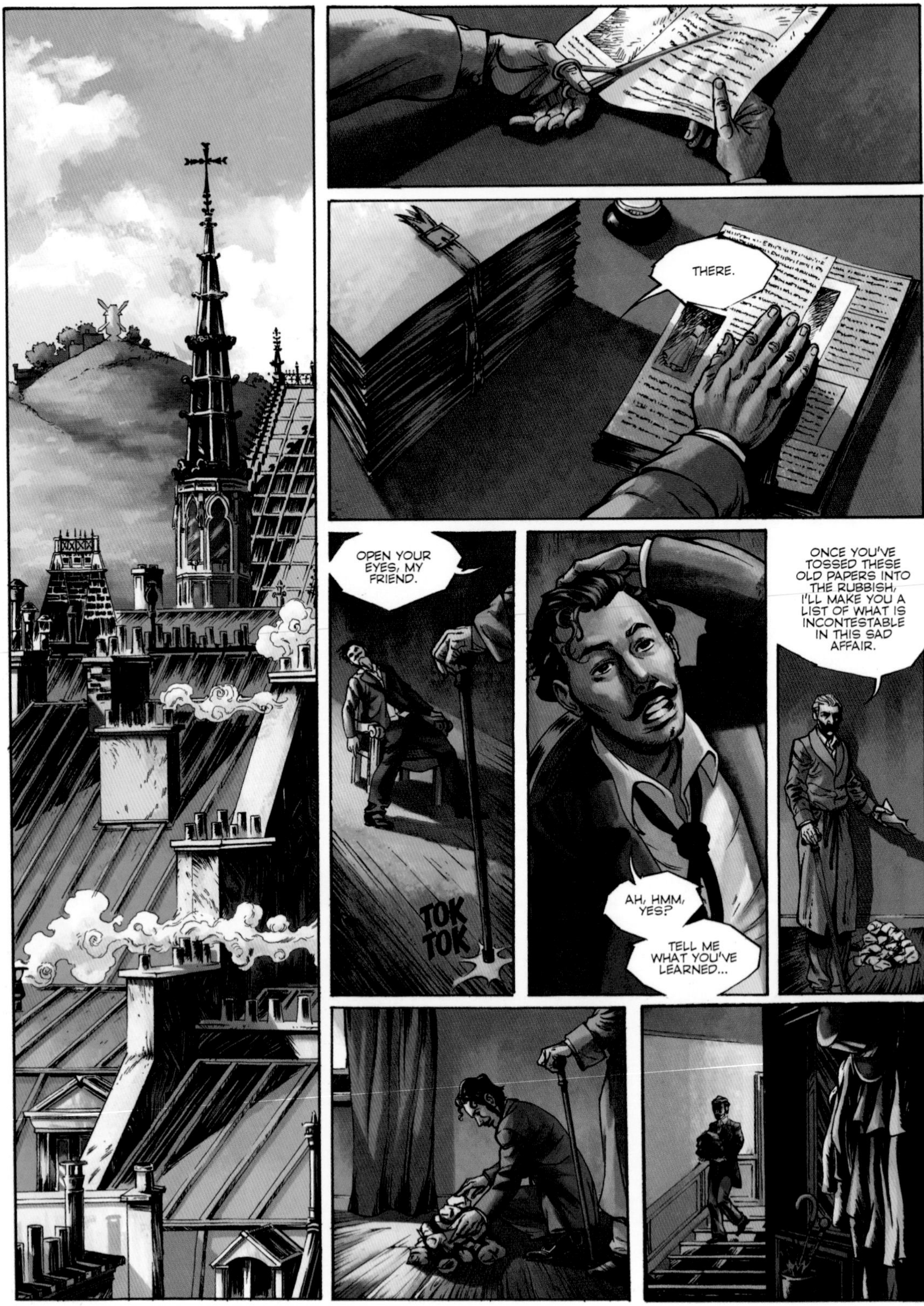
THERE.
OPEN YOUR EYES, MY FRIEND.
TOK TOK
AH, HMM, YES?
TELL ME WHAT YOU'VE LEARNED...
ONCE YOU'VE TOSSED THESE OLD PAPERS INTO THE RUBBISH, I'LL MAKE YOU A LIST OF WHAT IS INCONTESTABLE IN THIS SAD AFFAIR.

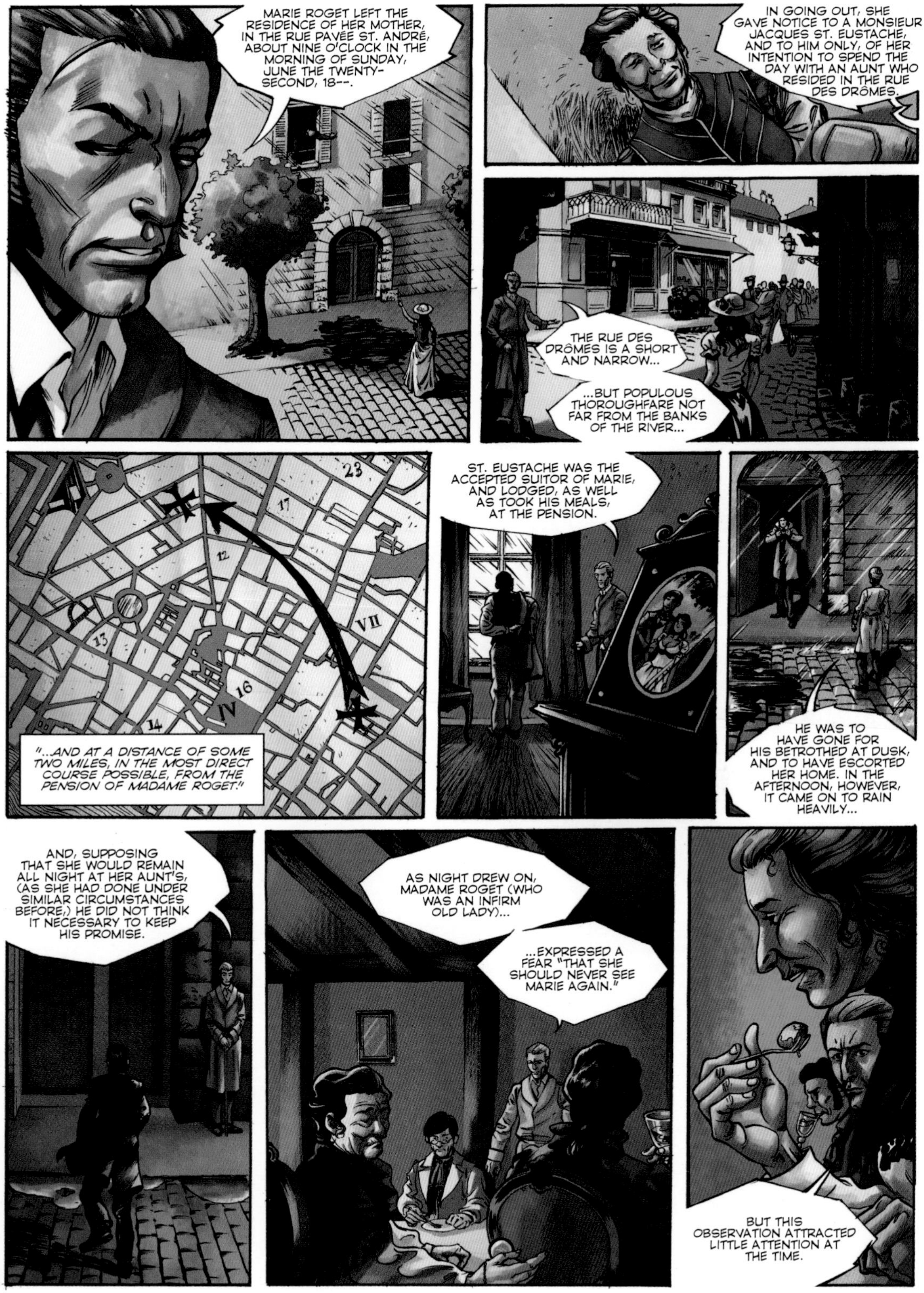

MARIE ROGET LEFT THE RESIDENCE OF HER MOTHER, IN THE RUE PAVÉE ST. ANDRÉ, ABOUT NINE O'CLOCK IN THE MORNING OF SUNDAY, JUNE THE TWENTY-SECOND, 18--.
IN GOING OUT, SHE GAVE NOTICE TO A MONSIEUR JACQUES ST. EUSTACHE, AND TO HIM ONLY, OF HER INTENTION TO SPEND THE DAY WITH AN AUNT WHO RESIDED IN THE RUE DES DRÔMES.
THE RUE DES DRÔMES IS A SHORT AND NARROW...
...BUT POPULOUS THOROUGHFARE NOT FAR FROM THE BANKS OF THE RIVER...
23
17
12
VII
13
16
IV
14
"...AND AT A DISTANCE OF SOME TWO MILES, IN THE MOST DIRECT COURSE POSSIBLE, FROM THE PENSION OF MADAME ROGET."
ST. EUSTACHE WAS THE ACCEPTED SUITOR OF MARIE, AND LODGED, AS WELL AS TOOK HIS MEALS, AT THE PENSION.
HE WAS TO HAVE GONE FOR HIS BETROTHED AT DUSK, AND TO HAVE ESCORTED HER HOME. IN THE AFTERNOON, HOWEVER, IT CAME ON TO RAIN HEAVILY...
AND, SUPPOSING THAT SHE WOULD REMAIN ALL NIGHT AT HER AUNT'S, (AS SHE HAD DONE UNDER SIMILAR CIRCUMSTANCES BEFORE,) HE DID NOT THINK IT NECESSARY TO KEEP HIS PROMISE.
AS NIGHT DREW ON, MADAME ROGET (WHO WAS AN INFIRM OLD LADY)...
...EXPRESSED A FEAR "THAT SHE SHOULD NEVER SEE MARIE AGAIN."
BUT THIS OBSERVATION ATTRACTED LITTLE ATTENTION AT THE TIME.

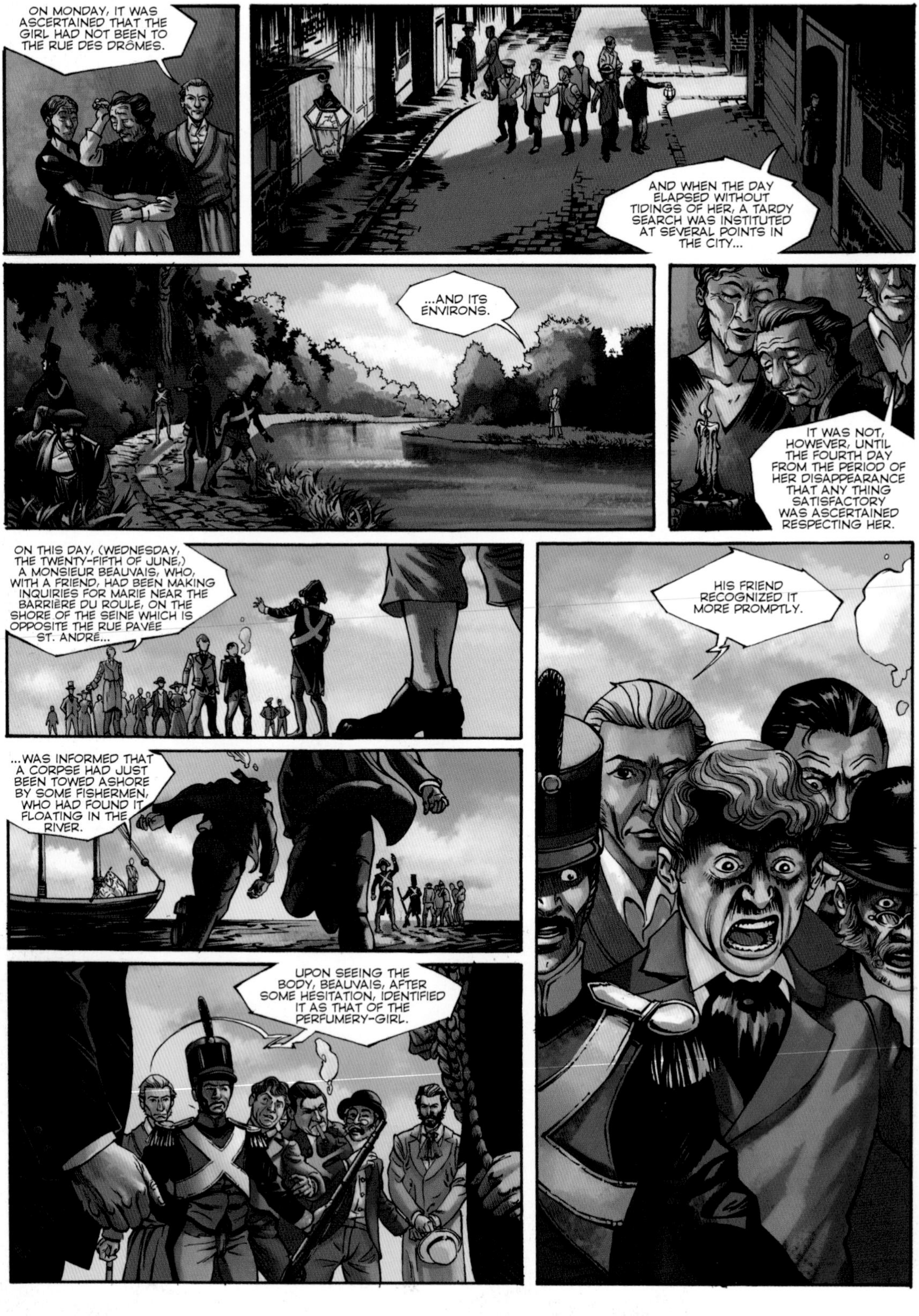

ON MONDAY, IT WAS ASCERTAINED THAT THE GIRL HAD NOT BEEN TO THE RUE DES DRÔMES.
AND WHEN THE DAY ELAPSED WITHOUT TIDINGS OF HER, A TARDY SEARCH WAS INSTITUTED AT SEVERAL POINTS IN THE CITY...
...AND ITS ENVIRONS.
IT WAS NOT, HOWEVER, UNTIL THE FOURTH DAY FROM THE PERIOD OF HER DISAPPEARANCE THAT ANY THING SATISFACTORY WAS ASCERTAINED RESPECTING HER.
ON THIS DAY, (WEDNESDAY, THE TWENTY-FIFTH OF JUNE,) A MONSIEUR BEAUVAIS, WHO, WITH A FRIEND, HAD BEEN MAKING INQUIRIES FOR MARIE NEAR THE BARRIÈRE DU ROULE, ON THE SHORE OF THE SEINE WHICH IS OPPOSITE THE RUE PAVÉE ST. ANDRÉ...
...WAS INFORMED THAT A CORPSE HAD JUST BEEN TOWED ASHORE BY SOME FISHERMEN, WHO HAD FOUND IT FLOATING IN THE RIVER.
UPON SEEING THE BODY, BEAUVAIS, AFTER SOME HESITATION, IDENTIFIED IT AS THAT OF THE PERFUMERY-GIRL.
HIS FRIEND RECOGNIZED IT MORE PROMPTLY.

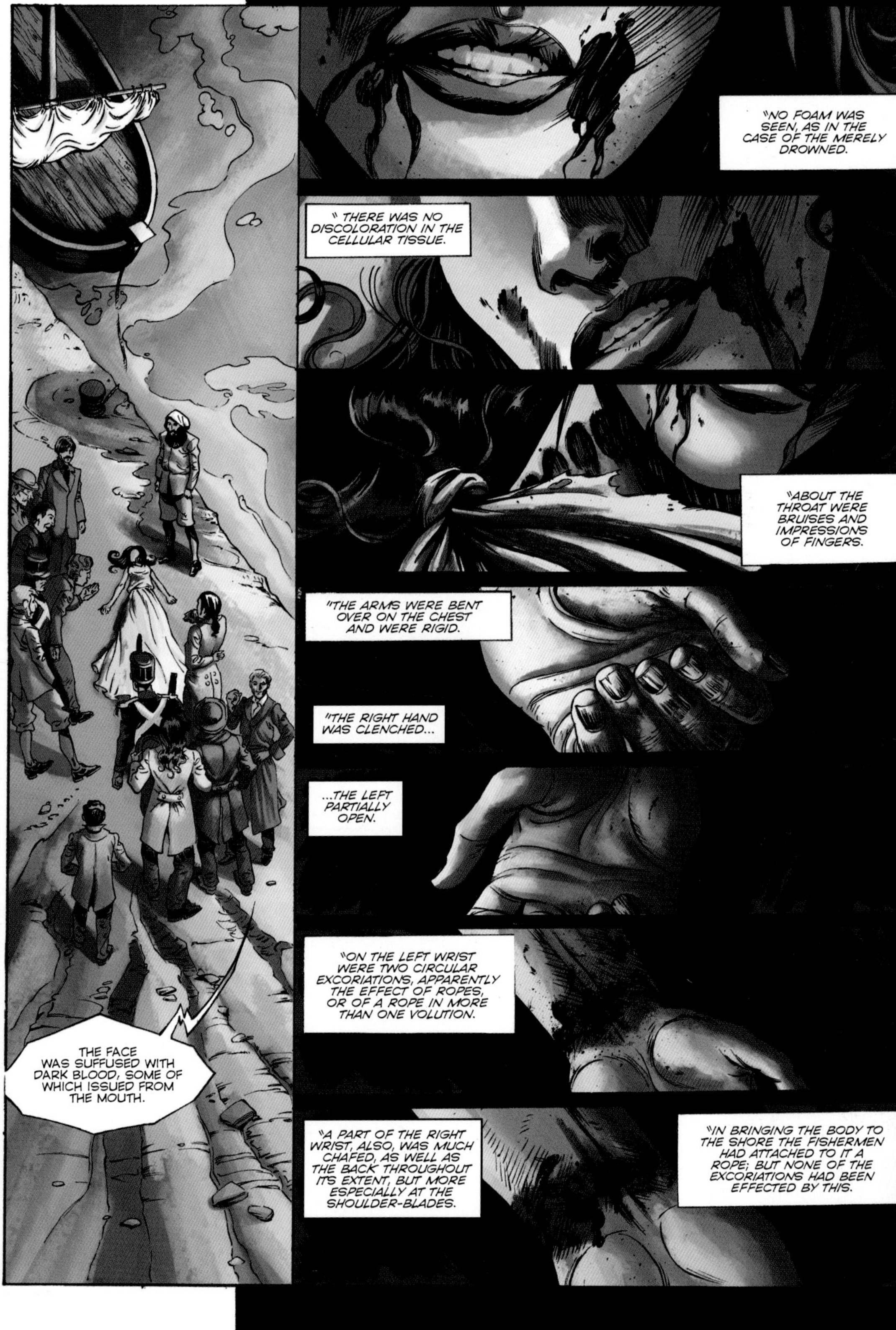
THE FACE WAS SUFFUSED WITH DARK BLOOD, SOME OF WHICH ISSUED FROM THE MOUTH.
"NO FOAM WAS SEEN, AS IN THE CASE OF THE MERELY DROWNED.
" THERE WAS NO DISCOLORATION IN THE CELLULAR TISSUE.
"ABOUT THE THROAT WERE BRUISES AND IMPRESSIONS OF FINGERS.
"THE ARMS WERE BENT OVER ON THE CHEST AND WERE RIGID.
"THE RIGHT HAND WAS CLENCHED...
...THE LEFT PARTIALLY OPEN.
"ON THE LEFT WRIST WERE TWO CIRCULAR EXCORIATIONS, APPARENTLY THE EFFECT OF ROPES, OR OF A ROPE IN MORE THAN ONE VOLUTION.
"A PART OF THE RIGHT WRIST, ALSO, WAS MUCH CHAFED, AS WELL AS THE BACK THROUGHOUT ITS EXTENT, BUT MORE ESPECIALLY AT THE SHOULDER-BLADES.
"IN BRINGING THE BODY TO THE SHORE THE FISHERMEN HAD ATTACHED TO IT A ROPE; BUT NONE OF THE EXCORIATIONS HAD BEEN EFFECTED BY THIS.

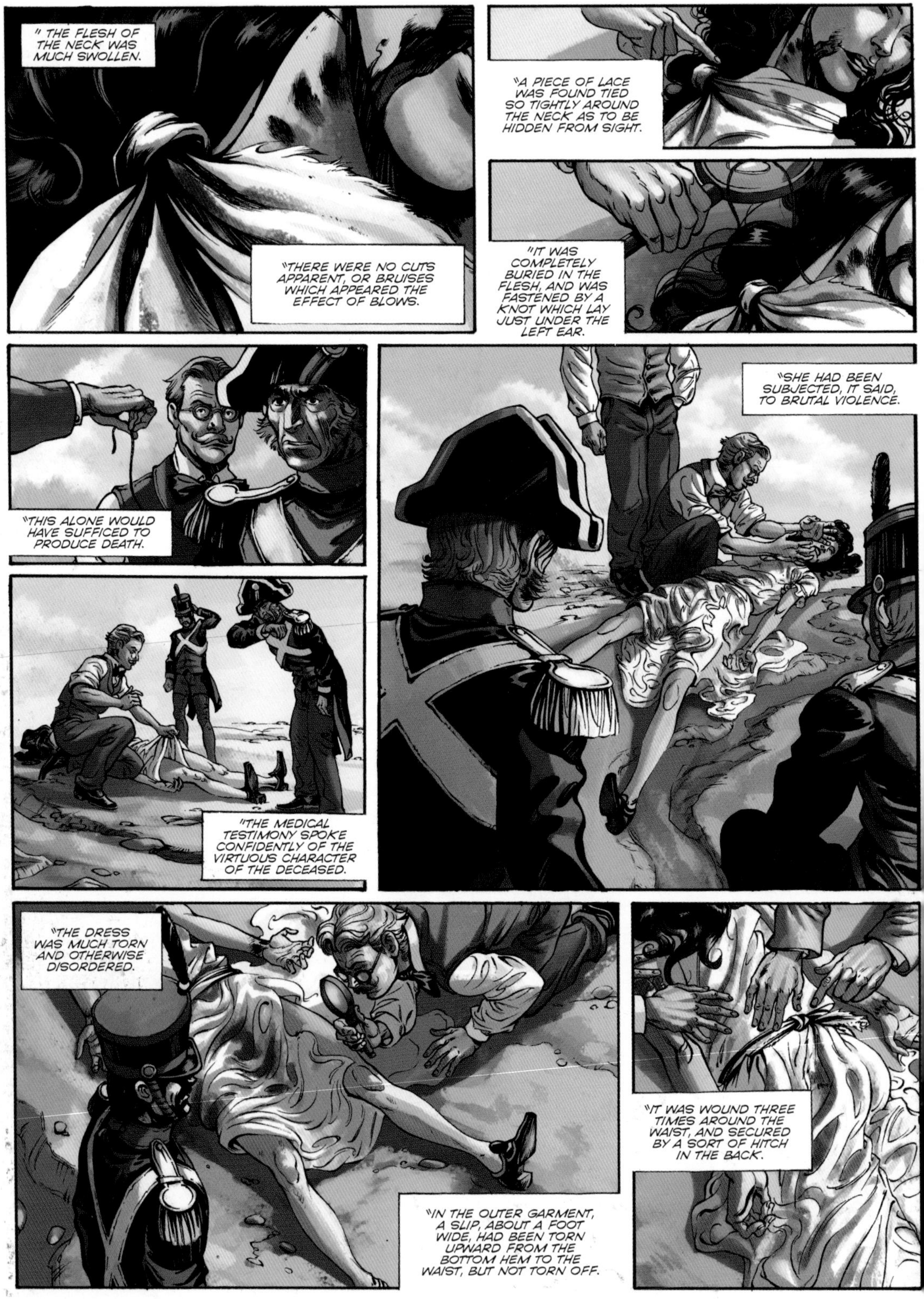
"THE FLESH OF THE NECK WAS MUCH SWOLLEN.
"THERE WERE NO CUTS APPARENT, OR BRUISES WHICH APPEARED THE EFFECT OF BLOWS.
"A PIECE OF LACE WAS FOUND TIED SO TIGHTLY AROUND THE NECK AS TO BE HIDDEN FROM SIGHT.
"IT WAS COMPLETELY BURIED IN THE FLESH, AND WAS FASTENED BY A KNOT WHICH LAY JUST UNDER THE LEFT EAR.
"THIS ALONE WOULD HAVE SUFFICED TO PRODUCE DEATH.
"THE MEDICAL TESTIMONY SPOKE CONFIDENTLY OF THE VIRTUOUS CHARACTER OF THE DECEASED.
"SHE HAD BEEN SUBJECTED, IT SAID, TO BRUTAL VIOLENCE.
"THE DRESS WAS MUCH TORN AND OTHERWISE DISORDERED.
"IN THE OUTER GARMENT, A SLIP, ABOUT A FOOT WIDE, HAD BEEN TORN UPWARD FROM THE BOTTOM HEM TO THE WAIST, BUT NOT TORN OFF.
"IT WAS WOUND THREE TIMES AROUND THE WAIST, AND SECURED BY A SORT OF HITCH IN THE BACK.

"IT WAS FOUND AROUND HER NECK, FITTING LOOSELY, AND SECURED WITH A HARD KNOT.

"THE KNOT BY WHICH THE STRINGS OF THE BONNET WERE FASTENED, WAS NOT A LADY'S, BUT A SLIP OR SAILOR'S KNOT.

"THE DRESS IMMEDIATELY BENEATH THE FROCK WAS OF FINE MUSLIN; AND FROM THIS A SLIP EIGHTEEN INCHES WIDE HAD BEEN TORN ENTIRELY OUT-- TORN VERY EVENLY AND WITH GREAT CARE.

"OVER THIS MUSLIN SLIP AND THE SLIP OF LACE, THE STRINGS OF A BONNET WERE ATTACHED; THE BONNET BEING APPENDED.

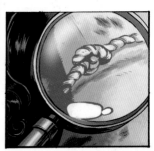

"AFTER THE RECOGNITION OF THE CORPSE, IT WAS NOT, AS USUAL, TAKEN TO THE MORGUE, (THIS FORMALITY BEING SUPERFLUOUS,) BUT HASTILY INTERRED NOT FAR FROM THE SPOT AT WHICH IT WAS BROUGHT ASHORE.

"MEANTIME, THE EXCITEMENT INCREASED HOURLY.

"A WEEKLY PAPER, HOWEVER, AT LENGTH TOOK UP THE THEME.

"THROUGH THE EXERTIONS OF BEAUVAIS, THE MATTER WAS INDUSTRIOUSLY HUSHED UP, AS FAR AS POSSIBLE; AND SEVERAL DAYS HAD ELAPSED BEFORE ANY PUBLIC EMOTION RESULTED.

"THE CORPSE WAS DISINTERRED, AND A RE-EXAMINATION INSTITUTED; BUT NOTHING WAS ELICITED BEYOND WHAT HAS BEEN ALREADY NOTED.

"THE CLOTHES, HOWEVER, WERE NOW SUBMITTED TO THE MOTHER AND FRIENDS OF THE DECEASED, AND FULLY IDENTIFIED AS THOSE WORN BY THE GIRL UPON LEAVING HOME.

"SEVERAL INDIVIDUALS WERE ARRESTED AND DISCHARGED. ST. EUSTACHE FELL ESPECIALLY UNDER SUSPICION; AND HE FAILED, AT FIRST, TO GIVE AN INTELLIGIBLE ACCOUNT OF HIS WHEREABOUTS DURING THE SUNDAY ON WHICH MARIE LEFT HOME."

"SUBSEQUENTLY, HOWEVER, HE SUBMITTED TO MONSIEUR G--, AFFIDAVITS, ACCOUNTING SATISFACTORILY FOR EVERY HOUR OF THE DAY IN QUESTION."

AS TIME PASSED AND NO DISCOVERY ENSUED, A THOUSAND CONTRADICTORY RUMORS WERE CIRCULATED, AND JOURNALISTS BUSIED THEMSELVES IN SUGGESTIONS. AMONG THESE, THE ONE WHICH ATTRACTED THE MOST NOTICE...

...WAS THE IDEA THAT MARIE ROGÊT STILL LIVED--THAT THE CORPSE FOUND IN THE SEINE WAS THAT OF SOME OTHER UNFORTUNATE.

THESE PASSAGES ARE LITERAL CITATIONS FROM L'ÉTOILE, A PAPER CONDUCTED, IN GENERAL, WITH MUCH ABILITY.

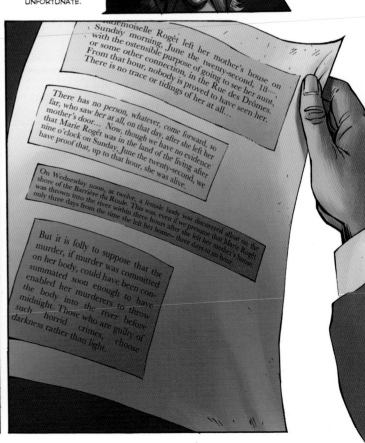

Mademoiselle Rogêt left her mother's house on Sunday morning, June the twenty-second, 18--, with the ostensible purpose of going to see her aunt, or some other connection, in the Rue des Drômes. From that hour, nobody is proved to have seen her. There is no trace or tidings of her at all...

There has no person, whatever, come forward, so far, who saw her at all, on that day, after she left her mother's door... Now, though we have no evidence that Marie Rogêt was in the land of the living after nine o'clock on Sunday, June the twenty-second, we have proof that, up to that hour, she was alive.

On Wednesday noon, at twelve, a female body was discovered afloat on the shore of the Barrière du Roule. This was, even if we presume that Marie Rogêt was thrown into the river within three hours after she left her mother's house, only three days from the time she left her home--three days to an hour.

But it is folly to suppose that the murder, if murder was committed on her body, could have been consummated soon enough to have enabled her murderers to throw the body into the river before midnight. Those who are guilty of such horrid crimes, choose darkness rather than light.

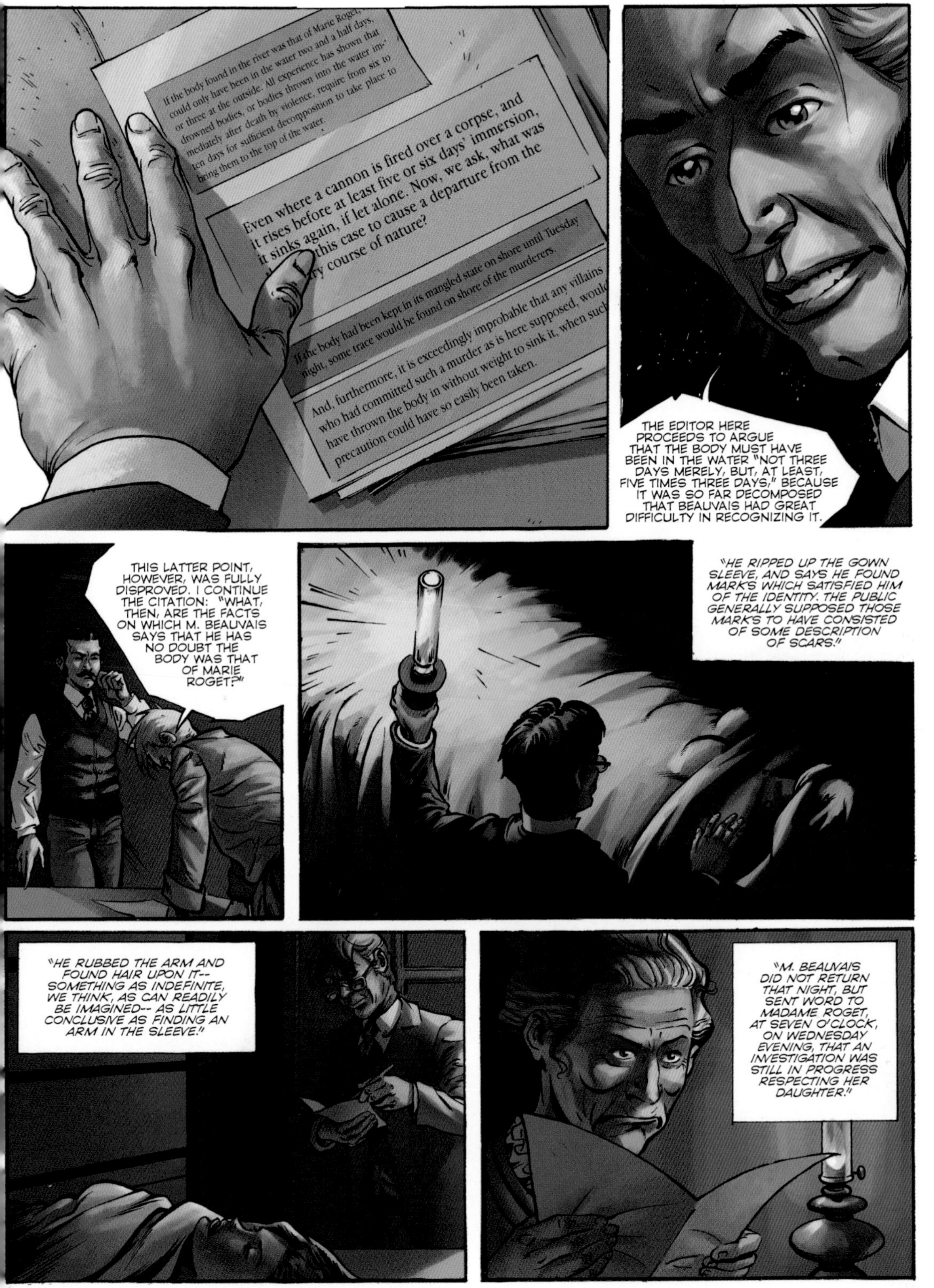
If the body found in the river was that of Marie Roget, could only have been in the water two and a half days, or three at the outside. All experience has shown that drowned bodies, or bodies thrown into the water immediately after death by violence, require from six to ten days for sufficient decomposition to take place to bring them to the top of the water.
Even where a cannon is fired over a corpse, and it rises before at least five or six days' immersion, it sinks again, if let alone. Now, we ask, what was
this case to cause a departure from the
course of nature?
If the body had been kept in its mangled state on shore until Tuesday night, some trace would be found on shore of the murderers.
And, furthermore, it is exceedingly improbable that any villains who had committed such a murder as is here supposed, would have thrown the body in without weight to sink it, when such precaution could have so easily been taken.
THE EDITOR HERE PROCEEDS TO ARGUE THAT THE BODY MUST HAVE BEEN IN THE WATER "NOT THREE DAYS MERELY, BUT, AT LEAST, FIVE TIMES THREE DAYS," BECAUSE IT WAS SO FAR DECOMPOSED THAT BEAUVAIS HAD GREAT DIFFICULTY IN RECOGNIZING IT.
THIS LATTER POINT, HOWEVER, WAS FULLY DISPROVED. I CONTINUE THE CITATION: "WHAT, THEN, ARE THE FACTS ON WHICH M. BEAUVAIS SAYS THAT HE HAS NO DOUBT THE BODY WAS THAT OF MARIE ROGET?"
"HE RIPPED UP THE GOWN SLEEVE, AND SAYS HE FOUND MARKS WHICH SATISFIED HIM OF THE IDENTITY. THE PUBLIC GENERALLY SUPPOSED THOSE MARKS TO HAVE CONSISTED OF SOME DESCRIPTION OF SCARS."
"HE RUBBED THE ARM AND FOUND HAIR UPON IT-- SOMETHING AS INDEFINITE, WE THINK, AS CAN READILY BE IMAGINED-- AS LITTLE CONCLUSIVE AS FINDING AN ARM IN THE SLEEVE."
"M. BEAUVAIS DID NOT RETURN THAT NIGHT, BUT SENT WORD TO MADAME ROGET, AT SEVEN O'CLOCK, ON WEDNESDAY EVENING, THAT AN INVESTIGATION WAS STILL IN PROGRESS RESPECTING HER DAUGHTER."

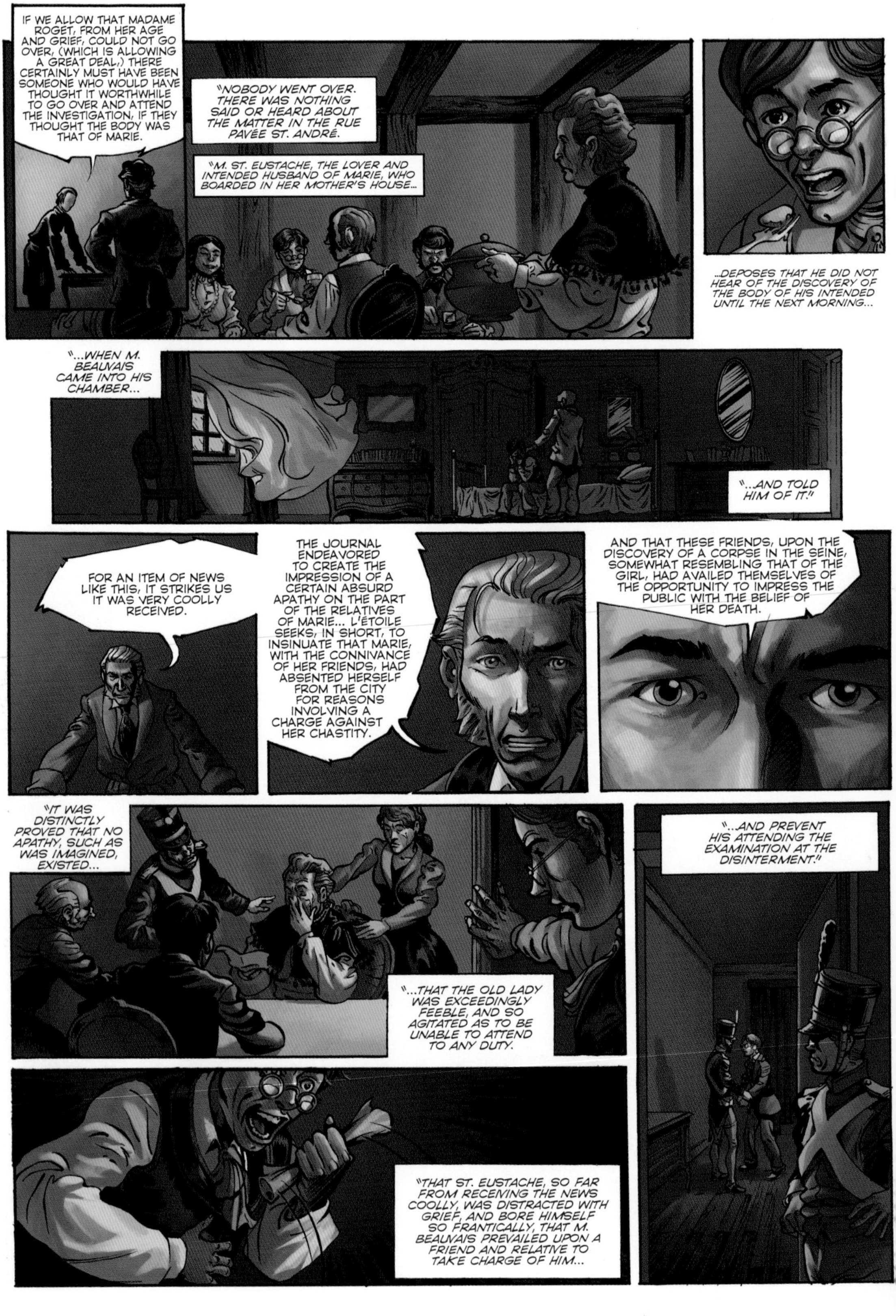

IF WE ALLOW THAT MADAME ROGET, FROM HER AGE AND GRIEF, COULD NOT GO OVER, (WHICH IS ALLOWING A GREAT DEAL,) THERE CERTAINLY MUST HAVE BEEN SOMEONE WHO WOULD HAVE THOUGHT IT WORTHWHILE TO GO OVER AND ATTEND THE INVESTIGATION, IF THEY THOUGHT THE BODY WAS THAT OF MARIE.
"NOBODY WENT OVER. THERE WAS NOTHING SAID OR HEARD ABOUT THE MATTER IN THE RUE PAVÉE ST. ANDRÉ.
"M. ST. EUSTACHE, THE LOVER AND INTENDED HUSBAND OF MARIE, WHO BOARDED IN HER MOTHER'S HOUSE...
...DEPOSES THAT HE DID NOT HEAR OF THE DISCOVERY OF THE BODY OF HIS INTENDED UNTIL THE NEXT MORNING...
"...WHEN M. BEAUVAIS CAME INTO HIS CHAMBER...
"...AND TOLD HIM OF IT."
FOR AN ITEM OF NEWS LIKE THIS, IT STRIKES US IT WAS VERY COOLLY RECEIVED.
THE JOURNAL ENDEAVORED TO CREATE THE IMPRESSION OF A CERTAIN ABSURD APATHY ON THE PART OF THE RELATIVES OF MARIE... L'ÉTOILE SEEKS, IN SHORT, TO INSINUATE THAT MARIE, WITH THE CONNIVANCE OF HER FRIENDS, HAD ABSENTED HERSELF FROM THE CITY FOR REASONS INVOLVING A CHARGE AGAINST HER CHASTITY.
AND THAT THESE FRIENDS, UPON THE DISCOVERY OF A CORPSE IN THE SEINE, SOMEWHAT RESEMBLING THAT OF THE GIRL, HAD AVAILED THEMSELVES OF THE OPPORTUNITY TO IMPRESS THE PUBLIC WITH THE BELIEF OF HER DEATH.
"IT WAS DISTINCTLY PROVED THAT NO APATHY, SUCH AS WAS IMAGINED, EXISTED...
"...THAT THE OLD LADY WAS EXCEEDINGLY FEEBLE, AND SO AGITATED AS TO BE UNABLE TO ATTEND TO ANY DUTY.
"THAT ST. EUSTACHE, SO FAR FROM RECEIVING THE NEWS COOLLY, WAS DISTRACTED WITH GRIEF, AND BORE HIMSELF SO FRANTICALLY, THAT M. BEAUVAIS PREVAILED UPON A FRIEND AND RELATIVE TO TAKE CHARGE OF HIM...
"...AND PREVENT HIS ATTENDING THE EXAMINATION AT THE DISINTERMENT."

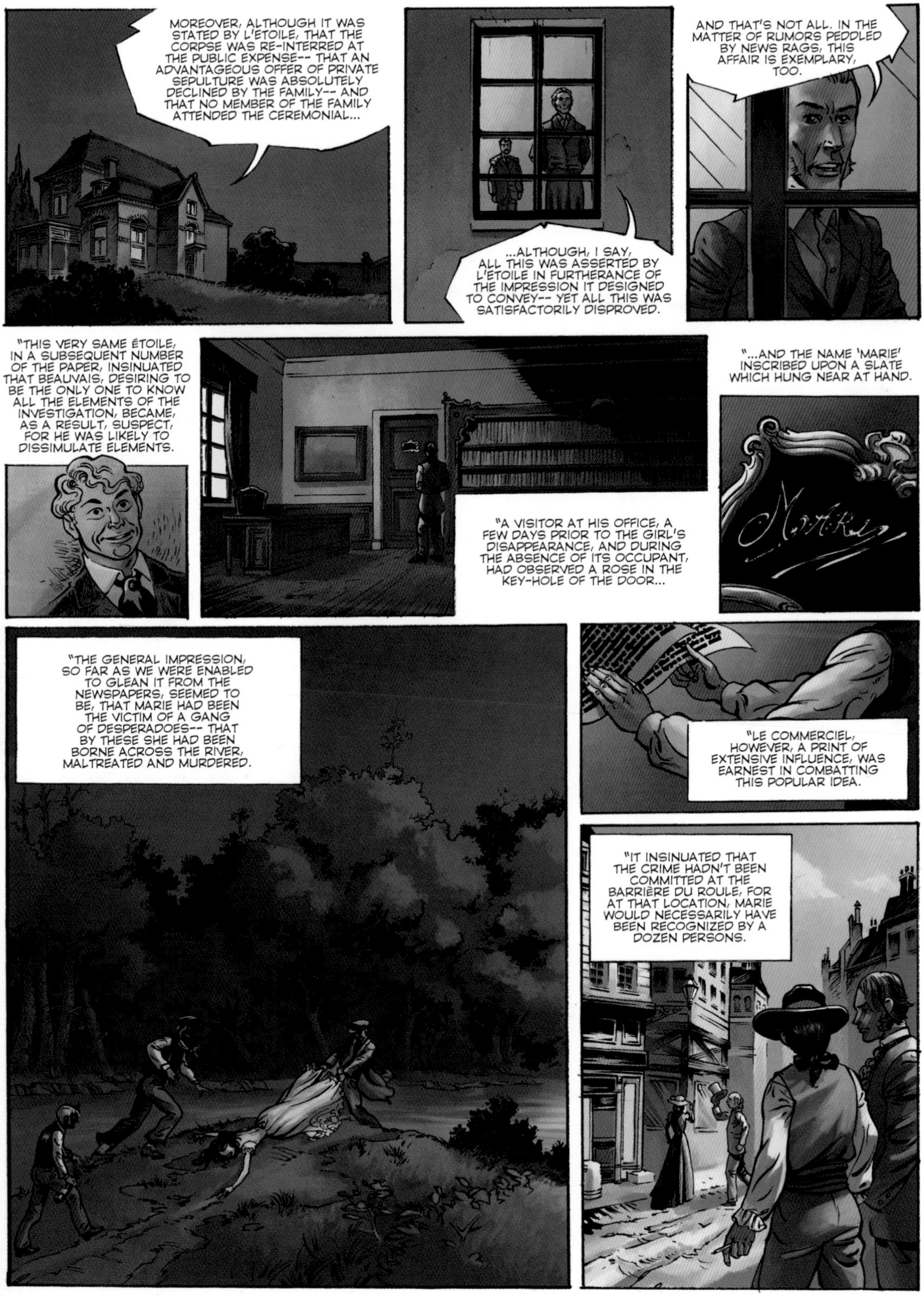

MOREOVER, ALTHOUGH IT WAS STATED BY L'ETOILE, THAT THE CORPSE WAS RE-INTERRED AT THE PUBLIC EXPENSE-- THAT AN ADVANTAGEOUS OFFER OF PRIVATE SEPULTURE WAS ABSOLUTELY DECLINED BY THE FAMILY-- AND THAT NO MEMBER OF THE FAMILY ATTENDED THE CEREMONIAL...
...ALTHOUGH, I SAY, ALL THIS WAS ASSERTED BY L'ETOILE IN FURTHERANCE OF THE IMPRESSION IT DESIGNED TO CONVEY-- YET ALL THIS WAS SATISFACTORILY DISPROVED.
AND THAT'S NOT ALL. IN THE MATTER OF RUMORS PEDDLED BY NEWS RAGS, THIS AFFAIR IS EXEMPLARY, TOO.
"THIS VERY SAME ÉTOILE, IN A SUBSEQUENT NUMBER OF THE PAPER, INSINUATED THAT BEAUVAIS, DESIRING TO BE THE ONLY ONE TO KNOW ALL THE ELEMENTS OF THE INVESTIGATION, BECAME, AS A RESULT, SUSPECT, FOR HE WAS LIKELY TO DISSIMULATE ELEMENTS.
"A VISITOR AT HIS OFFICE, A FEW DAYS PRIOR TO THE GIRL'S DISAPPEARANCE, AND DURING THE ABSENCE OF ITS OCCUPANT, HAD OBSERVED A ROSE IN THE KEY-HOLE OF THE DOOR...
"...AND THE NAME 'MARIE' INSCRIBED UPON A SLATE WHICH HUNG NEAR AT HAND.
"THE GENERAL IMPRESSION, SO FAR AS WE WERE ENABLED TO GLEAN IT FROM THE NEWSPAPERS, SEEMED TO BE, THAT MARIE HAD BEEN THE VICTIM OF A GANG OF DESPERADOES-- THAT BY THESE SHE HAD BEEN BORNE ACROSS THE RIVER, MALTREATED AND MURDERED.
"LE COMMERCIEL, HOWEVER, A PRINT OF EXTENSIVE INFLUENCE, WAS EARNEST IN COMBATTING THIS POPULAR IDEA.
"IT INSINUATED THAT THE CRIME HADN'T BEEN COMMITTED AT THE BARRIÈRE DU ROULE, FOR AT THAT LOCATION, MARIE WOULD NECESSARILY HAVE BEEN RECOGNIZED BY A DOZEN PERSONS.

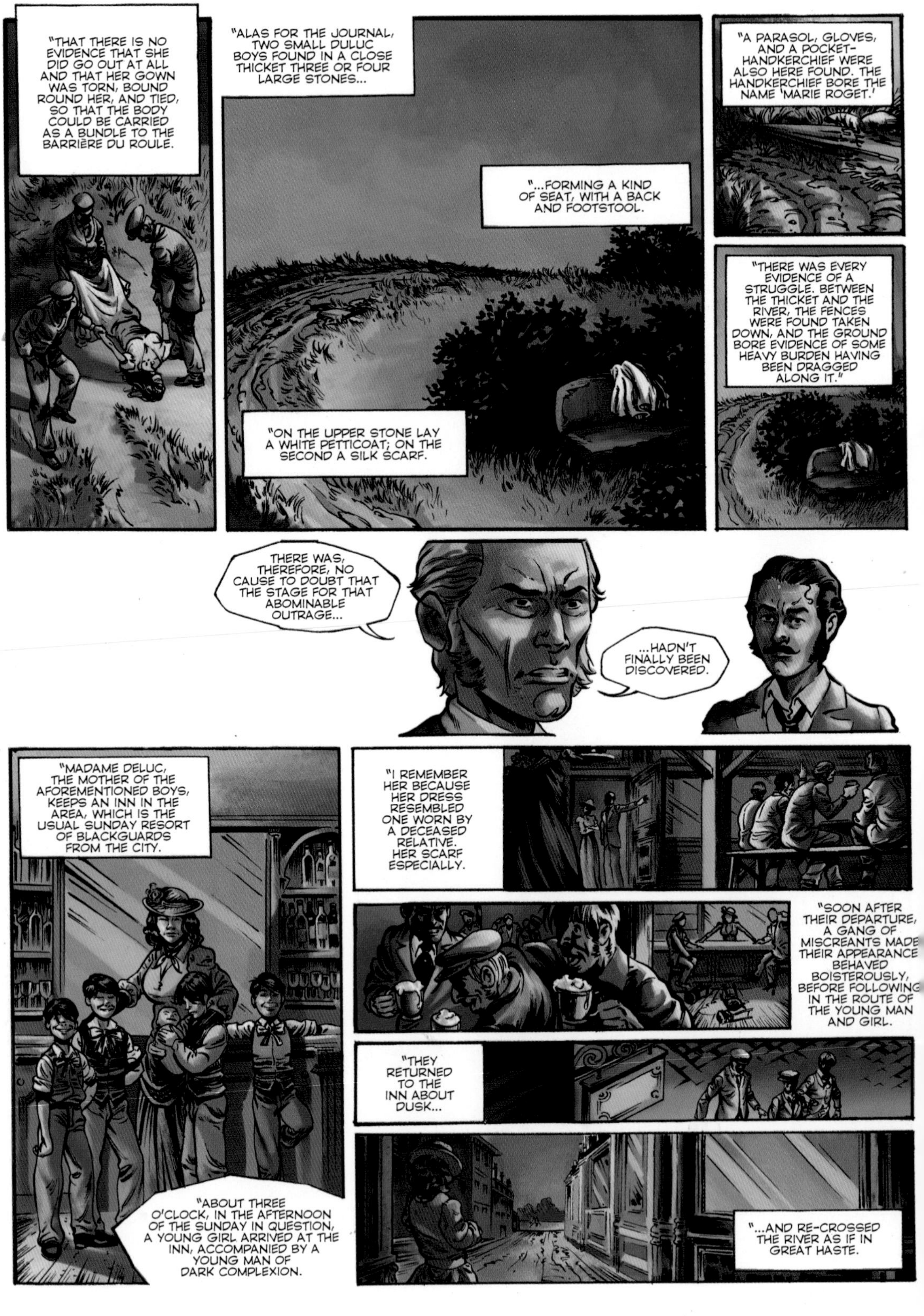
"THAT THERE IS NO EVIDENCE THAT SHE DID GO OUT AT ALL AND THAT HER GOWN WAS TORN, BOUND ROUND HER, AND TIED, SO THAT THE BODY COULD BE CARRIED AS A BUNDLE TO THE BARRIÈRE DU ROULE.
"ALAS FOR THE JOURNAL, TWO SMALL DULUC BOYS FOUND IN A CLOSE THICKET THREE OR FOUR LARGE STONES...
"...FORMING A KIND OF SEAT, WITH A BACK AND FOOTSTOOL.
"ON THE UPPER STONE LAY A WHITE PETTICOAT; ON THE SECOND A SILK SCARF.
"A PARASOL, GLOVES, AND A POCKET-HANDKERCHIEF WERE ALSO HERE FOUND. THE HANDKERCHIEF BORE THE NAME 'MARIE ROGET.'
"THERE WAS EVERY EVIDENCE OF A STRUGGLE. BETWEEN THE THICKET AND THE RIVER, THE FENCES WERE FOUND TAKEN DOWN, AND THE GROUND BORE EVIDENCE OF SOME HEAVY BURDEN HAVING BEEN DRAGGED ALONG IT."
THERE WAS, THEREFORE, NO CAUSE TO DOUBT THAT THE STAGE FOR THAT ABOMINABLE OUTRAGE...
...HADN'T FINALLY BEEN DISCOVERED.
"MADAME DELUC, THE MOTHER OF THE AFOREMENTIONED BOYS, KEEPS AN INN IN THE AREA, WHICH IS THE USUAL SUNDAY RESORT OF BLACKGUARDS FROM THE CITY.
"ABOUT THREE O'CLOCK, IN THE AFTERNOON OF THE SUNDAY IN QUESTION, A YOUNG GIRL ARRIVED AT THE INN, ACCOMPANIED BY A YOUNG MAN OF DARK COMPLEXION.
"I REMEMBER HER BECAUSE HER DRESS RESEMBLED ONE WORN BY A DECEASED RELATIVE. HER SCARF ESPECIALLY.
"SOON AFTER THEIR DEPARTURE, A GANG OF MISCREANTS MADE THEIR APPEARANCE BEHAVED BOISTEROUSLY, BEFORE FOLLOWING IN THE ROUTE OF THE YOUNG MAN AND GIRL.
"THEY RETURNED TO THE INN ABOUT DUSK...
"...AND RE-CROSSED THE RIVER AS IF IN GREAT HASTE.

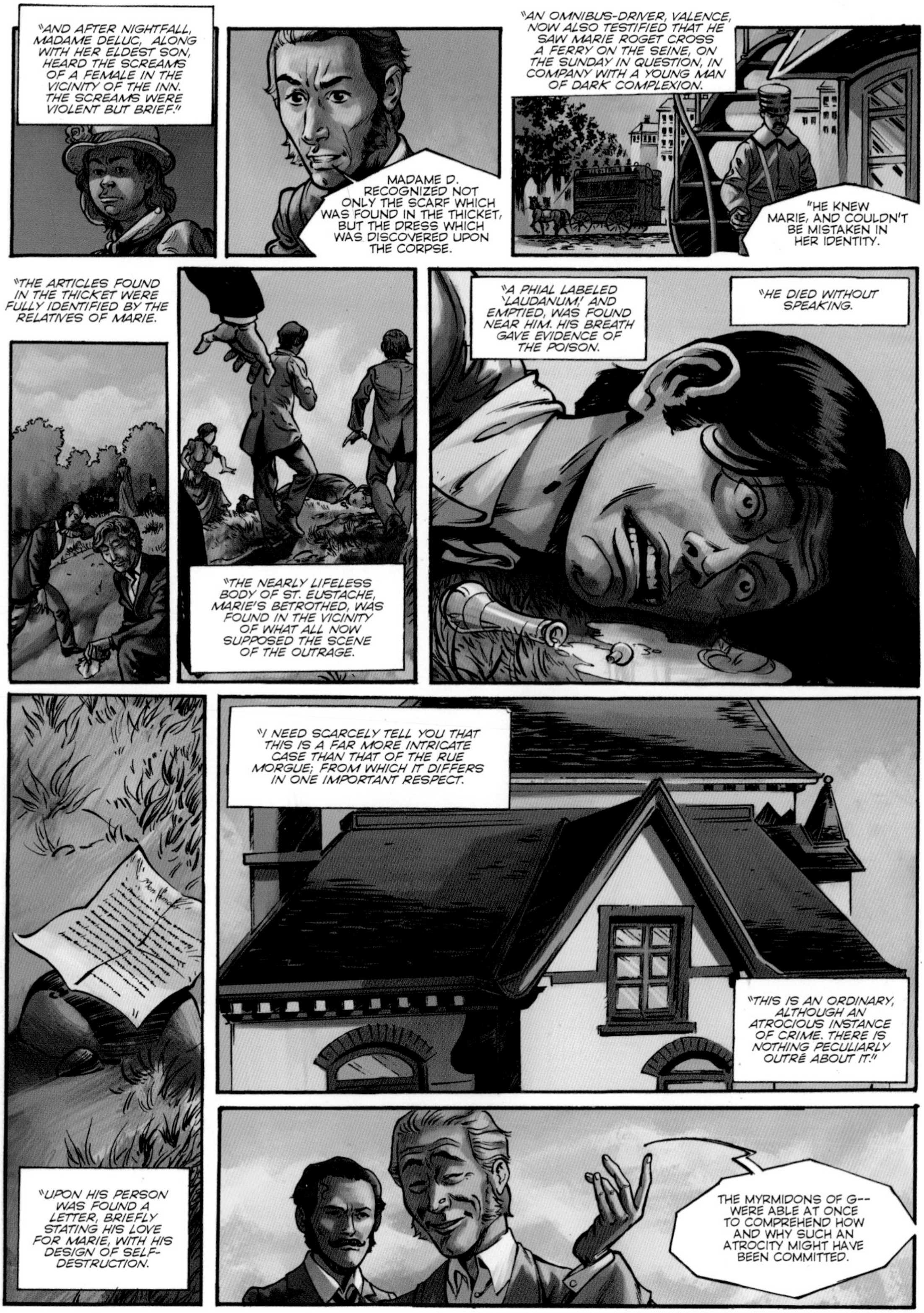
"AND AFTER NIGHTFALL, MADAME DELUC, ALONG WITH HER ELDEST SON, HEARD THE SCREAMS OF A FEMALE IN THE VICINITY OF THE INN. THE SCREAMS WERE VIOLENT BUT BRIEF."
MADAME D. RECOGNIZED NOT ONLY THE SCARF WHICH WAS FOUND IN THE THICKET, BUT THE DRESS WHICH WAS DISCOVERED UPON THE CORPSE.
"AN OMNIBUS-DRIVER, VALENCE, NOW ALSO TESTIFIED THAT HE SAW MARIE ROGET CROSS A FERRY ON THE SEINE, ON THE SUNDAY IN QUESTION, IN COMPANY WITH A YOUNG MAN OF DARK COMPLEXION.
"HE KNEW MARIE, AND COULDN'T BE MISTAKEN IN HER IDENTITY.
"THE ARTICLES FOUND IN THE THICKET WERE FULLY IDENTIFIED BY THE RELATIVES OF MARIE.
"THE NEARLY LIFELESS BODY OF ST. EUSTACHE, MARIE'S BETROTHED, WAS FOUND IN THE VICINITY OF WHAT ALL NOW SUPPOSED THE SCENE OF THE OUTRAGE.
"A PHIAL LABELED 'LAUDANUM,' AND EMPTIED, WAS FOUND NEAR HIM. HIS BREATH GAVE EVIDENCE OF THE POISON.
"HE DIED WITHOUT SPEAKING.
"UPON HIS PERSON WAS FOUND A LETTER, BRIEFLY STATING HIS LOVE FOR MARIE, WITH HIS DESIGN OF SELF-DESTRUCTION.
"I NEED SCARCELY TELL YOU THAT THIS IS A FAR MORE INTRICATE CASE THAN THAT OF THE RUE MORGUE; FROM WHICH IT DIFFERS IN ONE IMPORTANT RESPECT.
"THIS IS AN ORDINARY, ALTHOUGH AN ATROCIOUS INSTANCE OF CRIME. THERE IS NOTHING PECULIARLY OUTRÉ ABOUT IT."
THE MYRMIDONS OF G-- WERE ABLE AT ONCE TO COMPREHEND HOW AND WHY SUCH AN ATROCITY MIGHT HAVE BEEN COMMITTED.

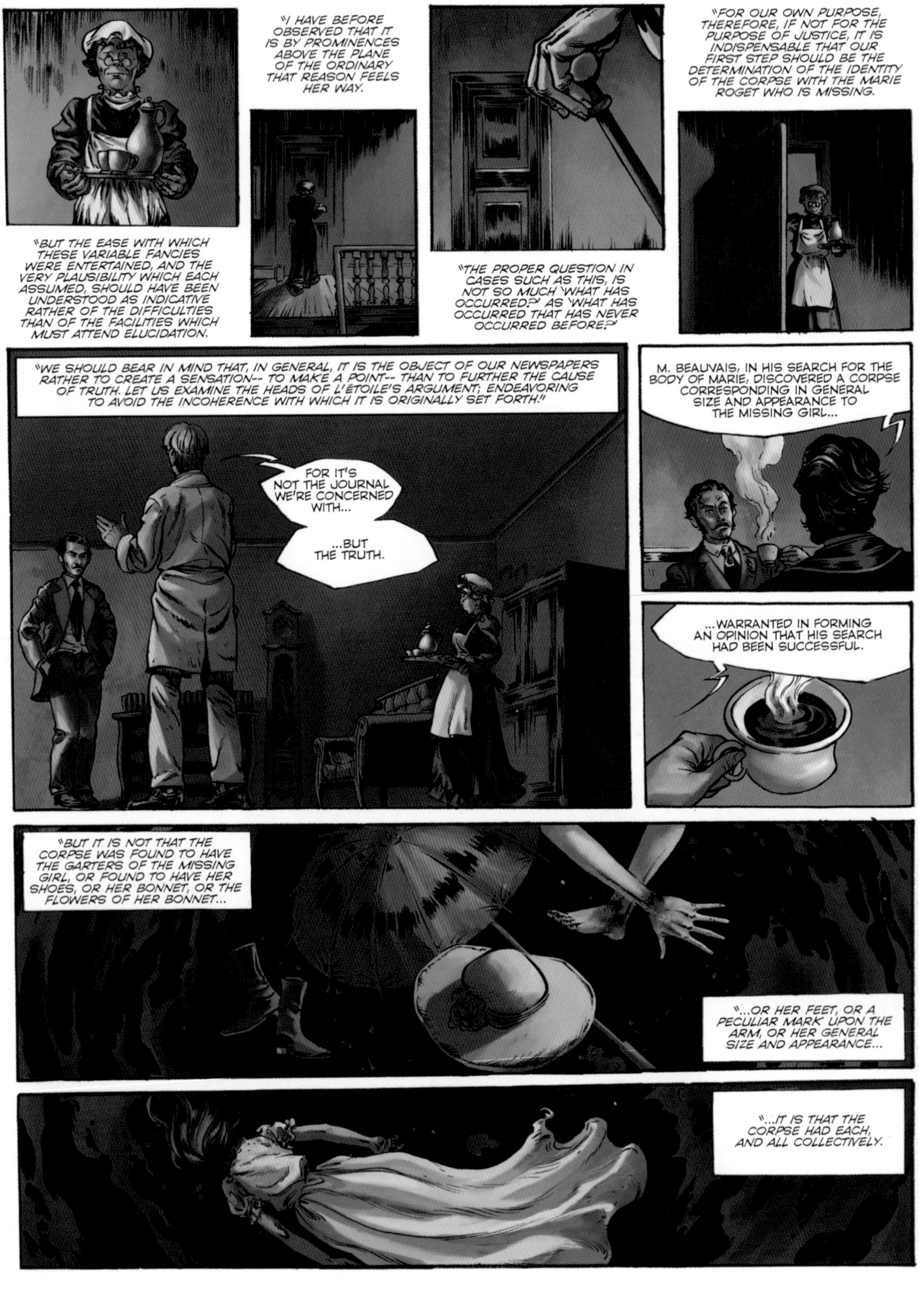
"I HAVE BEFORE OBSERVED THAT IT IS BY PROMINENCES ABOVE THE PLANE OF THE ORDINARY THAT REASON FEELS HER WAY.
"BUT THE EASE WITH WHICH THESE VARIABLE FANCIES WERE ENTERTAINED, AND THE VERY PLAUSIBILITY WHICH EACH ASSUMED, SHOULD HAVE BEEN UNDERSTOOD AS INDICATIVE RATHER OF THE DIFFICULTIES THAN OF THE FACILITIES WHICH MUST ATTEND ELUCIDATION.
"THE PROPER QUESTION IN CASES SUCH AS THIS, IS NOT SO MUCH 'WHAT HAS OCCURRED?' AS 'WHAT HAS OCCURRED THAT HAS NEVER OCCURRED BEFORE?'
"FOR OUR OWN PURPOSE, THEREFORE, IF NOT FOR THE PURPOSE OF JUSTICE, IT IS INDISPENSABLE THAT OUR FIRST STEP SHOULD BE THE DETERMINATION OF THE IDENTITY OF THE CORPSE WITH THE MARIE ROGET WHO IS MISSING.
"WE SHOULD BEAR IN MIND THAT, IN GENERAL, IT IS THE OBJECT OF OUR NEWSPAPERS RATHER TO CREATE A SENSATION-- TO MAKE A POINT-- THAN TO FURTHER THE CAUSE OF TRUTH. LET US EXAMINE THE HEADS OF L'ÉTOILE'S ARGUMENT; ENDEAVORING TO AVOID THE INCOHERENCE WITH WHICH IT IS ORIGINALLY SET FORTH."
FOR IT'S NOT THE JOURNAL WE'RE CONCERNED WITH...
...BUT THE TRUTH.
M. BEAUVAIS, IN HIS SEARCH FOR THE BODY OF MARIE, DISCOVERED A CORPSE CORRESPONDING IN GENERAL SIZE AND APPEARANCE TO THE MISSING GIRL...
...WARRANTED IN FORMING AN OPINION THAT HIS SEARCH HAD BEEN SUCCESSFUL.
"BUT IT IS NOT THAT THE CORPSE WAS FOUND TO HAVE THE GARTERS OF THE MISSING GIRL, OR FOUND TO HAVE HER SHOES, OR HER BONNET, OR THE FLOWERS OF HER BONNET...
"...OR HER FEET, OR A PECULIAR MARK UPON THE ARM, OR HER GENERAL SIZE AND APPEARANCE...
"...IT IS THAT THE CORPSE HAD EACH, AND ALL COLLECTIVELY.

"HE IS A BUSY-BODY, WITH MUCH OF ROMANCE AND LITTLE OF WIT. ANY ONE SO CONSTITUTED WILL READILY SO CONDUCT HIMSELF, UPON OCCASION OF REAL EXCITEMENT, AS TO RENDER HIMSELF LIABLE TO SUSPICION ON THE PART OF THE OVER-ACUTE, OR THE ILL-DISPOSED.

"I WOULD RESPOND TO THE EDITOR OF L'ÉTOILE THAT NOTHING IS MORE VAGUE THAN IMPRESSIONS OF INDIVIDUAL IDENTITY. EACH MAN RECOGNIZES HIS NEIGHBOR, YET THERE ARE FEW INSTANCES IN WHICH ANY ONE IS PREPARED TO GIVE A REASON FOR HIS RECOGNITION.

"IN RESPECT TO THE INSINUATIONS LEVELED AT BEAUVAIS, YOU WILL BE WILLING TO DISMISS THEM IN A BREATH. YOU HAVE ALREADY FATHOMED THE TRUE CHARACTER OF THIS GOOD GENTLEMAN.

"HE PERSISTS,' SAYS THE PAPER, 'IN ASSERTING THE CORPSE TO BE THAT OF MARIE, BUT CANNOT GIVE A CIRCUMSTANCE, IN ADDITION TO THOSE WHICH WE HAVE COMMENTED UPON, TO MAKE OTHERS BELIEVE.'

"THE SUSPICIOUS CIRCUMSTANCES WHICH INVEST HIM, WILL BE FOUND TO TALLY MUCH BETTER WITH MY HYPOTHESIS OF ROMANTIC BUSY-BODYISM...

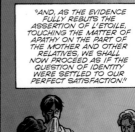

"...THAN WITH THE REASONER'S SUGGESTION OF GUILT.

"WE SHALL FIND NO DIFFICULTY IN COMPREHENDING THE ROSE IN THE KEY-HOLE; THE 'MARIE' UPON THE SLATE; THE 'ELBOWING THE MALE RELATIVES OUT OF THE WAY;' THE 'AVERSION TO PERMITTING THEM TO SEE THE BODY...'

"AND, AS THE EVIDENCE FULLY REBUTS THE ASSERTION OF L'ETOILE, TOUCHING THE MATTER OF APATHY ON THE PART OF THE MOTHER AND OTHER RELATIVES, WE SHALL NOW PROCEED AS IF THE QUESTION OF IDENTITY WERE SETTLED TO OUR PERFECT SATISFACTION."

"...THE CAUTION GIVEN TO MADAME B--, THAT SHE MUST HOLD NO CONVERSATION WITH THE GENDARME UNTIL HIS RETURN (BEAUVAIS); AND, LASTLY, HIS APPARENT DETERMINATION 'THAT NOBODY SHOULD HAVE ANYTHING TO DO WITH THE PROCEEDINGS EXCEPT HIMSELF.'

"IT SEEMS TO ME UNQUESTIONABLE THAT BEAUVAIS WAS A SUITOR OF MARIE'S; THAT SHE COQUETTED WITH HIM; AND THAT HE WAS AMBITIOUS OF BEING THOUGHT TO ENJOY HER FULLEST INTIMACY AND CONFIDENCE.

AND WHAT DO YOU THINK OF THE OPINIONS OF LE COMMERCIEL, WHICH IMPLIES THAT A PERSON SO WELL KNOWN TO THOUSANDS AS THIS YOUNG WOMAN WAS COULD NOT HAVE PASSED THREE BLOCKS WITHOUT SOMEONE HAVING SEEN HER?

"THIS IS THE IDEA OF A MAN LONG RESIDENT IN PARIS-- A PUBLIC MAN-- WHO SELDOM PASSES SO FAR AS A DOZEN BLOCKS FROM HIS OWN BUREAU, WITHOUT BEING RECOGNIZED AND ACCOSTED.

"AND, KNOWING THE EXTENT OF HIS PERSONAL ACQUAINTANCE WITH OTHERS, AND OF OTHERS WITH HIM, HE COMPARES HIS NOTORIETY WITH THAT OF THE PERFUMERY-GIRL, AND REACHES AT ONCE THE CONCLUSION THAT SHE, IN HER WALKS, WOULD BE EQUALLY LIABLE TO RECOGNITION WITH HIMSELF IN HIS.

"IN THIS PARTICULAR INSTANCE, IT WILL BE UNDERSTOOD AS MOST PROBABLE, THAT SHE PROCEEDED UPON A ROUTE OF MORE THAN AVERAGE DIVERSITY FROM HER ACCUSTOMED ONES."

BUT WHATEVER FORCE THERE MAY STILL APPEAR TO BE IN THE SUGGESTION OF LE COMMERCIEL, WILL BE MUCH DIMINISHED WHEN WE TAKE INTO CONSIDERATION THE HOUR AT WHICH THE GIRL WENT ABROAD. "IT WAS WHEN THE STREETS WERE FULL OF PEOPLE," SAYS LE COMMERCIEL.

"IT WAS CERTAINLY AT NINE O'CLOCK IN THE MORNING, BUT IT WAS A SUNDAY!"

"AT NINE ON SUNDAY, THE POPULACE ARE CHIEFLY WITHIN DOORS PREPARING FOR CHURCH."

AND WHAT ARE WE TO THINK OF THE ARTICLE IN LE SOLEIL?

THAT IT IS A VAST PITY ITS EDITOR WAS NOT BORN A PARROT-- IN WHICH CASE HE WOULD HAVE BEEN THE MOST ILLUSTRIOUS PARROT OF HIS RACE!

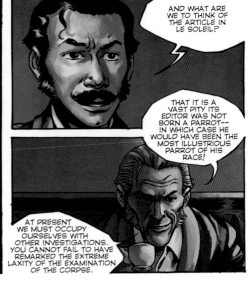

AT PRESENT WE MUST OCCUPY OURSELVES WITH OTHER INVESTIGATIONS. YOU CANNOT FAIL TO HAVE REMARKED THE EXTREME LAXITY OF THE EXAMINATION OF THE CORPSE.

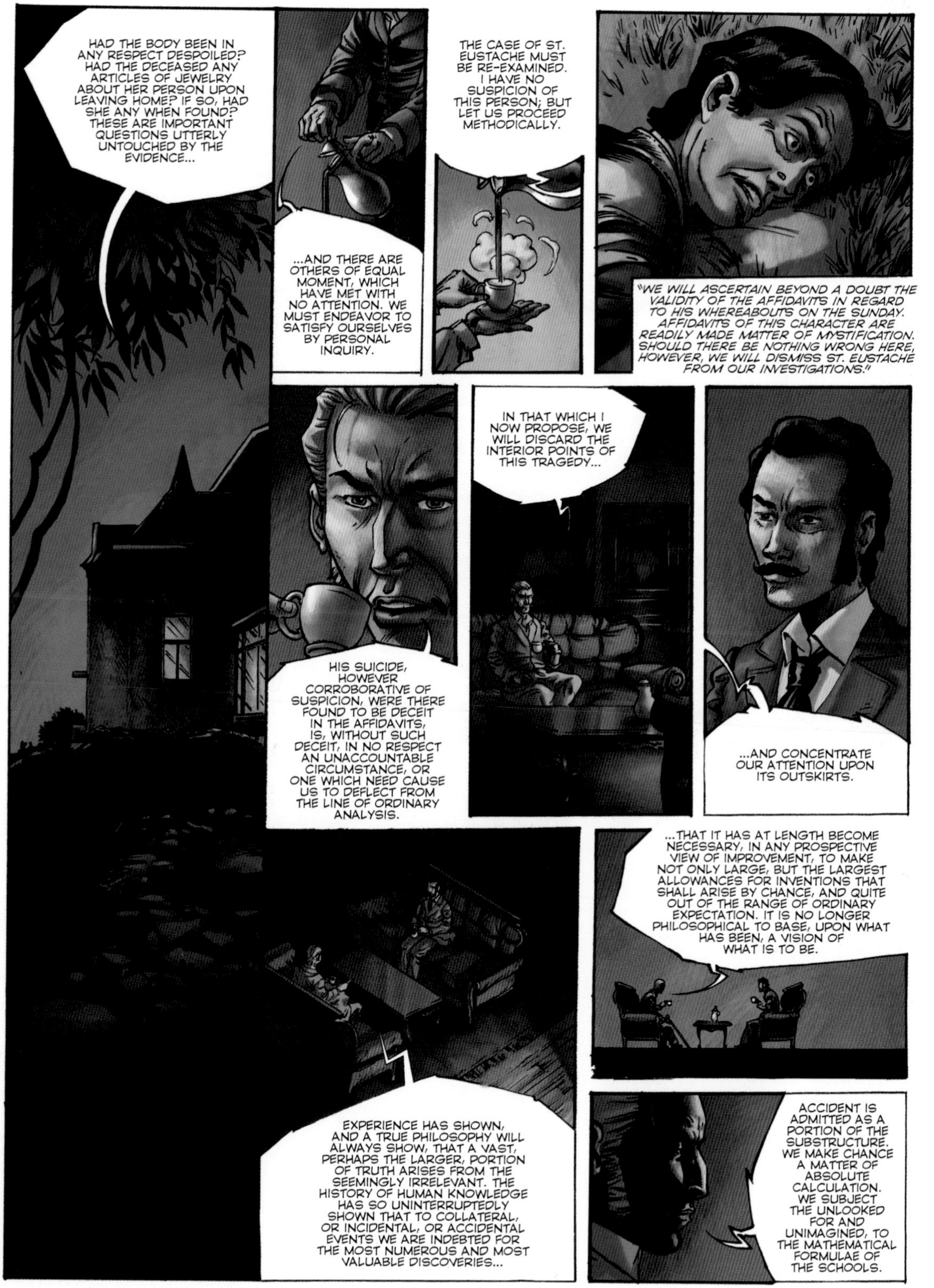
HAD THE BODY BEEN IN ANY RESPECT DESPOILED? HAD THE DECEASED ANY ARTICLES OF JEWELRY ABOUT HER PERSON UPON LEAVING HOME? IF SO, HAD SHE ANY WHEN FOUND? THESE ARE IMPORTANT QUESTIONS UTTERLY UNTOUCHED BY THE EVIDENCE...
...AND THERE ARE OTHERS OF EQUAL MOMENT, WHICH HAVE MET WITH NO ATTENTION. WE MUST ENDEAVOR TO SATISFY OURSELVES BY PERSONAL INQUIRY.
THE CASE OF ST. EUSTACHE MUST BE RE-EXAMINED. I HAVE NO SUSPICION OF THIS PERSON; BUT LET US PROCEED METHODICALLY.
"WE WILL ASCERTAIN BEYOND A DOUBT THE VALIDITY OF THE AFFIDAVITS IN REGARD TO HIS WHEREABOUTS ON THE SUNDAY. AFFIDAVITS OF THIS CHARACTER ARE READILY MADE MATTER OF MYSTIFICATION. SHOULD THERE BE NOTHING WRONG HERE, HOWEVER, WE WILL DISMISS ST. EUSTACHE FROM OUR INVESTIGATIONS."
HIS SUICIDE, HOWEVER CORROBORATIVE OF SUSPICION, WERE THERE FOUND TO BE DECEIT IN THE AFFIDAVITS, IS, WITHOUT SUCH DECEIT, IN NO RESPECT AN UNACCOUNTABLE CIRCUMSTANCE, OR ONE WHICH NEED CAUSE US TO DEFLECT FROM THE LINE OF ORDINARY ANALYSIS.
IN THAT WHICH I NOW PROPOSE, WE WILL DISCARD THE INTERIOR POINTS OF THIS TRAGEDY...
...AND CONCENTRATE OUR ATTENTION UPON ITS OUTSKIRTS.
EXPERIENCE HAS SHOWN, AND A TRUE PHILOSOPHY WILL ALWAYS SHOW, THAT A VAST, PERHAPS THE LARGER, PORTION OF TRUTH ARISES FROM THE SEEMINGLY IRRELEVANT. THE HISTORY OF HUMAN KNOWLEDGE HAS SO UNINTERRUPTEDLY SHOWN THAT TO COLLATERAL, OR INCIDENTAL, OR ACCIDENTAL EVENTS WE ARE INDEBTED FOR THE MOST NUMEROUS AND MOST VALUABLE DISCOVERIES...
...THAT IT HAS AT LENGTH BECOME NECESSARY, IN ANY PROSPECTIVE VIEW OF IMPROVEMENT, TO MAKE NOT ONLY LARGE, BUT THE LARGEST ALLOWANCES FOR INVENTIONS THAT SHALL ARISE BY CHANCE, AND QUITE OUT OF THE RANGE OF ORDINARY EXPECTATION. IT IS NO LONGER PHILOSOPHICAL TO BASE, UPON WHAT HAS BEEN, A VISION OF WHAT IS TO BE.
ACCIDENT IS ADMITTED AS A PORTION OF THE SUBSTRUCTURE. WE MAKE CHANCE A MATTER OF ABSOLUTE CALCULATION. WE SUBJECT THE UNLOOKED FOR AND UNIMAGINED, TO THE MATHEMATICAL FORMULAE OF THE SCHOOLS.

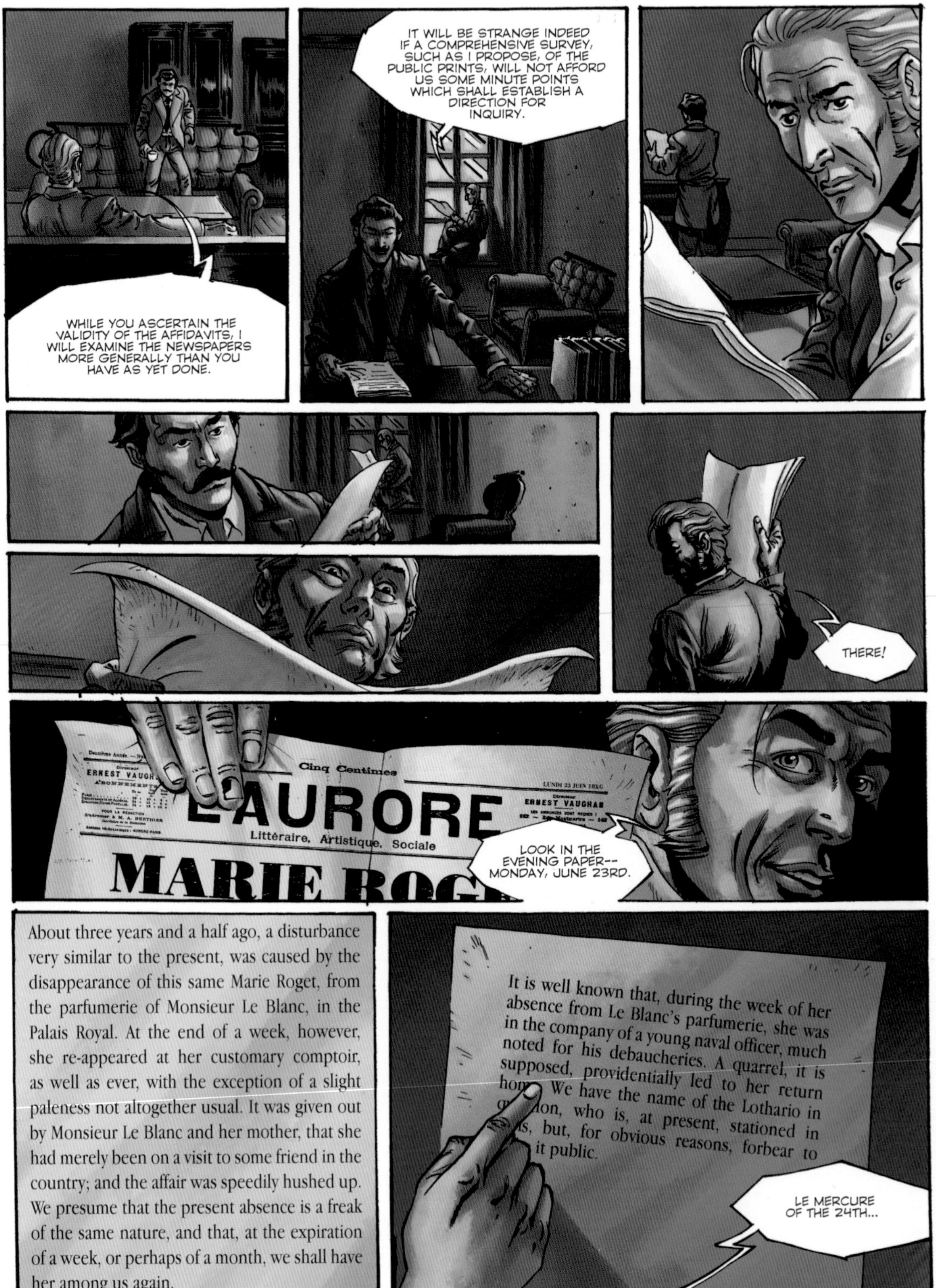

WHILE YOU ASCERTAIN THE VALIDITY OF THE AFFIDAVITS, I WILL EXAMINE THE NEWSPAPERS MORE GENERALLY THAN YOU HAVE AS YET DONE.
IT WILL BE STRANGE INDEED IF A COMPREHENSIVE SURVEY, SUCH AS I PROPOSE, OF THE PUBLIC PRINTS, WILL NOT AFFORD US SOME MINUTE POINTS WHICH SHALL ESTABLISH A DIRECTION FOR INQUIRY.
THERE!
Cinq Centimes
L'AURORE
Littéraire, Artistique, Sociale
LOOK IN THE EVENING PAPER--MONDAY, JUNE 23RD.
About three years and a half ago, a disturbance very similar to the present, was caused by the disappearance of this same Marie Roget, from the parfumerie of Monsieur Le Blanc, in the Palais Royal. At the end of a week, however, she re-appeared at her customary comptoir, as well as ever, with the exception of a slight paleness not altogether usual. It was given out by Monsieur Le Blanc and her mother, that she had merely been on a visit to some friend in the country; and the affair was speedily hushed up. We presume that the present absence is a freak of the same nature, and that, at the expiration of a week, or perhaps of a month, we shall have her among us again.
It is well known that, during the week of her absence from Le Blanc's parfumerie, she was in the company of a young naval officer, much noted for his debaucheries. A quarrel, it is supposed, providentially led to her return
LE MERCURE OF THE 24TH...

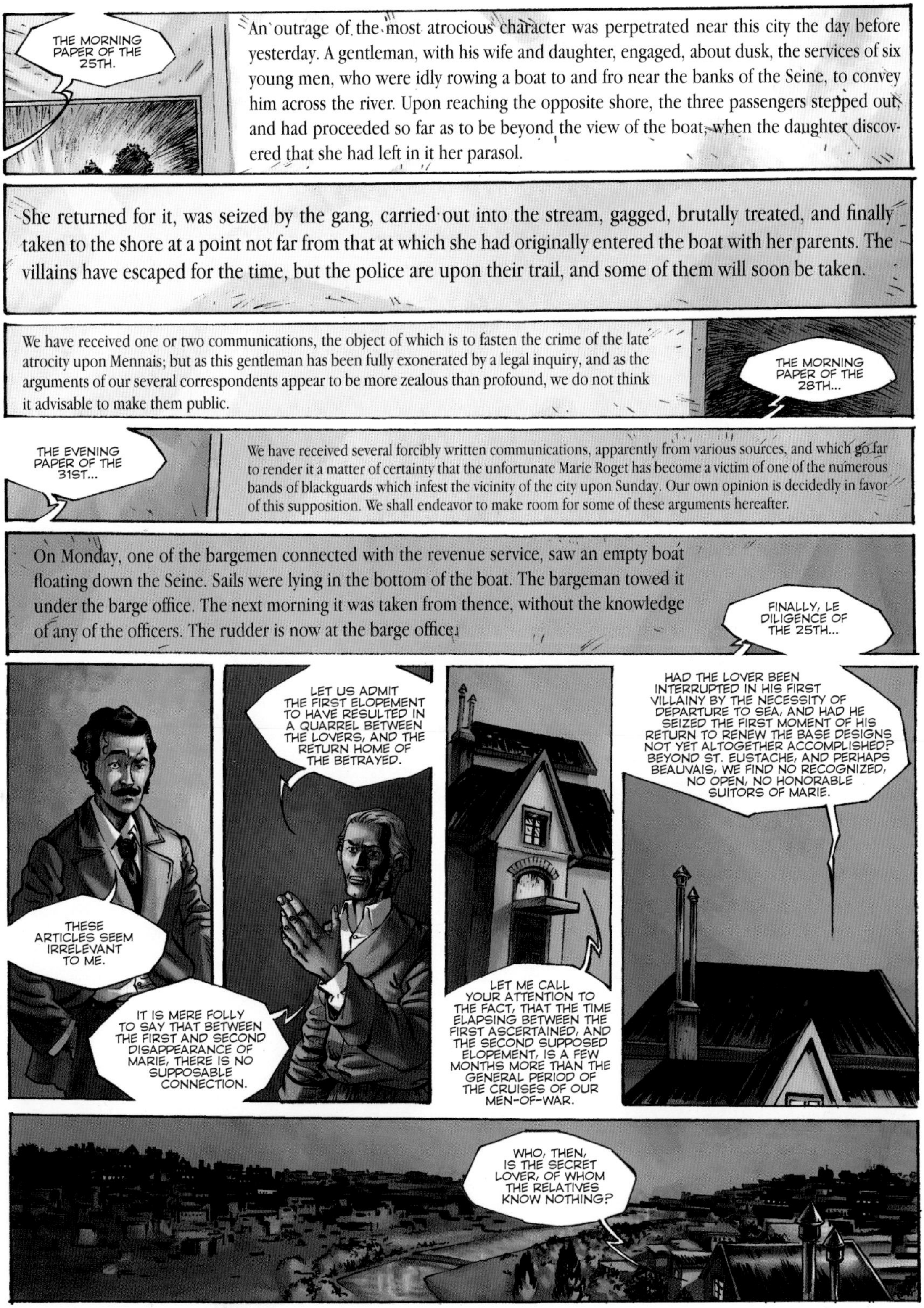
THE MORNING PAPER OF THE 25TH.
An outrage of the most atrocious character was perpetrated near this city the day before yesterday. A gentleman, with his wife and daughter, engaged, about dusk, the services of six young men, who were idly rowing a boat to and fro near the banks of the Seine, to convey him across the river. Upon reaching the opposite shore, the three passengers stepped out, and had proceeded so far as to be beyond the view of the boat, when the daughter discovered that she had left in it her parasol.
She returned for it, was seized by the gang, carried out into the stream, gagged, brutally treated, and finally taken to the shore at a point not far from that at which she had originally entered the boat with her parents. The villains have escaped for the time, but the police are upon their trail, and some of them will soon be taken.
We have received one or two communications, the object of which is to fasten the crime of the late atrocity upon Mennais; but as this gentleman has been fully exonerated by a legal inquiry, and as the arguments of our several correspondents appear to be more zealous than profound, we do not think it advisable to make them public.
THE MORNING PAPER OF THE 28TH...
THE EVENING PAPER OF THE 31ST...
We have received several forcibly written communications, apparently from various sources, and which go far to render it a matter of certainty that the unfortunate Marie Roget has become a victim of one of the numerous bands of blackguards which infest the vicinity of the city upon Sunday. Our own opinion is decidedly in favor of this supposition. We shall endeavor to make room for some of these arguments hereafter.
On Monday, one of the bargemen connected with the revenue service, saw an empty boat floating down the Seine. Sails were lying in the bottom of the boat. The bargeman towed it under the barge office. The next morning it was taken from thence, without the knowledge of any of the officers. The rudder is now at the barge office.
FINALLY, LE DILIGENCE OF THE 25TH...
THESE ARTICLES SEEM IRRELEVANT TO ME.
LET US ADMIT THE FIRST ELOPEMENT TO HAVE RESULTED IN A QUARREL BETWEEN THE LOVERS, AND THE RETURN HOME OF THE BETRAYED.
IT IS MERE FOLLY TO SAY THAT BETWEEN THE FIRST AND SECOND DISAPPEARANCE OF MARIE, THERE IS NO SUPPOSABLE CONNECTION.
LET ME CALL YOUR ATTENTION TO THE FACT, THAT THE TIME ELAPSING BETWEEN THE FIRST ASCERTAINED, AND THE SECOND SUPPOSED ELOPEMENT, IS A FEW MONTHS MORE THAN THE GENERAL PERIOD OF THE CRUISES OF OUR MEN-OF-WAR.
HAD THE LOVER BEEN INTERRUPTED IN HIS FIRST VILLAINY BY THE NECESSITY OF DEPARTURE TO SEA, AND HAD HE SEIZED THE FIRST MOMENT OF HIS RETURN TO RENEW THE BASE DESIGNS NOT YET ALTOGETHER ACCOMPLISHED? BEYOND ST. EUSTACHE, AND PERHAPS BEAUVAIS, WE FIND NO RECOGNIZED, NO OPEN, NO HONORABLE SUITORS OF MARIE.
WHO, THEN, IS THE SECRET LOVER, OF WHOM THE RELATIVES KNOW NOTHING?

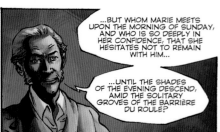
...BUT WHOM MARIE MEETS UPON THE MORNING OF SUNDAY, AND WHO IS SO DEEPLY IN HER CONFIDENCE, THAT SHE HESITATES NOT TO REMAIN WITH HIM...

...UNTIL THE SHADES OF THE EVENING DESCEND, AMID THE SOLITARY GROVES OF THE BARRIÈRE DU ROULE?

AND WHAT MEANS THE SINGULAR PROPHECY OF MADAME ROGET ON THE MORNING OF MARIE'S DEPARTURE?

"I FEAR THAT I SHALL NEVER SEE MARIE AGAIN!"

IF WE SUPPOSE MARIE NOT INTENDING TO RETURN, WE MAY IMAGINE HER THINKING THUS...

I AM TO MEET A CERTAIN PERSON FOR THE PURPOSE OF ELOPEMENT, OR FOR CERTAIN OTHER PURPOSES KNOWN ONLY TO MYSELF. IT IS NECESSARY THAT THERE BE NO CHANCE OF INTERRUPTION.

THERE MUST BE SUFFICIENT TIME GIVEN US TO ELUDE PURSUIT.

I WILL GIVE IT TO BE UNDERSTOOD THAT I SHALL VISIT AND SPEND THE DAY WITH MY AUNT AT THE RUE DES DRÔMES-- I WILL TELL ST. EUSTACHE NOT TO CALL FOR ME UNTIL DARK.

IN THIS WAY, MY ABSENCE FROM HOME FOR THE LONGEST POSSIBLE PERIOD, WITHOUT CAUSING SUSPICION OR ANXIETY, WILL BE ACCOUNTED FOR, AND I SHALL GAIN MORE TIME THAN IN ANY OTHER MANNER.

IF I BID ST. EUSTACHE CALL FOR ME AT DARK, HE WILL BE SURE NOT TO CALL BEFORE.

BUT, IF I WHOLLY NEGLECT TO BID HIM CALL, MY TIME FOR ESCAPE WILL BE DIMINISHED, SINCE IT WILL BE EXPECTED THAT I RETURN THE EARLIER, AND MY ABSENCE WILL THE SOONER EXCITE ANXIETY. NOW, IF IT WERE MY DESIGN TO RETURN AT ALL-- IF I HAD IN CONTEMPLATION MERELY A STROLL WITH THE INDIVIDUAL IN QUESTION--

IT WOULD NOT BE MY POLICY TO BID ST. EUSTACHE CALL; FOR, CALLING, HE WILL BE SURE TO ASCERTAIN THAT I HAVE PLAYED HIM FALSE...

...A FACT OF WHICH I MIGHT KEEP HIM FOREVER IN IGNORANCE, BY LEAVING HOME WITHOUT NOTIFYING HIM OF MY INTENTION...

...BY RETURNING BEFORE DARK, AND BY THEN STATING THAT I HAD BEEN TO VISIT MY AUNT IN THE RUE DES DRÔMES.

BUT, AS IT IS MY DESIGN NEVER TO RETURN-- OR NOT FOR SOME WEEKS-- OR NOT UNTIL CERTAIN CONCEALMENTS ARE EFFECTED-- THE GAINING OF TIME IS THE ONLY POINT ABOUT WHICH I NEED GIVE MYSELF ANY CONCERN.

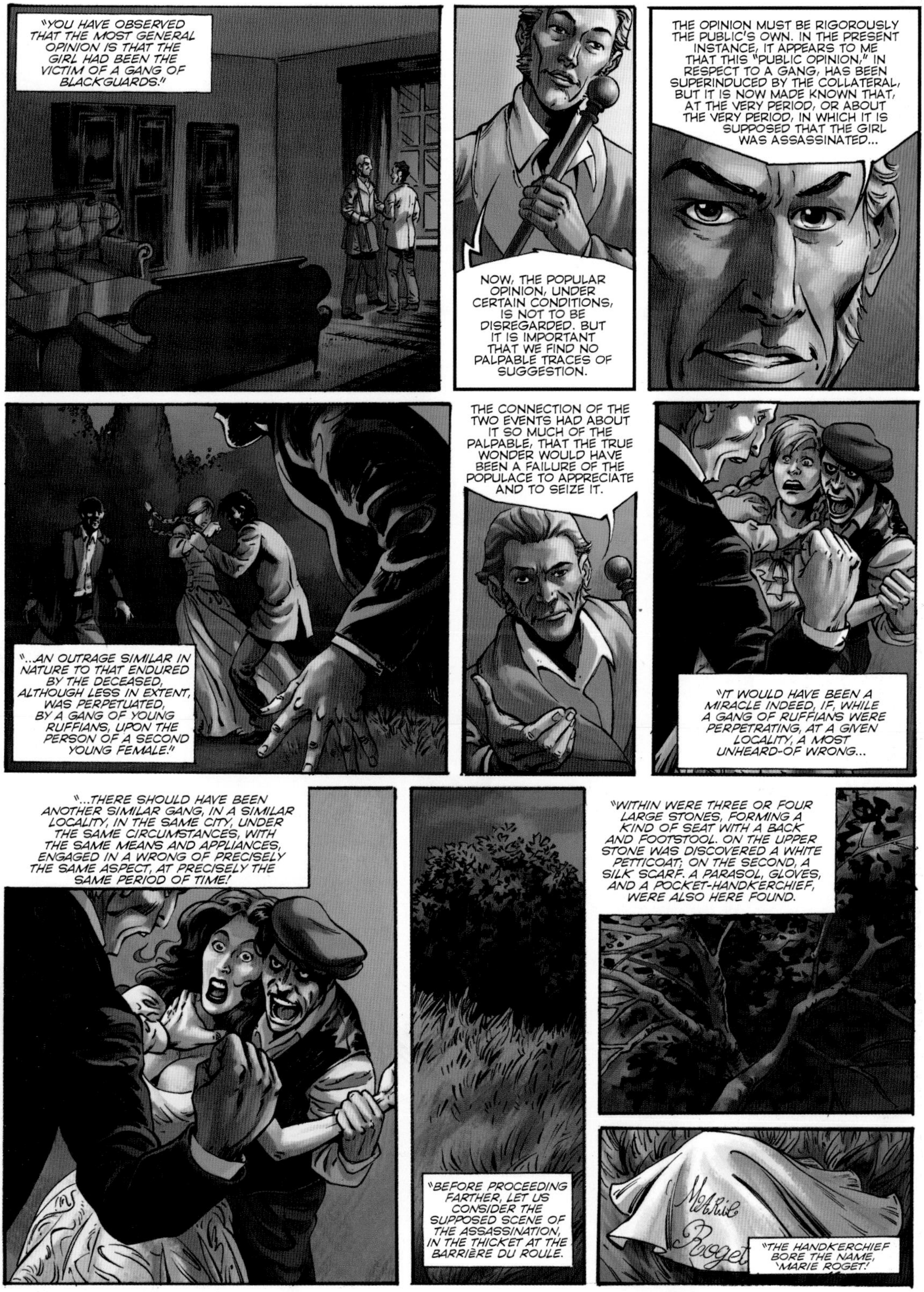
"YOU HAVE OBSERVED THAT THE MOST GENERAL OPINION IS THAT THE GIRL HAD BEEN THE VICTIM OF A GANG OF BLACKGUARDS."
NOW, THE POPULAR OPINION, UNDER CERTAIN CONDITIONS, IS NOT TO BE DISREGARDED. BUT IT IS IMPORTANT THAT WE FIND NO PALPABLE TRACES OF SUGGESTION.
THE OPINION MUST BE RIGOROUSLY THE PUBLIC'S OWN. IN THE PRESENT INSTANCE, IT APPEARS TO ME THAT THIS "PUBLIC OPINION," IN RESPECT TO A GANG, HAS BEEN SUPERINDUCED BY THE COLLATERAL, BUT IT IS NOW MADE KNOWN THAT, AT THE VERY PERIOD, OR ABOUT THE VERY PERIOD, IN WHICH IT IS SUPPOSED THAT THE GIRL WAS ASSASSINATED...
"...AN OUTRAGE SIMILAR IN NATURE TO THAT ENDURED BY THE DECEASED, ALTHOUGH LESS IN EXTENT, WAS PERPETUATED, BY A GANG OF YOUNG RUFFIANS, UPON THE PERSON OF A SECOND YOUNG FEMALE."
THE CONNECTION OF THE TWO EVENTS HAD ABOUT IT SO MUCH OF THE PALPABLE, THAT THE TRUE WONDER WOULD HAVE BEEN A FAILURE OF THE POPULACE TO APPRECIATE AND TO SEIZE IT.
"IT WOULD HAVE BEEN A MIRACLE INDEED, IF, WHILE A GANG OF RUFFIANS WERE PERPETRATING, AT A GIVEN LOCALITY, A MOST UNHEARD-OF WRONG...
"...THERE SHOULD HAVE BEEN ANOTHER SIMILAR GANG, IN A SIMILAR LOCALITY, IN THE SAME CITY, UNDER THE SAME CIRCUMSTANCES, WITH THE SAME MEANS AND APPLIANCES, ENGAGED IN A WRONG OF PRECISELY THE SAME ASPECT, AT PRECISELY THE SAME PERIOD OF TIME!
"BEFORE PROCEEDING FARTHER, LET US CONSIDER THE SUPPOSED SCENE OF THE ASSASSINATION, IN THE THICKET AT THE BARRIÈRE DU ROULE.
"WITHIN WERE THREE OR FOUR LARGE STONES, FORMING A KIND OF SEAT WITH A BACK AND FOOTSTOOL. ON THE UPPER STONE WAS DISCOVERED A WHITE PETTICOAT; ON THE SECOND, A SILK SCARF. A PARASOL, GLOVES, AND A POCKET-HANDKERCHIEF, WERE ALSO HERE FOUND.
"THE HANDKERCHIEF BORE THE NAME, 'MARIE ROGET.'

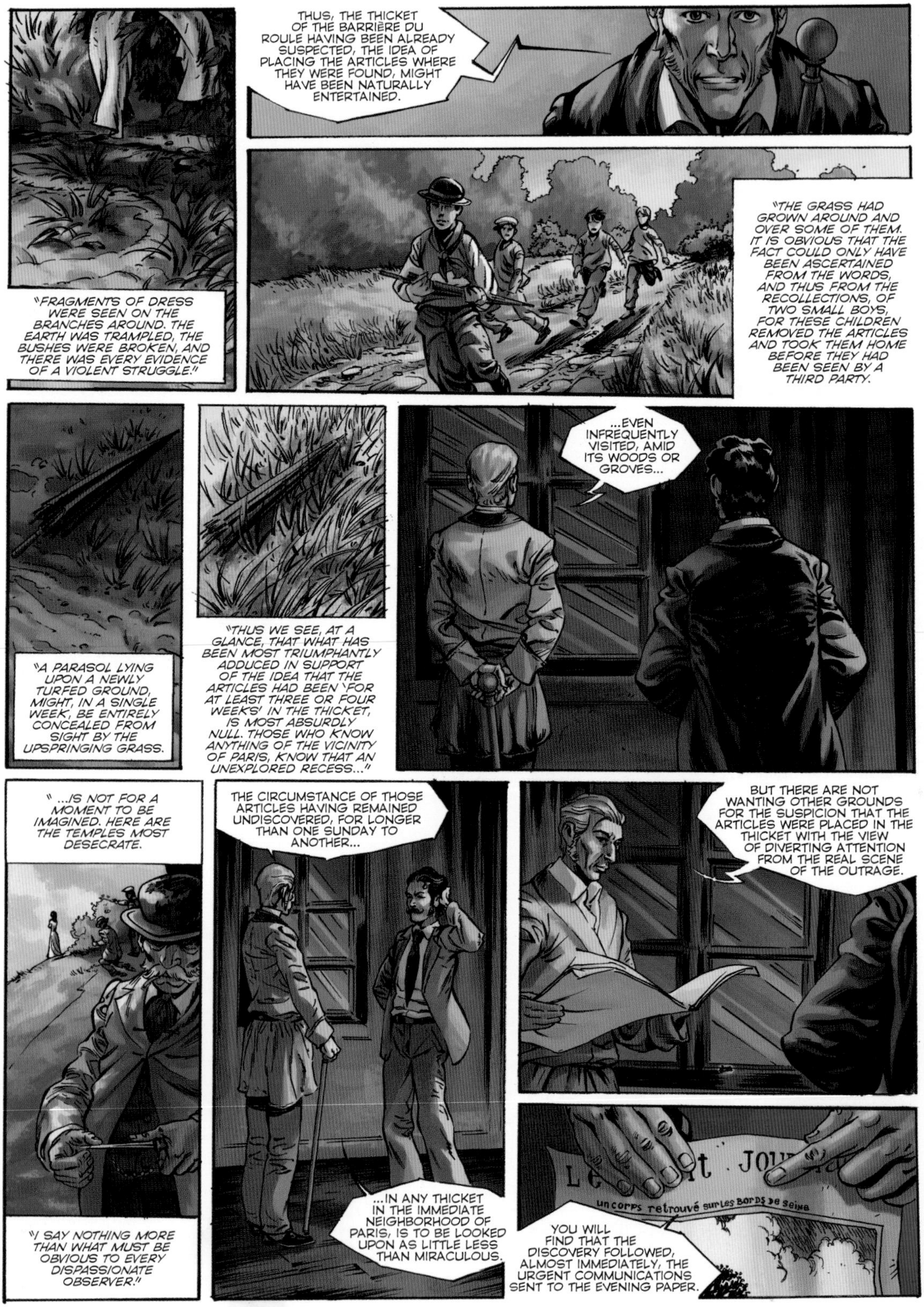
THUS, THE THICKET OF THE BARRIÈRE DU ROULE HAVING BEEN ALREADY SUSPECTED, THE IDEA OF PLACING THE ARTICLES WHERE THEY WERE FOUND, MIGHT HAVE BEEN NATURALLY ENTERTAINED.
"FRAGMENTS OF DRESS WERE SEEN ON THE BRANCHES AROUND. THE EARTH WAS TRAMPLED, THE BUSHES WERE BROKEN, AND THERE WAS EVERY EVIDENCE OF A VIOLENT STRUGGLE."
"THE GRASS HAD GROWN AROUND AND OVER SOME OF THEM. IT IS OBVIOUS THAT THE FACT COULD ONLY HAVE BEEN ASCERTAINED FROM THE WORDS, AND THUS FROM THE RECOLLECTIONS, OF TWO SMALL BOYS, FOR THESE CHILDREN REMOVED THE ARTICLES AND TOOK THEM HOME BEFORE THEY HAD BEEN SEEN BY A THIRD PARTY.
"A PARASOL LYING UPON A NEWLY TURFED GROUND, MIGHT, IN A SINGLE WEEK, BE ENTIRELY CONCEALED FROM SIGHT BY THE UPSPRINGING GRASS.
"THUS WE SEE, AT A GLANCE, THAT WHAT HAS BEEN MOST TRIUMPHANTLY ADDUCED IN SUPPORT OF THE IDEA THAT THE ARTICLES HAD BEEN 'FOR AT LEAST THREE OR FOUR WEEKS' IN THE THICKET, IS MOST ABSURDLY NULL. THOSE WHO KNOW ANYTHING OF THE VICINITY OF PARIS, KNOW THAT AN UNEXPLORED RECESS..."
...EVEN INFREQUENTLY VISITED, AMID ITS WOODS OR GROVES...
" ...IS NOT FOR A MOMENT TO BE IMAGINED. HERE ARE THE TEMPLES MOST DESECRATE.
"I SAY NOTHING MORE THAN WHAT MUST BE OBVIOUS TO EVERY DISPASSIONATE OBSERVER."
THE CIRCUMSTANCE OF THOSE ARTICLES HAVING REMAINED UNDISCOVERED, FOR LONGER THAN ONE SUNDAY TO ANOTHER...
...IN ANY THICKET IN THE IMMEDIATE NEIGHBORHOOD OF PARIS, IS TO BE LOOKED UPON AS LITTLE LESS THAN MIRACULOUS.
BUT THERE ARE NOT WANTING OTHER GROUNDS FOR THE SUSPICION THAT THE ARTICLES WERE PLACED IN THE THICKET WITH THE VIEW OF DIVERTING ATTENTION FROM THE REAL SCENE OF THE OUTRAGE.
un corps retrouvé sur les bords de seine
YOU WILL FIND THAT THE DISCOVERY FOLLOWED, ALMOST IMMEDIATELY, THE URGENT COMMUNICATIONS SENT TO THE EVENING PAPER.

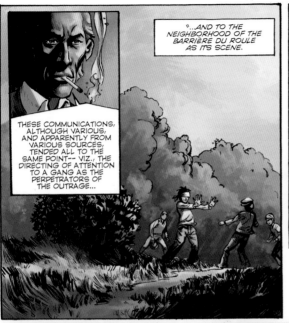

"...AND TO THE NEIGHBORHOOD OF THE BARRIÈRE DU ROULE AS ITS SCENE.

THESE COMMUNICATIONS, ALTHOUGH VARIOUS, AND APPARENTLY FROM VARIOUS SOURCES, TENDED ALL TO THE SAME POINT-- VIZ., THE DIRECTING OF ATTENTION TO A GANG AS THE PERPETRATORS OF THE OUTRAGE...

"ONE COULD LEGITIMATELY SUPPOSE THAT, IF THE BOYS HADN'T FOUND THE OBJECTS SOONER, IT'S BECAUSE THE OBJECTS IN QUESTION WEREN'T YET IN THE THICKET.

"AND, NOW, LET ME BEG YOUR NOTICE TO THE HIGHLY ARTIFICIAL ARRANGEMENT OF THE ARTICLES.

"HERE IS JUST SUCH AN ARRANGEMENT AS WOULD NATURALLY BE MADE BY A NOT-OVER-ACUTE PERSON WISHING TO DISPOSE THE ARTICLES NATURALLY."

BUT IT IS BY NO MEANS A REALLY NATURAL ARRANGEMENT. I SHOULD RATHER HAVE LOOKED TO SEE THE THINGS ALL LYING ON THE GROUND AND TRAMPLED UNDERFOOT.

"THERE WAS EVIDENCE,' IT IS SAID, 'OF A STRUGGLE; AND THE EARTH WAS TRAMPLED, THE BUSHES WERE BROKEN;'--BUT THE PETTICOAT AND THE SCARF ARE FOUND DEPOSITED AS IF UPON SHELVES."

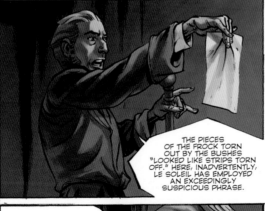

THE PIECES OF THE FROCK TORN OUT BY THE BUSHES "LOOKED LIKE STRIPS TORN OFF." HERE, INADVERTENTLY, LE SOLEIL HAS EMPLOYED AN EXCEEDINGLY SUSPICIOUS PHRASE.

THE PIECES, AS DESCRIBED, DO INDEED "LOOK LIKE STRIPS TORN OFF;" BUT PURPOSELY AND BY HAND.

TO TEAR A PIECE FROM THE INTERIOR, WHERE NO EDGE IS PRESENTED, COULD ONLY BE EFFECTED BY A MIRACLE THROUGH THE AGENCY OF THORNS, AND NO ONE THORN COULD ACCOMPLISH IT.

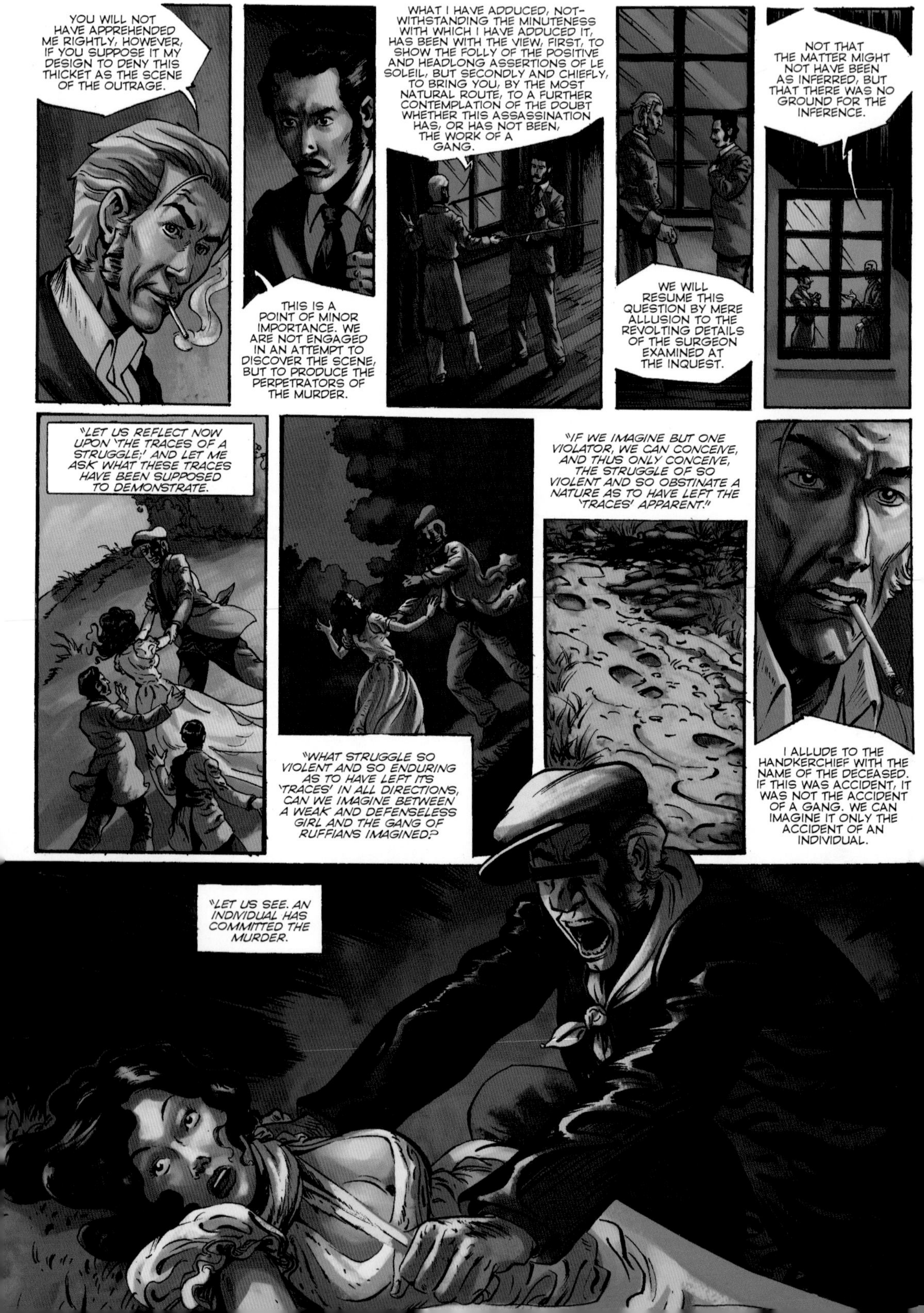
YOU WILL NOT HAVE APPREHENDED ME RIGHTLY, HOWEVER, IF YOU SUPPOSE IT MY DESIGN TO DENY THIS THICKET AS THE SCENE OF THE OUTRAGE.
THIS IS A POINT OF MINOR IMPORTANCE. WE ARE NOT ENGAGED IN AN ATTEMPT TO DISCOVER THE SCENE, BUT TO PRODUCE THE PERPETRATORS OF THE MURDER.
WHAT I HAVE ADDUCED, NOT-WITHSTANDING THE MINUTENESS WITH WHICH I HAVE ADDUCED IT, HAS BEEN WITH THE VIEW, FIRST, TO SHOW THE FOLLY OF THE POSITIVE AND HEADLONG ASSERTIONS OF LE SOLEIL, BUT SECONDLY AND CHIEFLY, TO BRING YOU, BY THE MOST NATURAL ROUTE, TO A FURTHER CONTEMPLATION OF THE DOUBT WHETHER THIS ASSASSINATION HAS, OR HAS NOT BEEN, THE WORK OF A GANG.
WE WILL RESUME THIS QUESTION BY MERE ALLUSION TO THE REVOLTING DETAILS OF THE SURGEON EXAMINED AT THE INQUEST.
NOT THAT THE MATTER MIGHT NOT HAVE BEEN AS INFERRED, BUT THAT THERE WAS NO GROUND FOR THE INFERENCE.
"LET US REFLECT NOW UPON 'THE TRACES OF A STRUGGLE;' AND LET ME ASK WHAT THESE TRACES HAVE BEEN SUPPOSED TO DEMONSTRATE.
"WHAT STRUGGLE SO VIOLENT AND SO ENDURING AS TO HAVE LEFT ITS 'TRACES' IN ALL DIRECTIONS, CAN WE IMAGINE BETWEEN A WEAK AND DEFENSELESS GIRL AND THE GANG OF RUFFIANS IMAGINED?
"IF WE IMAGINE BUT ONE VIOLATOR, WE CAN CONCEIVE, AND THUS ONLY CONCEIVE, THE STRUGGLE OF SO VIOLENT AND SO OBSTINATE A NATURE AS TO HAVE LEFT THE 'TRACES' APPARENT."
I ALLUDE TO THE HANDKERCHIEF WITH THE NAME OF THE DECEASED. IF THIS WAS ACCIDENT, IT WAS NOT THE ACCIDENT OF A GANG. WE CAN IMAGINE IT ONLY THE ACCIDENT OF AN INDIVIDUAL.
"LET US SEE. AN INDIVIDUAL HAS COMMITTED THE MURDER.

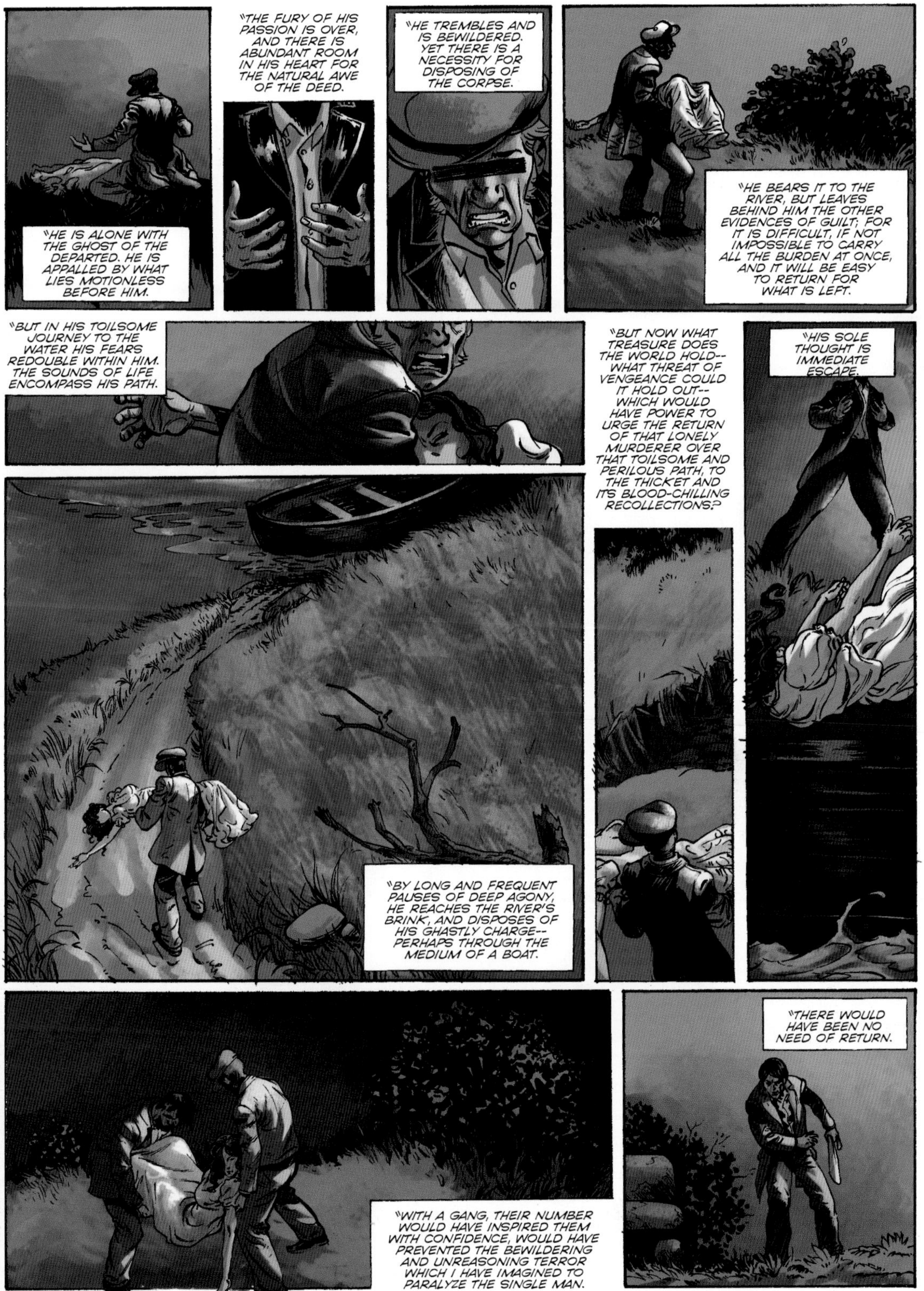
"HE IS ALONE WITH THE GHOST OF THE DEPARTED. HE IS APPALLED BY WHAT LIES MOTIONLESS BEFORE HIM.
"THE FURY OF HIS PASSION IS OVER, AND THERE IS ABUNDANT ROOM IN HIS HEART FOR THE NATURAL AWE OF THE DEED.
"HE TREMBLES AND IS BEWILDERED. YET THERE IS A NECESSITY FOR DISPOSING OF THE CORPSE.
"HE BEARS IT TO THE RIVER, BUT LEAVES BEHIND HIM THE OTHER EVIDENCES OF GUILT; FOR IT IS DIFFICULT, IF NOT IMPOSSIBLE TO CARRY ALL THE BURDEN AT ONCE, AND IT WILL BE EASY TO RETURN FOR WHAT IS LEFT.
"BUT IN HIS TOILSOME JOURNEY TO THE WATER HIS FEARS REDOUBLE WITHIN HIM. THE SOUNDS OF LIFE ENCOMPASS HIS PATH.
"BY LONG AND FREQUENT PAUSES OF DEEP AGONY, HE REACHES THE RIVER'S BRINK, AND DISPOSES OF HIS GHASTLY CHARGE-- PERHAPS THROUGH THE MEDIUM OF A BOAT.
"BUT NOW WHAT TREASURE DOES THE WORLD HOLD-- WHAT THREAT OF VENGEANCE COULD IT HOLD OUT-- WHICH WOULD HAVE POWER TO URGE THE RETURN OF THAT LONELY MURDERER OVER THAT TOILSOME AND PERILOUS PATH, TO THE THICKET AND ITS BLOOD-CHILLING RECOLLECTIONS?
"HIS SOLE THOUGHT IS IMMEDIATE ESCAPE.
"WITH A GANG, THEIR NUMBER WOULD HAVE INSPIRED THEM WITH CONFIDENCE, WOULD HAVE PREVENTED THE BEWILDERING AND UNREASONING TERROR WHICH I HAVE IMAGINED TO PARALYZE THE SINGLE MAN.
"THERE WOULD HAVE BEEN NO NEED OF RETURN.

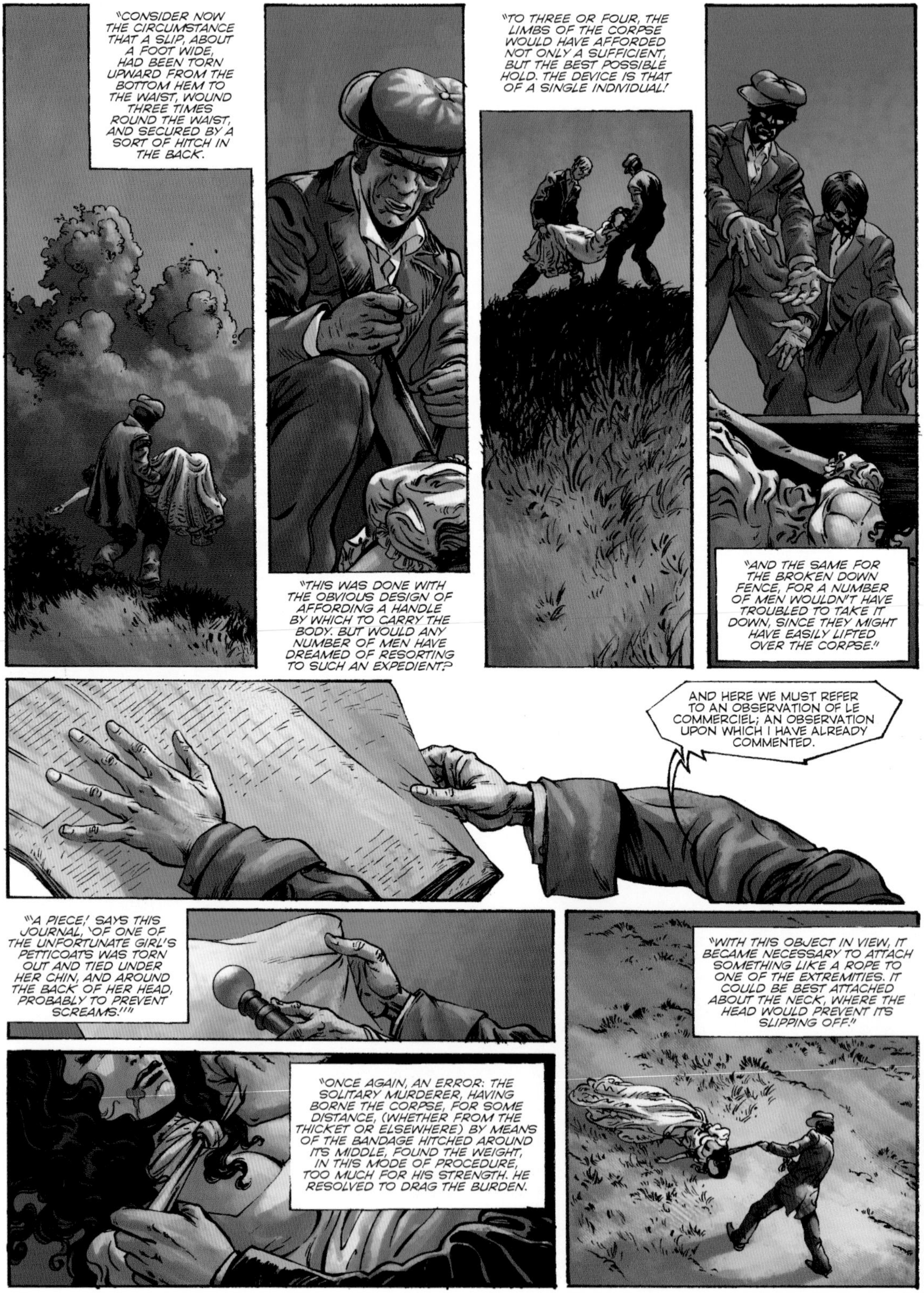
"CONSIDER NOW THE CIRCUMSTANCE THAT A SLIP, ABOUT A FOOT WIDE, HAD BEEN TORN UPWARD FROM THE BOTTOM HEM TO THE WAIST, WOUND THREE TIMES ROUND THE WAIST, AND SECURED BY A SORT OF HITCH IN THE BACK.
"THIS WAS DONE WITH THE OBVIOUS DESIGN OF AFFORDING A HANDLE BY WHICH TO CARRY THE BODY. BUT WOULD ANY NUMBER OF MEN HAVE DREAMED OF RESORTING TO SUCH AN EXPEDIENT?
"TO THREE OR FOUR, THE LIMBS OF THE CORPSE WOULD HAVE AFFORDED NOT ONLY A SUFFICIENT, BUT THE BEST POSSIBLE HOLD. THE DEVICE IS THAT OF A SINGLE INDIVIDUAL!
"AND THE SAME FOR THE BROKEN DOWN FENCE, FOR A NUMBER OF MEN WOULDN'T HAVE TROUBLED TO TAKE IT DOWN, SINCE THEY MIGHT HAVE EASILY LIFTED OVER THE CORPSE."
AND HERE WE MUST REFER TO AN OBSERVATION OF LE COMMERCIEL; AN OBSERVATION UPON WHICH I HAVE ALREADY COMMENTED.
"'A PIECE,' SAYS THIS JOURNAL, 'OF ONE OF THE UNFORTUNATE GIRL'S PETTICOATS WAS TORN OUT AND TIED UNDER HER CHIN, AND AROUND THE BACK OF HER HEAD, PROBABLY TO PREVENT SCREAMS.'"
"ONCE AGAIN, AN ERROR: THE SOLITARY MURDERER, HAVING BORNE THE CORPSE, FOR SOME DISTANCE, (WHETHER FROM THE THICKET OR ELSEWHERE) BY MEANS OF THE BANDAGE HITCHED AROUND ITS MIDDLE, FOUND THE WEIGHT, IN THIS MODE OF PROCEDURE, TOO MUCH FOR HIS STRENGTH. HE RESOLVED TO DRAG THE BURDEN.
"WITH THIS OBJECT IN VIEW, IT BECAME NECESSARY TO ATTACH SOMETHING LIKE A ROPE TO ONE OF THE EXTREMITIES. IT COULD BE BEST ATTACHED ABOUT THE NECK, WHERE THE HEAD WOULD PREVENT ITS SLIPPING OFF."

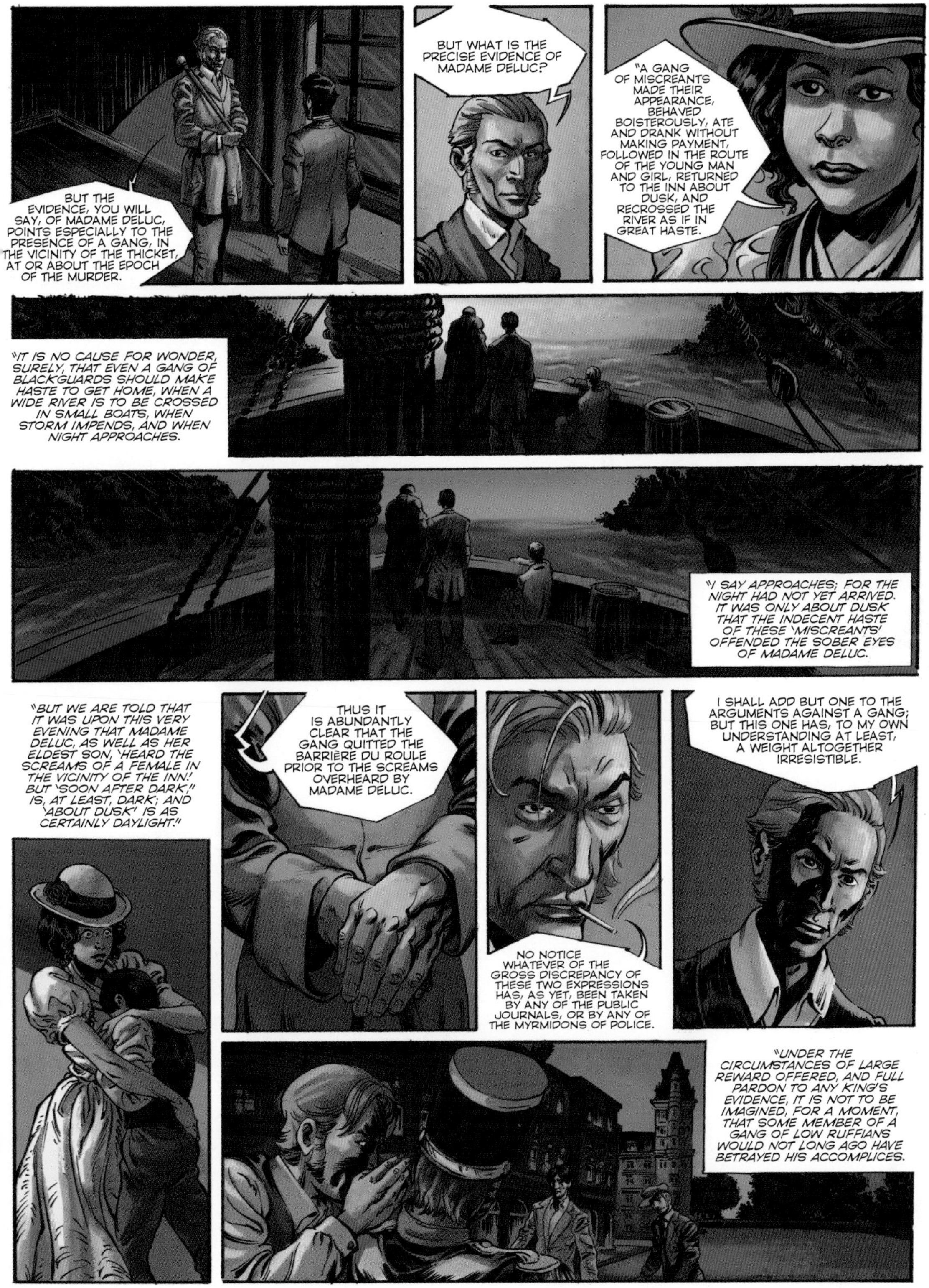
BUT THE EVIDENCE, YOU WILL SAY, OF MADAME DELUC, POINTS ESPECIALLY TO THE PRESENCE OF A GANG, IN THE VICINITY OF THE THICKET, AT OR ABOUT THE EPOCH OF THE MURDER.
BUT WHAT IS THE PRECISE EVIDENCE OF MADAME DELUC?
"A GANG OF MISCREANTS MADE THEIR APPEARANCE, BEHAVED BOISTEROUSLY, ATE AND DRANK WITHOUT MAKING PAYMENT, FOLLOWED IN THE ROUTE OF THE YOUNG MAN AND GIRL, RETURNED TO THE INN ABOUT DUSK, AND RECROSSED THE RIVER AS IF IN GREAT HASTE.
"IT IS NO CAUSE FOR WONDER, SURELY, THAT EVEN A GANG OF BLACKGUARDS SHOULD MAKE HASTE TO GET HOME, WHEN A WIDE RIVER IS TO BE CROSSED IN SMALL BOATS, WHEN STORM IMPENDS, AND WHEN NIGHT APPROACHES.
"I SAY APPROACHES; FOR THE NIGHT HAD NOT YET ARRIVED. IT WAS ONLY ABOUT DUSK THAT THE INDECENT HASTE OF THESE 'MISCREANTS' OFFENDED THE SOBER EYES OF MADAME DELUC.
"BUT WE ARE TOLD THAT IT WAS UPON THIS VERY EVENING THAT MADAME DELUC, AS WELL AS HER ELDEST SON, 'HEARD THE SCREAMS OF A FEMALE IN THE VICINITY OF THE INN.' BUT 'SOON AFTER DARK,' IS, AT LEAST, DARK; AND 'ABOUT DUSK' IS AS CERTAINLY DAYLIGHT."
THUS IT IS ABUNDANTLY CLEAR THAT THE GANG QUITTED THE BARRIÈRE DU ROULE PRIOR TO THE SCREAMS OVERHEARD BY MADAME DELUC.
NO NOTICE WHATEVER OF THE GROSS DISCREPANCY OF THESE TWO EXPRESSIONS HAS, AS YET, BEEN TAKEN BY ANY OF THE PUBLIC JOURNALS, OR BY ANY OF THE MYRMIDONS OF POLICE.
I SHALL ADD BUT ONE TO THE ARGUMENTS AGAINST A GANG; BUT THIS ONE HAS, TO MY OWN UNDERSTANDING AT LEAST, A WEIGHT ALTOGETHER IRRESISTIBLE.
"UNDER THE CIRCUMSTANCES OF LARGE REWARD OFFERED, AND FULL PARDON TO ANY KING'S EVIDENCE, IT IS NOT TO BE IMAGINED, FOR A MOMENT, THAT SOME MEMBER OF A GANG OF LOW RUFFIANS WOULD NOT LONG AGO HAVE BETRAYED HIS ACCOMPLICES.

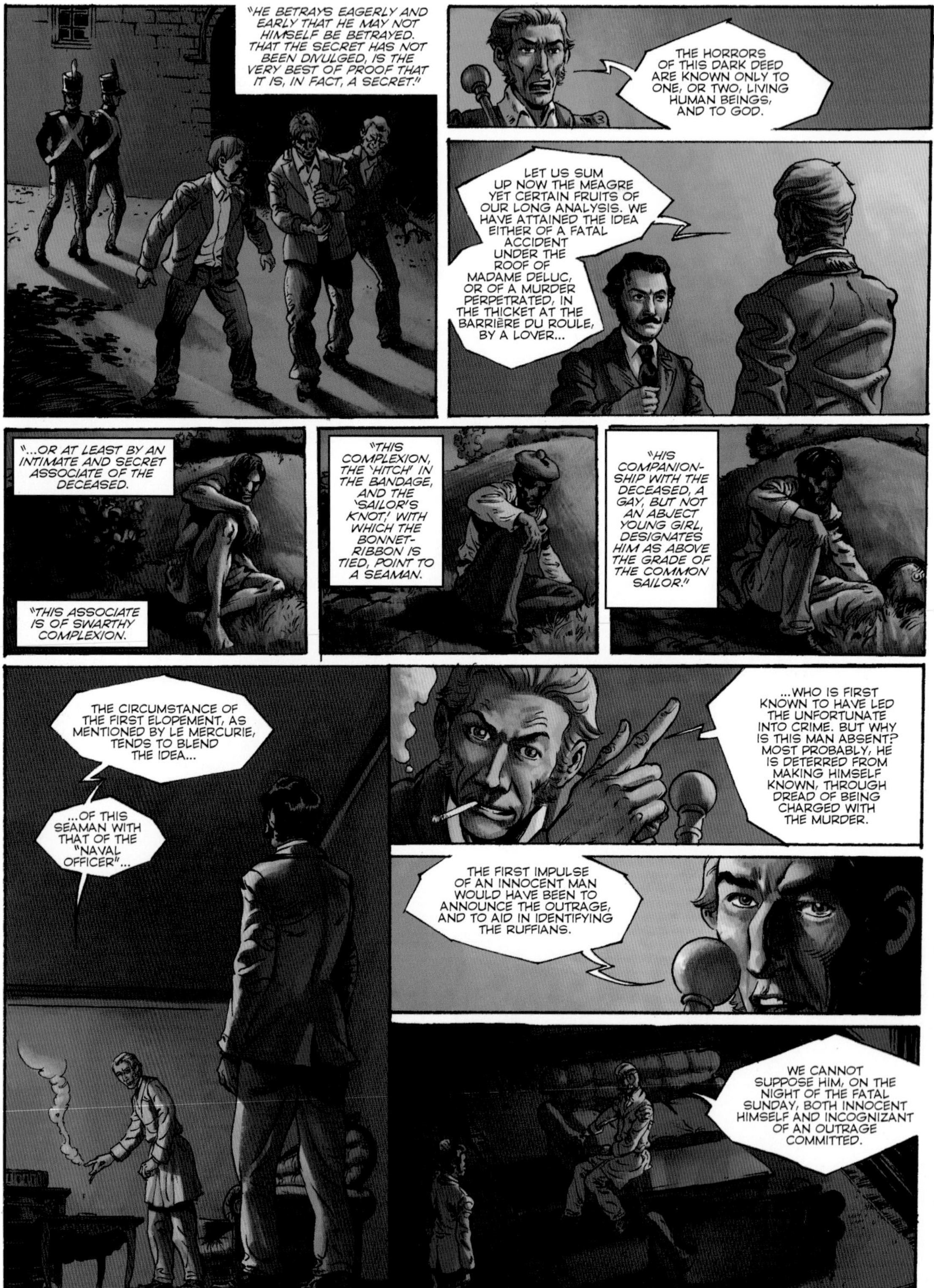
"HE BETRAYS EAGERLY AND EARLY THAT HE MAY NOT HIMSELF BE BETRAYED. THAT THE SECRET HAS NOT BEEN DIVULGED, IS THE VERY BEST OF PROOF THAT IT IS, IN FACT, A SECRET."
THE HORRORS OF THIS DARK DEED ARE KNOWN ONLY TO ONE, OR TWO, LIVING HUMAN BEINGS, AND TO GOD.
LET US SUM UP NOW THE MEAGRE YET CERTAIN FRUITS OF OUR LONG ANALYSIS. WE HAVE ATTAINED THE IDEA EITHER OF A FATAL ACCIDENT UNDER THE ROOF OF MADAME DELUC, OR OF A MURDER PERPETRATED, IN THE THICKET AT THE BARRIÈRE DU ROULE, BY A LOVER...
"...OR AT LEAST BY AN INTIMATE AND SECRET ASSOCIATE OF THE DECEASED.
"THIS ASSOCIATE IS OF SWARTHY COMPLEXION.
"THIS COMPLEXION, THE 'HITCH' IN THE BANDAGE, AND THE 'SAILOR'S KNOT,' WITH WHICH THE BONNET-RIBBON IS TIED, POINT TO A SEAMAN.
"HIS COMPANIONSHIP WITH THE DECEASED, A GAY, BUT NOT AN ABJECT YOUNG GIRL, DESIGNATES HIM AS ABOVE THE GRADE OF THE COMMON SAILOR."
THE CIRCUMSTANCE OF THE FIRST ELOPEMENT, AS MENTIONED BY LE MERCURIE, TENDS TO BLEND THE IDEA...
...OF THIS SEAMAN WITH THAT OF THE "NAVAL OFFICER"...
...WHO IS FIRST KNOWN TO HAVE LED THE UNFORTUNATE INTO CRIME. BUT WHY IS THIS MAN ABSENT? MOST PROBABLY, HE IS DETERRED FROM MAKING HIMSELF KNOWN, THROUGH DREAD OF BEING CHARGED WITH THE MURDER.
THE FIRST IMPULSE OF AN INNOCENT MAN WOULD HAVE BEEN TO ANNOUNCE THE OUTRAGE, AND TO AID IN IDENTIFYING THE RUFFIANS.
WE CANNOT SUPPOSE HIM, ON THE NIGHT OF THE FATAL SUNDAY, BOTH INNOCENT HIMSELF AND INCOGNIZANT OF AN OUTRAGE COMMITTED.

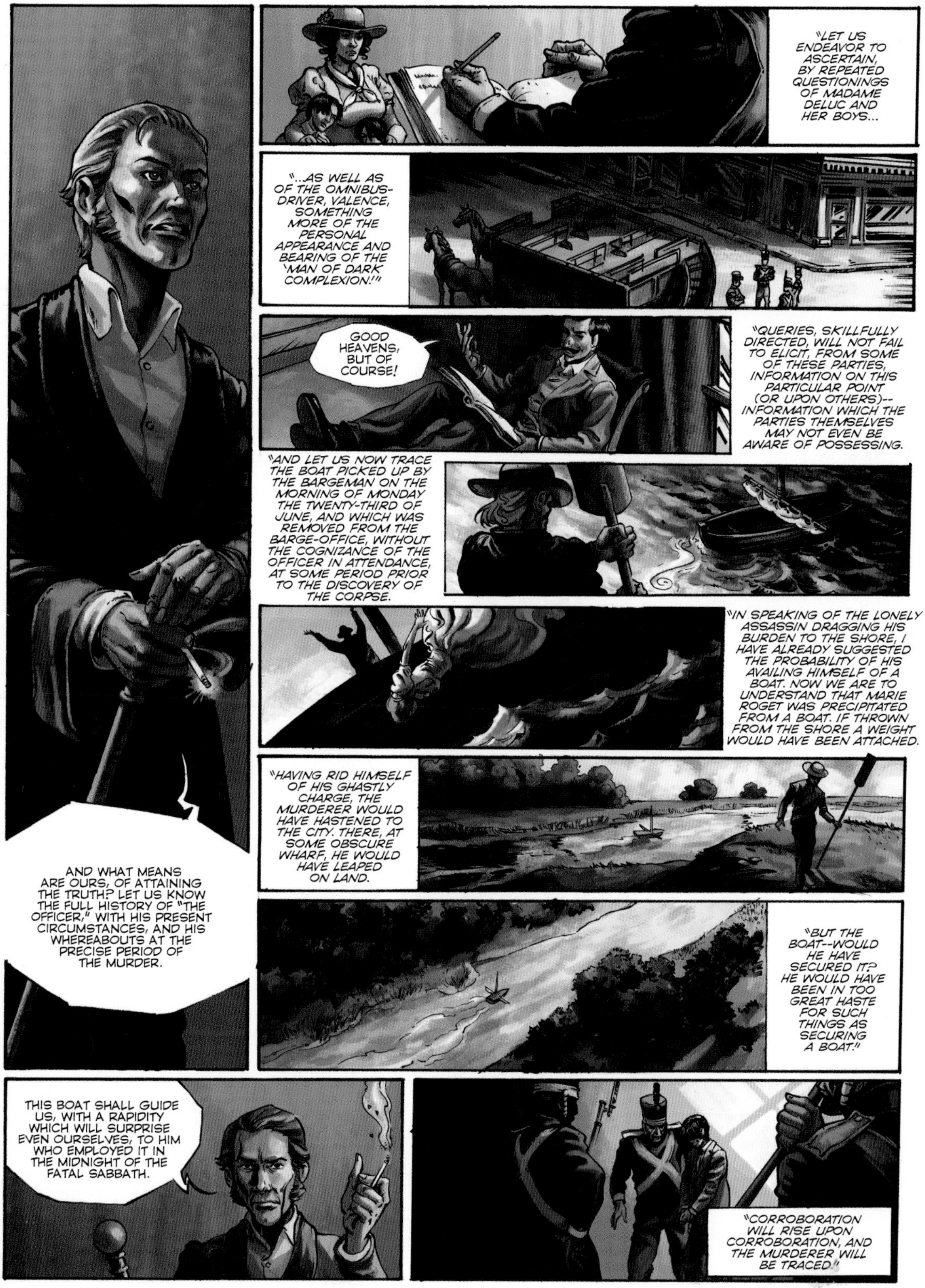
AND WHAT MEANS ARE OURS, OF ATTAINING THE TRUTH? LET US KNOW THE FULL HISTORY OF "THE OFFICER," WITH HIS PRESENT CIRCUMSTANCES, AND HIS WHEREABOUTS AT THE PRECISE PERIOD OF THE MURDER.
"LET US ENDEAVOR TO ASCERTAIN, BY REPEATED QUESTIONINGS OF MADAME DELUC AND HER BOYS...
"...AS WELL AS OF THE OMNIBUS-DRIVER, VALENCE, SOMETHING MORE OF THE PERSONAL APPEARANCE AND BEARING OF THE 'MAN OF DARK COMPLEXION.'"
GOOD HEAVENS, BUT OF COURSE!
"QUERIES, SKILLFULLY DIRECTED, WILL NOT FAIL TO ELICIT, FROM SOME OF THESE PARTIES, INFORMATION ON THIS PARTICULAR POINT (OR UPON OTHERS)--INFORMATION WHICH THE PARTIES THEMSELVES MAY NOT EVEN BE AWARE OF POSSESSING.
"AND LET US NOW TRACE THE BOAT PICKED UP BY THE BARGEMAN ON THE MORNING OF MONDAY THE TWENTY-THIRD OF JUNE, AND WHICH WAS REMOVED FROM THE BARGE-OFFICE, WITHOUT THE COGNIZANCE OF THE OFFICER IN ATTENDANCE, AT SOME PERIOD PRIOR TO THE DISCOVERY OF THE CORPSE.
"IN SPEAKING OF THE LONELY ASSASSIN DRAGGING HIS BURDEN TO THE SHORE, I HAVE ALREADY SUGGESTED THE PROBABILITY OF HIS AVAILING HIMSELF OF A BOAT. NOW WE ARE TO UNDERSTAND THAT MARIE ROGET WAS PRECIPITATED FROM A BOAT. IF THROWN FROM THE SHORE A WEIGHT WOULD HAVE BEEN ATTACHED.
"HAVING RID HIMSELF OF HIS GHASTLY CHARGE, THE MURDERER WOULD HAVE HASTENED TO THE CITY. THERE, AT SOME OBSCURE WHARF, HE WOULD HAVE LEAPED ON LAND.
"BUT THE BOAT--WOULD HE HAVE SECURED IT? HE WOULD HAVE BEEN IN TOO GREAT HASTE FOR SUCH THINGS AS SECURING A BOAT."
THIS BOAT SHALL GUIDE US, WITH A RAPIDITY WHICH WILL SURPRISE EVEN OURSELVES, TO HIM WHO EMPLOYED IT IN THE MIDNIGHT OF THE FATAL SABBATH.
"CORROBORATION WILL RISE UPON CORROBORATION, AND THE MURDERER WILL BE TRACED."

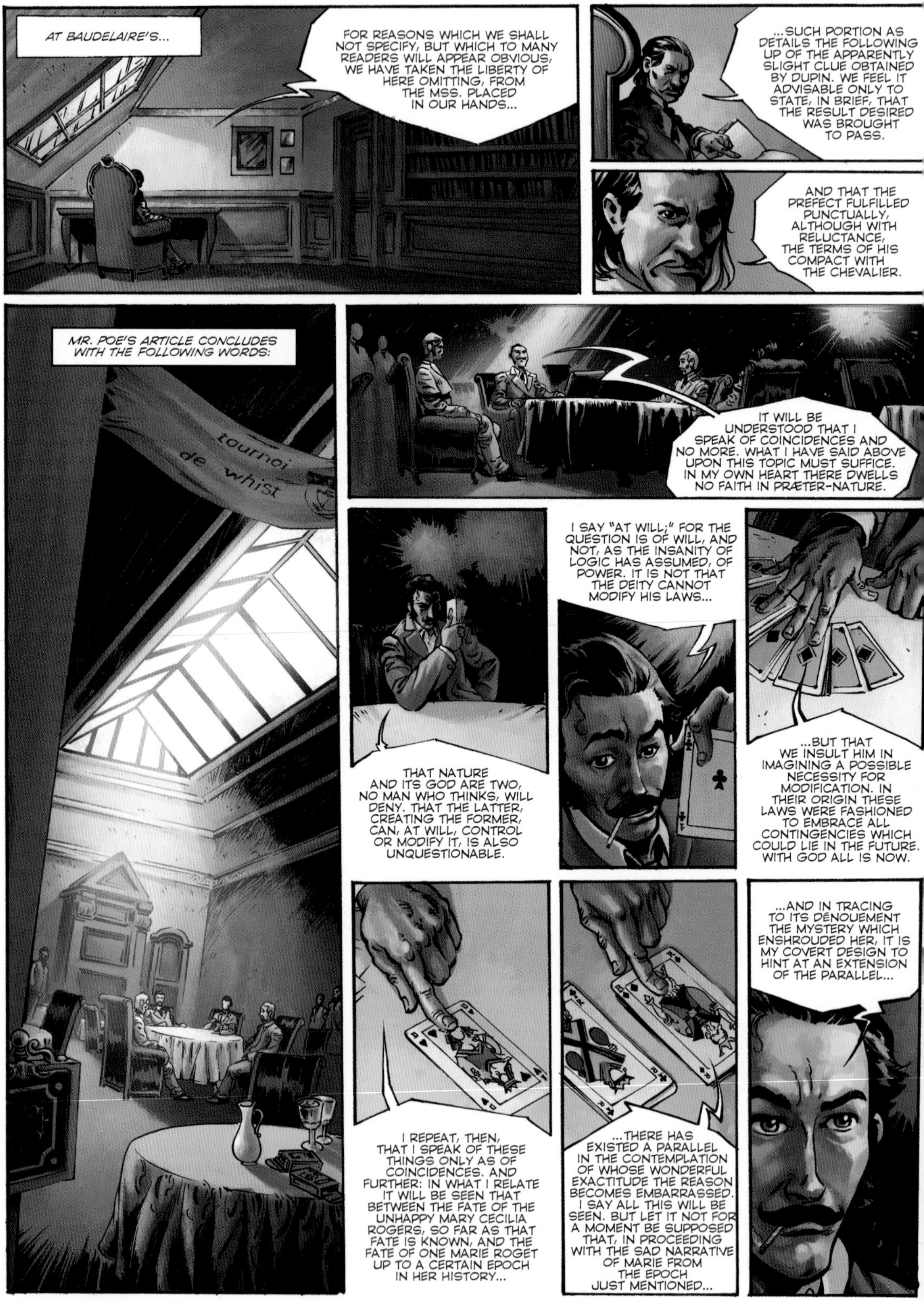
AT BAUDELAIRE'S...
FOR REASONS WHICH WE SHALL NOT SPECIFY, BUT WHICH TO MANY READERS WILL APPEAR OBVIOUS, WE HAVE TAKEN THE LIBERTY OF HERE OMITTING, FROM THE MSS. PLACED IN OUR HANDS...
...SUCH PORTION AS DETAILS THE FOLLOWING UP OF THE APPARENTLY SLIGHT CLUE OBTAINED BY DUPIN. WE FEEL IT ADVISABLE ONLY TO STATE, IN BRIEF, THAT THE RESULT DESIRED WAS BROUGHT TO PASS.
AND THAT THE PREFECT FULFILLED PUNCTUALLY, ALTHOUGH WITH RELUCTANCE, THE TERMS OF HIS COMPACT WITH THE CHEVALIER.
MR. POE'S ARTICLE CONCLUDES WITH THE FOLLOWING WORDS:
tournoi de whist
IT WILL BE UNDERSTOOD THAT I SPEAK OF COINCIDENCES AND NO MORE. WHAT I HAVE SAID ABOVE UPON THIS TOPIC MUST SUFFICE. IN MY OWN HEART THERE DWELLS NO FAITH IN PRÆTER-NATURE.
THAT NATURE AND ITS GOD ARE TWO, NO MAN WHO THINKS, WILL DENY. THAT THE LATTER, CREATING THE FORMER, CAN, AT WILL, CONTROL OR MODIFY IT, IS ALSO UNQUESTIONABLE.
I SAY "AT WILL;" FOR THE QUESTION IS OF WILL, AND NOT, AS THE INSANITY OF LOGIC HAS ASSUMED, OF POWER. IT IS NOT THAT THE DEITY CANNOT MODIFY HIS LAWS...
...BUT THAT WE INSULT HIM IN IMAGINING A POSSIBLE NECESSITY FOR MODIFICATION. IN THEIR ORIGIN THESE LAWS WERE FASHIONED TO EMBRACE ALL CONTINGENCIES WHICH COULD LIE IN THE FUTURE. WITH GOD ALL IS NOW.
I REPEAT, THEN, THAT I SPEAK OF THESE THINGS ONLY AS OF COINCIDENCES. AND FURTHER: IN WHAT I RELATE IT WILL BE SEEN THAT BETWEEN THE FATE OF THE UNHAPPY MARY CECILIA ROGERS, SO FAR AS THAT FATE IS KNOWN, AND THE FATE OF ONE MARIE ROGET UP TO A CERTAIN EPOCH IN HER HISTORY...
...THERE HAS EXISTED A PARALLEL IN THE CONTEMPLATION OF WHOSE WONDERFUL EXACTITUDE THE REASON BECOMES EMBARRASSED. I SAY ALL THIS WILL BE SEEN. BUT LET IT NOT FOR A MOMENT BE SUPPOSED THAT, IN PROCEEDING WITH THE SAD NARRATIVE OF MARIE FROM THE EPOCH JUST MENTIONED...
...AND IN TRACING TO ITS DÉNOUEMENT THE MYSTERY WHICH ENSHROUDED HER, IT IS MY COVERT DESIGN TO HINT AT AN EXTENSION OF THE PARALLEL...

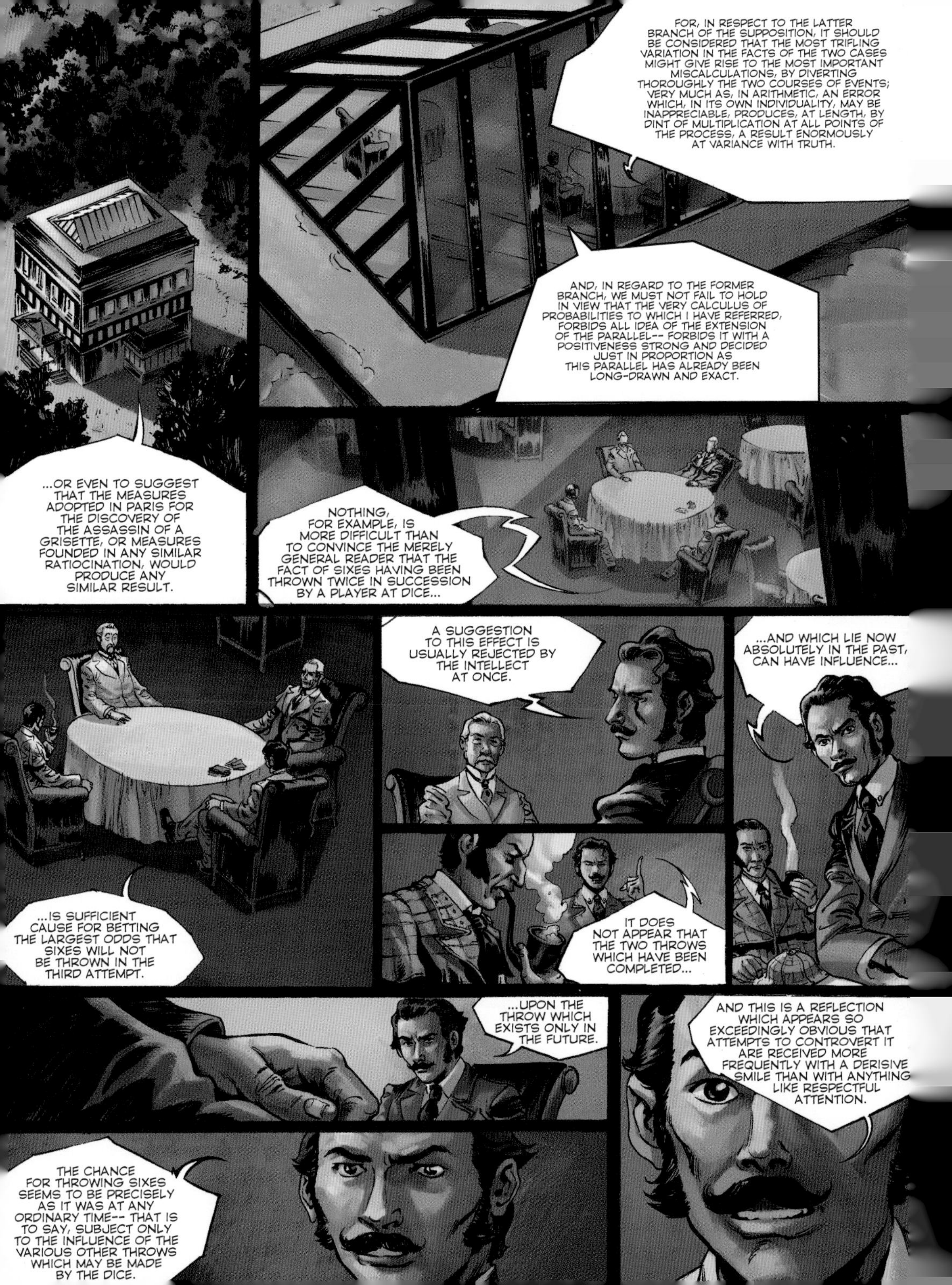
FOR, IN RESPECT TO THE LATTER BRANCH OF THE SUPPOSITION, IT SHOULD BE CONSIDERED THAT THE MOST TRIFLING VARIATION IN THE FACTS OF THE TWO CASES MIGHT GIVE RISE TO THE MOST IMPORTANT MISCALCULATIONS, BY DIVERTING THOROUGHLY THE TWO COURSES OF EVENTS; VERY MUCH AS, IN ARITHMETIC, AN ERROR WHICH, IN ITS OWN INDIVIDUALITY, MAY BE INAPPRECIABLE, PRODUCES, AT LENGTH, BY DINT OF MULTIPLICATION AT ALL POINTS OF THE PROCESS, A RESULT ENORMOUSLY AT VARIANCE WITH TRUTH.
AND, IN REGARD TO THE FORMER BRANCH, WE MUST NOT FAIL TO HOLD IN VIEW THAT THE VERY CALCULUS OF PROBABILITIES TO WHICH I HAVE REFERRED, FORBIDS ALL IDEA OF THE EXTENSION OF THE PARALLEL-- FORBIDS IT WITH A POSITIVENESS STRONG AND DECIDED JUST IN PROPORTION AS THIS PARALLEL HAS ALREADY BEEN LONG-DRAWN AND EXACT.
...OR EVEN TO SUGGEST THAT THE MEASURES ADOPTED IN PARIS FOR THE DISCOVERY OF THE ASSASSIN OF A GRISETTE, OR MEASURES FOUNDED IN ANY SIMILAR RATIOCINATION, WOULD PRODUCE ANY SIMILAR RESULT.
NOTHING, FOR EXAMPLE, IS MORE DIFFICULT THAN TO CONVINCE THE MERELY GENERAL READER THAT THE FACT OF SIXES HAVING BEEN THROWN TWICE IN SUCCESSION BY A PLAYER AT DICE...
...IS SUFFICIENT CAUSE FOR BETTING THE LARGEST ODDS THAT SIXES WILL NOT BE THROWN IN THE THIRD ATTEMPT.
A SUGGESTION TO THIS EFFECT IS USUALLY REJECTED BY THE INTELLECT AT ONCE.
IT DOES NOT APPEAR THAT THE TWO THROWS WHICH HAVE BEEN COMPLETED...
...AND WHICH LIE NOW ABSOLUTELY IN THE PAST, CAN HAVE INFLUENCE...
...UPON THE THROW WHICH EXISTS ONLY IN THE FUTURE.
THE CHANCE FOR THROWING SIXES SEEMS TO BE PRECISELY AS IT WAS AT ANY ORDINARY TIME-- THAT IS TO SAY, SUBJECT ONLY TO THE INFLUENCE OF THE VARIOUS OTHER THROWS WHICH MAY BE MADE BY THE DICE.
AND THIS IS A REFLECTION WHICH APPEARS SO EXCEEDINGLY OBVIOUS THAT ATTEMPTS TO CONTROVERT IT ARE RECEIVED MORE FREQUENTLY WITH A DERISIVE SMILE THAN WITH ANYTHING LIKE RESPECTFUL ATTENTION.

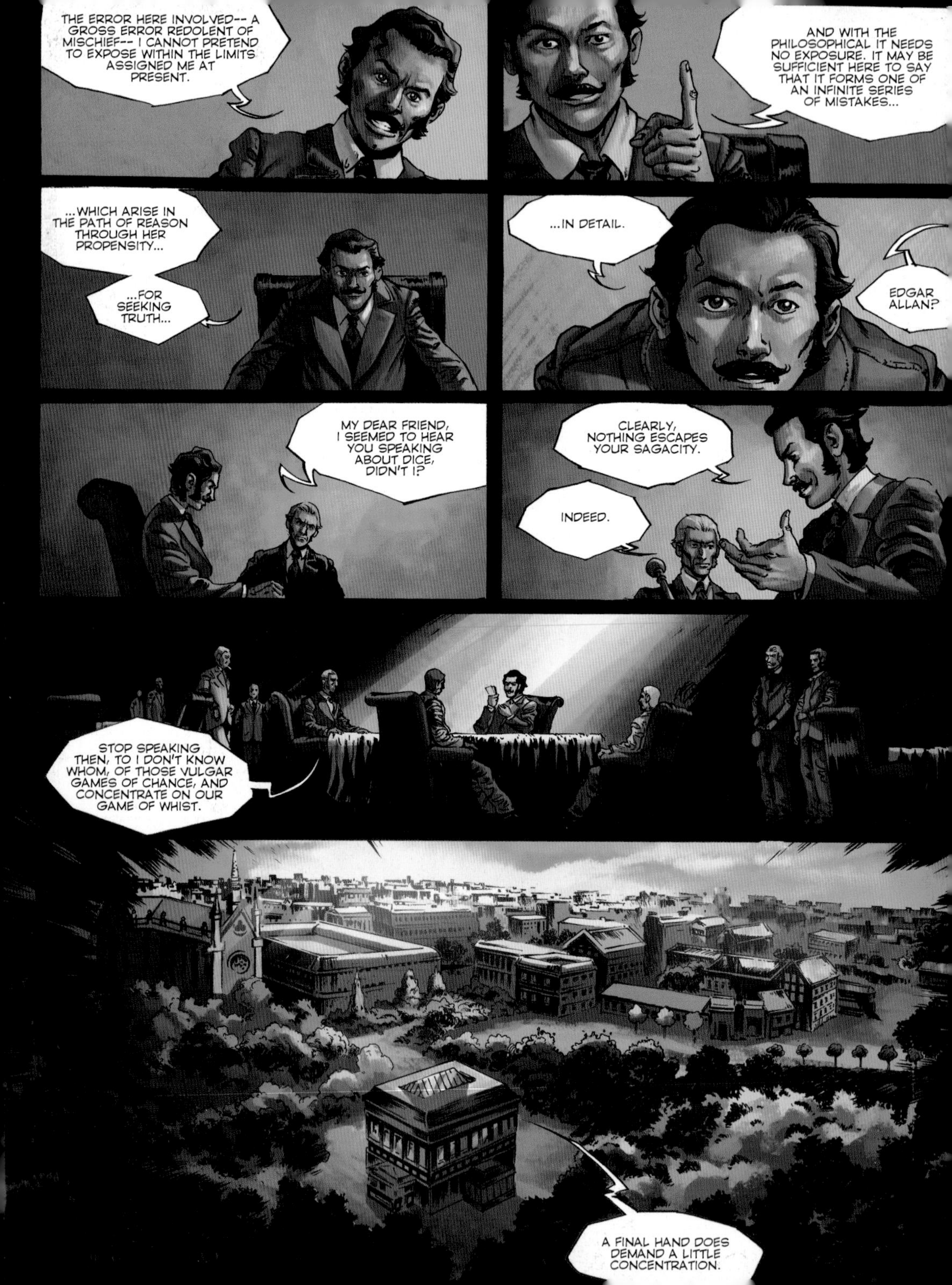
THE ERROR HERE INVOLVED-- A GROSS ERROR REDOLENT OF MISCHIEF-- I CANNOT PRETEND TO EXPOSE WITHIN THE LIMITS ASSIGNED ME AT PRESENT.
AND WITH THE PHILOSOPHICAL IT NEEDS NO EXPOSURE. IT MAY BE SUFFICIENT HERE TO SAY THAT IT FORMS ONE OF AN INFINITE SERIES OF MISTAKES...
...WHICH ARISE IN THE PATH OF REASON THROUGH HER PROPENSITY...
...FOR SEEKING TRUTH...
...IN DETAIL.
EDGAR ALLAN?
MY DEAR FRIEND, I SEEMED TO HEAR YOU SPEAKING ABOUT DICE, DIDN'T I?
CLEARLY, NOTHING ESCAPES YOUR SAGACITY.
INDEED.
STOP SPEAKING THEN, TO I DON'T KNOW WHOM, OF THOSE VULGAR GAMES OF CHANCE, AND CONCENTRATE ON OUR GAME OF WHIST.
A FINAL HAND DOES DEMAND A LITTLE CONCENTRATION.

# CLASSICS ILLUSTRATED GRAPHIC NOVELS
## AVAILABLE FROM PAPERCUTZ

#1 "GREAT EXPECTATIONS"

#2 "THE INVISIBLE MAN"

#3 "THROUGH THE LOOKING-GLASS"

#4 "THE RAVEN AND OTHER POEMS"

#5 "HAMLET"

#6 "THE SCARLET LETTER"

#7 "DR. JEKYLL & MR. HYDE"

#8 "THE COUNT OF MONTE CRISTO"

#9 "THE JUNGLE"

#10 "CYRANO DE BERGERAC"

#11 "THE DEVIL'S DICTIONARY AND OTHER WORKS"

#12 "THE ISLAND OF DOCTOR MOREAU"

#13 "IVANHOE"

#14 "WUTHERING HEIGHTS"

#15 "THE CALL OF THE WILD"

#16 "KIDNAPPED"

#17 "THE SECRET AGENT"

#18 "AESOP'S FABLES"

**CLASSICS ILLUSTRATED graphic novels are available only in hardcover for $9.95 each, except #8-18, $9.99 each. Available from booksellers everywhere.**

Or order from us. Please add $4.00 for postage and handling for the first book, add $1.00 for each additional book. MC, Visa, Amex accepted or make check payable to NBM Publishing. Send to: Papercutz, 160 Broadway, Suite 700, East Wing, New York, NY 10038.

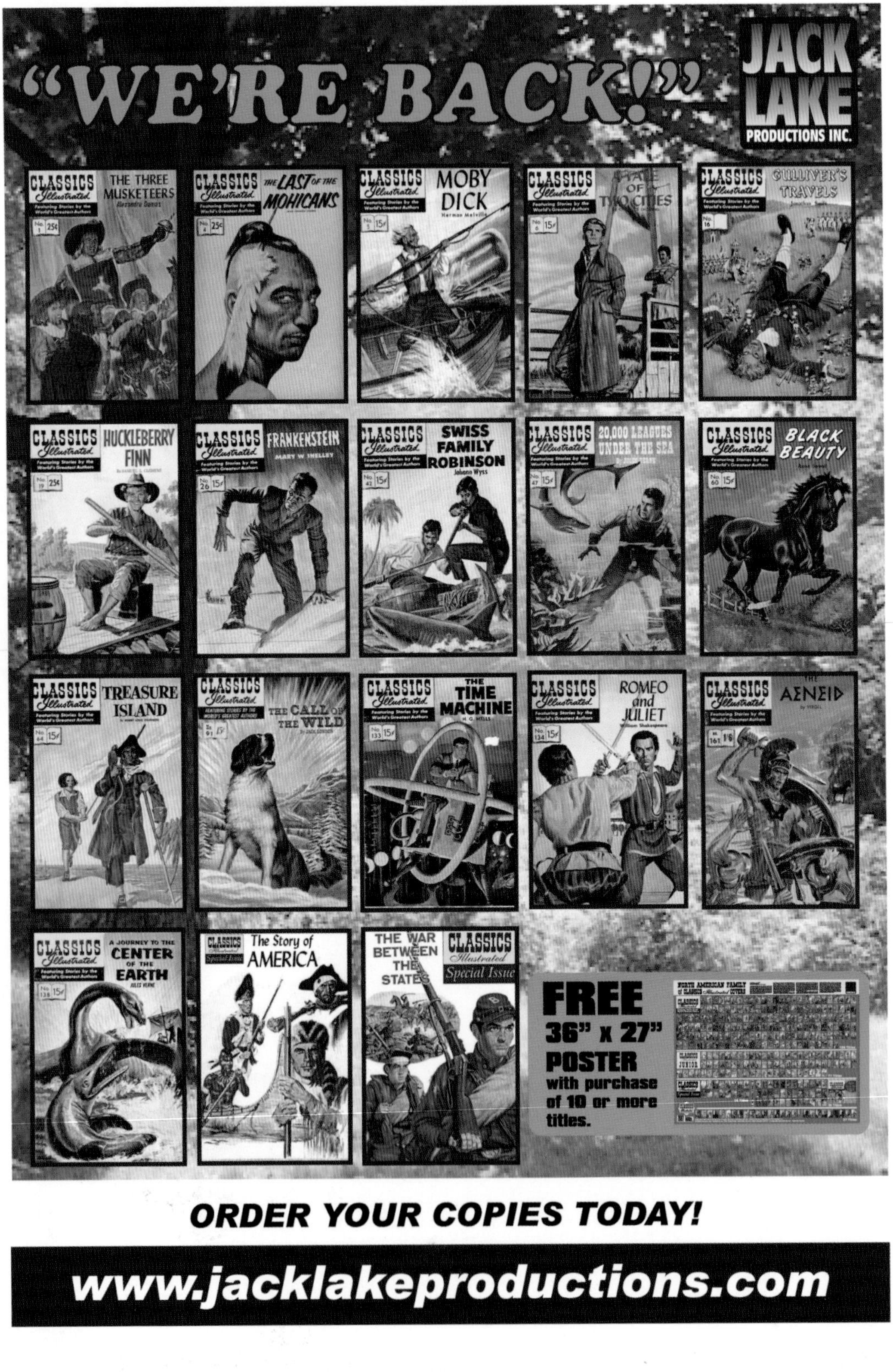
"WE'RE BACK!"
JACK LAKE PRODUCTIONS INC.
CLASSICS Illustrated
THE THREE MUSKETEERS
THE LAST OF THE MOHICANS
MOBY DICK
A TALE OF TWO CITIES
GULLIVER'S TRAVELS
HUCKLEBERRY FINN
FRANKENSTEIN
SWISS FAMILY ROBINSON
20,000 LEAGUES UNDER THE SEA
BLACK BEAUTY
TREASURE ISLAND
THE CALL OF THE WILD
THE TIME MACHINE
ROMEO and JULIET
THE AENEID
A JOURNEY TO THE CENTER OF THE EARTH
The Story of AMERICA
THE WAR BETWEEN THE STATES
Special Issue
FREE
36" x 27"
POSTER
with purchase of 10 or more titles.

# WATCH OUT FOR PAPERCUTZ

Welcome to the tragic tenth CLASSICS ILLUSTRATED DELUXE graphic novel from Papercutz, the company dedicated to publishing great graphic novels for all ages-- this graphic novel being a notable exception to the rule. While we believe the adaptations of the Poe tales collected here are all done faithfully and in good taste, the subject matter may be too mature for younger audiences. Rather than water things down, we decided to post an advisory on our back cover. Another problem is Poe's depiction of the character "Jupiter," in "The Gold Bug." Obviously, the character is little more than a racist stereotype by today's standards, although one could argue simply by giving Jupiter a speaking role, which was uncommon at the time the story was written, Poe was attempting a more human portrayal of an African-American character.

I'm Jim Salicrup, Editor-in-Chief of Papercutz, and I'm particularly pleased to be presenting adaptations of two of the three C. Auguste Dupin stories by Edgar Allan Poe. As you may know, the premiere Papercutz graphic novel series were THE HARDY BOYS and NANCY DREW, the famous teen sleuths. As with all fictional detectives, they follow in the footsteps of Poe's Dupin. As Arthur Conan Doyle wrote in the Preface of his 1902 book, "Adventures of Sherlock Holmes"…

"Edgar Allan Poe, who, in his carelessly prodigal fashion, threw out the seeds from which so many of our present forms of literature have sprung, was the father of the detective tale, and covered its limits so completely that I fail to see how his followers can find any fresh ground which they can confidently call their own."

So, in a strange way, Papercutz wouldn't even exist if it wasn't for Poe! Fittingly, in the final volume (#21) of the first Papercutz NANCY DREW series, the Girl Detective encounters a deranged man claiming to be a descendent of Poe—"Edwin Allan Poe." It's a clever story, written by Stefan Petrucha and Sarah Kinney, filled with many Poe references and featuring two detectives that Nancy's own success inspired—The Dana Girls. And like in "The Mystery of Marie Rogêt," it's also inspired by a real-life mystery. I especially enjoyed this first encounter between Nancy Drew and "Poe":

POE: Lenore?
NANCY DREW: No, Nancy Drew, Girl Detective.
POE: A detective? Ha! My own Dupin, now there's a detective!

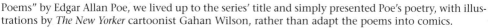

Edwin may've been crazy, but I'll agree with him about Dupin! Of course, Poe, the real one, was even better known for his more macabre tales and poems. In CLASSICS ILLUSTRATED #4 "The Raven and Other Poems" by Edgar Allan Poe, we lived up to the series' title and simply presented Poe's poetry, with illustrations by *The New Yorker* cartoonist Gahan Wilson, rather than adapt the poems into comics.

We hope to feature more Poe adaptations in the future, especially the third and final Dupin story, "The Purloined Letter," but in the meantime enjoy the two presented here, along with an adaptation of Poe's "The Gold-Bug." As for the Papercutz titles mentioned here, both NANCY DREW #22 and CLASSICS ILLUSTRATED #4 are still available from www.papercutz.com and are highly recommended to lovers of Poe, poetry, and girl detectives.

Now for something completely different! Coming up next in CLASSICS ILLUSTRATED DELUXE #11- "The Sea Wolf"! Don't miss it!

Thanks,

**Stay in Touch!**

EMAIL:     salicrup@papercutz.com
WEB:       www.papercutz.com
TWITTER:  @papercutzgn
FACEBOOK:  PAPERCUTZGRAPHICNOVELS
FAN MAIL:  Papercutz, 160 Broadway, Suite 700,
            East Wing, New York, NY 10038

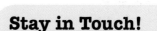

# EDGAR ALLAN POE
## (1809-1849)

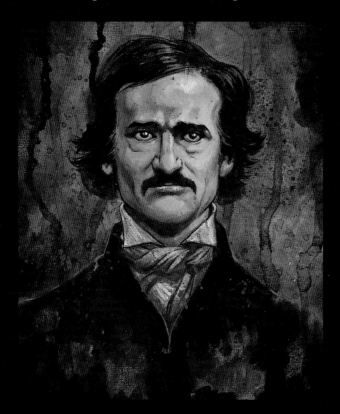

A n orphan-- the child of itinerant actors-- Edgar Poe was quite young when he was taken in by the Allans, wealthy Richmond merchants with whom he spent the majority of his youth. After a brief stint at the University of Virginia and attempts at a military career, Poe left his adoptive family and started his literary career humbly with the publication of the collection *"Tamerlane and Other Poems."* Little by little, he abandoned poetry for prose and began writing tales. In 1835, he started his career as a journalist and literary critic. After the failure of his novel *"The Narrative of Arthur Gordon Pym of Nantucket,"* Poe wrote his first collection of stories, the *"Tales of the Grotesque and Arabesque"* in 1840, which met with critical success.

It was in January of 1845, with the publication of *"The Raven,"* that Poe knew an immediate success. The premature death of his young bride aggravated his depressive tendencies, and his already fragile health felt the effects: he died two years later to general indifference. Edgar Poe would first be recognized and defended in France, in particular thanks to the translation of his work by Charles Baudelaire.